TWENTY YEARS
OF THE
CAINE PRIZE
FOR AFRICAN WRITING

with an introduction by Ben Okri

Interlink Books

An imprint of Interlink Publishing Group, Inc.
Northampton, Massachusetts

Twenty Years of the Caine Prize for African Writing

First published in 2020 in the USA by
INTERLINK BOOKS
An imprint of Interlink Publishing Group, Inc.
46 Crosby Street
Northampton, Massachusetts 01060
www.interlinkbooks.com

Book cover design by Pam Fontes-May, Interlink Publishing
Interior book design by New Internationalist

Library of Congress Cataloging-in-Publication data available
ISBN 978-1-62371-935-7

Printed and bound in the United States of America

To order our free 48-page, full-color catalog, please call us toll-free at 1-800-238-LINK, visit our website at www.interlinkbooks.com, or write to Interlink Publishing, 46 Crosby Street, Northampton, MA 01060

Twenty Years of the Caine Prize for African Writing

Contents

Introduction by Ben Okri

Maybe it was wisdom, maybe it was expediency, but the short-story form has turned out to be a regenerator of African literature. And one of the chief causes of that regeneration has been the Caine Prize for African Writing. It was instituted twenty years ago by Baroness Emma Nicholson as a way of honoring the memory of her husband, Michael Caine, who worked so tirelessly in Africa and was the Chairman of the Booker Prize. It began as one thing, but became another, as year after year, in June or July, were gathered young writers from all over the continent and all across the diaspora, who were shortlisted for what quickly became the pre-eminent prize for African writing.

The writers would gather for the announcement dinner in the Divinity School of the Bodleian Library in Oxford. The five shortlisted stories would be read out, dinner served, rich conversation followed, and at the end of the evening one writer would step forth as the recipient of the Prize. But the Prize has not just been about the recipients and the shortlisted writers. Its true value has been in creating a climate for African writing to flourish, nurturing a spirit of hope and encouragement, and fostering the sense that no matter where you came from, no matter how deprived your circumstances, if you could write you would be read, and if you could write well you would be celebrated.

And so, from the beginning, stories poured in from all over Africa and from all over the world. It turned out that African writers had much to say. They were bursting with stuff to say. They made up stories out of the vigorous, pullulating, rowdy, rich, and strange conditions of the continent—tales political, tales harrowing, tales humorous, tales told with vitality and passion and intelligence. People discovered themselves to be writers in the act of sending their submissions to the Caine Prize. It was a case of "if you build it they will come." In this case, the creation of the Caine Prize, the lure of publication, gave courage to hundreds of writers who otherwise might not have known where to send their fictions and their stories about the lives they were living or imagining.

The fact is that, in the 1990s, British and American publishers were not interested in the literature of Africa. There was the idea then that people wanted to read about their own kind, and that a place as far away and as outlandish as Africa could not possibly interest your average British or American readers. I remember in the 1980s, when I was publishing my early short stories, an editor saying to me, with all seriousness, and without an ounce of malice, merely stating an obvious fact, that:

"No one is going to buy your book. Look at the census. The numbers are not in your favor. Ordinary people are just not interested in Africa."

In short, I was wasting my time trying to be a writer. This was my editor, and he was an intelligent man. But I believed then, as I believe now, that good writing transcends barriers and that all people want to be enriched, challenged, diverted, entertained; and that true literature knows no boundaries, as it speaks to the human condition, not just to the condition of one place or time.

And events have borne me out. First the winning of the Booker Prize in 1991 and the hundreds of thousands of copies of *The Famished Road* sold, and then, in the new millennium, the explosion of African writing all around the world. Chimamanda Ngozi Adichie, NoViolet Bulawayo, Chika Unigwe, Teju Cole: all of the new generation, and most of them brought to the attention of the world through the Caine Prize. Those who were not shortlisted for the Prize benefited tremendously from the renewed attention that it brought to the literature of Africa.

It was up to the first panel of judges, which I chaired, to define what constituted African writing. There was an argument for restricting the Prize only to writers from the continent and of African birth. There was talk of making it a black African prize only. In the end we opted for the widest possible definition of African, including writers from the diaspora, of all colors, so long as there was a tangible connection with the continent of Africa. And this has proven to be the right course, for the Prize now reflects the panoramic presence of Africans on the globe.

But I think the real heart of the Prize's success is its choice of form. The choice of the short story was inspired. While the novel is the more expansive form, the short story is the more accessible. Everyone can attempt the short story. It lets you in. It lets you begin. It is not daunting. For this reason the short story allows people to venture into the miraculous rigors of literature. It is gentle on beginners and tough on seasoned practitioners. For people who have little time, the short story is manageable. You can hold the whole idea in your head. Most African writers began with the short story. Ngugi began by bluffing that he had written a short story and then wrote one to make his bluff real. Wole Soyinka began with short stories, as did Achebe, Marechera, Bessie Head, Nadine Gordimer, Cyprian Ekwensi, as well as Chekhov, Joyce, Baldwin, Hemingway, Woolf... Many writers began really with poetry, but the short story is the poetry of the prose form. That is to say, it is the form of compression and analogue. It stands always for something more than itself, it stands in a poetic relationship to reality. The short story is a small universe, and the ideal form in which to learn how to write. It is also the most democratic of forms and the most inclusive. It is one of the oldest forms. The ancient Egyptians, along with images of their gods and hymns of their culture, inscribed short stories on tombs and walls. Their poems and books of the dead and their wisdom tales are as enduring a legacy as their temples and pyramids.

But many begin with the short story and quickly run to the novel, as the form which brings most sustenance and financial reward. This is a shame. For the short story is a world unto itself and should never be regarded as a starting point for the novel. So many promising short-story writers never return to the short form again once they have been contaminated by the novel, which leads to more expansion and elaboration and diffusion. But the short story leads to more concentration, to greater clarity, and to creative integrity. The short story is the true home of our craft.

The short story is richly suited to the African experience, partly because of the storytelling nature of African life, and partly because of the way the form plays into the flow of African time. Whether in the cities or in the villages, whether it is in East or West or South or North Africa, something pulses through the varied and oddly unified life of the continent that lends itself to the framing that the short story excels at—the slicing of a portion of imaginative experience, the investigation of an enigma, the ebb and flow of clashes and consequences. Whether it is the celebration, the marketplace, the bus stop, the ritual, the family, the funeral, comradeship, grisly death, sexual awakening, the short story catches the experience, holds it at an angle, illuminates it.

The partial documentary nature of the form is also fruitful in a land where life bustles and experience is crowded and where, in a moment, significant events can fill out to bursting the boundaries of time. Life and imagination are so intermingled in African life that often it is not necessary to invent. Life does the inventing for you. Rather, more often, what is needed is restraint and craft, selection and art. The writer has to learn to let one thing stand for many others, when life offers a plethora of incidents. It is easy for the African literary temper to run to the gothic or the baroque, and the temptation to be dense, to match the sometimes density of reality, is always there. This is perhaps why the short form is salutary. It teaches the writer quite early on that they cannot say everything. Some things have to be suggested. They teach the writer to accept the excesses of reality, but to harness that with the discipline of art. It is a vital lesson to learn before they get unleashed on the novel, where you can say everything, but where it is best that you don't. Art, by its nature, is the tension of the infinite being expressed by the finite. Anything that exhausts its possibilities ruins its effectiveness, its art. To express too much is, in the end, to express nothing. And because it does not express everything, because it leaves space for the imaginative participation of the reader, the short story is the most collaborative of literary prose forms. In this, again, it is akin to poetry. The short story, well executed, awakens questions rather than gives answers, stimulates imaginative participation in a life beyond the story rather than gets the reader to travel to the end of its road. The short story builds roads that enable you to travel to your own places, to the hinterland of your own spirit and imagining. It never does all your traveling for you. In any case, the best journeys happen in the mind, in the subconscious, in the kingdom of the spirit where the real reading and the real experiencing take place.

It is in this way that the short form lends itself to the political, the social, the contemplative, the anecdotal, the cultural. It is because it can be a perfect mirror of life that it serves on so many levels. It can be a mood, a memory, an aesthetic throb, a thought experiment, an enigma, a glimpse of a mental state, a scene broken off from a complex historical moment, a record of something terrible witnessed, a note of an obsession, or the testing of a philosophical hypothesis in a fictional guise. The elasticity of the form is astounding. There is almost nothing it cannot do. The short story can seem like a short play. It can be an exegesis, in which nothing happens except the somewhat dramatic journey of an idea. Sometimes short stories make me think of those sonatas that begin the music in you when they end, and long afterwards you are vibrating to those harmonies which were begun in you and which continue in the underground of your subsequent existence. If there was ever a form that begins its work in you most powerfully when it is finished it is the short story. It somehow presses you forward into a life beyond its pages, making you hum and thrill with the silence of its after melodies.

Perhaps, for that reason, it is an ideal form for the posing of inexhaustible questions. In some odd way, the brevity multiplies the questions. And perhaps the form also trains one indirectly in the art of asking oblique questions.

Our time is one of vagueness and the blurring of truth. Language slides into imprecision and the public use of words encourages the sense that public figures use words to conceal rather than to reveal. The language is under great strain and the poisoning of language poisons the general spirit. Where is truth to be found? The short story rescues language from imprecision, because in a good story every word counts. Not only does every word count, but every word carries its true weight. There is no room for faking in a short story. The slightest word or phrase that is not right immediately betrays itself. Every false note shows. It is a matter of tone and harmonies and tautness. It is a form that is in a way purely about the truth of telling and construction. It is one of the greatest tools for reflecting the human condition and the human experience as it is lived.

This is why the Caine Prize has been so fruitful; the chosen form for the Prize is itself fruitful, coming as it does from the innumerable fountains of experience.

Is there anything more I would like to see from the Prize? I would like the winning stories not always to be measured by length or by weight of theme. It would be progressive to see more experimental short stories win. It would be great to see winning stories that are only two pages long, highly worked, and absolutely true. It would be wonderful to see more comic stories win.

For twenty years now, the prize has celebrated the best of new African writing. It has conducted influential workshops and readings across the African continent. In the process, it has revealed to the world the dizzying array of talent that had just been waiting for the opportunity to dream and to elevate their craft.

For twenty years, the Caine Prize has been this engine for African literary regeneration. Under the new leadership of Ellah Wakatama Allfrey, fresh horizons beckon.

The Prize began small and began with the small. But, as my mother never tired of telling me, from little acorns mighty oaks grow.

Ben Okri
June 2019

The Museum

Leila Aboulela—winner of the 2000 Caine Prize

At first Shadia was afraid to ask him for his notes. The earring made her afraid. And the straight long hair that he tied up with a rubber band. She had never seen a man with an earring and such long hair. But then she had never known such cold, so much rain. His silver earring was the strangeness of the West, another culture-shock. She stared at it during classes, her eyes straying from the white scribbles on the board. Most times she could hardly understand anything. Only the notation was familiar. But how did it all fit together? How did *this* formula lead to *this*? Her ignorance and the impending exams were horrors she wanted to escape. His long hair, a dull color between yellow and brown, different shades. It reminded her of a doll she had when she was young. She had spent hours combing that doll's hair, stroking it. She had longed for such straight hair. When she went to Paradise she would have hair like that. When she ran it would fly behind her, if she bent her head down it would fall over like silk and sweep the flowers on the grass. She watched his ponytail move as he wrote and then looked up at the board. She pictured her doll, vivid suddenly after years, and felt sick that she was day-dreaming in class, not learning a thing.

The first days of term, when the classes started for the MSc in Statistics, she was like someone tossed around by monstrous waves. Battered, as she lost her way to the different lecture rooms, fumbled with the photocopying machine, could not find anything in the library. She could scarcely hear or eat or see. Her eyes bulged with fright, watered from the cold. The course required a certain background, a background she didn't have. So she floundered, she and the other African students, the two Turkish girls, and the men from Brunei. Asafa, the short, round-faced Ethiopian, said, in his grave voice, as this collection from the Third World whispered their anxieties in grim Scottish corridors, the girls in nervous giggles, "Last year, last year a Nigerian on this very same course committed suicide. *Cut his wrists.*"

Us and them, she thought. The ones who would do well, the ones who would crawl and sweat and barely pass. Two predetermined groups. Asafa, generous and wise (he was the oldest) leaned and whispered to Shadia, "The Spanish girl is good. Very good." His eyes bulged redder than Shadia's. He cushioned his fears every night in the university pub, she only cried. Their countries were next-door neighbors but he had never been to Sudan, and Shadia had never been to Ethiopia. "But we meet in Aberdeen!" she had shrieked when this information was exchanged, giggling furiously. Collective fear had its euphoria.

"That boy Bryan," said Asafa, "is excellent."

"The one with the earring?"

Asafa laughed and touched his own unadorned ear. "The earring doesn't mean anything. He'll get the Distinction. He did his undergraduate here, got First Class Honors. That gives him an advantage. He knows all the lecturers, he knows the system."

So the idea occurred to her of asking Bryan for the notes of his graduate year. If she strengthened her background in stochastic processes and time series, she would be better able to cope with the new material they were bombarded with every day. She watched him to judge if he was approachable. Next to the courteous Malaysian students, he was devoid of manners. He mumbled and slouched and did not speak with respect to the lecturers. He spoke to them as if they were his equal. And he did silly things. When he wanted to throw a piece of paper in the bin, he squashed it into a ball and from where he was sitting he aimed it at the bin. If he missed, he muttered under his breath. She thought that he was immature. But he was the only one who was sailing through the course.

The glossy handbook for overseas students had explained about the "famous British reserve" and hinted that they should be grateful, things were worse further south, less "hospitable." In the cafeteria, drinking coffee with Asafa and the others, the picture of "hospitable Scotland" was something different. Badr, the Malaysian, blinked and whispered, "Yesterday our windows got smashed, my wife today is afraid to go out."

"Thieves?" asked Shadia, her eyes wider than anyone else's.

"Racists," said the Turkish girl, her lipstick chic, the word tripping out like silver, like ice.

Wisdom from Asafa, muted, before the collective silence, "These people think they own the world…" and around them the aura of the dead Nigerian student. They were ashamed of that brother they had never seen. He had weakened, caved in. In the cafeteria, Bryan never sat with them. They never sat with him. He sat alone, sometimes reading the local paper. When Shadia walked in front of him he didn't smile. "These people are strange… One day they greet you, the next day they don't."

On Friday afternoon, as everyone was ready to leave the room after Linear Models, she gathered her courage and spoke to Bryan. He had spots on his chin and forehead, was taller than her, restless, as if he was in a hurry to go somewhere else. He put his calculator back in its case, his pen in his pocket. She asked him for his notes and his blue eyes behind his glasses took on the blankest look she had ever seen in her life. What was all the surprise for? Did he think she was an insect, was he surprised that she could speak?

A mumble for a reply, words strung together. So taken aback, he was. He pushed his chair back under the table with his foot.

"Pardon?"

He slowed down, separated each word, "Ah'll have them for ye on Monday."

"Thank you." She spoke English better than him! How pathetic. The whole of him was pathetic. He wore the same shirt every blessed day. Gray and white stripes.

* * *

On the weekends, Shadia never went out of the halls and unless someone telephoned long distance from home, she spoke to no-one. There was time to remember Thursday nights in Khartoum, a wedding to go to with Fareed, driving in his red Mercedes. Or the club with her sisters. Sitting by the pool drinking lemonade with ice, the waiters all dressed in white. Sometimes people swam at night, dived in the water dark like the sky above. Here, in this country's weekend of Saturday and Sunday, Shadia washed her clothes and her hair. Her hair depressed her. The damp weather made it frizz up after she straightened it with hot tongs. So she had given up and now wore it in a bun all the time, tightly pulled back away from her face, the curls held down by pins and Vaseline Tonic. She didn't like this style, her corrugated hair, and in the mirror her eyes looked too large. The mirror in the public bathroom, at the end of the corridor to her room, had printed on it "This is the face of someone with HIV." She had written about this mirror to her sister, something foreign and sensational like hail and cars driving on the left. But she hadn't written that the mirror made her feel as if she had left her looks behind in Khartoum.

On the weekends, she made a list of the money she had spent, the sterling enough to keep a family alive back home. Yet she might fail her exams after all that expense, go back home empty-handed without a degree. Guilt was cold like the fog of this city. It came from everywhere. One day she forgot to pray in the morning. She reached the bus-stop and then realized that she hadn't prayed. That morning folded out like the nightmare she sometimes had, of discovering that she had gone out into the street without any clothes.

In the evening, when she was staring at multidimensional scaling, the telephone in the hall rang. She ran to answer it. Fareed's cheerful greeting. "Here, Shadia, Mama and the girls want to speak to you." His mother's endearments, "They say it's so cold where you are…"

Shadia was engaged to Fareed. Fareed was a package that came with the 7Up franchise, the paper factory, the big house he was building, his sisters and widowed mother. Shadia was going to marry them all. She was going to be happy and make her mother happy. Her mother deserved happiness after the misfortunes of her life. A husband who left her for another woman. Six girls to bring up. People felt sorry for her mother. Six girls to educate and marry off.

But your Lord is generous, each of the girls, it was often said, was lovelier than the other. They were clever, too; dentist, pharmacist, architect, and all with the best of manners.

"We are just back from looking at the house," Fareed's turn again to talk. "It's coming along fine, they're putting the tiles down…"

"That's good, that's good," her voice strange from not talking to anyone all day.

"The bathroom suites. If I get them all the same color for us and the girls and Mama, I could get them on a discount. Blue, the girls are in favor of blue," his voice echoed from one continent to another. Miles and miles.

"Blue is nice. Yes, better get them all the same color." He was building a block of flats, not a house. The ground floor flat for his mother and the girls until they married, the first floor for him and Shadia. The girls' flats on the two top floors would be rented out. When Shadia had first got engaged to Fareed, he was the son of rich man. A man with the franchise for 7Up and the paper factory which had a monopoly in ladies' sanitary towels. Fareed's sisters never had to buy sanitary towels, their house was abundant with boxes of Pinky, fresh from the production line. But Fareed's father died of an unexpected heart attack soon after the engagement party (500 guests at the Hilton). Now Shadia was going to marry the rich man himself. You are a lucky, lucky girl, her mother said and Shadia rubbed soap in her eyes so that Fareed would think she had been weeping about his father's death.

There was not time to talk about her course on the telephone, no space for her anxieties. Fareed was not interested in her studies. He had said, "I am very broad-minded to allow you to study abroad. Other men would not have put up with this…" It was her mother who was keen for her to study, to get a postgraduate degree from Britain and then have a career after she got married. "This way," her mother had said, "you will have your in-laws' respect. They have money but you will have a degree. Don't end up like me. I left my education to marry your father and now…" Many conversations ended with her mother bitter, with her mother saying, "No-one suffers like I suffer," and making Shadia droop. At night her mother howled in her sleep, noises that woke Shadia and her sisters.

No, on the long-distance line, there was no space for her worries. Talk about the Scottish weather. Picture Fareed, generously perspiring, his stomach straining the buttons of his shirt. Often she had nagged him to lose weight, with no success. His mother's food was too good, his sisters were both overweight. On the long-distance line, listen to the Khartoum gossip as if listening to a radio play.

* * *

On Monday, without saying anything, Bryan slid two folders across the table towards her as if he did not want to come near her, did not want to talk to her. She wanted to say, "I won't take till you hand them to me politely." But, smarting, she said, "Thank you very much." She had manners. She was well brought up.

Back in her room, at her desk, the clearest handwriting she had ever seen. Sparse on the pages, clean. Clear and rounded like a child's, the tidiest notes. She cried over them, wept for no reason. She cried until she wet one of the pages, stained the ink, blurred one of the formulas. She dabbed at it with a tissue but the paper flaked and became transparent. Should she apologize about the stain, say that she was drinking water, say that it was rain? Or should she just keep quiet, hope he wouldn't notice? She chided herself for all that concern. He wasn't concerned about wearing the same shirt every day. She was giving him too much attention thinking about him. He was just an immature and closed-in sort of character. He probably came from a small town, his parents were probably poor, low-class. In Khartoum, she never mixed with people like that. Her mother liked her to be friends with people who were higher up. How else were she and her sisters going to marry well? She must study the notes and stop crying over this boy's handwriting. His handwriting had nothing to do with her, nothing to do with her at all.

Understanding after not understanding is fog lifting, is pictures swinging into focus, missing pieces slotting into place. It is fragments gelling, a sound vivid whole, a basis to build on. His notes were the knowledge she needed, the gaps. She struggled through them, not skimming them with the carelessness of incomprehension, but taking them in, making them a part of her, until in the depth of concentration, in the late hours of the nights, she lost awareness of time and place and at last when she slept she became epsilon and gamma and she became a variable making her way through discrete space from state i to state j.

* * *

It felt natural to talk to him. As if now that she had spent hours and days with his handwriting she knew him in some way. She forgot the offense she had taken when he had slid his folders across the table to her, all the times he didn't say hello.

In the computer room, at the end of the Statistical Packages class, she went to him and said, "Thanks for the notes. They are really good. I think I might not fail, after all. I might have a chance to pass." Her eyes were dry from all the nights she had stayed up. She was tired and grateful.

He nodded and they spoke a little about the Poisson distribution, queuing theory. Everything was clear in his mind, his brain was a clear pane of glass, where all the concepts were written out boldly and neatly. Today, he seemed more at ease talking to her, though he still shifted about from foot to foot, avoided her eyes.

He said, "Do ye want to go for a coffee?"

She looked up at him. He was tall and she was not used to speaking to people with blue eyes. Then she made a mistake. Perhaps because she had been up late last night, she made that mistake. Perhaps there were other reasons for that mistake. The mistake of shifting from one level to another.

"I don't like your earring."

The expression in his eyes, a focusing, no longer shifting away. He lifted his hand to his ear and tugged the earring off. His earlobe without the silver looked red and scarred.

She giggled because she was afraid, because he wasn't smiling, wasn't saying anything. She covered her mouth with her hand then wiped her forehead and eyes. A mistake was made and it was too late to go back. She plunged ahead, careless now, reckless, "I don't like your long hair."

He turned and walked away.

* * *

The next morning, Multivariate Analysis, and she came in late, disheveled from running and the rain. The professor, whose name she wasn't sure of (there were three who were McSomething), smiled unperturbed. All the lecturers were relaxed and urbane, in tweed jackets and polished shoes. Sometimes she wondered how the incoherent Bryan, if he did pursue an academic career, was going to transform himself into a professor like that. But it was none of her business.

Like most of the other students, she sat in the same seat in every class. Bryan sat a row ahead, which was why she could always look at his hair. But he had cut it, there was no ponytail today! Just his neck and the collar of the gray and white striped shirt.

Notes to take down. *In discriminant analysis, a linear combination of variables serves as the basis for assigning cases to groups...*

She was made up of layers. Somewhere inside, deep inside, under the crust of vanity, in the untampered-with essence, she would glow and be in awe, and be humble and think, this is just for me, he cut his hair for me. But there were other layers, bolder, more to the surface. Giggling. Wanting to catch hold of a friend. Guess what? You wouldn't *believe* what this idiot did!

Find a weighted average of variables... The weights are estimated so that they result in the best separation between the groups.

After the class he came over and said very seriously, without a smile. "Ah've cut my hair."

A part of her hollered with laughter, sang, you stupid boy, you stupid boy, I can see that, can't I?

She said, "It looks nice." She had said the wrong thing and her face felt hot and she made herself look away so that she would not know his reaction. It was true, though, he did look nice; he looked decent now.

* * *

She should have said to Bryan, when they first held their coffee mugs in their hands and were searching for an empty table, "Let's sit with Asafa and the others." Mistakes follow mistakes. Across the cafeteria, the Turkish girl saw them together and raised her perfect eyebrows, Badr met Shadia's eyes and quickly looked away. Shadia looked at Bryan and he was different, different without the earring and the ponytail, transformed in some way. If he would put lemon juice on his spots... but it was none of her business. Maybe the boys who smashed Badr's windows looked like Bryan, but with fiercer eyes, no glasses. She must push him away from her. She must make him dislike her.

He asked her where she came from and when she replied, he said, "Where's that?"

"Africa," with sarcasm. "Do you know where *that* is?"

His nose and cheeks, under the rim of his glasses, went red. Good, she thought, good. He will leave me now in peace.

He said, "Ah know Sudan is in Africa, I meant where exactly in Africa."

"North-east, south of Egypt. Where are *you* from?"

"Peterhead. It's north of here. By the sea."

It was hard to believe that there was anything north of Aberdeen. It seemed to her that they were on the northernmost corner of the world. She knew better now than to imagine suntanning and sandy beaches for his "by the sea." More likely dismal skies, pale bad-tempered people shivering on the rocky shore.

"Your father works in Peterhead?"

"Aye, he does."

She had grown up listening to the proper English of the BBC World Service only to come to Britain and find people saying "yes" like it was said back home in Arabic, aye.

"What does he do, your father?"

He looked surprised, his blue eyes surprised, "Ma dad's a joiner."

Fareed hired people like that to work on the house. Ordered them about.

"And your mother?" she asked.

He paused a little, stirred sugar in his coffee with a plastic spoon. "She's a lollipop lady."

Shadia smirked into her coffee, took a sip.

"My father," she said proudly, "is a doctor, a specialist." Her father was a gynaecologist. The woman who was his wife now had been one of his patients. Before that, Shadia's friends had teased her about her father's job, crude jokes that made her laugh. It was all so sordid now.

"And my mother," she blew the truth up out of proportion, "comes from a very big family. A ruling family. If you British hadn't colonized us, my mother would have been a princess now."

"Ye walk like a princess," he said.

What a gullible, silly boy! She wiped her forehead with her hand, said, "You mean I am conceited and proud?"

"No, Ah didnae mean that, no..." The packet of sugar he was tearing open tipped from his hand, its contents scattered over the table. "Ah shit... sorry..." He tried to scoop up the sugar and knocked against his coffee mug, spilling a little on the table.

She took out a tissue from her bag, reached over and mopped up the stain. It was easy to pick up all the bits of sugar with the damp tissue.

"Thanks," he mumbled and they were silent. The cafeteria was busy, full of the humming, buzzing sound of people talking to each other, trays and dishes. In Khartoum, she avoided being alone with Fareed. She preferred it when they were with others; their families, their many mutual friends. If they were ever alone, she imagined that her mother or her sister was with them, could hear them, and spoke to Fareed with that audience in mind.

Bryan was speaking to her, saying something about rowing on the River Dee. He went rowing on the weekends, he belonged to a rowing club.

To make herself pleasing to people was a skill Shadia was trained in. It was not difficult to please people. Agree with them, never dominate the conversation, be economical with the truth. Now here was someone whom all these rules needn't apply to.

She said to him, "The Nile is superior to the Dee. I saw your Dee, it is nothing, it is like a stream. There are two Niles, the Blue and the White, named after their colors. They come from the south, from two different places. They travel for miles, over countries with different names, never knowing they will meet. I think they get tired of running alone, it is such a long way to the sea. They want to reach the sea so that they can rest, stop running. There is a bridge in Khartoum and under this bridge the two Niles meet and if you stand on the bridge and look down you can see the two waters mixing together."

"Do ye get homesick?" he asked and she felt tired now, all this talk of the river running to rest in the sea. She had never talked like that before. Luxury words, and the question he asked.

"Things I should miss I don't miss. Instead I miss things I didn't think I would miss. The *azan*, the Muslim call to prayer from the mosque, I don't know if you know about it. I miss that. At dawn it used to wake me up. I would hear *prayer is better than sleep* and just go back to sleep, I never got up to pray." She looked down at her hands on the table. There was no relief in confessions, only his smile, young, and something like wonder in his eyes.

"We did Islam in school," he said, "Ah went on a trip to Mecca." He opened out his palms on the table.

"What!"

"In a book."

"Oh."

The coffee was finished. They should go now. She should go to the library before the next lecture and photocopy previous exam papers. Asafa, full of helpful advice, had shown her where to find them.

"What is your religion?" she asked.

"Dunno, nothing I suppose."

"That's terrible! That's really terrible!" Her voice was too loud, concerned.

His face went red again and he tapped his spoon against the empty mug.

Waive all politeness, make him dislike her. Badr had said, even before his windows got smashed, that here in the West they hate Islam. Standing up to go, she said flippantly, "Why don't you become a Muslim then?"

He shrugged, "Ah wouldnae mind traveling to Mecca, I was keen on that book."

Her eyes filled with tears. They blurred his face when he stood up. In the West they hate Islam and he... She said, "Thanks for the coffee" and walked away but he followed her.

"Shadiya, Shadiya," he pronounced her name wrong, three syllables instead of two, "there's this museum about Africa. I've never been before. If you'd care to go, tomorrow..."

* * *

No sleep for the guilty, no rest, she should have said no, I can't go, no I have too much catching up to do. No sleep for the guilty, the memories come from another continent. Her father's new wife, happier than her mother, fewer worries. When Shadia visits she offers fruit in a glass bowl, icy oranges and guava, soothing in the heat. Shadia's father hadn't wanted a divorce, hadn't wanted to leave them, he wanted two wives not a divorce. But her mother had too much pride, she came from fading money, a family with a "name." Of the new wife her mother says, bitch, whore, the dregs of the earth, a nobody.

Tomorrow, she need not show up at the museum, even though she said that she would. She should have told Bryan she was engaged to be married, mentioned it casually. What did he expect from her? Europeans had different rules, reduced, abrupt customs. If Fareed knew about this... her secret thoughts like snakes... Perhaps she was like her father, a traitor. Her mother said that her father was devious. Sometimes Shadia was devious. With Fareed in the car, she would deliberately say, "I need to stop at the grocer, we need things at home." At the grocer he would pay for all her shopping and she would say, "No, you shouldn't do that, no, you are too generous, you are embarrassing me." With the money she saved, she would buy a blouse for her mother, nail varnish for her mother, a magazine, imported apples.

* * *

It was strange to leave her desk, lock her room and go out on a Saturday. In the hall the telephone rang. It was Fareed. If he knew where she was going now... Guilt was like a hard-boiled egg stuck in her chest. A large cold egg.

"Shadia, I want you to buy some of the fixtures for the bathrooms. Taps and towel hangers. I'm going to send you a list of what I want exactly and the money..."

"I can't, I can't."

"What do you mean you can't? If you go into any large department store..."

"I can't, I wouldn't know where to put these things, how to send them."

There was a rustle on the line and she could hear someone whispering, Fareed distracted a little. He would be at work this time in the day, glass bottles filling up with clear effervescent, the words 7Up written in English and Arabic, white against the dark green.

"You can get good things, things that aren't available here. Gold would be good. It would match..."

Gold. Gold toilet seats!

"People are going to burn in Hell for eating out of gold dishes, you want to sit on gold!"

He laughed. He was used to getting his own way, not easily threatened, "Are you joking with me?"

"No."

In a quieter voice, "This call is costing..."

She knew, she knew. He shouldn't have let her go away. She was not coping with the whole thing, she was not handling the stress. Like the Nigerian student.

"Shadia, gold-colored, not gold. It's smart."

"Allah is going to punish us for this, it's not right..."

"Since when have you become so religious!"

* * *

Bryan was waiting for her on the steps of the museum, familiar-looking against the strange gray of the city, streets where cars had their headlamps on in the middle of the afternoon. He wore a different shirt, a navy-blue jacket. He said, not looking at her, "Ah was beginning to think you wouldnae turn up."

There was no entry fee to the museum, no attendant handing out tickets. Bryan and Shadia walked on soft carpets, thick blue carpets that made Shadia want to take off her shoes. The first thing they saw was a Scottish man from Victorian times. He sat on a chair surrounded with possessions from Africa, overflowing trunks, an ancient map strewn on the floor of the glass cabinet. All the light in the room came from this and other glass cabinets, gleamed on the wax. Shadia turned away, there was an ugliness in the lifelike wispiness of his hair, his determined expression, the way he sat. A hero who had gone away and come back, laden, ready to report.

Bryan began to conscientiously study every display cabinet, read the posters on the wall. She followed him around and thought that he was studious, careful and studious, that was why he did so well in his degree. She watched the intent expression on his face as he looked at everything. For her the posters were an effort to read, the information difficult to take in. It had been so long since she had read anything outside the requirements of the course. But she persevered, saying the words to herself, moving her lips... *During the 18th and 19th centuries, northeast Scotland made a disproportionate impact on the world at large by contributing so many skilled and committed individuals... In serving an empire they gave and received, changed others and were themselves changed and often returned home with tangible reminders of their experiences.*

The tangible reminders were there to see, preserved in spite of the years. Her eyes skimmed over the disconnected objects out of place and time. Iron and copper, little statues. Nothing was of her, nothing belonged to her life at home, what she missed. Here was Europe's vision, the clichés about Africa; cold and old.

She had not expected the dim light and the hushed silence. Apart from Shadia and Bryan, there was only a man with a briefcase, a lady who took down notes, unless there were others out of sight on the second floor. Something electrical, the heating or the lights, gave out a humming sound like that of an air conditioner. It made Shadia feel as if they were in an airplane without windows, detached from the world outside.

"He looks like you, don't you think?" she said to Bryan. They stood in front of a portrait of a soldier who died in the first year of this century. It was the color of his eyes and his hair. But Bryan did not answer her, did not agree with her. He was preoccupied with reading the caption. When she looked at the portrait again, she saw that she was mistaken. That strength in the eyes, the purpose, was something Bryan didn't have. They had strong faith in those days long ago.

Biographies of explorers who were educated in Edinburgh; doctors, courage, they knew what to take to Africa: Christianity, commerce, civilization. They knew what they wanted to bring back;

cotton watered by the Blue Nile, the Zambezi River. She walked after Bryan, felt his concentration, his interest in what was before him and thought, "In a photograph we would not look nice together."

She touched the glass of a cabinet showing papyrus rolls, copper pots. She pressed her forehead and nose against the cool glass. If she could enter the cabinet, she would not make a good exhibit. She wasn't right, she was too modern, too full of mathematics.

Only the carpet, its petroleum blue, pleased her. She had come to the museum expecting sunlight and photographs of the Nile, something to appease her homesickness, a comfort, a message. But the messages were not for her, not for anyone like her. A letter from West Africa, 1762, an employee to his employer in Scotland. An employee trading European goods for African curiosities. *It was difficult to make the natives understand my meaning, even by an interpreter, it being a thing so seldom asked of them, but they have all undertaken to bring something and laughed heartily at me and said I was a good man to love their country so much...*

Love my country so much. She should not be here, there was nothing for her here. She wanted to see minarets, boats fragile on the Nile, people. People like her father. Times she had sat in the waiting room of his clinic, among pregnant women, the pain in her heart because she was going to see him in a few minutes. His room, the air conditioner and the smell of his pipe, his white coat. When she hugged him, he smelled of Listerine mouthwash. He could never remember how old she was, what she was studying, six daughters, how could he keep track? In his confusion, there was freedom for her, games to play, a lot of teasing. She visited his clinic in secret, telling lies to her mother. She loved him more than she loved her mother. Her mother who did everything for her, tidied her room, sewed her clothes from *Burda* magazine. Shadia was 25 and her mother washed everything for her by hand, even her panties and bras.

"I know why they went away," said Bryan, "I understand why they traveled." At last he was talking. She had not seen him intense before. He spoke in a low voice, "They had to get away, to leave here..."

"To escape from the horrible weather..." she was making fun of him. She wanted to put him down. The imperialists who had humiliated her history were heroes in his eyes.

He looked at her. "To escape…" he repeated.

"They went to benefit themselves," she said, "people go away because they benefit in some way…"

"I want to get away," he said.

She remembered when he had opened his palms on the table and said, "I went on a trip to Mecca." There had been pride in his voice.

"I should have gone somewhere else for the course," he went on, "a new place, somewhere down south."

He was on a plateau, not like her. She was punching and struggling for a piece of paper that would say she was awarded an MSc from a British university. For him, the course was a continuation.

"Come and see," he said, and he held her arm. No one had touched her before, not since she had hugged her mother goodbye. Months now in this country and no one had touched her.

She pulled her arm away. She walked away, quickly up the stairs. Metal steps rattled under her feet. She ran up the stairs to the next floor. Guns, a row of guns aiming at her. They had been waiting to blow her away. Scottish arms of centuries ago, gunfire in the service of the empire.

Silver muzzles, a dirty gray now. They must have shone prettily once, under a sun far away. If they blew her away now, where would she fly and fall? A window that looked out at the hostile sky. She shivered in spite of the wool she was wearing, layers of clothes. Hell is not only blazing fire, a part of it is freezing cold, torturous ice and snow. In Scotland's winter you live a glimpse of this unseen world, feel the breath of it in your bones.

There was a bench and she sat down. There was no one here on this floor. She was alone with sketches of jungle animals, words on the wall. The dead speaking out, not of what they know now, but their ignorance of old. A diplomat away from home, in Ethiopia in 1903, Asafa's country long before Asafa was born. *It is difficult to imagine anything more satisfactory or better worth taking part in than a lion drive. We rode back to camp feeling very well indeed. Archie was quite right when he said that this was the first time since we have started that we have really been in Africa—the real Africa of jungle inhabited only by game, and plains where herds of antelope meet your eye in every direction.*

"Shadiya, don't cry." He still pronounced her name wrong because she had not shown him how to say it properly.

He sat next to her on the bench, the blur of his navy jacket blocking the guns, the wall-length pattern of antelope herds. She should explain that she cried easily, there was no need for the alarm on his face. His awkward voice, "Why are you crying?" He didn't know, he didn't understand. He was all wrong, not a substitute...

"They are telling you lies in this museum," she said. "Don't believe them. It's all wrong. It's not jungles and antelopes, it's people. We have things like computers and cars. We have 7Up in Africa and some people, a few people, have bathrooms with golden taps... I shouldn't be here with you. You shouldn't talk to me..."

He said, "Museums change, I can change..."

He didn't know it was a steep path she had no strength for. He didn't understand. Many things, years and landscapes, gulfs. If she was strong she would have explained and not tired of explaining. She would have patiently taught him another language, letters curved like the epsilon and gamma he knew from mathematics. She would have showed him that words could be read from right to left. If she was not small in the museum, if she was really strong, she would have made his trip to Mecca real, not only in a book.

Love Poems

Helon Habila—winner of the 2001 Caine Prize

In the middle of his second year in prison, Lomba got access to pencil and paper and he started a diary. It was not easy. He had to write in secret, mostly in the early mornings when the night warders, tired of peeping through the door bars, waited impatiently for the morning shift. Most of the entries he simply headed with the days of the week; the exact dates, when he used them, were often incorrect. The first entry was in July 1997, a Friday.

Friday, July 1997

Today I begin a diary, to say all the things I want to say, to myself, because here in prison there is no one to listen. I express myself. It stops me from standing in the center of this narrow cell and screaming at the top of my voice. It stops me from jumping up suddenly and bashing my head repeatedly against the wall. Prison chains not so much your hands and feet as it does your voice.

I express myself. I let my mind soar above these walls to bring back distant, exotic bricks with which I seek to build a more endurable cell within this cell. Prison. Misprison. Dis. Un. Prisoner. See? I write of my state in words of derision, aiming thereby to reduce the weight of these walls from my shoulders, to rediscover my nullified individuality. Here in prison, loss of self is often expressed as anger. Anger is the baffled prisoner's attempt to recrystallize his slowly dissolving self. The anger

31

creeps on you, like twilight edging out the day. It builds in you silently until one day it explodes in violence, surprising you. I saw it happen in my first month in prison. A prisoner, without provocation, had attacked an unwary warder at the toilets. The prisoner had come out of a bath-stall and there was the warder before him, monitoring the morning ablutions. Suddenly the prisoner leaped upon him, pulling him by the neck to the ground, grinding him into the black, slimy water that ran in the gutter from the toilets. He pummeled the surprised face repeatedly until other warders came and dragged him away. They beat him to a pulp before throwing him into solitary.

Sometimes the anger leaves you as suddenly as it appeared; then you enter a state of tranquil acceptance. You realize the absolute puerility of your anger: it was nothing but acid, cancer, eating away your bowels in the dark. You accept the inescapability of your fate; and with that, you learn the craft of cunning. You learn ways of surviving—surviving the mindless banality of the walls around you, the incessant harassment from the warders; you learn to hide money in your anus, to hold a cigarette inside your mouth without wetting it. And each day survived is a victory against the jailor, a blow struck for freedom.

My anger lasted a whole year. I remember the exact day it left me. It was a Saturday, a day after a failed escape attempt by two convicted murderers. The warders were more than usually brutal that day; the inmates were on tenterhooks, not knowing from where the next blow would come. We were lined up in rows in our cell, waiting for hours to be addressed by the prison superintendent. When he came, his scowl was hard as rock, his eyes were red and singeing, like fire. He paced up and down before us, systematically flagellating us with his harsh, staccato sentences. We listened, our heads bowed, our hearts quaking.

When he left, an inmate, just back from a week in solitary, broke down and began to weep. His hands shook, as if with a life of their own. "What's going to happen next?" he wailed, going from person to person, looking into each face, not waiting for an answer. "We'll be punished. If I go back there I'll die. I can't. I can't." Now he was standing before me, a skinny mass of eczema inflammations, and ringworm, and snot. He couldn't be more than twenty. I thought, what did he do to end up in this dungeon? Then, without thinking, I reached out and patted his shoulder. I even smiled. With a confidence I did not feel I said kindly, "No one will take you back."

He collapsed into my arms, soaking my shirt with snot and tears and saliva. "Everything will be all right," I repeated over and over. That was the day the anger left me.

* * *

In the over two months that he wrote before he was discovered and his diary seized, Lomba managed to put in quite a large number of entries. Most of them were poems, and letters to various persons from his by now hazy, pre-prison life—letters he can't have meant to send. There were also long soliloquies and desultory interior monologs. The poems were mostly love poems; fugitive lines from poets he had read in school: Donne, Shakespeare, Graves, Eliot, etc. Some were his original compositions rewritten from memory; but a lot were fresh creations—tortured sentimental effusions to women he had known and admired, and perhaps loved. Of course they might be imaginary beings, fabricated in the smithy of his prison-fevered mind. One of the poems reads like a prayer to a much doubted, but fervently hoped for God:

Lord, I've had days black as pitch
And nights crimson as blood

But they have passed over me, like water
Let this one also pass over me, lightly,
Like a smooth rock rolling down the hill,
Down my back, my skin, like soothing water.

That, he wrote, was the prayer on his lips the day the cell door opened without warning and the superintendent, flanked by two baton-carrying warders, entered.

Monday, July

I had waited for this; perversely anticipated it with each day that passed, with each surreptitious sentence that I wrote. I knew it was me he came for when he stood there, looking bigger than life, bigger than the low, narrow cell. The two dogs with him licked their chops and growled menacingly. Their eyes roved hungrily over the petrified inmates caught sitting, or standing, or crouching; laughing, frowning, scratching—like figures in a movie still.

"Lomba, step forward!" his voice rang out suddenly. In the frozen silence it sounded like glass breaking on concrete, but harsher, without the tinkling. I was on my mattress on the floor, my back propped against the damp wall. I stood up. I stepped forward.

He turned the scowl on me. "So, Lomba. You are."

"Yes. I am Lomba," I said. My voice did not fail me. Then he nodded, almost imperceptibly, to the two dogs. They bounded forward eagerly, like game hounds scenting a rabbit, one went to a tiny crevice low in the wall, almost hidden by my mattress. He threw aside the mattress and poked two fingers into the triangular crack. He came out with a thick roll of papers. He looked triumphant as he handed it to the superintendent. Their informer had been exact. The other hound reached unerringly into a tiny hole in the sagging, rain-designed ceiling and brought out another tube of papers.

"Search. More!" the superintendent barked. He unrolled the tubes. He appeared surprised at the number of sheets in his hands. I was. I didn't know I had written so much. When they were through with the holes and crevices the dogs turned their noses to my personal effects. They picked my mattress and shook and sniffed and poked. They ripped off the tattered cloth on its back. There were no papers there. They took the pillow-cum-rucksack (a jeans trouser-leg cut off at mid-thigh and knotted at the ankle) and poured out the contents onto the floor. Two threadbare shirts, one trouser, one plastic comb, one toothbrush, one half-used soap, and a pencil. This is the sum of my life, I thought, this is what I've finally shrunk to; the detritus after the explosion: a comb, a toothbrush, two shirts, one trouser, and a pencil. They swooped on the pencil before it had finished rolling on the floor, almost knocking heads in their haste.

"A pencil!" the superintendent said, shaking his head, exaggerating his amazement. The prisoners were standing in a tight, silent arc. He walked the length of the arc, displaying the papers and pencil, clucking his tongue. "Papers. And pencil. In prison. Can you believe that? In my prison!"

I was sandwiched between the two hounds, watching the drama in silence. I felt removed from it all. Now the superintendent finally turned to me. He bent a little at the waist, pushing his face into mine. I smelt his grating smell; I picked out the white roots beneath his carefully dyed mustache. "I will ask. Once. Who gave you. Papers?" He spoke like that, in jerky, truncated sentences. I shook my head. I did my best to meet his red hot glare. "I don't know."

Some of the inmates gasped, shocked; they mistook my answer for reckless intrepidity. They thought I was foolishly trying to protect my source. But in a few other eyes I saw sympathy. They understood that I had really forgotten from where the papers came.

"Hmm," the superintendent growled. His eyes were on the papers in his hands, he kept folding and unfolding them. I was surprised he had not pounced on me yet. Maybe he was giving me a spell to reconsider my hopeless decision to protect whoever it was I was protecting. The papers. They might have blown in through the door bars on the sentinel wind that sometimes patrolled the prison yard in the evenings. Maybe a sympathetic warder, seeing my yearning for self-expression emblazoned like neon on my face, had secretly thrust the roll of papers into my hands as he passed me in the yard. Maybe—and this seems more probable—I bought them from another inmate (anything can be bought here in prison: from marijuana to a gun). But I had forgotten.

In prison, memory short-circuit is an ally to be cultivated at all costs.

"I repeat. My question. Who gave you the papers?" he thundered into my face, spraying me with spit. I shook my head. "I have forgotten."

I did not see it, but he must have nodded to one of the hounds. All I felt was the crushing blow on the back of my neck, where it meets the head. I pitched forward, stunned by pain and the unexpectedness of it. My face struck the door bars and I fell before the superintendent's boots. I saw blood where my face had touched the floor. I waited. I stared, mesmerized, at the reflection of my eyes in the high gloss of the boots' toecaps. One boot rose and descended on my neck, grinding my face into the floor.

"So, you won't. Talk. You think you are. Tough," he shouted. "You are. Wrong. Twenty years! That is how long I have been dealing with miserable bastards like you. Let this be an example to all of you. Don't. Think you can deceive me. We have our sources of information. You can't. This insect will be taken to solitary and he will be properly dealt with. Until. He is willing to. Talk."

I imagined his eyes rolling balefully round the tight, narrow cell, branding each of the 60 inmates separately. The boot pressed down harder on my neck; I felt a tooth bend at the root.

"Don't think because you are political. Detainees you are untouchable. Wrong. You are all rats. Saboteurs. Anti-government rats. That is all. Rats."

But the superintendent was too well versed in the ways of torture to throw me into solitary that very day. I waited two days before they came and blindfolded me and took me away to the solitary section. In the night. Forty-eight hours. In the first 24 hours I waited with my eyes fixed to the door, bracing myself whenever it opened; but it was only the cooks bringing the meal, or the number-check warders come to count the inmates for the night, or the slop-disposal team. In the second 24 hours I bowed my head into my chest and refused to look up. I was tired. I refused to eat or speak or move.

I was rehearsing for solitary.

They came, around ten in the night. The two hounds. Banging their batons on the door bars, shouting my name, cursing and kicking at anyone in their path. I hastened to my feet before they reached me, my trouser-leg rucksack clutched like a shield in my hands. The light of their torch on my face was like a blow.

"Lomba!"

"Come here! Move!"

"Oya, out. Now!"

I moved, stepping high over the stirring bodies on the floor. A light fell on my rucksack.

"What's that in your hand, eh? Where you think say you dey carry am go? Bring am. Come here! Move!"

Outside. The cell door clanked shut behind us. All the compounds were in darkness. Only security lights from poles shone at the sentry posts. In the distance the prison wall loomed huge and merciless, like a mountain. Broken bottles. Barbed wire. Then they threw the blindfold over my head. My hands instinctively started to rise, but they were held and forced behind me and cuffed.

"Follow me."

One was before me, the other was behind, prodding me with his baton. I followed the footsteps, stumbling.

At first it was easy to say where we were. There were eight compounds within the prison yard; ours was the only one reserved for political detainees. There were four other Awaiting Trial Men's compounds surrounding ours. Of the three compounds for convicted criminals, one was for lifers and one, situated far away from the other compounds, was for condemned criminals. Now we had passed the central lawn where the warders conduct their morning parade. We turned left towards the convicted prisoners' compound, then right towards... we turned right again, then straight... I followed the boots, now totally disoriented. I realized that the forced march had no purpose to it, or rather its purpose was not to reach anywhere immediately. It was part of the torture. I walked. On and on. I bumped into the front warder whenever he stopped abruptly.

"What? You no de see? Idiot!"

Sometimes I heard their voices exchanging pleasantries and amused chuckles with other warders. We marched for over 30 minutes; my slippered feet were chipped and bloody from hitting into stones. My arms locked behind me robbed me of balance and often I fell down, then I'd be prodded and kicked. At some places—near the light poles—I was able to see brief shimmers of light. At other places the darkness was thick as walls, and eerie. I recalled the shuffling, chain-clanging steps we heard late at night through our cell window. Reluctant, sad steps. Hanging victims going to the hanging room; or their ghosts returning. We'd lie in the dark, stricken by immobility as the shuffling grew distant and finally faded away. Now we were on concrete, like a corridor. The steps in front halted. I waited. I heard metal knock against metal, then the creaking of hinges. A hand took my wrist, cold metal touched me as the handcuffs were unlocked. My hands felt light with relief. I must have been standing right before the cell door because when a hand on my back pushed me forward I stumbled inside. I was still blindfolded, but I felt the consistency of the darkness change: it grew thicker, I had to wade through it to feel the walls, the bunk, the walls and walls. That was all: walls so close together that I felt like a man in a hole. I reached down and touched the bunk. I sat down. I heard the door close. I heard footsteps retreating. When I removed the blindfold the darkness remained the same, only now a little air touched my face. I closed my eyes. I don't know how long I remained like that, hunched forward on the bunk, my sore, throbbing feet on the floor, my elbows on my knees, my eyes closed. As if realizing how close I was to tears, the smells got up from their corners, shook the dust off their buttocks and lined up to make my acquaintance—to distract me from my sad thoughts. I shook their hands one by one: Loneliness Smell, Anger Smell, Waiting Smell, Masturbation Smell, Fear Smell. The most noticeable was Fear Smell, it filled the tiny room from floor to ceiling, edging out the others. I did not cry. I opened my lips and slowly, like a Buddhist chanting his mantra, I prayed:

Let this one also pass over me, lightly,
Like a smooth rock rolling down the hill
Down my back, my skin, like soothing water.

* * *

He was in solitary for three days. This is how he described the cell in his diary: *The floor was about six feet by ten, and the ceiling was about seven feet from the floor. There were exactly two pieces of furniture: the iron bunk with its tattered, lice-ridden mat, and the slop bucket in the corner.*

His only contacts with the outside were in the nights when his mess of beans, once daily, at 6:00PM, was pushed into the cell through a tiny flap at the bottom of the wrought iron door, and at precisely 8:00PM when the cell door was opened for him to take out the slop bucket and take in a fresh one. He wrote that the only way he distinguished night from day was by the movement of his bowels—in hunger or in purgation. Once a day.

Then on the third day, late in the evening, things began to happen. Like Nichodemus, the superintendent came to him, covertly, seeking knowledge.

Third Day. Solitary Cell
When I heard metal touch the lock on the door I sat down from my blind pacing. I composed my countenance. The door opened, bringing in unaccustomed rays of light. I blinked. *"Oh, sweet light. May your face meeting mine bring me good fortune."* When my eyes adjusted to the light, the superintendent was standing on the threshold—the cell entrance was a tight, lighted frame around his looming form. He advanced into the cell and stood in the center, before my disadvantaged position on the bunk. His legs were planted apart, like an A. He looked like a cartoon figure: his jodhpurs-like uniform trousers emphasized the skinniness of his calves, where they disappeared into the glass-glossy boots. His stomach bulged and hung like a belted sack. He cleared his voice. When I looked at his face I saw his blubber lips twitching with the effort of an attempted smile. But he couldn't quite carry it off. He started to speak, then stopped abruptly and began to pace the tiny space before the bunk. When he returned to his original position he stopped. Now I noticed the sheaf of papers in his hands.

He gestured in my face with it.

"These. Are the. Your papers." His English was more disfigured than usual: soaking wet with the effort of saying whatever it was he wanted to say. "I read. All. I read your file again. Also. You are journalist. This is your second year. Here. Awaiting trial. For organizing violence. Demonstration against. Anti-government demonstration against the military legal government."

He did not thunder as usual.

"It is not true."

"Eh?" The surprise on his face was comical. "You deny?"

"I did not organize a demonstration. I went there as a reporter."

"Well..." He shrugged. "That is not my business. The truth. Will come out at your. Trial."

"But when will that be? I have been forgotten. I am not allowed a lawyer, or visitors. I have been awaiting trial for two years now..."

"Do you complain? Look. Twenty years I've worked in prisons all over this country. Nigeria. North. South. East. West. Twenty years. Don't be stupid. Sometimes it is better this way. How. Can you win a case against government? Wait. Hope."

Now he lowered his voice, like a conspirator: "Maybe there'll be another coup, eh? Maybe the leader will collapse and die; he is mortal after all. Maybe a civilian government will come. Then. There will be amnesty for all political prisoners. Amnesty. Don't worry. Enjoy yourself."

I looked at him planted before me like a tree, his hands clasped behind him, the papier-mâché smile on his lips. *Enjoy yourself.* I turned the phrase over and over in my mind.

When I lay to sleep rats kept me awake, and mosquitoes, and lice, and hunger, and loneliness. The rats bit at my toes and scuttled around in the low ceiling, sometimes falling onto my face from the holes in the ceiling. *Enjoy yourself.*

"Your papers," he said, thrusting them at me once more. I was not sure if he was offering them to me. "I read them. All. Poems. Letters. Poems, no problem. The letters, illegal. I burned them. Prisoners sometimes smuggle out letters to the press to make us look foolish. Embarrass the government. But the poems are harmless. Love Poems. And diaries. You wrote the poems for your girl, isn't it?" He bent forward; he clapped a hand on my shoulder. I realized with wonder that the man, in his awkward, flatfooted way, was making overtures of friendship to me. My eyes fell on the boot that had stepped on my neck just five days ago. What did he want?

"Perhaps because I work in Prison. I wear uniform. You think I don't know poetry, eh? Soyinka, Okigbo, Shakespeare."

It was apparent that he wanted to talk about poems, but he was finding it hard to begin.

"What do you want?" I asked.

He drew back to his full height. "I write poems too. Sometimes," he added quickly when the wonder grew and grew on my face. He dipped his hand into his jacket pocket and came out with a foolscap paper. He unfolded it and handed it to me.

"Read."

It was a poem; handwritten. The title was written in capital letters: "MY LOVE FOR YOU." Like a man in a dream I ran my eyes over the bold squiggles. After the first stanza, I saw that it was a thinly veiled imitation of one of my poems. I sensed his waiting. He was hardly breathing. I let him wait. Lord, I can't remember another time when I had felt so good. So powerful. I was Samuel Johnson and he was an aspiring poet waiting anxiously for my verdict, asking tremulously: "Sir, is it poetry, is it Pindar?"

I wanted to say, with as much sarcasm as I could put into my voice: "Sir, your poem is both original and interesting, but the part that is interesting is not original, and the part that is original is not interesting."

But all I said was, "Not bad, you need to work on it some more."

The eagerness went out of his face and for a fleeting moment the scowl returned. "I promised my lady a poem. She is educated, you know. A teacher. You will write a poem for me. For my lady."

"You want me to write a poem for you?" I tried to mask the surprise, the confusion, and yes, the eagerness in my voice. He was offering me a chance to write.

"I am glad you understand. Her name is Janice. She has been to a university. She has class. Not like other girls. She teaches in my son's school. That is how we met."

Even jailors fall in love, I thought inanely.

"At first she didn't take me seriously. She thought I only wanted to use her and dump her. And. Also. We are of different religion. She is Christian, I am Muslim. But no problem. I love her. But she still doubted. I did not know what to do. Then I saw one of your poems... yes, this one."

He handed me the poem. "It said everything I wanted to tell her."

It was one of my earliest poems, rewritten from memory.

"'Three Words.' I gave it to her yesterday when I took her out."

"You gave her my poem?"

"Yes."

"You... you told her you wrote it?"

"Yes, yes, of course. I wrote it again in my own hand," he said, unabashed. He had been speaking in a rush; now he drew himself together and, as though to reassert his authority, began to pace the room, speaking in a subdued, measured tone.

"I can make life easy for you here. I am the prison superintendent. There is nothing I cannot do, if I want. So write. The poem. For me."

There is nothing I cannot do: You can get me cigarettes, I am sure, and food. You can remove me from solitary. But can you stand me outside these walls free under the stars? Can you connect the tips of my upraised arms to the stars so that the surge of liberty passes down my body to the soft downy grass beneath my feet?

I asked for paper and pencil. And a book to read.

* * *

He was removed from the solitary section that day. The pencil and papers came, the book too. But not the one he had asked for. He wanted Wole Soyinka's prison notes, *The Man Died*; but when it came it was *A Brief History of West Africa*. While writing the poems in the cell, Lomba would sometimes let his mind wander; he'd picture the superintendent and his lady out on a date, how he'd bring out the poem and unfold it and hand it to her and say boldly, "I wrote it for you. Myself."

They sit outside on the veranda at her suggestion. The light from the hanging, wind-swayed Chinese lanterns falls softly on them. The breeze blowing from the lagoon below smells fresh to her nostrils; she loves its dampness on her bare arms and face. She looks across the circular table, with its vase holding a single rose petal, at him. He appears nervous. A thin film of sweat covers his forehead. He removes his cap and dabs at his forehead with a white handkerchief.

"Do you like it, a Chinese restaurant?" he asks, like a father anxious to please his favorite child. It is their first outing together. He pestered her until she gave in. Sometimes she is at a loss what to make of his attentions. She sighs. She turns her plump face to the deep blue lagoon. A white boat with dark stripes on its sides speeds past; a figure is crouched inside, almost invisible. Her light, flower-patterned gown shivers in the light breeze. She watches him covertly. He handles his chopsticks awkwardly, but determinedly.

"Waiter!" he barks, his mouth full of fish, startling her. "Bring another bottle of wine!"

"No. I am all right, really," she says firmly, putting down her chopsticks.

After the meal, which has been quite delicious, he lifts the tiny, wine-filled porcelain cup before him and says: "To you. And me."

She sips her drink, avoiding his eyes.

"I love you, Janice. Very much. I know you think I am not serious. That I only want to suck. The juice and throw away the peel. No." He suddenly dips his hand into the pocket of his well-ironed white kaftan and brings out a yellow paper.

"Read and see." He pushes the paper across the table to her. "I wrote it. For you. A poem."

She opens the paper. It smells faintly of sandalwood. She looks at the title: "Three Words." She reaches past the vase with its single, white rose petal, past the wine bottle, the wine glasses, and covers his hairy hand with hers briefly. "Thank you."

She reads the poem, shifting in her seat towards the swaying light of the lantern:

Three Words

When I hear the waterfall clarity of your laughter,
When I see the twilight softness of your eyes,

I feel like draping you all over myself, like a cloak,
To be warmed by your warmth.

Your flower petal innocence, your perennial
Sapling resilience—your endless charms
All these set my mind on wild flights of fancy:
I add word unto word,
I compare adjectives and coin exotic phrases
But they all seem jaded, corny, unworthy
Of saying all I want to say to you.

So I take refuge in these simple words
Trusting my tone, my hand in yours, when I
Whisper them, to add depth and new
Twists of meaning to them. Three words:
I love you.

With his third or fourth poem for the superintendent, Lomba began to send Janice cryptic messages. She seemed to possess an insatiable appetite for love poems. Every day a warder came to the cell, in the evening, with the same request from the superintendent: "The poem." When he finally ran out of original poems, Lomba began to plagiarize the masters from memory. Here are the opening lines of one:

Janice, your beauty is to me
Like those treasures of gold…

Another one starts:
I wonder, my heart, what you and I
Did till we loved…

But it was Lomba's bowdlerization of Sappho's "Ode" that brought the superintendent to the cell door:

A peer of goddesses she seems to me
The lady who sits over against me
Face to face,
Listening to the sweet tones of my voice,
And the loveliness of my laughing.
It is this that sets my heart fluttering
In my chest,
For if I gaze on you but for a little while
I am no longer master of my voice,
And my tongue lies useless
And a delicate flame runs over my skin
No more do I see with my eyes;
The sweat pours down me
I am all seized with trembling
And I grow paler than the grass
My strength fails me
And I seem little short of dying.

He came to the cell door less than twenty minutes after the poem had reached him, waving the paper in the air, a real smile splitting his granite face.

"Lomba, come out!" he hollered through the iron bars. Lomba was lying on his wafer-thin mattress, on his back, trying to imagine figures out of the rain designs on the ceiling. The door officer hastily threw open the door.

The superintendent threw a friendly arm over Lomba's shoulders. He was unable to stand still. He walked Lomba up and down the grassy courtyard.

"This poem. Excellent. With this poem. After. I'll ask her for marriage." He was incoherent in his excitement. He raised the paper and read aloud the first line, straining his eyes in the dying light: "'A peer of goddesses she seems to me.' Yes. Excellent. She will be happy. Do you think I should ask her for. Marriage. Today?"

He stood before Lomba, bent forward expectantly, his legs planted in their characteristic A-formation.

"Why not?" Lomba answered. A passing warder stared at the superintendent and the prisoner curiously. The twilight fell dully on the broken bottles studded in the concrete of the prison wall.

"Yes. Why not. Good." The superintendent walked up and down, his hands clasped behind him, his head bowed in thought. Finally he stopped before Lomba and declared gravely: "Tonight. I'll ask her."

Lomba smiled at him, sadly. The superintendent saw the smile; he did not see the sadness.

"Good. You are happy. I am happy too. I'll send you a packet of cigarette. Two packets. Today. Enjoy. Now go back inside."

He turned abruptly on his heels and marched away.

July

Janice came to see me two days after I wrote her the Sappho. I thought, she has discovered my secret messages, my scriptive Morse tucked innocently in the lines of the poems I've written her.

Two o'clock is compulsory siesta time. The opening of the cell door brought me awake. My limbs felt heavy and lifeless. I feared I might have an infection. The warder came directly to me. "Oya, get up. The superintendent wan see you." His skin was coarse, coal black. He was fat and his speech came out in labored gasps.

"Oya, get up. Get up," he repeated impatiently.

I was in that lethargic, somnambulistic state condemned people surely fall into when, in total inanition and despair, they await their fate—without fear or hope, because nothing could be changed. No dew-wet finger of light would come poking into the parched gloom of the abyss they tenanted. I did not want to write any more poems for the superintendent's lover. I did not want any more of his cigarettes. I was tired of being pointed at behind my back, of being whispered about by the other inmates as the superintendent's informer, his fetch-water. I wanted to recover my lost dignity. Now I realize that I really had no "self" to express; that self had flown away from me the day the chains touched my hands; what is left here is nothing but a mass of protruding bones and unkempt hair and tearful eyes; an asshole for shitting and farting; and a penis that in the mornings grows turgid in vain. This left-over self, this sea-bleached wreck panting on the iron-filing sands of the shores of this penal island is nothing but hot air, and hair, and ears cocked, hopeful...

So I said to the warder: "I don't want to see him today. Tell him I'm sick."

The fat face contorted. He raised his baton in Pavlovian response. "What!" But our eyes met. He was smart enough to decipher the bold "No Trespassing" sign written in mine. Smart enough to obey. He moved back, shrugging. "Na you go suffer!" he blustered, and left.

I was aware of the curious eyes staring at me. I closed mine. I willed my mind over the prison walls to other places. Free. I dreamed of standing under the stars, my hands raised, their tips touching the blinking, pulsating electricity of the stars. My naked body surging with the surge. The rain would be falling. There'd be nothing else: just me and rain and stars and my feet on the wet downy grass earthing the electricity of freedom.

He returned almost immediately. There was a smirk on his fat face as he handed me a note. I recognized the superintendent's clumsy scrawl. It was brief, a one-liner: *Janice is here. Come. Now.* Truncated, even in writing. I got up and pulled on my sweat-grimed shirt. I slipped my feet into my old, worn-out slippers. I followed the warder. We passed the parade ground, and the convicted men's compound. An iron gate, far to our right, locked permanently, led to the women's wing of the prison. We passed the old laundry, which now served as a barbershop on Saturdays—the prison's sanitation day. A gun-carrying warder opened a tiny door in the huge gate that led into a foreyard where the prison officials had their offices. I had been here before, once, on my first day in prison. There were cars parked before the offices, cadets in their well-starched uniforms came and went, their young faces looking comically stern. Female secretaries with time on their hands stood in the corridors gossiping. The superintendent's office was not far from the gate;

a flight of three concrete steps led up to a thick wooden door, which bore the single word: SUPERINTENDENT.

My guide knocked on it timidly before turning the handle.

"The superintendent wan see am," he informed the secretary. She barely looked up from her typewriter; she nodded. Her eyes were bored, uncurious.

"Enter," the warder said to me, pointing to a curtained doorway beside the secretary's table. I entered. A lady sat in one of the two visitors' armchairs. Her back to the door; her elbows rested on the huge Formica-topped table before her. Janice. She was alone. When she turned, I noted that my mental image of her was almost accurate. She was plump. Her face was warm and homely. She came half-way out of her chair, turning it slightly so that it faced the other chair. There was a tentative smile on her face as she asked: "Mr. Lomba?"

I almost said no, surprised by the "mister." I nodded. She pointed at the empty chair. "Please sit down."

She extended a soft, pudgy hand to me. I took it and marveled at its softness. She was a teacher; the hardness would be in the fingers: the tips of the thumb and the middle finger, and the side of the index finger.

"Muftau... the superintendent, will be here soon. He just stepped out," she said. Her voice was clear, a little high-pitched. Her English was correct, each word carefully pronounced and projected. Like in a classroom. I was struck by how clean she looked, squeaky-clean; her skin glowed like a child's after a bath. She had obviously taken a lot of trouble with her appearance: her blue evening dress looked almost new, a slash of red lipstick extended to the left cheek after missing the curve of the lip. She crossed and uncrossed her legs, tapping the left foot on the floor. She was nervous. That was when I realized I had not said a word since I entered.

"Welcome to the prison," I said, unable to think of anything else.

She nodded. "Thank you. I told Muftau I wanted to see you. The poems, I just knew it wasn't him writing them. I went along with it for a while, but later I told him."

She opened the tiny handbag in her lap and took out some

papers. The poems. She put them on the table and unfolded them, smoothing out the creases, uncurling the edges. "After the Sappho I decided I must see you. It was my favorite poem in school, and I like your version of it."

"Thank you," I said. I liked her directness, her sense of humor.

"So I told him—look, I know who the writer is, he is one of the prisoners, isn't he? That surprised him. He couldn't figure out how I knew. But I was glad he didn't deny it. I told him that. And if we are getting married, there shouldn't be secrets between us, should there?"

Ah, I thought, so my Sappho has worked the magic. Aloud, I said, "Congratulations."

She nodded. "Thanks. Muftau is a nice person, really, when you get to know him. His son, Farouk, was in my class—he's finished now—really, you should see them together. So touching. I know he has his awkward side, and that he was once married—but I don't care. After all, I have a little past too. Who doesn't?" She added the last quickly, as if scared she was revealing too much to a stranger. Her left hand went up and down as she spoke, like a hypnotist, like a conductor. After a brief pause, she continued:

"After all the pain he's been through with his other wife, he deserves some happiness. She was in the hospital a whole year before she died."

Muftau. The superintendent had a name, and a history, maybe even a soul. I looked at his portrait hanging on the wall, he looked young in it, serious-faced and smart, like the cadet warders outside. I turned to her and said suddenly and sincerely: "I am glad you came. Thanks."

Her face broke into a wide, dimpled smile. She was actually pretty. A little past her prime, past her sell-by date, but still nice, still viable. "Oh, no. I am the one that should be glad. I love meeting poets. I love your poems. Really I do."

"Not all of them are mine."

"I know—but you give them a different feel, a different tone. And also, I discovered your S.O.S. I had to come..." She picked the poems off the table and handed them to me. There were thirteen of them. Seven were my originals, six were purloined. She had carefully underlined in red ink certain lines in some of them—the same line, actually, recurring.

There was a waiting-to-be-congratulated smile on her face as she awaited my comment.

"You noticed," I said.

"Of course I did. S.O.S. It wasn't apparent at first. I began to notice the repetition with the fifth poem. 'Save my soul, a prisoner.'"

Save my soul, a prisoner... The first time I put down the words, in the third poem, it had been non-deliberate, I was just making alliteration. Then I began to repeat it in the subsequent poems. But how could I tell her that the message wasn't really for her, or for anyone else? It was for myself, perhaps, written by me to my own soul, to every other soul, the collective soul of the universe.

I said to her: "The first time I wrote it, an inmate had died. His name was Thomas. No, he wasn't sick. He just started vomiting after the afternoon meal, and before the warders came to take him to the clinic, he died. Just like that. He died. Watching his stiffening face, with the mouth open and the eyes staring, as the inmates took him out of the cell, an irrational fear had gripped me. I saw myself being taken out like that, my lifeless arms dangling, brushing the ground. The fear made me sit down, shaking uncontrollably amidst the flurry of movements and voices excited by the tragedy. I was scared. I felt certain I was going to end up like that. Have you ever felt like that, certain that you were going to die? No? I did. I was going to die. My body would end up in some anonymous mortuary, and later in an unmarked grave, and no one would know. No one would care. It happens every day here. I am a political detainee, if I die I am just one antagonist less. That was when I wrote the S.O.S. It was just a message in a bottle, thrown without much hope into the sea..." I stopped speaking when my hands started to shake. I wanted to put them in my pocket to hide them from her. But she had seen it. She left her seat and came to me. She took both my hands in hers.

"You'll not die. You'll get out alive. One day it will all be over," she said. Her perfume, mixed with her female smell, rose into my nostrils; flowery, musky. I had forgotten the last time a woman had stood so close to me. Sometimes, in our cell, when the wind blows from the female prison, we'll catch distant sounds of female screams and shouts and even laughter. That is the closest we ever come to women. Only when the wind blows, at the right time, in the right direction. Her hands on mine, her smell, her presence, acted like fire on some huge, prehistoric glacier locked deep in my chest. And when her hand touched my head and the back of my neck, I wept.

When the superintendent returned my sobbing face was buried in Janice's ample bosom, her hands were on my head, patting, consoling, like a mother, all the while cooing softly, "One day it will finish."

I pulled away from her. She gave me her handkerchief.

"What is going on? Why is he crying?"

He was standing just within the door—his voice was curious, with a hint of jealousy. I wiped my eyes; I subdued my body's spasms. He advanced slowly into the room and went round to his seat. He remained standing, his hairy hands resting on the table.

"Why is he crying?" he repeated to Janice.

"Because he is a prisoner," Janice replied simply. She was still standing beside me, facing the superintendent.

"Well. So. Is he realizing that just now?"

"Don't be so unkind, Muftau."

I returned the handkerchief to her.

"Muftau, you must help him."

"Help. How?"

"You are the prison superintendent. There's a lot you can do."

"But I can't help him. He is a political detainee. He has not even been tried."

"And you know that he is never going to be tried. He will be kept here forever, forgotten." Her voice became sharp and indignant. The superintendent drew back his seat and sat down. His eyes were lowered. When he looked up, he said earnestly, "Janice. There's nothing anyone can do for him. I'll be implicating myself.

Besides, his lot is far easier than that of other inmates. I give him things. Cigarettes. Soap. Books. And I let him. Write."

"How can you be so unfeeling! Put yourself in his shoes—two years away from friends, from family, without the power to do anything you wish to do. Two years in CHAINS! How can you talk of cigarettes and soap, as if that were substitute enough for all that he has lost?" She was like a teacher confronting an erring student. Her left hand tapped the table for emphasis as she spoke.

"Well." He looked cowed. His scowl alternated rapidly with a smile. He stared at his portrait on the wall behind her. He spoke in a rush. "Well. I could have done something. Two weeks ago. The Amnesty International. People came. You know, white men. They wanted names of. Political detainees held. Without trial. To pressure the government to release them."

"Well?"

"Well." He still avoided her stare. His eyes touched mine and hastily passed. He picked a pen and twirled it between his fingers, the pen slipped out of his fingers and fell to the floor.

"I didn't. Couldn't. You know... I thought he was comfortable. And, he was writing the poems, for you..." His voice was almost pleading. Surprisingly, I felt no anger at him. He was just Man. Man in his basic, rudimentary state, easily moved by the powerful emotions, like love, lust, anger, greed, fear; but totally dumb to the finer, acquired emotions like pity and mercy and humor, and justice.

Janice slowly picked up her bag from the table. There was enormous dignity to her movements. She clasped the bag under her left arm. Her words were slow, almost sad. "I see now that I've made a mistake. You are not really the man I thought you were..."

"Janice." He stood up and started coming round to her, but a gesture stopped him.

"No. Let me finish. I want you to contact these people. Give them his name. If you can't do that, then forget you ever knew me."

Her hand brushed my arm as she passed me to the door. He

started after her, then stopped halfway across the room. We stared in silence at the curtained doorway, listening to the sound of her heels on the bare floor till it finally died away. He returned slowly to his seat and slumped into it. The wood creaked audibly in the quiet office.

"Go," he said, not looking at me.

The above is the last entry in Lomba's diary. There's no record of how far the superintendent went to help him regain his freedom, but like he told Janice, there was very little he could have done for a political detainee—especially since about a week after that meeting a coup was attempted against the military leader, General Sani Abacha, by some officers close to him. There was an immediate crackdown on all pro-democracy activists, and the prisons all over the country swelled with political detainees. A lot of those already in detention were transferred randomly to other prisons around the country—for security reasons. Lomba was among them. He was transferred to Agodi Prison in Ibadan. From there he was moved to the far north, a small desert town called Gashuwa. There was no record of him after that.

A lot of these political prisoners died in detention, although only the prominent ones made the headlines—people like Moshood Abiola and General Yar Adua.

But somehow it is hard to imagine that Lomba died, a lot seems to point to the contrary. His diary, his economical expressions, show a very sedulous character at work. A survivor. The years in prison must have taught him not to hope too much, not to despair too much, that for the prisoner nothing kills as surely as too much hope or too much despair. He had learned to survive in tiny atoms, piecemeal, a day at a time. It is probable that in 1998, when the military dictator, Abacha, died, and his successor, General Abdulsalam Abubakar, dared to open the gates to democracy, and to liberty for the political detainees, Lomba was in the ranks of those released.

This is how it might have happened: Lomba was perhaps seated in a dingy cell in Gashuwa, his eyes closed, his mind soaring above the glass-studded prison walls, mingling with the stars and the rain in elemental union of freedom; then the door clanked open, and when he opened his eyes, it was Liberty standing over him, smiling kindly, extending an arm.

And Liberty said softly, "Come. It is time to go."

And they left, arm in arm.

Discovering Home

Binyavanga Wainaina—winner of the 2002 Caine Prize

Cape Town, June 1995

There is a problem. Somebody has locked themselves in the toilet. The upstairs bathroom is locked and Frank has disappeared with the keys. There is a small riot at the door, as drunk women with smudged lipstick and crooked wigs bang on the door.

There is always that point at a party when people are too drunk to be having fun; when strange smelly people are asleep on your bed; when the good booze runs out and there is only Sedgwick's Brown Sherry and a carton of sweet white wine; when you realize that all your roommates have gone and all this is your responsibility; when the DJ is slumped over the stereo and some strange person is playing "I'm a Barbie girl, in a Barbie Wo-o-orld" over and over again.

I have been working here, in Observatory, Cape Town, for two years and rarely breached the boundary of my clique. Fear, I suppose, and a feeling that I am not quite ready to leave a place that has let me be anything I want to be—and provided not a single predator. That is what this party is all about:

I am going home for a year.

So maybe this feeling that my movements are being guided is explicable. This time tomorrow, I will be sitting next to my mother. We shall soak each other up. Flights to distant places always arouse in me a peculiar awareness: that what we refer to as reality—not the substance, but the organization of reality—is really a strand as thin as the puffy white lines that planes leave behind as they fly.

It will be so easy—I will wonder why I don't do this every day. I hope to be in Kenya for thirteen months. I intend to travel as much as possible and finally to attend my grandparents' 60th wedding anniversary in Uganda in December.

There are so many possibilities that could overturn this journey, yet I will get there. If there is a miracle in the idea of life it is this: that we are able to exist for a time—in defiance of chaos. Later, we often forget how dicey everything was: how the tickets almost didn't materialize; how the event almost got postponed. Phrases swell, becoming bigger than their context and speak to us with TRUTH. We wield this series of events as our due, the standard for gifts of the future. We live the rest of our lives with the utter knowledge that there is something deliberate, a vein in us that transports everything into place—*if* we follow the stepping stones of certainty.

After the soft light and mellow manners of Cape Town, Nairobi is a shot of whisky. We drive from the airport into the City Center; around us, matatus: those brash, garish minibus-taxis, so irritating to every Kenyan except those who own one, or work for one. I can see them as the best example of contemporary Kenyan Art. The best of them get new paint jobs every few months. Oprah seems popular right now, and Gidi Gidi Maji Maji, one of the hottest bands in Kenya, and the inevitable Tupac. The colored lights, and fancy horn and the purple interior lighting; the Hip Hop blaring out of speakers I will never afford.

This is Nairobi! This is what you do to get ahead: make yourself boneless, and treat your straitjacket as if it is a game, a challenge. The city is now all on the streets, sweet-talk and hustle. Our worst recession ever has just produced brighter, more creative matatus.

It is good to be home.

In the afternoon, I take a walk down River Road, all the way to Nyamakima. This is the main artery of movement to and from Public Transport Vehicles. It is ruled by manambas (taxi touts) and their image is cynical—every laugh is a sneer, the city is a war or a game. It is a useful face to carry, here where humanity invades all the space you do not claim with conviction.

The desperation that is for me the most touching is the expressions of the people who come from the rural areas into the City Center to sell their produce: thin-faced, with the massive cheekbones common amongst Kikuyus—so dominating they seem like an appendage to be embarrassed about—something that draws attention to their faces, when attention is the last thing they want. Anywhere else those faces are beauty. Their eyes dart about in a permanent fear, unable to train themselves to a background of so much chaos. They do not know how to put on a glassy expression.

Those who have been in the fresh produce business for long are immediately visible: mostly old women in khanga sarongs with weary take-it-or-leave-it voices. They hang out in groups, chattering away constantly, as if they want no quiet where the fragility of their community will reveal itself.

* * *

I am at home. The past eight hours are already receding into the forgotten; I was in Cape Town this morning, I am in Nakuru, Kenya now.

Blink.

Mum looks tired and her eyes are sleepier than usual. She has never seemed frail, but does so now. I decide that it is I who is growing, changing, and my attempts at maturity make her seem more human.

I make my way to the kitchen: the Nandi woman still rules the corridor.

After ten years, I can still move about with ease in the dark. I stop at that hollow place, the bit of wall on the other side of the fireplace. My mother's voice, talking to my dad, echoes in the corridor. None of us has her voice: if crystal was water solidified, her voice would be the last splash of water before it solidifies.

Light from the kitchen brings the Nandi woman to life. She is a painting.

I was terrified of her when I was a kid. Her eyes seemed so alive and the red bits growled at me menacingly. Her broad face announced an immobility that really scared me; I was stuck there, fenced into a tribal reserve by her features. *Rings on her ankles and bells on her nose, she will make music wherever she goes.*

Why? Did I sense, so young, that her face could never translate into acceptability? That, however disguised, it could not align itself to the program I aspired to? In Kenya there are two sorts of people. Those on one side of the line will wear third-hand clothing till it rots, they will eat dirt, but school fees will be paid. On the other side of the line live people you may see in coffee-table books. Impossibly exotic and much fewer in number than the coffee-table books suggest. They are like an old and lush jungle that continues to flourish its leaves and unfurl extravagant blooms, refusing to realize that somebody cut off the water—often somebody from the other side of the line.

These two groups of people are fascinated by one another. We, the modern ones, are fascinated by the completeness of the old ones. To us it seems that everything is mapped out and defined for them—and everybody is fluent in those definitions. The old ones are not much impressed with our society, or manners—what catches their attention is our tools, the cars and medicines and telephones and wind-up dolls and guns.

In my teens, I was set alight by the poems of Senghor and Okot P'Bitek; the Nandi woman became my Negritude. I pronounced her beautiful, marveled at her cheekbones and mourned the lost wisdom in her eyes, but I still would have preferred to sleep with Pam Ewing or Iman.

It was a source of terrible fear for me that I could never love her. I covered that betrayal with a complicated imagery that had no connection to my gut: O Nubian Princess, and other bad poetry. She moved to my bedroom for a while, next to the kente wall-hanging, but my mother took her back to her pulpit.

Over the years, I learned to look at her amiably. She filled me with a lukewarm nostalgia for things lost. I never again attempted to look beyond her costume.

She is younger than me now; I can see that she has a girlishness about her. Her eyes are the artist's only real success—they suggest mischief, serenity, vulnerability and a weary wisdom. Today, I don't need to bludgeon my brain with her beauty, it just sinks in, and I am floored by lust: It makes me feel like I have desecrated something.

Then I see it.

Have I been such a bigot? Everything. The slight smile, the angle of her head and shoulders, the mild flirtation with the artist: *I know you want me, I know something you don't.*

Mona Lisa: not a single thing says otherwise. The truth is that I never saw the smile: her thick lips created such a war between my intellect and emotions that I never noticed the smile.

The artist is probably not African, not only because of the obvious Mona Lisa business but also because, for the first time, I realize that the woman's expression is *inaccurate*. In Kenya, you will only see such an expression in girls who went to private schools, or who are brought up in the richer surburbs of the larger towns.

That look, that toying slight smile could not have happened with an actual Nandi woman. In the portrait, she has covered her vast sexuality with a shawl of ice, letting only the hint of smile reveal that she has a body that can quicken: a flag on the moon. The artist has got the dignity right but the sexuality is European: it would be difficult for an African artist to get that wrong.

The lips too seem wrong. There's an awkwardness about them, as if a shift of aesthetics has taken place on the plane of muscles between her nose and her mouth. Also, the mouth strives too hard for symmetry, as if to apologize for its thickness. That mouth is meant to break open like the flesh of a ripe mango; restraint of expression is not common in Kenya and certainly not among the Nandi.

I turn, and head for the kitchen. I cherish the kitchen at night. It is cavernous, chilly and echoing with night noises that are muffled by the vast spongy silence outside. After so many years in cupboard-sized South African kitchens, I feel more thrilled than I should.

On my way back to my room, I turn and face the Nandi woman thinking of the full circle since I left. When I left, White people ruled South Africa. When I left, Kenya was a one-party dictatorship. When I left, I was relieved that I had escaped the burdens and guilts of being in Kenya, of facing my roots, and repudiating them. Here I am, looking for them again.

I know, her red-rimmed eyes say. *I know.*

A fluid disposition: Masailand, August 1995

A few minutes ago, I was sleeping comfortably in the front of a Landrover Discovery. Now I have been unceremoniously dumped by the side of the road as the extension officer makes a mad dash for the night comforts of Narok town. Driving at night in this area is not a bright idea.

It is an interesting aspect of traveling to a new place that, for the first few moments, your eyes cannot concentrate on the particular. I am overwhelmed by the glare of dusk, by the shiver of wind on undulating acres of wheat and barley, by the vision of mile upon mile of space free from our wirings. So much is my focus derailed that when I return to myself I find, to my surprise, that my feet are not off the ground—that the landscape had grabbed me with such force it sucked up the awareness of myself for a moment.

It occurs to me that there is no clearer proof of the subjectivity (or selectivity) of our senses than at moments like this. Seeing is always only noticing. We pass our eyes upon the landscapes of our familiars and choose what to acknowledge.

There are rotor-blades of cold chopping away in my nostrils. The silence, after the non-stop drone of the car, is as persistent as cobwebs, as intrusive as the loudest of noises. I have an urge to claw it away.

I am in Masailand.

Not television Masailand—rolling grasslands, lions, and acacia trees.

We are high up in the Mau Hills. Here there aren't vast fields of grain—there are forests. Here impenetrable weaves of highland forest dominated by bamboo cover the landscape. Inside them, there are many elephants, which come out at night and leave enormous pancakes of shit on the road. When I was a kid, I used to think that elephants use dusty roads as toilet paper like cats—sitting on the sand with their haunches and levering themselves forward with their forelegs.

Back on the *choosing to see* business: I know, chances are I will see no elephants for the weeks I am here. I will see people. It occurs to me that if I was White, chances are I would choose to see elephants— and this would be a very different story. That story would be about the wide, empty spaces people from Europe yearn to get lost in, rather than the cozy surround of kin we Africans generally seek.

Whenever I read something by some White writer who stopped by Kenya, I am astounded by the amount of game that appears for breakfast at their patios and the snakes that drop into the baths and the lions that terrorize their calves. I have seen one snake in my life. I don't know anybody who has ever been bitten by one.

The cold air is really irritating. I want to breathe in—suck up the moist mountain-ness of the air, the smell of fever tree and dung—but the process is just too painful. What do people do in wintry places? Do they have some sort of nasal sensodyne?

I can see our ancient Massey Ferguson wheezing up a distant hill. They are headed this way. Relief!

* * *

A week later, I am on a tractor, freezing my butt off, as we make our way from the wheat fields and back to camp. We've been supervising the spraying of wheat and barley in the fields my father leases here.

There isn't much to look forward to at night here, no pubs hidden in the bamboo jungle. You can't even walk about freely at night because the areas outside are full of stinging nettles. We will be in bed by seven to beat the cold. I will hear stories about frogs that sneak under one's bed and turn into beautiful women who entrap you. I will hear stories about legendary tractor drivers—people who could turn the jagged roof of Mt. Kilimanjaro into a neat afro. I will hear about Masai people—about so-and-so, who got 14,000 rand for barley grown on his land, and how he took off to the Majengo Slums in Nairobi, leaving his wife and children behind, to live with a prostitute for a year. When the money ran out, he discarded his suit, pots and pans, and furniture. He wrapped a blanket around himself and walked home, whistling happily all the way.

Most of all, I will hear stories about Ole Kamaro, our landlord, and his wife Eddah (names changed).

My dad has been growing wheat and barley in this area since I was a child. All this time, we have been leasing a portion of Ole Kamaro's land to keep our tractors and things and to make Camp. I met Eddah when she had just married Ole Kamaro. She was his fifth wife, thirteen years old. He was very proud of her. She was the daughter of some big time chief near Mau Narok *and she could read and write!* Ole Kamaro bought her a pocket radio and made her follow him about with a pen and pencil everywhere he went, taking notes.

I remember being horrified by the marriage—she was so young! My sister Ciru was eight and they played together one day. That night, my sister had a terrible nightmare that my dad had sold her to Ole Kamaro in exchange for 50 acres.

Those few years of schooling were enough to give Eddah a clear idea of the basic tenets of Empowerment. By the time she was eighteen, Ole Kamaro had dumped the rest of his wives.

Eddah leased out his land to Kenya Breweries and opened a bank account where all the money went.

Occasionally, she gave her husband pocket money.

Whenever he was away, she took up with her lover, a wealthy young Kikuyu shopkeeper from the other side of the hill who kept her supplied with essentials like soap, matches and paraffin.

Eddah was the local chairwoman of KANU (Kenya's Ruling Party) Women's League and so remained invulnerable to censure from the conservative elements around. She also had a thriving business, curing hides and beading them elaborately for the tourist market at the Mara. Unlike most Masai women, who disdain growing of crops, she had a thriving market garden with maize, beans, and various vegetables. She did not lift a finger to take care of this garden. Part of the co-operation we expected from her as landlady meant that our staff had to take care of that garden. Her reasoning was that Kikuyu men are cowardly women anyway and they do farming so-oo well.

Something interesting is going on today and the drivers are nervous. There is a tradition amongst Masai that women are released from all domestic duties a few months after giving birth. The women are allowed to take over the land and claim any lovers that they choose. For some reason I don't quite understand, this all happens at a particular season—and this season begins today. I have been warned to keep away from any bands of women wandering about.

We are on some enormous hill and I can feel the old Massey Ferguson tractor wheezing. We get to the top, turn to make our way down, and there they are: led by Eddah, a troop of about 40 women marching towards us dressed in their best traditional clothing.

Eddah looks imperious and beautiful in her beaded leather cloak, red khanga wraps, rings, necklaces and earrings. There is an old woman amongst them, she must be 70 and she is cackling in toothless glee. She takes off her wrap and displays her breasts—they resemble old gym socks.

Mwangi, who is driving, stops, and tries to turn back, but the road is too narrow: on one side there is the mountain, and on the other, a yawning valley. Kipsang, who is sitting in the trailer with me, shouts "Aiii Mwangi Bwana! DO NOT STOP!"

It seems that the modernized version of this tradition involves men making donations to the KANU Women's Group. Innocent enough, you'd think—but the amount of these donations must satisfy them or they will strip you naked and do unspeakable things to your body.

So we take off at full speed. The women stand firm in the middle of the road. We can't swerve. We stop.

Then Kipsang saves our skins by throwing a bunch of coins onto the road. I throw down some notes and Mwangi (renowned across Masailand for his stinginess) empties his pockets, throws down notes and coins. The women start to gather the money, the tractor roars back into action and we drive right through them.

I am left with the picture of the toothless old lady diving to avoid the tractor. Then standing, looking at us and laughing, her breasts flapping about like a Flag of Victory.

*   *   *

I am in bed, still in Masailand.

I pick up my father's *World Almanac and Book of Facts 1992*. The language section has new words, confirmed from sources as impeccable as the *Columbia Encyclopedia* and the *Oxford English Dictionary*. The list reads like an American Infomercial: Jazzercize, Assertiveness-Training, Bulimarexic, Microwavable, Fast-tracker.

There is a word there—*skanking*: it is a style of West Indian dancing to reggae music, in which the body bends forward at the waist and the knees are raised and the hands claw the air in time to the beat.

I have some brief flashes of ourselves in 40 years' time, in some generic Dance Studio. We are practicing for the Senior Dance Championships, plastic smiles on our faces as we skank across the room.

The tutor checks the movement: shoulder up, arms down, move this way, move that: Claw, baby. Claw!

In time to the beat, dancing in this style.

Langat and Kariuki have lost their self-consciousness around me, and are chatting away about Eddah Ole Kamaro, our landlady.

"Eh! She had 10,000 shillings and they went and stayed in a Hotel in Narok for a week. Ole Kamaro had to bring in another woman to look after the children!"

"He! But she sits on him!"

Their talk meanders slowly, with no direction—just talk, just connecting, and I feel that tight wrap of time loosen, the anxiety of losing time fades and I am a glorious vacuum for a while just letting what strikes my mind strike my mind, then sleep strikes my mind.

* * *

Ole Kamaro is slaughtering a goat today! For me!

We all settle on the patch of grass between the two compounds. Ole Kamaro makes quick work of the goat and I am offered the fresh kidney to eat. It tastes surprisingly good. It tastes of a slippery warmth, an organic cleanliness.

Ole Kamaro introduces me to his sister-in-law, tells me proudly that she is in Form Four. Eddah's sister—I spotted her this morning staring at me from the tiny window in their Manyatta. It was disconcerting at first—a typically Masai stare—unembarrassed, not afraid to be vulnerable. Then she noticed that I had seen her, and her eyes narrowed and became sassy—street-sassy, like a girl from Eastlands in Nairobi.

So I am now confused how to approach her. Should my approach be one of exaggerated politeness, as is traditional, or with a casual cool, as her second demeanor requested? I would have opted for the latter but her uncle is standing eagerly next to us.

She responds by lowering her head and looking away. I am painfully embarrassed. I ask her to show me where they tan their hides.

We escape with some relief.

"So where do you go to school?"

"Oh! At St. Teresa's Girls in Nairobi."

"Eddah is your sister?"

"Yes."

We are quiet for a while. English was a mistake. Where I am fluent, she is stilted. I switch to Swahili and she pours herself into another person: talkative, aggressive, a person who must have a Tupac t-shirt stashed away somewhere.

"Arhh! It's so boring here! Nobody to talk to! I hope Eddah comes home early."

I am still stunned. How bold and animated she is, speaking *Sheng*, a very hip street language that mixes Swahili and English.

"Why didn't you go with the women today?"

She laughs, "I am not married. Ho! I'm sure they had fun! They are drinking Muratina somewhere here I am sure. I can't wait to get married."

"Kwani? You don't want to go to university and all that?"

"Maybe, but if I'm married to the right guy, life is good. Look at Eddah—she is free—she does anything she wants. Old men are good. If you feed them, and give them a son, they leave you alone."

"Won't it be difficult to do this if you are not circumcised?"

"Kwani, who told you I'm not circumcised? I went last year."

I am shocked, and it shows. She laughs.

"He! I nearly shat myself! But I didn't cry!"

"Why? Si, you could have refused."

"Ai! If I would have refused, it would mean that my life here was finished. There is no place here for someone like that."

"But..."

I cut myself short. I am sensing this is her compromise—to live two lives fluently. As it is with people's reasons for their faiths and choices—trying to disprove her is silly. As a Masai, she will see my statement as ridiculous.

In Sheng, there is no way for me to bring it up that would be diplomatic; in Sheng, she can only present this with a hard-edged bravado, it is humiliating. I do not know of any way we can discuss this successfully in English. If there is a courtesy every Kenyan practices, it is that none of us ever questions each other's contradictions—we all have them, and destroying someone's face is sacrilege.

There is nothing wrong with being what you are not in Kenya—just be it successfully. Almost every Kenyan joke is about somebody who thought they had mastered a new persona and ended up ridiculous. For us, life is about having a fluid disposition.

You can have as many as you want.

Christmas in Bufumbira, 20 December 1995

The drive through the Mau Hills, past the Rift Valley and onwards to Kisumu is a drag. I haven't been this way for ten years, but my aim is to be in Uganda. We arrive in Kampala at ten in the evening. We have been on the road for over eight hours.

This is my first visit to Uganda, a land of incredible mystery for me. I grew up with her myths and legends and her horrors—narrated with the intensity that only exiles can muster. It is my first visit to my mother's ancestral home, the occasion is her parents' 60th wedding anniversary.

It will be the first time that she and her ten surviving brothers and sisters have been together since the early 1960s. The first time that my grandparents will have all their children and most of their grandchildren at home together—more than a hundred people are expected.

My mother, and the many visitors who came to visit, always filled my imagination with incredible tales of Uganda. I heard how you had to wriggle on your stomach to see the Kabaka; how the Tutsi king in Rwanda (who was seven feet tall) was once given a bicycle as a present. Because he couldn't walk on the ground (being a king and all), he was carried everywhere, on his bicycle, by his bearers.

Apparently, in the old kingdom in Rwanda, Tutsi women were not supposed to exert themselves or mar their beauty in any way. Some women had to be spoon-fed by their Hutu servants and wouldn't leave their huts for fear of sunburn.

I was told about a trip my grandfather took when he was young, with an uncle, where he was mistaken for a Hutu servant and taken away to stay with the goats. A few days later his uncle asked about him and his hosts were embarrassed to confess that they didn't know he was "one of us."

It has been a year of mixed blessings for Africa. This is the year that I sat at Newlands Stadium during the Rugby World Cup in the

Cape and watched South Africans reach out to each other before giving New Zealand a hiding. Mandela, wearing the Number Six rugby jersey, managed to melt away for one incredible night all the hostility that had gripped the country since he was released from jail. Black people, for a long time supporters of the All Blacks, embraced the Springboks with enthusiasm. For just one night most South Africans felt a common Nationhood.

It was the year that I returned to my home, Kenya, to find people so way beyond cynicism that they looked back on their cynical days with fondness.

Uganda is different: this is a country that has not only reached the bottom of the hole countries sometimes fall into, it has scratched through that bottom and free-fallen again and again, and now it has rebuilt itself and swept away the hate. This country gives me hope that this continent is not incontinent.

This is the country I used to associate with banana trees, old and elegant kingdoms, rot, Idi Amin, and hopelessness. It was an association I had made as a child, when the walls of our house would ooze and leak whispers of horror whenever a relative or friends of the family came home, fleeing from Amin's literal and metaphorical crocodiles.

I am rather annoyed that the famous Seven Hills of Kampala are not as clearly defined as I had imagined they would be. I have always had a childish vision of a stately city filled with royal paraphernalia. I had expected to see elegant people dressed in flowing robes, carrying baskets on their heads and walking arrogantly down streets filled with the smell of roasting bananas; and Intellectuals from a 1960s dream, burning the streets with their Afrocentric rhetoric.

Images formed in childhood can be more than a little bit stubborn.

Reality is a better aesthetic. Kampala seems disorganized, full of potholes, bad management, and haphazardness. The African city that so horrifies the West. The truth is that it is a city being overwhelmed by enterprise. I see smiles, the shine of healthy skin, and teeth; no layabouts lounging and plotting at every street corner. People do not walk about with walls around themselves as they do in Nairobbery.

All over, there is a frenzy of building: a blanket of paint is slowly spreading over the city, so it looks rather like one of those Smirnoff adverts where inanimate things get breathed to Technicolor by the sacred burp of 30 per cent or so of clear alcohol.

It is humid, and hot, and the banana trees flirt with you, swaying gently like fans offering a coolness that never materializes.

Everything smells musky, as if a thick, soft steam has risen like a broth. The plants are enormous. Mum once told me that when traveling in Uganda in the 1940s and 1950s, if you were hungry you could simply enter a banana plantation and eat as much as you wished—you didn't have to ask anybody, but you were not allowed to carry so much as a single deformed banana out of the plantation.

* * *

We are booked in at the Catholic Guesthouse. As soon as I have dumped my stuff on the bed, I call up an old school friend, who promises to pick me up.

Musoke comes at six and we go to find food. We drive past the famous Mulago Hospital and into town. He picks up a couple of friends and we go to a place called Yakubu's.

We order a couple of beers, lots of roast pork brochettes and sit in the car. The brochettes are delicious. I like them so much, I order more. Nile beer is okay, but nowhere near Kenya's Tusker.

The sun is drowned suddenly and it is dark.

* * *

We get onto the highway to Entebbe. On both sides of the road, people have built flimsy houses: bars, shops, and cafés line the road the whole way. What surprises me is how many people are out, especially teenagers, guided hormones flouncing about, puffs of fog surrounding their huddled faces. It is still hot outside and paraffin lamps light the fronts of all these premises.

I turn to Musoke and ask, "Can we stop at one of those pubs and have a beer?"

"Ah! Wait till we get to where we are going, it's much nicer than this dump!"

"I'm sure it is; but you know, I might never get a chance to drink in a real Entebbe pub, not those bourgeois places. Come on, I'll buy a round."

Magic words.

The place is charming. Ugandans seem to me to have a knack for making things elegant and comfortable, regardless of income. In Kenya, or South Africa, a place like this would be dirty, and buildings would be put together with a sort of haphazard self-loathing; sort of like saying "I won't be here long, why bother?"

The inside of the place is decorated simply, mostly with reed mats. The walls are well finished, and the floor, simple cement, has no cracks or signs of misuse. Women in traditional Baganda dress serve us.

I find Baganda women terribly sexy. They carry about with them a look of knowledge, a proud and naked sensuality, daring you to satisfy them.

Also, they don't seem to have that generic cuteness many city women have, that I have already begun to find irritating. Their features are strong; their skin is a deep, gleaming copper and their eyes are large and oil-black.

Baganda women traditionally wear a long, loose Victorian-style dress. It fulfills every literal aspect the Victorians desired, but manages despite itself to suggest sex. The dresses are usually in bold colors. To emphasize their size, many women tie a band just below their buttocks (which are often padded).

What makes the difference is the walk.

Many women visualize their hips as an unnecessary evil, an irritating accessory that needs to be whittled down. I guess, a while back, women looked upon their hips as a cradle for the depositing of desire, for the nurturing of babies. Baganda women see their hips as great ball bearings; rolling, supple things moving in lubricated circles—so they make excellent Dombolo dancers. In those loose dresses, their hips brushing the sides of the dress as they move, they are a marvel to watch.

Most appealing is the sense of stature they carry about them. Baganda women seem to have found a way to be traditional and powerful at the same time—most of the ones I know grow more beautiful with age and many compete with men in industry without seeming to compromise themselves as women.

* * *

I sleep on the drive from Kampala to Kisoro.

We leave Kisoro and begin the drive to St. Paul's Mission, Mutolere. My sister Ciru is sitting next to me. She is a year younger than me. Chiqy, my youngest sister, has been to Uganda before and is taking full advantage of her vast experience to play the adult tour guide. At her age, cool is a god.

I have the odd feeling we are puppets in some Christmas story. It is as if a basket-weaver were writing this story; tightening the tension on the papyrus strings every few minutes, and superstitiously refusing to reveal the ending (even to herself) until she has tied the very last knot.

We are now in the mountains. The winding road and the dense papyrus in the valleys seem to entwine me, ever tighter, into my fictional weaver's basket. Every so often, she jerks her weaving to tighten it.

I look up to see the last half-hour of road winding along the mountain above us. We are in the Bufumbira range now, driving through Kigaland on our way to Kisoro, the nearest town to my mother's home.

There is an alien quality to this place. It does not conform to any African topography that I am familiar with. The mountains are incredibly steep and resemble inverted ice-cream cones: a hoe has tamed every inch of them.

It is incredibly green.

In Kenya, "green" is the ultimate accolade a person can give land: green is scarce, green is wealth, fertility.

Bufumbira green is not a tropical green, no warm musk, like in Buganda; it is not the harsh green of the Kenyan savannah, either: that two-month-long green that compresses all the elements of life—millions of wildebeest and zebra, great carnivores feasting during the rains, frenzied ploughing and planting, and dry riverbeds overwhelmed by soil and bloodstained water; and Nairobi underwater.

It is not the green of grand waste and grand bounty that my country knows. This is a mountain green, cool and enduring. Rivers and lakes occupy the cleavage of the many mountains that surround us.

Mum looks almost foreign now; her Kinyarwanda accent is more pronounced, and her face is not as reserved as usual. Her beauty, so exotic and head-turning in Kenya, seems at home here. She does not stand out here, she belongs; the rest of us seem like tourists.

As the drive continues, I become imbued with the sense of where we are. We are no longer in the history of Buganda, of Idi Amin, of the Kabakas, or civil war, Museveni and Hope.

We are now on the outskirts of the theater where the Hutus and the Tutsis have been performing for the world's media. My mother has always described herself as a Mufumbira, one who speaks Kinyarwanda. She has always avoided talking about the differences.

I am glad she has, because it saves me from trying to understand. I am not here about genocide or hate. Enough people have been here for that (try typing "Tutsi" on any search engine).

I am here to be with family.

I ask my mother where the border with Rwanda is. She points it out, and points out the Congo as well. They are both nearer than I thought. Maybe this is what makes this coming together so urgent. How amazing life seems when it stands around death. There is no grass as beautiful as the blades that stick out after the first rain.

As we move into the forested area, I am enthralled by the smell and by the canopy of mountain vegetation. I join the conversation in the car. I have become self-conscious about displaying my dreaminess and absent-mindedness these days.

I used to spend hours gazing out of car windows, creating grand battles between battalions of clouds. I am aware of a conspiracy to get me back to Earth, to get me to be more practical. My parents are pursuing this cause with little subtlety, aware that my time with them is limited. It is necessary for me to believe that I am putting myself on a gritty road to personal success when I leave home. Cloud travel is well and good when you have mastered the landings. I never have. I must live, not dream about living.

We are in Kisoro, the main town of the district, weaving through roads between people's houses. We are heading towards Uncle Kagame's house.

The image of a dictatorial movie director manipulating our movements replaces that of the basket-weaver in my mind. I have a dizzy vision of a supernatural moviemaker slowing down the action before the climax by examining tiny details instead of grand scenes.

I see a continuity presenter in the fifth dimension saying: "And now it's our Christmas movie: a touching story about the reunion of a family torn apart by civil war and the genocide in Rwanda. This movie is sponsored by Sobbex, hankies for every occasion" (repeated in Zulu, then a giggle and a description of the soapie that will follow).

My fantasy escalates and there is a motivational speaker/aerobics instructor shouting at Christmas TV viewers: "Jerk those tear glands, baby!"

I am still dreaming when we get to my uncle's place.

I am at my worst, half in dream, clumsy, tripping and unable to focus. I have learned to move my body resolutely at such times, but it generally makes things worse. Tea and every possible thing we could want will be available to us on demand (and so we must not demand).

My uncle Gerald Kagame and his wife both work at the mission hospital. I discover it is their formidable organizational skills that have made this celebration possible. There are already around 100 visitors speaking five or six languages.

Basically, the Binyavangas have taken over the Kisoro town and business is booming. During such an event, hotels are not an option. The church at St. Paul's is booked, the dorms are booked, homes have been hijacked, and so on.

We are soon driving through my grandfather's land. In front of us is a saddle-shaped hill with a large, old, imposing church ruling the view. My mother tells us that my grandfather donated this land for the building of the church. The car squishes and slides up the muddy hills, progress impeded by a thick mat of grass.

I see Ankole cattle grazing, their enormous horns like regal crowns.

"Look, that's the homestead. I know this place."

It is a small brick house. I can see the surge of family coming towards the car. After the kissing and hugging, the crowd parts for my grandparents. They seem tall but aren't, just lean and fit. Age and time have made them start to look alike.

My grandmother stretches a long-fingered hand to Ciru's cheek and exclaims: "She still has a big forehead!"

How do you keep track of 60 grandchildren?

She embraces me. She is very slender and I feel she will break. Her elegance surrounds me and I can feel a strong pull to dig into her, burrow in her secrets, see with her eyes. She is a quiet woman, and unbending, even taciturn—and this gives her a powerful charisma. Things not said. Her resemblance to my mother astounds me.

My grandfather is crying and laughing, exclaiming when he hears that Chiqy and I are named after him and his wife (Kamanzi and Binyavanga). We drink rgwagwa (banana wine) laced with honey. It is delicious, smoky and sweet.

Ciru and Chiqy are sitting next to my grandmother. I see why my grandfather was such a legendary schoolteacher: his gentleness and love of life are palpable.

At night, we split into our various age groups and start to bond with one another. Of the cousins, Manwelli, the eldest, is our unofficial leader. He works for the World Bank.

Aunt Rosaria and her family are the coup of the ceremony. They were feared dead during the war in Rwanda and hid for months in their basement, helped by a friend who provided food. They all survived; they walk around carrying expressions that are more common in children—delight, sheer delight at life.

Her three sons spend every minute bouncing about with the high of being alive. They dance at all hours, sometimes even when there is no music. In the evenings, we squash into the veranda, looking out as far as the Congo, and they entertain us with their stand-up routines in French and Kinyarwanda; the force of their humor carries us all to laughter. Manwelli translates one skit for me: they imitate a vain Tutsi woman who is pregnant and is kneeling to make a confession to the shocked priest:

"Oh please, God, let my child have long fingers, and a gap between the teeth; let her have a straight nose and be ta-a-all. Oh lord, let her not have (gesticulations of a gorilla prowling) a mashed banana nose like a Hutu. Oh please, I shall be your grateful servant!"

The biggest disappointment so far is that my Aunt Christine has not yet arrived. She has lived with her family in New York since the early 1970s. We all feel her loss keenly as it was she who urged us all years ago to gather for this occasion at any cost.

She and my Aunt Rosaria are the senior aunts, and they were very close when they were younger. They speak frequently on the phone and did so especially during the many months that Aunt Rosaria and her family were living in fear in their basement. They are, for me, the summary of the pain the family has been through over the years. Although they are very close, they haven't met since 1961. Visas, wars, closed borders and a thousand triumphs of chaos have kept them apart. We are all looking forward to their reunion.

As is normal on traditional occasions, people stick with their peers; so I have hardly spoken to my mother the past few days. I find her in my grandmother's room, trying, without much success, to get my grandmother to relax and let her many daughters and granddaughters do the work.

I have been watching Mum from a distance for the past few days. At first, she seemed a bit aloof from it all; but now she's found fluency with everything and she seems far away from the Kenyan Mother we know. I can't get over the sight of her cringing and blushing as my grandmother machine-guns instructions to her. How alike they are. I want to talk with her more, but decide not to be selfish, that I am trying to establish possession of her. We'll have enough time on the way back.

I've been trying to pin down my grandfather, to ask him about our family's history. He keeps giving me this bewildered look when I corner him, as if he is asking, "Can't you just relax and party?"

Last night, he toasted us all and cried again before dancing to some very hip gospel rap music from Kampala. He tried to get Grandmother to join him but she beat a hasty retreat.

Gerald is getting quite concerned that when we are all gone, they will find it too quiet.

We hurtle on towards Christmas. Booze flows, we pray, chat, and bond under the night rustle of banana leaves. I feel as if I am filled with magic and I succumb to the masses. In two days, we feel a family. In French, Swahili, English, Kikuyu, Kinyarwanda, Kiganda and Ndebele we sing one song, a multitude of passports in our luggage.

At dawn on 24 December I stand smoking in the banana plantation at the edge of my grandfather's hill and watch the mists disappear. Uncle Chris saunters up to join me. I ask: "Any news about Aunt Christine?"

"It looks like she might not make it. Manwelli has tried to get in contact with her and failed. Maybe she couldn't get a flight out of New York. Apparently the weather is terrible there."

The day is filled with hard work. My uncles have convinced my grandfather that we need to slaughter another bull as meat is running out. The old man adores his cattle but reluctantly agrees. He cries when the bull is killed.

There is to be a church service in the sitting room of my grandfather's house later in the day.

The service begins and I bolt from the living room, volunteering to peel potatoes outside.

About halfway through the service, I see somebody staggering up the hill, suitcase in hand and muddied up to her ankles. It takes me an instant to guess. I run to her and mumble something. We hug. Aunt Christine is here.

The plot has taken me over now. Resolution is upon me. The poor woman is given no time to freshen up or collect her bearings. In a minute we have ushered her into the living room. She sits by the door, facing everybody's back. Only my grandparents are facing her. My grandmother starts to cry.

Nothing is said, the service motors on. Everybody stands up to sing. Somebody whispers to my Aunt Rosaria. She turns and gasps soundlessly. Others turn. We all sit down. Aunt Rosaria and Aunt Christine start to cry. Aunt Rosaria's mouth opens and closes in disbelief. My mother joins them, and soon everybody is crying.

The Priest motors on, fluently. Unaware.

Weight of Whispers

Yvonne Adhiambo Owuor—
winner of the 2003 Caine Prize

The collection of teeth on the man's face is a splendid brown. I have never seen such teeth before. Refusing all instruction, my eyes focus on dental contours and craters. Denuded of any superficial pretense—no braces, no fillings, no toothbrush—it is a place where small scavengers thrive.

"Evidence!" The man giggles.

A flash of green and my US$50 disappears into his pocket. His fingers prod: shirt, coat, trousers. He finds the worked snake-skin wallet. No money in it, just a picture of Agnethe-mama, Lune and Chi-Chi, elegant and unsmiling, diamonds in their ears, on their necks and wrists. The man tilts the picture this way and that, returns the picture into the wallet. The wallet disappears into another of his pockets. The man's teeth gleam.

"Souvenir." Afterwards, a hiccupping "*Greeeheeereeehee*" not unlike a National Geographic hyena, complete with a chorus from the pack.

"Please… it's… my mother… all I have."

His eyes become thin slits, head tilts and the veins on his right eye pulse. His nostrils flare, an indignant goat.

A thin sweat-trail runs down my spine, the backs of my knees tingle. I look around at the faceless others in the dank room. His hand grabs my goatee and twists. My eyes smart. I lift up my hand to wipe them. The man sees the gold insignia ring, glinting on my index finger.

The ring of the royal household. One of only three. The second belonged to my father. Agnethe-mama told me that when father appeared to her in a dream to tell her he was dead, he was still wearing it. The third... no one has ever spoken about.

The policeman's grin broadens. He pounces. Long fingers. A girl would cut her hair for fingers like his. He spits on my finger, and draws out the ring with his teeth; the ring I have worn for eighteen years—from the day I was recognized by the priests as a man and a prince. It was supposed to have been passed on to the son I do not have. The policeman twists my hand this way and that, his tongue caught between his teeth; a study of concentrated avarice.

"Evidence!"

Gargoyles are petrified life-mockers, sentries at entry points, sentinels of sorrow, spitting at fate. I will try to protest.

"It is sacred ring... Please... please." To my shame, my voice breaks.

"Evidence!"

Cheek: nerve, gall, impertinence, brashness.

Cheek: the part of my face he chose to brand.

Later on, much later on, I will wonder what makes it possible for one man to hit another for no reason other than the fact that he can. But now, I lower my head. The sum total of what resides in a very tall man who used to be a prince in a land eviscerated.

* * *

Two presidents died when a missile launched from land forced their plane down. A man of note, a prince, had said, on the first day, that the perpetrators must be hunted down. That evil must be purged from lives. That is all the prince had meant. It seems someone heard something else. It emerges later on, when it is too late, that an old servant took his obligation too far, in the name of his prince.

We had heard rumor of a holocaust, of a land haemorrhaging to death. Everywhere, hoarse murmurs, eyes white and wide with an arcane fear. Is it possible that brothers would machete sisters-in-law to stew-meat-size chunks in front of nephews and nieces?

It was on the fifth day after the presidents had disintegrated with their plane that I saw that the zenith of existence cannot be human.

In the seasons of my European sojourn, Brussels, Paris, Rome, Amsterdam, rarely London, a city I could accommodate a loathing for, I wondered about the unsaid; hesitant signals and interminable reminders of *"What They Did."* Like a mnemonic device, the swastika would grace pages and/or screens, at least once a week, unto perpetuity. I wondered.

I remembered a conversation in Krakow with an academician, a man with primeval eyes. A pepper-colored, quill-beard obscured the man's mouth, and seemed to speak in its place. I was, suddenly, in the thrall of an irrational fear; that the mobile barbs would shoot off his face and stab me.

I could not escape.

I had agreed to offer perspectives on his seminal work, a work in progress he called, "A Mystagogy of Human Evil." I had asked, meaning nothing, a prelude to commentary:

"Are you a Jew?"

So silently, the top of his face fell, flowed towards his jaw, his formidable mustache-beard lank, his shoulders shaking, his eyes flooded with tears. But not a sound emerged from his throat. Unable to tolerate the tears of another man, I walked away.

Another gathering, another conversation, with another man. Mellowed by the well-being engendered by a goblet of Rémy Martin, I ventured an opinion about the sacrificial predilection of being; the necessity of oblation of men by men to men.

"War is the excuse," I said. I was playing with words, true, but, oddly the exchange petered into mumbles of "Never Again."

A year later, at a balcony party, when I asked the American Consul in Luxembourg to suggest a book which probed the slaughter of Germans during World War Two, she said:

"By whom?"

Before I could answer, she had spun away, turning her back on me as if I had asked "Cain, where is your brother?"

What had been Cain's response?

To my amusement, I was, of course, never invited to another informal diplomatic gathering. Though I would eventually relinquish my European postings—in order to harness, to my advantage, European predilection for African gems—over *après-diner* Drambuie, now and again, I pondered over what lay beneath the unstated.

Now, my world has tilted into a realm where other loaded silences lurk. And I can sense why some things must remain buried in silence, even if they resuscitate themselves at night in dreams where blood pours out of phantom mouths. In the empire of silence, the "turning away" act is a vain exorcism of a familiar daemon which invades the citadels we ever change, we constantly fortify. Dragging us back through old routes of anguish, it suggests: "Alas, human, your nature relishes fratricidal blood."

But to be human is to be intrinsically, totally, resolutely good. Is it not?

Nothing entertains the devil as much as this protestation.

* * *

Roger, the major-domo, had served in our home since before my birth 37 years ago. He reappeared at our door on the evening of the fifth day after the death of the two presidents. He had disappeared on the first day of the plane deaths. The day he resurfaced, we were celebrating the third anniversary of my engagement to Lune. I had thought a pungent whiff which entered the room with his presence was merely the Gorgonzola cheese Lune had been unwrapping.

Roger says:

"*J'ai terminé. Tout a été nettoyé.*" It is done. All has been cleaned.

"What, Roger?"

"The dirt." He smiles.

The bottle of Dom Pérignon Millésimé in my hand, wavers. I observe that Roger is shirtless, his hair stands in nascent, accidental dreadlocks. The bottom half of his trousers are torn, and his shoeless left foot, swollen. His fist is black and caked with what I think is tar. And in his wake, the smell of smoldering matter. Roger searches the ground, hangs his head, his mouth tremulous:

"They are coming... Sir."

Then Roger stoops. He picks up the crumbs of *petits fours* from the carpet; he is fastidious about cleanliness. The Dom Pérignon Millésimé drops from my hand, it does not break, though its precious contents soak into the carpet. Roger frowns, his mouth pursed. He also disapproves of waste.

* * *

In our party clothes and jewelry, with what we had in our wallets, and two packed medium-size Chanel cases, we abandoned our life at home. We counted the money we had between us: US$3,723. In the bank account, of course, there was more. There was always more. As President of the Banque Locale, I was one of three who held keys to the vault, so to say. Two weeks before the presidents died, I sold my Paris apartment. The money was to be used to expand our bank into Zaire. We got the last four of the last eight seats on the last flight out of our city. We assumed then, it was only right that it be so. We landed at the Jomo Kenyatta International Airport in Nairobi, Kenya, at 10:00PM.

I wondered about Kenya. I knew the country as a transit lounge and a stop-over base on my way to and out of Europe. It was only after we got a three-month visitor's pass that I realized that Kenya was an Anglophone country. Fortunately, we were in transit. Soon, we would be in Europe, among friends.

I am Boniface Louis R. Kuseremane. It has been long since anyone called me by my full name. The "R" name cannot be spoken aloud. In the bustle and noises of the airport, I glance at Agnethe-mama, regal, graying, her diamond earrings dance, her nose is slightly raised, her forehead unlined. My mother, Agnethe, is a princess in transit. She leans lightly against Lune, who stands, one foot's heel touching the toes of the other, one arm raised and then drooping over her shoulder.

I met Lune on the funeral day of both her parents, royal diplomats who had died in an unfortunate road crash. She was then, as she is now, not of Earth. Then, she seemed to be hovering atop her parents' grave, deciding whether to join them, fly away or stay. I asked her to leave the *corps ballet* in France where she was studying—to stay with me, forever. She agreed and I gained a sibylline fiancée.

"*Chéri, que faisons-nous maintenant?*" What do we do now? Lune asks, clinging to my mother's hand. Her other arm curved into mine. Chi-Chi, my sister, looks up at me, expecting the right answer, her hand at her favorite spot, my waistband—a childhood affectation that has lingered into her twentieth year. Chi-Chi, in thought, still sucks on her two fingers.

"*Bu-bu,*" Chi-Chi always calls me Bu-Bu. "*Bu-Bu, dans quel pays sommes-nous?*"

"Kenya," I tell her.

Chi-Chi is an instinctive contemplative. I once found her weeping and laughing, awed, as it turns out, by the wings of a monarch butterfly.

Low voiced, almost a whisper, the hint of a melody, my mother's voice. "*Bonbon, je me sens très fatiguée, où dormons-nous cette nuit?*"

Agnethe-mama was used to things falling into place before her feet touched the ground. Now she was tired. Now she wanted her bed immediately. Without thinking about it, we checked into a suite of the Nairobi Hilton. We were, after all, going to be in this country for just a few days.

* * *

"Mama, such ugliness of style!" Lune's summation of Kenyan fashion, of Kenyan hotel architecture. Mama smiles and says nothing. She twists her sapphire bracelet, the signal that she agrees.

"Why do I not see the soul of these people? Bonbon... are you sleeping?" Chi-Chi asks.

"Shh," I say.

Two days later, Agnethe-mama visited the jewelry shop downstairs. Not finding anything to suit her tastes, she concluded: "Their language and manner are not as sweet and gentle as ours."

She straightens her robes, eyes wide with the innocence of an unsubtle put-down.

"Mama!" I scold. The women giggle as do females who have received affirmation of their particular and unassailable advantage over other women.

* * *

A week has passed already. In the beginning of the second one, I am awakened by the feeling I had when I found my country embassy gates here locked and blocked. The feeling of a floor shifting beneath one's feet. There is no one in authority. The ambassador is in exile. Only a guard. Who should I speak to? A blank stare. I need to arrange our papers to go to Europe. A blank stare. A flag flutters in the courtyard. I do not recognize it. Then I do. It is my country's flag, someone installed it upside down. It flies at half-mast. An inadvertent act, I believe. Shifting sands: I am lost in this sea of English and I suspect that at 5,000 Kenyan shillings I have spent too much for a 30-kilometer taxi ride. Old friends have not returned phone calls.

The lines here are not reliable.

* * *

Lune is watching me, her long neck propped up by her hands. Her hair covers half her face. It is always a temptation to sweep it away from her eyes, a warm silk. When the tips of my fingers stroke her hair, the palms of my hand skim her face. Lune becomes still, drinking, feeling and tasting the stroking.

Soon, we will leave.

But now, I need to borrow a little money: US$5,000. It will be returned to the lender, of course, after things settle down. Agnethe, being a princess, knows that time solves all problems. Nevertheless she has ordered me to dispatch a telegram to sovereigns in exile, those who would be familiar with our quandary and could be depended on for empathy, cash assistance and even accommodation. The gratitude felt would extend generation unto generation.

Eight days later, Agnethe-mama sighs; a hiss through the gap of her front teeth. She asks, her French rolling off her tongue like an old scroll: "When are we leaving, Bonbon?"

A mother's ambush. I know what she really wants to know.

"Soon," I reply.

"Incidentally," she adds, folding Lune's lace scarf, "What of the response of our friends in exile... ah! Not yet... a matter of time," she says, answering herself.

"Agnethe-mama," I should have said, "We must leave this hotel... to save money."

It is simpler to be silent.

* * *

A guard with red-rimmed eyes in a dark blue uniform watches me counting out fifteen 1,000-Kenyan-shilling notes. The eyes of the president on the notes blink with every sweep of my finger. The Indian lady in a pink sari with gold trim, the paint flaking off, leans over the counter, her eyes empty. My gold bracelet has already disappeared. Two days from this moment, while standing with Celeste on Kenyatta Avenue, where many of my people stand and seek news of home, or just stand and talk the language of home or hope that soon we will return home, I discover that 15,000 Kenyan shillings is insufficient compensation for a 24-carat, customized gold and sapphire bracelet. Celeste knew of another jeweler who would pay me 100,000 for the bracelet.

I return to confront the Indian lady, she tells me to leave before I can speak. She dials a number and shouts, high-voiced, clear: "Police." I do not want trouble so I leave the jewelry shop, unable to speak, but not before I see her smile. Not before I hear her scold the guard with the red-rimmed eyes.

"Why you let *takataka* to come in, *nee*?"

Outside the shop, my hands are shaking. I have to remind myself to take the next step and the next step and the next step. My knees are light. I am unable to look into the eyes of those on the streets. What is my mind doing getting around the intricacies of a foreign currency? I have to get out with my family. Soon.

The newspaper on the streets, a vendor flywhisks dust fragments away. A small headline reads: "Refugees: Registration commences at the UNHCR."

The Kuseremanes are not refugees. They are visitors, tourists, people in transit, universal citizens with an affinity... well... to Europe.

Kuseremane, Kuseremane, Kuseremane... Unbeknown to me, one whisper had started gathering other whispers around it.

* * *

The Netherlands, the Belgians, the French, the British are processing visa applications. They have been processing them for three, four, five... nine days. At least they smile with their teeth as they process the visa applications. They process them until I see that they will be processed unto eternity, if only Agnethe, Chi-Chi, Lune, and I could wait that long. There are other countries in the world.

Chi-Chi's ramblings yield an array of useless trivia:

In Nairobi, a woman can be called *Aunti* or *chilé*, a president called *Moi*, pronounced Moyi, a national anthem that is a prayer, and twenty shillings is a *pao*.

"But Bu-Bu... So many faces... So many spirits gather here..."

We must leave soon.

* * *

The American embassy visa section woman has purple hair. Her voice evokes the grumbling of a he-toad which once lived in the marsh behind our family house in the country. One night, in the middle of its anthem, I had said; "*Ça suffit !*" Enough!

Roger led the gardeners in the hunt which choked the croak out of the toad. At dawn, Roger brought the severed head to me, encased in an old cigar case which he had wiped clean.

I cannot believe what this purple-hair woman has asked of me.

"What?"

"Bank details... bank statement... how much money."

My eyes blink, lashes entangle. Could it be possible another human being can simply ask over the counter, casually and with certainty of response, for intimate details of another person's life?

I look around the room. Is it to someone else she addresses this question?

"And title deed. Proof of domicile in country of origin... And letter from employer."

Has she not looked at my passport in her hands?

"I'm not Kenyan."

She folds her papers, bangs them on the table and frowns as if I have wasted her time. She tosses my passport out of her little window into my hands that are outstretched, a supplication on an altar of disbelief.

"All applications made at source country... next!"

"Madame... my country... is..."

"Next!"

Woven in the seams of my exit are the faces in the line winding from the woman's desk, into the street. Children, women, and men, faces lined with... hope? I must look at that woman again, that purveyor of hope. So I turn. I see a stately man, his beard gray. His face as dark as mine. He stoops over the desk—a posture of abnegation. So that is what I looked like to the people in the line. I want to shout to the woman: I am Boniface Kuseremane, a prince, a diplomat.

I stumble because it is here, in this embassy, that the fire-streaking specter of the guns which brought down two presidents find their mark in my soul. Like the eminent-looking man in a pin-striped suit, I am now a beggar.

* * *

We have US$520 left. My head hurts. When night falls, my mind rolls and rings. I cannot sleep.

The pharmacist is appealing in her way, but wears an unfortunate weave that sits on her head like a mature thorn bush. Eeeh! The women of this land! I frown. The frown makes the girl jump when she sees me. She covers her mouth with both her hands and gasps. I smile. She recovers:

"Sema!"

"Yes, sank you. I not sleep for sree nights and I feel..." I plane my hands, rocking them against my head. She says nothing, turns around, counts out ten Piritons and seals the envelope: "Three, twice a day, 200 shillings."

These Kenyans and their shillings!

It is possible that tonight I will sleep. The thought makes me laugh. A thin woman wearing a red and black choker glances up at me, half-smiling. I smile back.

I cannot sleep. I have taken five of the white pills. Lune, beside me in the large bed, is also awake.

"*Qu'est-ce que c'est?*" What is it?

"*Rien.*" Nothing.

Silence. Her voice, tiny. "I am afraid."

I turn away from her, to my side. I raise my feet, curling them beneath my body. I, too, am afraid. In the morning, the white Hilton pillow beneath my head is wet with tears. They cannot be mine.

* * *

The sun in Nairobi in May is brutal in its rising. A rude glory. My heart longs to be eased into life with the clarion call of an African rooster. Our gentle sunrises, rolling hills. Two months have passed. A month ago, we left the hotel. I am ashamed to say we did not pay our bill. All we had with us was transferred into and carried out in laundry bags. We left the hotel at intervals of three hours. We also packed the hotel towels and sheets. It was Lune's idea. We had not brought our own. We left our suitcases behind. They are good for at least US$1,500. Agnethe-mama is sure the hotel will understand.

We moved into a single-roomed place with an outside toilet in River Road. I have told Agnethe-mama, Lune, and Chi-Chi not to leave the room unless I am with them. Especially Chi-Chi.

"Bu-Bu, when are we leaving?"

Soon, Agnethe-mama. Soon, Lune. Soon, Chi-Chi.

Chi-Chi has learned to say "*Tafadhali, naomba maji.*" She asks for water this way, there are shortages.

We must leave soon.

Every afternoon, a sudden wind runs up this street, lifting dust, and garbage and plastic bags and whispers.

Kuseremane, Kuseremane, Kuseremane.

I turn to see if anyone else hears my name.

Sometimes, I leave the room to walk the streets, for the sake of having a destination. I walk, therefore I am. I walk therefore I cannot see six expectant eyes waiting for me to pull out an airplane from my pocket.

Ah! But tonight! Tonight, Club Balafon. I am meeting a compatriot and friend, René Katilibana. We met as I stood on the edge of Kenyatta Avenue, reading a newspaper I had rented from the vendor for five Kenya shillings. Four years ago, René needed help with a sugar deal. I facilitated a meeting which proved lucrative for him. René made a million francs. He offered me 50,000 in gratitude. I declined. I had enjoyed humoring a friend. I am wearing the Hugo Boss mauves and the Hervé handkerchief. I am hopeful, a good feeling to invoke.

"*Où vas-tu, chéri?*" Where are you going? A ubiquitous question I live with.

I stretch out my arms, Lune flies into them as she always does. She wraps her arms around me. Her arms barely span my waist.

I tell her; "I am hopeful today. Very hopeful."

I still have not heard from the friends I have called. Every night, their silence whispers something my ears cannot take hold of. Deceptive murmurings. This country of leering masses—all eyes, hands and mouths, grasping and feeding off graciousness—invokes paranoia.

My friends will call as soon as they are able to. They will.

I realize this must be one of those places I have heard about; where international phone calls are intercepted and deals struck before the intended, initial recipient is reached.

* * *

A contact, Félicien, who always knows even what he does not know, tells me that a list of *génocidaires* has been compiled and it is possible a name has been included. *Kuseremane.* Spelled out by a demure man, an aide he had said he was.

Soon we will be gone. To Europe, where the wind's weight of whispers do not matter; where wind, and all its suggestions have been obliterated.

Even as she stays in the room, Chi-Chi leaves us more often than ever, a forefinger in her mouth. She has no filters. I worry that the soul of this place is soaking into her.

The city clock clicks above my head into the 2:00AM position. Rain has seeped into my bones and become ice. My knees burn. The rainwater squelches in my feet. My Hugo Boss suit is ruined now, but I squeeze the water from the edges.

Club Balafon was a microcosm of home and the Zaïroise band was nostalgic and superior. The band slipped into a song called "*Chez*

Mama." The hearth of home. The women were beautiful and our laughter loud. It was good to taste good French cognac served in proper glasses. We lamented the fact that Kenyans are on the whole, so unchic.

And then René asked me where I was and what I was doing. I told him I needed his help, a loan. US$5,000, to be returned when things settle down back home. He listened and nodded and ordered for me a Kenyan beer named after an elephant. He turned to speak to Pierre who introduced him to Jean-Luc. I touched his shoulder to remind him of my request. He said in French: I will call you. He forgot to introduce me to Pierre and Jean-Luc. Two hours later, he said, in front of Pierre, Jean-Luc, and Michel: "Refresh my memory, who are you?"

My heart threatens to pound a way out of my chest. Then the band dredges up an old anthem of anguish, which, once upon a time, had encapsulated all our desires. *Ingénues Francophones* in Paris, giddy with hope. This unexpected evocation of fragile, fleeting longings drives me into an abyss of remembering.

"L'indépendance, ils l'ont obtenue/La table ronde, ils l'ont gagnée..."
Indépendance Cha-cha, the voice of Joseph Kabasellé.

Then, we were, vicariously, members of Kabasellé's *"Le Grand Kalle."* All of us, for we were bursting with dreams encapsulated in a song.

Now, at Balafon, the exiles were silent, to accommodate the ghosts of saints:

Bolikango... Kasavubu... Lumumba... Kalondji... Tshombe...

I remember heady days in Paris; hair parted, like the statement we had become, horn-rimmed glasses worn solely for aesthetic purposes, dark-suited, black-tied, dark-skinned radicals moving in a cloud of enigmatic French colognes. In our minds and footsteps, always, the *slow, slow, quick, quick slow,* mambo to rumba, of Kabasellé's *Indépendance Cha-cha.*

"L'indépendance, ils l'ont obtenue...
La table ronde, ils l'ont gagnée..."

I dance at Club Balafon, my arms around a short girl who wears yellow braids. She is from Kenya and is of the opinion that "Centro African" men are *soooo* good. And then the music stops. There can be no other footnote, so the band packs their musical tools as quietly as we leave the small dance floor.

When I looked, René, Pierre, Jean-Luc, Michel, and Emanuel were gone. Perhaps this was not their song.

"Which way did they go?" I ask the guard in black with red stripes on his shoulder. He shrugs. He says they entered into a blue Mercedes. Their driver had been waiting for them. He thinks they went to the Carnivore. It is raining as I walk back to River Road. Three fledglings are waiting for me, trusting that I shall return with regurgitated good news.

I am Boniface Kuseremane. Refresh my memory, who are you? There are places within, where a sigh can hide. It is cold and hard and smells of fear. In my throat something cries, "*hrgghghg.*" I cannot breathe. And then I can. So I hum:

"*Mhhhh… L'indépendance, ils l'ont obtenue…*"

It is odd, the sounds that make a grown man weep.

* * *

I sleep and dream of whispers. They have crossed the borders and arrived in Nairobi. Like many passing snakes. *Kuseremane. Kuseremane. Kuseremane. Kuseremane. Kuseremane.*

But we left on the fifth day!

Now whenever I approach Kenyatta Avenue, they, my people, disperse. Or disappear into shops. Or avert their eyes. If I open a conversation, there is always a meeting that one is late for. Once, on the street, a woman started wailing like an old and tired train when she saw me. Her fingers extended, like the tip of a sure spear, finding its mark.

Kuseremane. Kuseremane. Kuseremane. Kuseremane. Kuseremane.
The whispers have found a human voice.

I can tell neither Agnethe-mama, nor Chi-Chi, nor Lune. I tell them to stay where they are; that the city is not safe.

Agnethe wants to know if the brother-monarchs-in-exile have sent their reply.

"Soon," I say.

One morning, in which the sun shone pink, I found that a certain sorrow had become a tenant of my body and weighed it down on the small blue safari bed, at the end of which my feet hang. The sun has come into the room, but it hovers above my body and cannot pierce the shadow covering my life. A loud knock on the door, so loud the door shakes. I do not move, so Lune glides to the door.

"*Reo ni Reo, ni siku ya maripo.* Sixi hundred ant sevente shirrings." Kenyans and their shillings! The proprietor scratches his distended belly. His fly is undone and the net briefs he wears peek through. I want to smile.

Lune floats to my side, looks down at me. I shut my eyes. From the door a strangely gentle, "I donti af all dey."

I open my eyes.

Lune slips her hand into my coat pocket. How did she know where to look? She gives him the money, smiling as only she can. The proprietor thaws. He counts shillings. Then he smiles, a beatific grin.

I have shut my eyes again.

And then a hand—large, soft, warm—strokes my face, my forehead. Silence, except for the buzzing of a blue fly. Agnethe-Mama is humming "*Sur le Pont d'Avignon.*" I used to fall asleep wondering how it was possible to dance on the Avignon bridge. Soon, we will know. When we leave.

I slept so deeply that when I woke up I thought I was at home in my bed and for a full minute I wondered why Roger had not come in with fresh orange juice, eggs and bacon, croissants and coffee. I wondered why mama was staring down at me, hands folded. Lune looks as if she has been crying. Her eyes are red-rimmed. She has become thin, the bones of her neck jut out. Her fingers are no longer manicured. There! Chi-Chi. Her face has disappeared into her eyes which are large and black and deep. I look back at Agnethe-mama and see then that her entire hair front is gray. When did this happen?

"We must register. As refugees. Tell UNHCR we are here."

Now I remember that we are in Kenya; we are leaving Kenya soon. Am I a refugee?

"You slept the sleep of the dead, *mon fils.*" Agnethe said, lowering the veil from her head. If only she knew how prophetic her words were. Being a princess once married to her prince, she would have been more circumspect. I have woken up to find the world has

91

shifted, moved, aged, and I with it. Today I will try to obtain work. There cannot be too many here who have a PhD in Diplomacy or a Masters in Geophysics. The immigration offices will advise me. In four days we will have been here three and a half months.

The sun is gentle and warm. The rain has washed the ground. Kenyans are rushing in all directions. A street child accosts me. I frown. He runs away and pounces on an Indian lady. Everybody avoids the child and the lady, rushing to secret fates. Destiny. Who should I meet at the immigration office but Yves Fontaine, a former college mate. We had been at the Sorbonne together. He was studying art but dropped out in the third year. We were drawn together by one of life's ironies. He was so white, so short, and so high voiced. I was so tall, so black, and deep voiced. We became acquainted rather than friendly because it was a popular event to have the two of us pose for photographs together. It did not bother me. It did not bother him.

"Yves!"

"Boni-papa." His name for me. Boni-papa. We kiss each other three times on either cheek.

"It is inevitable we meet again?"

"It is inevitable."

"What are you doing here?"

"A visa renewal... I am chief technician for the dam in the valley."

"Ah, you did engineering?"

Yves shrugs "Pfff. *Non*. It is not necessary here." The sound of a stamp hitting the desk unnecessarily hard. A voice.

"Whyves Fontana."

Yves changes his posture, his nose rises, he whose nose was always in the ground avoiding eyes so he would not be carried off by campus clowns.

"*Ouais?*" It is an arrogant *oui*. The type of *oui* Yves would never have tried at the Sorbonne.

"Your resident visa."

Yves grabs his passport, swivels on his feet and exits. But first he winks at me.

"Next!" The voice shouts. I am next.

* * *

From outside the window of a travel agency, on Kaunda Street, a poster proclaims:

"Welcome to your own private wilderness." At the bottom of the poster: "Nature close at hand: Walking safaris available." The picture in the foreground is that of a horse, a mountain, and a tall, slender man wrapped in a red blanket, beads in his ears. It is all set within a watermark of the map of Kenya. I keep walking.

Beneath the steeple where the midday Angelus bells clang, I sit and watch the lunchtime prayer crowds dribble into the Minor Basilica. The crowds shimmer and weave behind my eyelids.

The immigration officer demanded papers. He would not listen to me. I told him about my PhD and he laughed out loud. He said:

"*Ati PhD. PhD gani? Wewe refugee, bwana!*"

He whispers that he is compelled by Section 3(f) of the immigration charter to report my illegal presence. He cracks his knuckles. Creak crack. He smiles quickly. Fortunately, all things are possible. The cost of silence is US$500. I have 3,000 shillings.

He took it all. But he returned 50 shillings for "bus fare."

"Eh, your family... where are they?"

"Gone," I say.

"*Si* I'll see you next week? Bring all your documents... eh. Write your address here." A black book. Under "name" I write René Katilibana. Address, Club Balafon. He watches every stroke of my pen.

A resumption of knuckle cracking. His eyes deaden into a slant.

"To not return... is to ask for the police to find you." He turns his head away. He calls: "Next!"

I have used five shillings to buy small round green sweets from a mute street vendor. Good green sweets which calm hunger grumbles. A few more days and we will be leaving. I have resolved not to bother compiling a curriculum vitae.

I join the flow into the church, sitting at the back. Rhythm of prayer, intonation of priests; I sleep sitting before the altar of a God whose name I do not know.

Chi-Chi says: "They laugh at themselves... They are shy... they hide in noise... but they are shy."

Who?

"Kenya people."

We must leave soon.

* * *

We woke up early, Agnethe, Chi-Chi, Lune and I, and walked to Westlands, 45 minutes' walk away from our room just before River Road. We reached the gates of the UNHCR bureau at 10:00AM. We were much too late because the lists of those who would be allowed entry that day had been compiled. The rest of us would have to return the next day. We did, at 7:00AM. We were still too late because the lists of those who would be allowed entry had already been compiled. We returned at 4:00AM. But at 2:00PM. we discovered we were too late because the lists of those who would be allowed in had already been compiled. I decided to ask the guard at the gate, with long, black hair and an earring, a genuine sapphire.

"How can list be compiled? We are here for sree days."

"New arrivals?" he asks.

"Yes?"

"A facilitation fee is needed to help those who are compiling the list."

"Facilitation fee?"

"Yes. That's all."

"And what is zis facilitation fee?"

"US$200 per person."

"And if one... he does not have US$200?"

"Then unfortunately, the list is full."

"But the UN... Sir?"

He raises his brow.

I told Lune and Chi-Chi. They told Agnethe. Agnethe covered her face and wailed. It is fortunate she wailed when a television crew arrived. The guard saw the television crew and realized that the list was not full. Five UN staffers wearing large blue badges appeared from behind the gate and arranged us into orderly lines, shouting commands here and commands there. Three desks materialized at the head of the queue as did three people who transferred our names and addresses into a large black book. After stamping our wrists we were sent to another table to collect our Refugee Registration Numbers. Chi-Chi returned briefly from her spirit realm to say: "Is it not magical how so full a list becomes so empty in so short a time?"

* * *

"*Toa Kitambulisho!*" I know this to be a request for identification. A policeman, one of three, grunted to me. I shivered. I was standing outside the hotel building watching street vendors fight over plastic casings left behind by an inebriated hawker. I was smoking my fifth Sportsman cigarette in two hours.

"*Sina.*" I don't have an identity card.

"*Aya! Toa kitu kidogo.*" I did not understand the code. Something small, what could it be? A cigarette. One each. It was a chilly evening. The cigarettes were slapped out of my hand. I placed my hand up and the second policeman said:

"Resisting arrest."

A fourth one appeared and the second policeman said:

"Illegal alien... resisting arrest."

They twisted my arm behind my back and, holding me by my waistband, the trouser crotch cutting into me, I was frog-marched across town. Some people on the street laughed loudly, pointing at the tall man with his trouser lines stuck between the cracks of his bottom.

"Please... please, *chef*... I'll walk quietly." My hand is raised, palm up. "Please."

Someone, the third one I think, swipes my head with a club. In a sibilant growl.

"Attempted escape."

A litany of crimes.

"What's your name?"

"I... I..." Silence. Again, I try. "I... I... I..."

"Aaaaaaa... aaaaii... eee." It amuses them.

What is my name? I frown. What is my name?

I was once drinking a good espresso in a café in Breda, in the Netherlands, with three European business contacts. Gem dealers.

We were sipping coffee at the end of a well-concluded deal. A squat African man wearing spectacles danced into the café. He wore a black suit, around his neck a gray scarf, in his hand a colorful and large bag, like a carpet bag. Outside, it was cold. So easy to recall the feeling of well-being a hot espresso evokes in a small café where the light is muted and the music a gentle jazz and there is a knowing that outside it is cold and gray and windy.

The squat African man grinned like an ingratiating hound, twisting and distorting his face, raising his lips and from his throat a thin high sound would emerge: "Heee heee heee, heh heh heh."

Most of the café turned back to their coffees and conversations. One man in a group of three put out his foot. The squat African man stumbled, grabbed his back to him. Rearranged himself and said to the man: "Heee heee heee, heh heh heh."

He flapped his arm up and down. I wondered why, and then it dawned on me. He was simulating a monkey. He flapped his way to where I was, my acquaintances and I.

Sweat trickled down my spine. I think it was the heat in the café.

"What is your country of origin?" I ask him. Actually, I snarl the question at him and I am surprised by the rage in my voice.

He mumbles, his face staring at the floor. He lowers his bag, unzips it and pulls out ladies' intimate apparel designed and colored in the manner of various African animals. Zebra, leopard, giraffe and colobus. There is a crocodile-skin belt designed for the pleasure of particular sado-masochists. At the bottom of the bag a stack of posters and sealed magazines. Nature magazines? I think I see a mountain on one. I put out my free hand for one. It is not a mountain, it is an impressive arrangement of an equally impressive array of Black male genitalia. I let the magazine slide from my hand and he stoops to pick it up, wiping it against the sleeve of his black coat.

"Where are you from?" I ask in Dutch.

"Rotterdam."

"No, man... your origin?"

"Sierra Leone."

"Have you no shame?"

His head jerks up, his mouth opens and closes, his eyes meet mine for the first time. His eyes are wet. It is grating that a man should cry.

"Broda." he savors the word. "Broda... it's fine to see de eyes of anoda man... it is fine to see de eyes."

Though his Dutch is crude, he read sociology in Leeds and mastered it. He is quick to tell me this. He has six children. His wife, Gemma, is a beautiful woman. On a good day he makes 200 guilders, it is enough to supplement the Dutch state income and it helps sustain the illusions of good living for remnants of his family back home. He refuses to be a janitor, he tells me. To wear a uniform to clean a European toilet? No way. This is why he is running his own enterprise.

"I be a Business Mon."

"Have you no shame?"

"Wha do ma childs go?"

"You have a master's degree from a good University. Use it!"

Business man picks up his bags. He is laughing, so deeply, so low, a different voice. He laughs until he cries. He wipes his eyes.

"Oh mah broda... tank you for de laughing... tank you... you know... Africans we be overeducated fools. Dem papers are for to wipe our bottom. No one sees your knowing when you has no feets to stand in."

He laughs again, patting his bag, smiling in reminiscence.

"My broda for real him also in Italy. Bone doctor. Specialist. Best in class. Wha he do now? Him bring Nigeria woman for de prostitute." Business man chortles.

"Maybe he fix de bone when dem break."

I gave him 20 guilders. "For the children."

It was when Joop van Vuuren, the gem dealer, idly, conversationally asked me what the business man's name was that I remembered I had not asked and he had not told me.

In exile we lower our heads so that we do not see in the mirror of another's eyes, what we suspect: that our precarious existence rests entirely on the whim of another's tolerance of our presence. A phrase crawls into my mind: "Psychic Oblation." But what does it mean?

* * *

"What is your name?"

97

I can smell my name. It is the smell of salt and the musk of sweat. It is... surprise... surprise... remembered laughter and a woman calling me "*Chéri...*"

I want to say... I want to say Yves Fontaine. As Yves Fontaine I would not be a vagrant immigrant, a pariah. As Yves Fontaine I would be "expatriate" and therefore desirable. As Yves Fontaine I do not need an identity card.

"I... I... My... I..." Silence.

The sibilant hoarseness of the Superintendent: "Unco-oparatif. Prejudicing infestigesons."

* * *

Agnethe-mama saw it happen. She had just raised her shawl to uncover her face so that she could shout at me to bring her some paracetamol for her headache. At first she thought she was reliving an old tale. Three men had arrived for her husband. She crawled up the stairs, lying low lest she be seen. Lune told me mama had sat on the bed rocking to and fro and moaning a song and whispering incantations she alone knew words to. In the four days I was away, making an unscheduled call on the Kenyan government, my mother's hair deepened from gray to white. We did not know that her blood pressure began its ascent that first day. Time, as she had always believed, would accomplish the rest.

It was at their station that the policemen found all manner of evidence in my pocket. All of which they liked and kept. After three days I was charged with "loitering with intent." At the crucial moment, the proprietor turned up with my refugee registration card. My case was dismissed and I was charged to keep the peace.

Lune paid the proprietor with her engagement ring. Whatever he had obtained from the sale of the ring caused him to put an arm around me, call me brother and drag me into a bar where he bought me three beers. He said: "*Pole.*" Sorry.

He said we did not need to pay rent for three months. He wanted to know if we had any more jewelry to sell. I said no. He bought me another beer. He slides a note into my pocket before he leaves. A thousand shillings.

The UNHCR are shifting people out of Kenya, resettlement in third countries. Soon, it will be us. Agnethe-mama now wakes up in the night, tiptoes to my bed. When she sees it is me, she whispers: *"Mwami,"* My Lord.

Sunday is a day in which we breathe a little easier in this place. There are fewer policemen and diffident laughter hiding in hearts' surfaces. It is simpler on Sunday to find our kind, my people in an African exile. We visit churches. Agnethe, Chi-Chi always go in. Lune sometimes joins them and sometimes joins me. I am usually sitting beneath a tree, on a stone bench, walking the perimeter wall and, if it is raining, sitting at the back of the church watching people struggling for words and rituals indicating allegiance to a God whose face they do not know. The hope peddlers become rich in a short while, singing, "Cheeeeessus!." Even the devastated destitute will tithe to commodified gods, sure that in the theatrics of frothing messengers, hope is being doled out. Investing in an eternal future? I do not have a coin to spare. Not now, maybe later, when all is quiet and normal, I will evaluate the idea of a Banker God created in the fearful image of man.

After church, to Agnethe's delight, she found Maria. Maria and Agnethe used to shop in Paris together. Once, they by-passed France and landed in Haiti. Maria's brother was an associate of Baby Doc's wife. They returned home unrepentant to their husbands and children; they treated their daring with the insouciance it deserved. It was fortunate Agnethe met Maria here because it was from Maria we learned that the Canadian government had opened its doors to those of us in Kenya.

Chi-Chi emerged from her sanctuary to say "Bu-Bu... patterns of life... somewhere lines meet, *non?*"

A statement of fact. I am hopeful.

Maria was living well. Her brother had settled in Kenya years ago. His wife was from Kenya. Maria was with them.

"Is Alphonse with you?"

Agnethe, being a princess, had been unaware that after the two presidents had died, one never asked one's compatriots where so and so was. If one did not see so and so, one did not ask until the party spoken to volunteered the information of whereabouts. Alphonse was not with Maria. That was all Maria said. Even if Agnethe was a princess, because she was a princess in exile, she read nuances. She kept her mouth shut, and looked to the ground.

Maria's brother, Professor George, and his wife and his two children were going to the Nairobi Animal Orphanage. Did we want to visit animals with them?

"Oh yes. Unfortunately... as you imagine... money is..."

"Don't worry, it is my pleasure," Professor George said.

So we went to meet animals. We met Langata the leopard who did not want people staring at him while he slept. Langata felt the intimacy of sleep is sacred and should be recognized as such. Apparently, he told Chi-Chi this. So Chi-Chi told us. Professor George glared at her. Chi-Chi refused to look at the animals. Lune said animals lived behind fences to protect them from humans. Agnethe-mama was surprised to find that her dead prince did indeed look like a lion. She and Maria stared at Simba who stared back at them as if he knew he was being compared to a prince and the prince was increasingly found to be lacking.

"Why the name 'Professor George'?" I said to Professor George.

"They find it hard to say Georges Nsibiriwa."

"'They' were his wife's people. I sensed the 'and' so I said: "And?"

Professor George walked quietly, he pointed out the difference between a Thomson's gazelle and a Grant's gazelle. Something about white posteriors. At a putrid pool, in which sluggish algae brewed a gross green soup, in between withered reeds and a hapless hyacinth, Professor George sighed and smiled. A dead branch, half-submerged, floated on the surface of the pool.

"Ah. Here we are... look... in the place you find yourself... in the time... camouflage!" A glorious pronouncement.

Surreptitious glance. Professor George then picks up a twig and throws it into the pond. From within the depths, what had been the dead branch twisted up a surge of power. Its jaws snapped the twig in two; a white underbelly displayed before transforming itself once again into a dead branch, half-submerged, floating on the surface of the pool.

"Ah! See! Camouflage... place dictates form, *mon ami*. Always."

I start to tell him about the police.

Professor George nods. "Yes... yes... it is the time." And he asks if I have heard word from Augustine, a mutual friend who lives in Copenhagen.

"Augustine has changed address, it seems."

Professor George says: "Yes... it is the time."

I need to ask something. "You have heard about the list?"

He looks up at me, his face a question. *"Les génocidaires?* Ah yes... but I pay no attention."

The relief of affirmation. A name's good can be invoked again. So I tell him, "Ah! It's difficult, *mon ami*, and... Agnethe-mama doesn't know."

"Know what?"

"Our name is on the list."

With the same agility that the crocodile used to become a log again, Professor George pulls away from the fence. He wipes his hand, the one I had shaken, against his shirt. He steps away, one step at a time, then he turns around and trots, like a donkey, shouting, looking over his shoulder at me:

"Maria! We leave... now!"

The first lesson of exile—camouflage. When is a log... not a log? When a name is not a name.

* * *

On Monday we were outside the UNHCR at 4.30am. We hope that the list is not full. It is not. Instead there is a handwritten sign leading to an office of many windows which says "Relocations, Resettlement." At the front, behind the glass, are three men and two women with blue badges that say UNHCR. They have papers in front of them. Behind them, four men, a distance away. They watch us all, their bodies still. I straighten my coat and stand a little taller.

We are divided into two groups, men and women: the women are at the front. The women are divided into three groups: Young Girls, Young Women, Old Women.

At the desks, where there is a desk sign which says "Records Clerk," they write out names and ages, previous occupation and country of origin and of course, the RRN—refugee registration number. Those who do not have an RRN must leave, obtain one in room 2004 and return after two weeks.

Later, flash! And a little pop. Our faces are engraved on a piece of paper. Passport photograph. Movement signified, we are leaving.

"Next," the photographer says. Defiance of absence. Photographer, do you see us at all? Inarticulation as defense. Let it pass. Soon, we will be gone from this place.

The Young Women are commanded to hand over babies to the Old Women. Young Girls and Young Women are taken into another room. A medical examination, we are informed. We are told to wait outside the office block, the gate. Perhaps we will be examined another day.

* * *

Agnethe-mama and I are sitting on a grassy patch opposite a petrol station. Agnethe bites at her lips. Then she tugs my sleeve.

"Bonbon... do other monarchs-in-exile live in Canada?"

"Perhaps."

Chi-Chi and Lune emerge, holding hands. It is two hours later and the sun hovers, ready to sink into darkness. They do not look at either of us. We walk back, silently. Chi-chi has hooked her hand into my waistband. Lune glides ahead of us all, her stride is high, the balance of her body undisturbed. A purple matatu, its music "thump thumping," slows down and a tout points north with a hand gesture. I decline. It speeds off in a series of "thump thumps." Agnethe frowns. We walk in silence. Long after the matatu has gone, Agnethe says, her face serene again:

"The reason they are like that... these Kenyans... is because they do not know the cow dance."

* * *

When Lune dipped her hand into my coat pocket while I slept and took out 800 shillings, returning in an hour with a long mirror, I should have listened to the signal from the landscape.

Chi-Chi used Lune's mirror to cut her hair. She cut it as if she were hacking a dress. She stepped on and kicked her shorn locks. Agnethe-mama covered her mouth, she said nothing as if she understood something. For Lune, the mirror evokes memories of ballet technique. She executes all her movements with her legs rotated outward. Agnethe-mama looks to the mirror so she can turn away and not look.

Two weeks later, I kick the mirror down. I smash it with my fists. They bleed. Agnethe screamed once, covering her mouth. Silence enters our room. Silence smells of the Jevanjee Garden roasted Kenchic chicken; one pack feeds a frugal family of four for three days.

On the third day, I find Lune looking down at me.

"It was mine. It was mine." She smiles suddenly and I am afraid.

From across the room, Agnethe-mama; "Ah Bonbon... still... no word from the kings-in-exile?"

The anger with which the rain launches itself upon this land, the thunder which causes floors to creak sparks a strange foreboding in me. That night, while we were eating cold beans and maize dinner, Lune pushed her plate aside, looked at me, a gentle, graceful crane, her hands fluttering closed, a smile in her eyes.

"*Chéri*, we can leave soon, but it depends on a certain... co-operation."

"Co-operation?"

"A condition from the medical examination."

Agnethe looks away. Chi-Chi clutches her body, staving off in her way something she is afraid of.

"How do we co-operate?" I am afraid to know.

"By agreeing to be examined," she laughs, high, dry, cough-laugh, "...examined by the officials at their homes for a night."

"I see." I don't. Silence. Agnethe is rocking herself to and fro. She is moaning a song. I know the tune. It is from the song new widows sing when the body of their dead spouse is laid on a bier.

Annals of war decree that conquest of landscapes is incomplete unless the vanquished's women are "taken." Where war is crudest, the women are discarded afterwards for their men to find. Living etchings of emasculation. Lune has not finished yet. I sense I am being taunted for my ineffectuality by this woman who would be my wife.

"Now… it has been discussed with family, it is not a question of being forced."

A recitation. I lower my head. The incongruity of tears. A persistent mosquito buzzes near my ear. The food on my plate is old. Lune leaves the table, pushing back her chair, she places her feet in a parallel arrangement, one in front of the other, the heel of a foot in line with the toes of the other. Her right arm extends in front of her body, and the left is slightly bent and raised. She moves the weight of her body over the left foot and bends the left knee. She raises her right heel, pointing the toe. Her body is bent toward the extended knee. She holds the pose and says: *"Pointe tendue!"*

Conscious now, I read the gesture. She will perform as she must, on this stage. I can only watch.

"No."

Now Chi-Chi raises her head, like a beautiful cat. I know the look; tentative hope, tendrils reaching out and into life. Lune closes her feet, the heel of one now touching the toes of the other; she pushes up from the floor and jumps, her legs straight, feet together and pointed. She lands and bows before me. Then she cracks and cries, crumbling on the floor.

Outside, the window, the drone of traffic which never stops and the cackle of drunkards. Creeping up the window a man's voice singing:

"Chupa na debe. Mbili kwa shilling tano. Chupa na debe."

Bottle and tin, two for five shillings, bottle and tin, Kenyans and their shillings.

* * *

I stood on the balcony staring at the traffic, counting every red car I could see. Nine so far. Behind me, Agnethe approached. In front of my face she dangled her wedding ring.

"Sell it."

"No."

She let it fall at my feet.

We used the money to leave the room on River Road. We went to a one-roomed cottage with a separate kitchen and an outside toilet. It was in Hurlingham, the property of a former government secretary, Mr. Wamathi, a drinking acquaintance of the proprietor. I observed that his gardening manners were undeveloped; he had subdivided his quarter-acre plot, cutting down old African olive trees and uprooting the largest bougainvillea I had ever seen, on the day we arrived. He was going to put up a block of flats. Mr. Wamathi was delirious with glee about selling the trees to the "City Canjo" for 15,000 shillings. His laughter was deep, rounded and certain with happiness.

He laughed and I felt hope joining us.

Agnethe started tending a small vegetable patch. Her eyes gleamed when the carrot tops showed. Lune made forays into a nearby mall, an eye-fest of possibilities satiating her heart, extending her wants. Chi-Chi, over the fence, befriended an Ethiopian resident who introduced her to his handsome brother, Matteo.

The day Chi-Chi met Matteo she slipped her hand into my waistband, looking up at me she said: "He... can... see..."

Every day I tried to contact home, seeking cash for four air tickets on a refugee pass. Word appeared in dribs and drabs. Detail gleaned from conversations heard, strangers approached and newspapers slyly read.

The bank? Burned down. The money? Missing from the safes. And once, the sound of a name accused, accursed: *Kuseremane.*

But hadn't we left on the fifth day?

The day flows on. I sit in different cafés, telling the waiters that I am waiting for a friend. Thirty minutes in some cafés. In the more confident ones, the ones which are sure of their identity, I can wait for a full hour before I make a face, glance at my non-existent watch, frown as if tardy friends are a source of annoyance and I exit.

Whispers had floated over the land of hills and nestled in valleys and refused to leave, had in fact given birth to volleys of sound. Now tales had been added of a most zealous servant instructed by an heir to sluice stains.

"Ah! Roger. *Mon oncle...*"

Excoriating women's wombs, crushing fetal skulls, following the instructions of a prince.

They said.

Today I woke up as early as the ones who walk to work maneuvering

105

the shadows of dawn, crochet-covered radios against ears, in pockets, or tied to bicycle saddles. Sometimes music, rumba. And in the dawn dark I can forget where I am and let others' footsteps show me the way. I hear Franklin Bukaka's plea, pouring out of so many radios, tenderly carried in so many ways. *"Aye! Afrika, O! Afrika..."*

I return from so many journeys like this and one day, I find Agnethe-mama lying on her back in her vegetable patch. At first I think she is soaking up the sun. Then I remember Agnethe-mama never let the sun touch her skin. An African princess, melanin management was an important event of toilette. I lean over her body. Then, head against her chest, I cannot hear a heartbeat.

I carry my mother and run along the road. The evening traffic courses past. Nairobi accommodates. Room for idiosyncrasies. So to those who pass by, it is not strange that a tall, tall man should carry a slender woman in his arms.

At the first hospital. "My mother... she is not heart beating... help."

"12,000-shilling deposit, Sir."

"But my mother…"

"Try Kenyatta."

At Kenyatta, they want a 4,000-shilling deposit and I will still have to wait, one of about 300 people waiting for two doctors to see them. I do not have 4,000 shillings.

"Where can I go?"

"Enda Coptic." Go to the Copts.

"Tafadhali… please, where are they?"

"Ngong Road."

"How far….?"

"Next!"

* * *

Agnethe sighs, opens her eyes and asks:

"Have the monarchs-in-exile sent our reply yet, Bonbon?"

"Soon... mama."

She had suffered a mild stroke.

I return to the cottage to pack a bag for mama. Exile blurs lines. So a son, such as I, can handle a mother's underwear. Agnethe-mama told Chi-Chi once, in my hearing, that all in a woman may fall apart, may become unmatched, but never her underwear. I place sets of underwear for Agnethe; black, brown and lacy purple.

* * *

Kuseremane, Kuseremane, Kuseremane.

It seems that the whispers have infringed upon the place where my tears hide. I cannot stop bawling, sniveling like a lost ghoul. My shoulders bounce with a life of their own. Lune watches me, her eyes veiled in a red, feral glow.

At 6:00PM I rejoin a river of workers returning to so many homes. To be one of many, is to be, anyway, if only for a moment. The sun is setting and has seared into the sky a golden trail; it has the look of a machete wound bleeding yellow light. It is an incongruous time to remember Roger's blackened hands.

Agnethe has taken to sitting in the garden rocking her body, to and fro, to and fro. She does not hum. But sometimes, in between the fro and to, she asks:

"Have the brother sovereigns sent a letter?"

"Soon."

At night, Chi-Chi shakes me awake, again. My pillow is soaked, my face wet. Not my tears.

The next morning, I left the cottage before sunrise. I have learned of hidden places; covered spaces which the invisible inhabit. The Nairobi Arboretum. The monkeys claim my attention, as does the frenzied moaning of emptied people calling out to frightened gods for succor. Now, it starts to rain. I walk rapidly, then start to jog, the mud splattering my already-stained coat. The other hidden place is through the open doors of a Catholic Church. Hard wooden benches, pews upon which a man may kneel, cover his eyes and sleep or cry unheeded before the presence that is also an absence.

* * *

My return coincides with Mr. Wamathi's winding his way into the house. He rocks on his feet:

107

"Habe new yearghh." "Year" ends with a burp and belch.

"Happy New Year." It is July and cold and time is relative.

Agnethe outside, uncovered. Rocking to and fro. She clutches thin arms about herself, shivering.

"Aiiee, mama!" I lean down to lift her up.

"*Bonbon, il fait froid, oui?*" It is cold.

"Lune? Chi-Chi? Lune?" Why is mama sitting out in the night alone?

"*Où est* Lune... Chi-Chi, mama?"

Agnethe stares up at the sky, from my arms.

"*Bonbon... il fait froid.*" Two anorexic streams glide down, past high cheekbones and nestle at the corner of her mouth. She looks up and into my eyes. The resolute eyes of an ancient crone. Now... now the cold's tendrils insinuate themselves, searing horror in my heart.

Chi-Chi returned first. She stumbled through the door, her body shuddering. She is wiping her hand up and down her body, ferociously, as if wiping away something foul only she can sense.

"Everything has a pattern... Bu-Bu, *non?*" She gives me the folded papers.

Three *laissez-passer.* Tickets to rapture. Let them pass. It favors Agnethe, Boniface and Chi-Chi Kuseremane.

I am not there.

I watch from afar, the ceiling I think, as the tall man tears the papers to shreds. I am curious about the weeping woman with shorn hair crawling on the ground gathering the fragments to her chest. I frown when I see the tall, dark man lift his hand up, right up and bring it crashing into the back of the girl who falls to the floor, lies flat on her belly and stops crying. She is staring into herself where no one else can reach her. A sound at the door. The tall, tall man walks up to his fiancée. Who bows low, the end of a performance. She too has a clutch of papers in her hand. The tall man sniffs the girl as if he were a dog and he bites her on the cheek, the one upon which another man's cologne lingers. Where the teeth marks are, the skin has broken. Drops of blood. Lune laughs.

"We can leave any time now."

"*Putaine!*"

She giggles. "But I shall live, *chéri...* we shall live... we shall live well."

Agnethe-mama heaves herself up from the bed and brushes her long white hair. I return to the body of the tall, black man whose arms are hanging against his side, his head bowed. He sees that Lune's feet are close, the heel of one touching the toes of the other. She slowly raises hands over her head, paper clutched in the right, she rounds her arms slightly, *en couronne*—in a crown.

Paper fragments, a mosaic on the floor. I stoop, the better to stare at them. I pick up my sister. She is so still. But then she asks, eyes wide with wanting to know: "Bu-Bu… there's a pattern in everything. *Oui?*"

"*Oui*, Ché-Ché." A childhood name, slips easily out of my mouth. Now when she smiles, it reaches her eyes. She touches my face with her hand.

* * *

That night, or more accurately, the next morning, it was 3:00AM, Agnethe went to the bathroom outside. Returning to the room she had stepped into and slid in a puddle. She stepped out again to clean her feet and then she screamed and screamed and screamed.

"Ahh! Ahh! Ahhhee!"

She points at the rag upon which she has wiped her feet. It is covered in fresh blood. She points into the room, at the floor. I return to look. Lune is now awake. Lights in the main house are switched on and Mr. Wamathi appears in the doorway, a knobkerrie in his hand.

"Where, where?" he shouts.

The neighborhood dogs have started to howl. The sky is clear and lit up by a crescent moon. I remember all this because I looked up as I carried my bleeding sister, my Chi-Chi-Ché-Ché, into Mr. Wamathi's car, cushioned by towels and blankets while her blood poured out.

At the hospital emergency wing where we had been admitted quickly, a tribute to Mr. Wamathi's threats, I watched the splayed legs of my sister, raised and stirruped. My sister, led to and stripped bare in the wilderness of lives altered when two presidents were shot to the ground from the sky. I remember a blow bestowed on a back by a defenseless brother-prince.

How can a blow be unswung?

109

A doctor and a nurse struggle to bring to premature birth a child we did not know existed. Chi-Chi's eyes are closed. Her face still. When she left us I felt a tug on my waistband as in days of life and her body lost its shimmer, as if a light within had gone off for good. She left with her baby.

The child's head was between her legs. A boy or girl, only the head was visible and one arm, small fists slightly open as if beckoning. Skin like cream coffee. The offspring of African exiles. An enigma solved. The Ethiopians had abruptly disappeared from the radar of our lives and Chi-Chi had said nothing. The dying child of African exiles in an African land. I stroked the baby's wet head. Did baby come to lure Chi-Chi away? A word shimmers into my heart: fratricide. I douse it with the coldness of my blood. I am shivering. A distant voice... mine.

"Leave them... leave the children." Keep them together... the way they are.

Landscape speaks. The gesture of an incomplete birth. Of what have we to be afraid? Metamorphoses of being. There must be another way to live.

"Is there a priest?" Even the faithless need a ritual to purge them of the unassailable scent of mystery.

"What shall we do with the body?"

A body... my sister. When did a pool of blood become this... absence? They let me cover her face after I have kissed her eyes shut.

Vain gesture.

Agnethe and Lune are outside, waiting. Islands in their hope. I open the door to let them in, gesturing with my hand. They step into the room and I step out. I let the door close behind me and try to block out the screams emanating from within. Staccato screams. Screams in a crescendo and then a crushing moan.

A nurse offers forms to be filled in.

"Nairobi City Mortuary."

It will cost 8,000 Kenyan shillings to rent space for Chi-Chi. I do not have 8,000 shillings. It's okay, the nurse says. I can pay it tomorrow at the mortuary.

Eeeh! Kenyans and their shillings.

Nurse turns: *"Pole."* Sorry.

But Mr. Wamathi makes an arrangement with his wives, and they find 35,000 shillings for Agnethe.

Is this it?

Later. After all the bluster of being... this? A body in a box, commended to the soil.

A brother's gesture: 12 torches alight in a sister's cheap coffin. Chi-Chi and her Nameless One will see in the dark.

* * *

It is a challenge to match paper fragments so that they match just right. It is fortunate there are words on the paper, it makes it easier. Three *laissez-passer*. Chi-Chi's is complete, almost new.

Lune has returned to my bed. Agnethe's resumed her rocking, which has accelerated in both speed and volume. Her eyes are brown and a ceaseless rivulet of tears drips onto her open palm. But she smiles at us, Lune and me, and does not utter a word. Sometimes her eyes have a film of white over them as if she had become a medium, in constant communion with the dead. Sometimes I imagine that they look at me with reproach. I look to the ground; the quest for patterns.

I have lost the feeling of sleep. I will not touch Lune nor can I let her touch me. It is the ghost of another man's cologne which lingers in my dreams and haunts my heart. I am bleeding in new places. But we are leaving.

"Bu-Bu, everything has a pattern, *non?*"

We will be leaving for Canada on Saturday night.

* * *

Agnethe shocked us by dying on Friday morning in my arms as I entered the gates of the Coptic hospital. On the streets, as before, no one found it strange, the idea of a tall, tall man carrying a slender woman in his arms. A pattern had been established, a specific madness accommodated.

When Agnethe-mama left, the energy of her exit made me stumble.

"Ah! Bonbon! Ah!" she says.

At the Coptic gate, "*Mwami!*"

She leaves with such force, her head is thrown back against my arms.

Agnethe-mama.

The Copts cannot wrench her from my arms. They let me sit in their office and rock my mother to and fro, to and fro. I am humming a song. It is the melody of "*Sur le pont d'Avignon*" where we shall dance.

At the cottage, old bags with few belongings are packed. On the bed, a manila bag with Agnethe's clothes, the bag she was packing when her body crumbled to the ground.

"*Où est maman?*" Lune asks. Where is mama?

I stretch out my arms and she lifts her hand to her long silk hair and draws it away from her face. She rushes into my arms and burrows her face into my shoulder.

"Forgive me."

We do what we can to live. Even the man whose cologne stayed on her face. I have no absolution to give. So I tell her instead that Agnethe has just died. And when Lune drops to the ground like a shattered rock, I slap her awake, harder than necessary on the cheek upon which another man's cologne had strayed and stayed. She does not move, but her eyes are open. Arms above her head, hair over her face.

She smirks. "I'm leaving. I am living."

She grabs my arm, a woman haunted by the desire for tomorrow where all good is possible. "I am leaving."

"*Ma mère... Lune-chérie.*"

Lune covers her ears, shuts her eyes.

For the most fleeting of moments, I enter into her choice. To slough the skin of the past off. To become another life form. I look around the room. Agnethe-mama's slippers by the bed. What traces have they left on the surface of the earth? The gossip of landscape. It is getting clear. I stoop low and kiss Lune on her forehead. In the pattern of things, there is a place in which the body of a princess may rest. Isn't there?

A Coptic priest, a Coptic doctor, Lune and I, Mr. and Mrs. Wamathi—

the sum total of those gathered around Agnethe-mama. Lune's airplane bags are over her shoulders, her plane ticket in her purse. In four hours' time she will be in a plane taking her to the Canada of her dreams. We forgot grave-diggers must be paid, their spades attached to Kenya shillings. So I will cover my mother's grave myself, when the others are gone.

* * *

A plane departs from Nairobi. Kenya Airways to London. From London, Air Canada to Ottawa.

I have been laughing for an hour now. True, the laughter is interspersed with hot, sour, incessant streams of tears. Squatting on my mother's grave. The unseen now obvious.

Life peering out of lives. Life calling life to dance. Life, the voyeur. I will start dancing now.

"L'indépendance, ils l'ont obtenue/ La table ronde, ils l'ont gagnée…"

"Mhhhh… Mhhhh… Mhh… Mhh… Mhhhh."

"L'indépendance, ils l'ont obtenue…"

Kabasellé laughs.

Who can allay the summon of life to life? The inexorable attraction for fire. The soul knows its keeper. Inexorable place, space and pace. I see. I see.

There!

Life aflame in a fire-gold sun. And dust restoring matter to ash. The ceaseless ardor for life now requited:

"Mhhhh… Mhhhh… Mhh… Mhh… Mhhhh."

"L'indépendance, ils l'ont obtenue/ La table ronde, ils l'ont gagnée…"

"Cha-cha-cha!"

Thus began the first day of my second life.

* * *

One day, a letter trudged to Kenya from Canada. Its first line is:

"Chéri, please, let me know the date of your arrival."

A tall, tall man straightens the lapels of a fading Hugo Boss coat. He cradles a shovel, listening to the sighing sentences of dust fragments filling a new grave. In his heart, an old phrase bubbles to the fore:

Soon.

Another week, another letter: "...when is your flight arriving?"

And another the week after that, and the next, until a year has gone and then six months more.

I have joined the sentinels of the cemetery; an assorted collection of life's creatures, through which life gazes at life. Devoted dogs, gypsy cats, two birds which perch over certain graves, a hundred unobtrusive trees and, of course, spirits caught between worlds. Living gargoyles guarding entry points through which humans pass, dreaming in the day about shy, wise, night shadows with which conversations broken off at dawn can resume.

The discovery of listening...

Catching landscape in its surreptitious gestures—patterns which point to meaning...

Waiting for the return of a name set ablaze when fire made dust out of two presidents' bodies...

I live in the silence-scope and perform the rituals of return, for life. Where I am, the bereaved know they will find, if they visit, that the reminder of their beloved's existence—the grave—is safe, that life watches and leaves signs on tombs; mostly flowers, sometimes trees.

I prefer trees.

Soon now, the wind-borne whispers will fall silent.

Seventh Street Alchemy

Brian Chikwava—winner of the 2004 Caine Prize

By 5:00AM most of Harare's struggling inhabitants are out of their hovels. They are on their way to innumerable places to waylay the dollars they so desperately need to stave hunger off their doorsteps. Trains and commuter omnibuses burst with exploitable human material. Its excess finds its way onto bicycles, or simply self-propels, tilling earth with bare, frost-bitten feet all the way to the city center or industrial areas.

The modes of transport are diverse, poverty the trendsetter. Like a colony of hungry ants, it crawls over the multitudes scattered along the city roads, ravaging all etches of dignity that only a few years back stood resilient. Threadbare resignation is concealed underneath threadbare shirts, together with socks and underpants that resemble a ruthless termite job. In spite of poverty's glorious march into every household, the will to be dignified by underpants and socks remains intact.

Activities in the city center tend towards the paranormal. A voodoo economy flourishes as daylight dwindles: fruit and vegetable vendors slash their prices by half and still fail to sell. The following morning the same material is carted back onto the streets, selling at higher than the previous day's peak rates. In some undertakings the enthusiasm to participate is expressed in wads of notes; in some, simple primitive violence—or the threat of its use—is common currency. As the idea of ensuring that your demands are backed up by violence is fast gaining hold among the city's prowlers, business carried out in pin-striped suits is fleeing the city center, ill-equipped to deal with the proliferation of scavenger tactics. Pigeons too have joined the new street entrepreneurs: they relieve themselves on pedestrians when least expected and never alight on the same street corner for more than two days in a row.

Even the supposedly civilized, well-to-do section of the population, a pitiful lot typified by their indefatigable amiability, now finds itself anchored down by a State whose methods of governance involve incessant roguery. Instead of facing up to their circumstances with a modicum of honor, they weekly hurl themselves into churches to petition a disinterested God to subvert the laws of the universe in their favor.

At the corner of Samora Machel Avenue and Seventh Street, in a flat whose bedroom is adorned with two newspaper cuttings of the President, lives a 52-year-old quasi-prostitute with 37 teeth and a pair of six-inch-heeled perspex platform shoes. It has been decades since she realized that, armed with a vagina and a will to survive, destitution could never lay claim to her. With these weapons of destruction she has continued to fortify her liberty against poverty and society. Fiso is her name and like a lot of the city's inhabitants she has conjured that death is mere spin, nobody ever really dies.

On the night a street kid got knocked down by a car it was a tranquil hour. A discerning ear would have been able to hear two flies fornicating several meters away. But to Anna Shava, a civil servant, soaked to the bone with matrimonial distress, the flies would have had to be inside her nose to get her attention. Her tearful departure from home after another scuffle with her husband set in motion a violent symphony of events. Security guards who scurried off the streets for safety could not have imagined that an exasperated spouse in a car vibrating to the frenzied rhythms of her anguished footwork could beget such upheaval.

Right in the middle of the lane, at the corner of Samora Machel Avenue and Seventh Street, a street kid staggers from left to right, struggling to tear himself out of a stupor acquired by sniffing glue all day. The car devours the tarmac, and in a screech of tires the corner is gobbled up together with the small figure endeavoring to grasp reality. Sheet metal grudgingly gives in to a dent, bones snap, glass shatters. The kid never had a chance. His soul's departure is punctuated by one final baritone fart relinquishing life. Protruding out of the kid's back pocket is a tube of Z68 glue.

A couple of blocks from the scene, blue lights flashed from a police car while two officers shared the delicate task of trying to convince a grouchy young musician to part with some of his dollars for having gone though red traffic lights.

"You've been having a good time. That's no problem. But you must understand we also need something to keep us happy while doing our rounds," one of the officers said with a well-drilled, venal smile before continuing. "Since you are a musician we know you can't afford much, Stix, but if you could just make us happy with a couple of Nando's takeaways..."

Anna, realizing that they were not going to pay her any attention without some effort on her part, marched over to the officers. "Will you please come to my help, haven't you seen what happened?" she said, donning that look of nefarious servitude that she often inspired on the faces of applicants at the immigration office. She knew better than anybody that being nice to people in authority could render purchasable otherwise priceless rights, and simplify one's life.

"We are off duty now. Madam, call Central Police Station," one of the officers yodeled over. Returning to her car and periodically glancing over her shoulder in disbelief, she saw the offending driver stick out of his window a clenched handful of notes to pacify the vultures that had taken positions around his throttled freedom. His liberties resuscitated, he sped off in his scarlet ramshackle car.

Two days before, Anna, no less fed up with her errant husband, had followed him to the city's most popular rhumba club. She had found him leaning against the bar, with men she did not recognize. They talked at the top of their voices in the dim smudged lighting. Her husband, who had been tapping his foot to the sound of loud Congolese music, recoiled at the sight of her. Befuddled, he grappled with the embarrassment of having been tracked down to a night-club crawling with prostitutes. And then there was the thought of his mates saying that his balls had long been liberated from him and safely deposited in his wife's bra. His impulse was to thump her thoroughly, but lacking essential practice, he could not lift a finger.

"What do you want?" he asked, icily.

"Buy me a drink, too," she brushed the question aside.

He stared at Anna as she grinned. Outrage lay not far beneath such grins—experience had schooled him. Reluctantly, he turned to the bar to order her a Coke, struggling to affect an air of ascendancy in the eyes of his peers. He tossed a 500-dollar note at the bartender, as if oblivious to his wife's presence.

Half an hour later when Anna visited the ladies' toilet, transgression would catch up with her husband. There, a lady with graying hair, standing with what looked like a couple of prostitutes, cut short her conversation to remark innocently, "Be careful with that man. He's a problem when it comes to paying up. Ask these girls. Make sure he pays you before you do anything or he will make excuses like, 'I didn't think you were that kind of girl.'"

Anna was transfixed, hoping—pretending—that the words were directed at someone else.

"You could always grab his cellphone, you know," the woman added kindly.

That woman was Fiso who, at the time Anna ran into a street kid, was engrossed in the common ritual of massaging her dementia. Having spent a whole day struggling to sell vegetables—a relatively new engagement imposed on her by the autumn of her street life—she was exhausted and was not bothered by the screeching tires down the road. It did not occur to her that what had registered in her ears was an incident precipitated by her well-meaning advice.

Beside her, sharing her bed, lay her daughter, Sue, a 26-year-old flea-market vendor. In the midst of her mother's furious campaign against a pair of rogue mosquitoes, which relentlessly circled their heads before attacking, Sue came to the tired realization that in spite of all the years on the streets, her mother still had undepleted stocks of a compulsive disorder from her youthful days.

In the sooty darkness, her mother blindly clapped, hoping to deal one or both of them a fatal blow. Precision, however, remained in inverse proportion to determination. The mosquitoes circled, mother waited, her desire to snuff out a life inflated. They would dive, she would clap. Sound and futility reigned supreme. At last, jumping off the bed, Fiso switched on the light. A minute later, one of the mosquitoes, squashed by a sandal, was a smudge of blood on the President's face, but Fiso could not be bothered to make good the insignia of her patriotism. A few months before, she would have wiped the blood away. But the novelty of affecting patriotic sentiment in the hope of dreaming herself out of prostitution to the level of First Lady had long worn off.

The following morning, Sue switched on her miniature radio, to be confronted by the continuously recycled maxims of State propaganda, which ranged from the importance of being a sovereign nation to defending the gains of independence in the face of a "neocolonialist onslaught." Leaning against the sink, she failed to grasp the value of the messages to her life. She gulped her tea and went to the Union Avenue flea market. There, among other vendors slugging it out for survival, she could at least learn where to get the next bag of sugar or cooking oil.

On the same Saturday afternoon that marked the climax to Anna's marital woes, Stix, a struggling, young jazz pianist, had a call from his friend, Shamiso, inviting him to an impromptu dinner at Mvura Restaurant. Her friends and elements of her "tribe," as she liked to refer to her cousins, were to be part of the company. With only the prospect of being part of a nondescript crowd at a glum, low-key music festival in the Harare Gardens, Stix committed himself to Shamiso's plans. At 7:30PM, he made his way to the restaurant. By midnight, he had made a pathetic retreat to his flat, having shared part of his meager income with two police officers fortunate enough to witness him driving through red lights. From his flat he had called Shamiso, and threatened to cremate her for inviting him to a restaurant where they would be saddled with a bill of over $15,000 each. That it was a restaurant with "melted Mars bar" on its dessert menu wickedly swelled his appetite for arson.

"So don't say you have not been warned about Mvura Restaurant," Stix said to Fiso the day after the incident. "If, however, out of curiosity you decide to go there, your experience will approximate to something like this: you get there, the car park is full of cars with diplomatic registration plates and there is not even space to open the car doors. At this point a security guard..." Stix pauses to light his cigarette, "...will run like a demon to find your parking space—but since you don't own a car, Fiso, you won't experience that bit."

"So you're not going to take me there?" Fiso asks, but Stix ignores her and continues.

"You may be at a table where you sit back to back with the Japanese ambassador, and you will be confronted by a waiter wielding a menu without prices. By the end of the evening you will be sorry. Never assume that such restaurants price their food reasonably!"

Fiso listened, thinking what a curious person Stix was, and well aware that save for living in the same dilapidated block of flats, they did not have much in common. The nice restaurants, elitist concerts and well-dressed friends existed only in the stories that Stix told her on their doorsteps on sluggish afternoons. They were just another spectral reality that Stix was fond of invoking. And after an hour or two of reciprocal balderdash, one of them would just stand up and walk into his or her flat, leaving the other to wean themselves from that hallucinogenic indulgence.

Defining one's relationship with the world demands daily renegotiating one's existence. So far-reaching are the consequences of neglecting exigencies imposed by this, that those unwilling or unable to participate eventually find themselves trapped in a parallel universe, the existence of which is not officially recognized. These are the people who never die, Sue and her mother being a quintessential sample. Sue has no birth certificate because her mother does not have one. Officially they were never born and so will never die. For how do authorities issue a death certificate when there is no birth certificate?

Several other official declarations only perfect the parallel existence of most of Harare's residents. Officially basic food commodities are affordable because prices are State-controlled. Officially no one starves because there is plenty of food on supermarket shelves. And if it is not there, it is officially somewhere, being hoarded by Enemies of the State. With all its innumerable benefits, who would not want to exist in this other world spawned by the authorities—where your situation does not daily remind you what a liability your mouth and stomach are? It was therefore towards this official existence that Sue and her mother strove. Fed up with galloping food prices in their parallel universe, they took a chance and tried to take the leap into official existence.

It was an ordinary Monday morning when mother and daughter walked to the Central Registry offices hoping to get birth certificates, metal IDs and, eventually, passports. Sue had been told she could make a good income buying things from South Africa and selling them at the flea markets. But because the benefit of her deathless existence did not also confer upon her freedom of movement across national boundaries, she needed a passport. Fiso had decided to assist her daughter and get herself a passport too. Little did they know that they would find the door out of their parallel existence shut, and bolted.

By mid-afternoon Fiso was on her doorstep relating the events of the morning to Stix. Back in her humble flat, she felt better having spent half a day surrounded by the smell of dust, apathy and defeat.

Such were the Central Registry offices: an assemblage of Portakabins that had outlived its lifespan a dozen times over. With people enduring never-ending queues, just to have their dignity thrown out of rickety windows by sadistic officials, inevitably a refugee camp ambience prevailed.

"If your mother and father are dead and you do not have their birth certificates, then there is nothing that I can do," the man in office number 28 had said, his fat fist thumping the desk. He wore a blue and yellow striped tie that dug painfully into his fat neck, accentuating the degradation of his torn collar.

"But what am I supposed to do?" Fiso asked, exasperated.

"Woman, just do as I say. I need one of your parents' birth or death certificates to process your application. You are wasting my time. You never listen. What's wrong with you people?"

"Aaaah, you are useless! Every morning you tell your wife that you are going to work when all you do is frustrate people!" Fiso stormed out of the office. Having learned the false nature of authority and law from the streets, she was certain that he was her only obstacle. Men, she knew, could have the most perverse idiosyncrasies and at least one vice. In her experience, doctors, lawyers and the most genteel of politicians could gleefully discard their masks to become the most brutal perverts. It was a male trait, an official trait, and it accounted for her failure to acquire the papers she and her daughter needed.

Fiso's parents had died long back in deep rural Zhombe where peasant life had confined them to a radius of less than a hundred kilometers, and where an innate suspicion of anything involving paperwork was nurtured. Back in the Forties, stories of people having their names changed by authorities horrified semi-literate peasants such as Fiso's parents, who swore they would never have anything to do with the wicked authorities of that era.

"We were told to go to office number 28, but there was no one there. After about 40 minutes, we went back to the office that had referred us, but there was no one there either. Returning to office number 28, and seeking help from an official who was strolling past we were told, 'Look? Can't you see that jacket? It means he is not far away. Wait for him.' So we waited—for three hours—only to be told to bring one of my parents' death or birth certificates."

"Civil servants are like that, Fiso. They all have two jobs you know," Stix said, mildly. Fiso was being too naive for a seasoned sex purveyor, he thought.

"Look: a Japanese firm is making big money generating electricity out of sewage waste. All you have to do to bring your electricity bill down is shit a lot!" Stix, his eyes on the newspaper, was trying to steer the conversation in another direction.

That afternoon, it was Fiso who disappeared into her flat first, inexplicably regretting that she had let Stix have sex with her a couple of months before. They had been drunk, and she had found herself naked and collapsing onto Stix's bed, his fiendish shaft plumbing her hard-wearing orifice.

"Ey, you! That's not a good starting point!" was her only protest, and she cursed the alcohol that still swirled inside her head.

"If you'd been a virgin, Fiso, I would have washed my penis with milk, just for you," Stix said after contenting himself. Fiso ignored the remark. More incensed with herself than with Stix, she simply decided to sleep over the anger in the hope that it would go.

In Harare, vegetable vendors can yield useful connections. After Fiso and Sue had failed to get their papers, a woman at the Central Registry was brought to the attention of Fiso by a fellow vendor. This woman, a relative, could assist her to get any form of ID for a fee. Because the vendor and her relative went to the same church, she suggested that this would be the ideal place to introduce Fiso.

Less than a hundred meters from the church building, a man of Fiso's age stood by a corner selling single cigarettes and bananas. Fiso, sensing her increasingly disagreeable nerves, sought to calm them down with a cigarette.

"Sekuru," she addressed the man. "How much are your cigarettes?"

"I'm not your Sekuru. Harare does not have any Sekurus. They are all in the rural areas. If you desire a Sekuru then make one for yourself out of cardboard."

"How much are your cigarettes?" she asked again, avoiding the contentious term.

"Fifteen dollars."

She quietly retrieved three brand-new five-dollar coins from her purse, handed them over and picked a Madison Red from among the many on display. Contentedly lighting the cigarette and avoiding eye contact, she heard the man ask, "What time is it?"

"If you need a watch why don't you make yourself one out of cardboard?" she retorted, and walked away, victorious.

With what panache does fate deliver the person of a harlot into a church building? Cockroaches appear through the cracks in the walls and wave their antennae in response to an almost primeval call. The priest, beneath his holy regalia, shudders, aware of the relative paleness of his cloistered virtues in the face of a salvation cobbled together on street corners. Against the tide of attrition of the human condition, what man of cloth can offer a soul a better salvation than the sheer dogged will to live? In the priest's mind, however, such sentiments only manifested themselves in vague notions of jealousy and contempt.

As Fiso strolled in carefree, the holy man recoiled, the congregation's heads turned, and the devil chuckled. A Dynamos Football Club T-shirt, fluorescent green mini-skirt and six-inch-high perspex platform shoes upstaged the holy word.

Destructive distillation is a process by which a substance is subjected to a high temperature with the absence of oxygen so that it simply degenerates into its several constituent substances without burning. After her silent confessions and having received the body and blood of Christ, Mrs. Shava found herself subjected to destructive distillation by an ogling congregation. Like anyone being introduced to a person of dubious appearance on sanctified premises, she degenerated into her constituent attributes of self-righteousness and caution.

"The church services are short here—or was I late?" Fiso remarked after being introduced to Mrs. Shava by her vending friend.

"No, we're not like those Pentecostal churches, we're less fanatical," Mrs. Shava said, unable to look Fiso straight in the eyes and bewildered, her mind whirling with an elliptical sense of déjà vu as she wondered where they had met before. She could also feel the stares of the congregation pecking at her back from several meters away. She resented them but neither did she like talking to Fiso.

However, having listened to her plight, she agreed to help her out. Everyone had to live, after all.

"Eeeek, ahh, it's complicated," Mrs. Shava moaned, a technique that she had perfected after helping several people. "It's no easy task," she continued, wanting to justify her fee.

"I understand, but I must have a birth certificate. And my daughter cannot get one if I don't have one—and she needs a passport."

"I can try, but it is a risk, I could lose my job." Mrs. Shava assumed a pious expression. Fiso knew that it was time to tie up her end of the deal. She understood what Mrs. Shava meant when she said that success depended on a number of factors; Fiso knew it meant one thing only.

"I understand it's a big risk, but I intend to reward you for your efforts." Fiso glanced at her friend for clues but the vendor's face was as blank as a hospital wall. "I don't know what you would like, but I'll leave you to decide, my sister."

Mrs. Shava's lips parted dispassionately to reveal her white teeth. "Okay, call me on Wednesday and I will see if it's all right for you to come to my office. People at my workplace will be on strike but I can't risk my job. If it's okay, I'll give you the forms, you fill them in and I'll take them back. And don't forget my fee: $15,000!" She smiled for the first time and turned to walk away.

"Uhh, huh, your phone number at work?" Fiso stammered.

"Nyasha will give it to you, I have to see someone else," came the reply.

Fiso turned to Nyasha, and they smiled at each other.

Contentedly walking off, Mrs. Shava could not have guessed that in less than a minute she would be caressed by more poltergeistic echoes of a recent past. She was walking out of the church premises when Stix stopped by to pick up Fiso in his scarlet car. A shiver descended Mrs. Anna Shava's spine as she recalled the night she killed the street kid. Fiso's face, though, defiantly refused to fit into the jigsaw puzzle, and Mrs. Shava could only watch in bewilderment as the old harlot jumped into the car, which rattled away, accelerating sideways like a crab.

In a mortuary at the central hospital, clad in a blue suit, white shirt, and seemingly asphyxiated by the tie around its neck, lies a slightly overweight corpse. A cellphone is still stuck in one of the pockets and when it rings for the third time, it is answered by a being who, after years as a mortuary cleaner, picking his wages from its floor, has become indifferent to death.

"Hullo, Central Hospital," he answers.

"Hullo, I'm looking for my husband, is that his phone you are using? Who are you? Is he there?"

"Aah, I don't know, but unless this is the body of a thief who stole the phone from your husband, your husband is dead. The police shot him in the head. They said he was rioting in the city center."

The previous night Anna's husband had not returned from work. That he would have come to such a rough end, no one could have guessed. But being in the insurance industry he would have appreciated it if he'd been told that the value of his life was equivalent to twenty condoms, and in all likelihood would not have contested such a settlement being awarded to Anna. His death, though, had consequences that reverberated through to Fiso, because on the day she was supposed to call Mrs. Shava, grief and its attendant ceremonies had already claimed her. Then on Monday, having spent all night at Piri-Piri, the city's sleaziest night-club, Fiso decided to take the Central Registry juggernaut head-on. Suffering from a hangover, and caring not about consequences, she went straight to the Registrar General's office.

"I've been trying to get a birth certificate and can't, because your staff members only care about getting bribes!" The Registrar

General's secretary remained calm, picked up the phone and dialed, but before she had uttered a word, the RG had emerged from his office. Being a constant target of ridicule by the press as the man heading one of the most inefficient and corrupt government departments, he was very sensitive to criticism.

"How can I help you, lady?" he demanded impatiently.

"I only need a birth certificate, but your staff is only interested in frustrating people into paying bribes!"

"Those are serious allegations." The RG's interest lay only in smothering public objections.

"All I want is a birth certificate, Sir. My womanhood is an old rag. I've paid the price of living. Please do not waste my time, I'm too old for that."

The Registrar nearly had convulsions. "Sandra, call security!" he ordered.

The secretary fumbled, dropped her pen and spilt her coffee.

"Your staff members all want bribes. I come to you and all you do is get rid of me! I suppose you want a bribe too? What else can you do apart from sitting on your empty scrotum all day?"

In a little less than half an hour, Fiso was behind police bars facing a charge of public disorder. The police, however, soon found their case stalling. There was no way of establishing her identity because she did not have an ID. After she told the investigating officer that she was trying to get just such an ID when she was arrested, the officer called the Registrar General who offered to quickly process an ID, if it was in the interest of facilitating the course of justice. That afternoon Fiso was bundled into the back of a Land Rover Defender in handcuffs and taken to the Central Registry to make an application for an ID. Predictably she refused to co-operate, so she was later thrown back into the vehicle and taken to the police cells.

Two days went by, each bringing a new face into the cell she shared with six other women. On the third day two cellmates went for trial and never returned—either freed or sent to Chikurubi Maximum. Then a new inmate arrived. From her appearance one would have surmised that she was a teenager picked up from the vicinity of a village while herding goats. It was her carefree disposition that won her the attention of the other cellmates.

"What are those for?" she asked, looking up at the left corner of the cell. The officer who had brought her had hardly locked up.

No immediate answer came until the officer had disappeared.

"Those are CCTV cameras," someone finally answered her.

"What is CCTV?" the girl asked again.

"Closed Circuit Television. It enables them to watch us from their offices all the time on one of their televisions."

Later in the evening when another new face was brought in, the goat-herd girl asked the officer: "Is it true that you have a TV and that you are watching us?"

The officer just continued with his duty of locking up the gate as if nothing had been said. Goat-girl was, however, unfazed.

"I think you people are going to be in trouble when the President finds out that you are wasting TVs on criminals. I'm sure he would like to be watched on TVs too. Or watch himself so that he's safe from assassins and perverts?"

After five days in the cell Fiso was cautioned and released without charge—not even that of failing to produce an ID. The investigating officer, seeing that the case was going nowhere, had managed to convince his superior to release her with just one statement: "It's only an aging whore."

Monday Morning

Segun Afolabi—winner of the 2005 Caine Prize

"I want to piss," the boy said in their language. He held his mother's hand as they walked, but his feet skipped to and fro. The mother scanned the area, but she could not find a place for her son; there were too many people beside the trees, talking, laughing. "Take the boy to the edge of the water so he can piss," she said to her husband.

The boy and his father hurried towards the lake. The father was glad to see that his son could find relief. They did not notice how people looked at them with their mouths turned down. Sour. The eyes narrowed to slits.

The breeze blew and the ducks and swans floated past. The boy was afraid of them, but his need to evacuate was urgent. Steam rose from the stream that emerged from him as it fell into the water, and he marveled at this. There was so much that was new to understand here. He had seen on the television at the hostel how water could become hard like glass, but the lake was not like that. The swans pushed their powerful legs and the ducks dipped their heads beneath the surface. The father held on to his son's jacket so he would not fall in. There were bits of flotsam at the bank where the water rippled. The boy looked away, a little disgusted, and gazed into the clean center of the lake.

They came away from the water's edge and joined the mother and the boy's brother, and the boy from the hostel whose name was Emmanuel. The father looked at his wife and the children. He wondered at how beautiful everything was in this place with the whispering leaves and the green grass like a perfect carpet and the people so fine in their Sunday clothes. He thought, With God's help it can surely happen. You are distraught, time passes and you are away from it. You can begin to reflect and observe. It was difficult now, to think of artillery and soldiers and flies feeding on abandoned corpses.

The little one laughed and said, "My piss made fire in the water," but the mother slapped his shoulder. "It's enough," she said.

They joined the people on the path as they strolled through Regent's Park. Only Emmanuel wanted to walk on the grass, but he did not dare because the father had forbidden it. He was a feeble man, Emmanuel thought, so timid in this new place, but his sons were different. Bolder. They had already grasped some of the new language.

A breeze gathered up leaves and pushed the crowds along. A clump of clouds dragged across the sun. People pulled their clothes tight around themselves. The mother adjusted her scarf so there were no spaces for the wind to enter. She reached across with her good hand to secure her husband's baseball cap. The area in the center of his scalp was smooth as marble and he felt the cold easily. She shoved her mittened hand back into her coat pocket and watched the children as they drifted further away. After a moment she called, "Ernesto, come away from there," to her eldest boy. They had wandered towards an area where people were playing a game with a ball and a piece of wood, and she did not want there to be any trouble. Not today, not on Sunday. She knew his friend was leading him to places he would not have ventured on his own and she feared there would be difficulties ahead. The youngest boy skipped between them: the mother and father, his brother, the brother's best friend. He was her little one and she would hold on to him for as long as she was able.

The father sighed and called out to his children. The cold was setting in again and their walk was too leisurely. They would have to return to the hostel before the sun disappeared. He called to Ernesto, "Come, it is time for us to go. Tell your brother." It would take at least half an hour for them to walk back.

Ernesto turned to Alfredo, the little one, who giggled as they played a game among themselves—*Kill the Baron*. The friend, Emmanuel, ran about them, laughing, until the father called again. "We are going back, you hear me? Ernesto, hold your brother! We go!"

Emmanuel looked at him. He did not speak their language, but regardless, he thought the father was a stupid man—too fat, too quiet. The boy had lost his own father in his own country in his own village home. Now he could only see the faults in them, the other fathers, their weaknesses, what they did not understand. He had thought his father remarkable at one time, but with his own eyes he had seen him cut down, destroyed. They were all foolish and clumsy, despite their arrogance. He would never become such a man himself.

The children trailed behind the mother and father as they navigated paths that took them to the edge of the park. As they came to the road, Alfredo raced to walk beside his mother, and a passing car screeched to a halt.

"Keep 'em off the road, for fuck's sake!" the driver shouted.

The mother held her son, and the father looked at the driver without expression. The boy had not run across the road, but the driver had made an assumption, and now he did not want to lose face.

"Keep the buggers off the road!" he shouted again and shook his head when there was no response.

The father glanced at the mother who only shrugged and held her boy. Emmanuel turned to the driver and waved an apology on behalf of the father, grinning to indicate he understood. But he did not know the appropriate words, and the driver failed to notice or did not care for the gesture. He sped away, complaining bitterly to his passenger. There were people on the pavement who had seen the incident, who now stood watching. The mother and father did not understand the signs and gestures the people used. They did not feel the indignation. They knew only that they were scrutinized and they were sometimes puzzled by this, but they were not overwhelmed.

They trudged along the main road near the building where the books lived. The huge railway stations teemed with people. In the mornings sometimes, the father walked in the vicinity of the stations. At night the area was forsaken, but during the day, workers emerged in their thousands. Often he looked at them and it seemed impossible that he could ever be a part of this. The people moved as if they were all one river, and they flowed and they did not stop.

"Here is the one!" Alfredo squealed to Emmanuel when they came to the glass hotel. "I will live here!"

"You're crazy," Emmanuel said to the boy. But he could not fail to notice the guests in the lobby, the people sipping tea in the café, the lights warm, the atmosphere congenial.

The sign at the building read Hotel Excelsior, but this was not a hotel. The orange carpet was threadbare, the linen was stained with the memory of previous guests, the rooms sang with the clamor of too many people. When they had arrived, the mother knew it was not a place to become used to. They had their room, the four of them, and it was enough: the bed, the two narrow cots. There was warmth even though the smell of the damp walls never left them. They could not block out the chatter and groans of other occupants. In the mornings the boys feasted on hot breakfasts in the basement dining room where there was a strange hum of silence as people ate. They were gathering strength after years of turmoil in other places. This was the best part of the day.

As they approached the hostel, the sky was already turning even though it was still afternoon. Men and women walked up and down the road, but they did not have a destination. They glanced at the family with eyes like angry wounds. A woman knelt on the pavement with her head upturned, swaying, and when the family passed, Alfredo could see that she was dazed. The mother cupped her hand against his face so he could no longer look at her. Another man guided a woman in a miniskirt hurriedly by the elbow. He was shouting at her. He crossed the road so he would not have to meet the family and then re-crossed it after they had passed. Every day they saw these people, the lost ones, who seemed to hurt for the things they were looking for but could not find. The mother wondered sometimes, Have they never been young like my boys? Where does innocence flee? She wanted to be away from this place, away from the Excelsior. She wanted her family's new life to begin.

The father had begun to work. He could not wait for any bureaucratic decision when there were people who relied on him for food and shelter, for simple things: his mother, his sister and her family, his wife's people. It had begun easily enough. A man at the hostel had told him there was work on a construction site in the south of the city. They did not ask for your papers there, he said. It was a way to help yourself, and if it ended, well, there were other places to work. It was important not to be defeated, he warned, even though you were disregarding the rules. The man had been an architect in his own country, but now he did the slightest thing in order to help himself. He was ebullient, and when the father looked at him and listened, he was filled with hope.

Four of them journeyed from the Excelsior to the building site in the south. Every day they took their breakfast early and joined the people who became a river on their way to work. The job was not complex, but one could easily become disheartened by the cold and the routine. The father dreamed of the day when he could return to his own occupation, to the kitchen where he handled meat and vegetables and the spices he loved so much. He had not touched any ingredients for many months now and sometimes he was afraid he would forget what he had learned. But already it was ingrained in him and he could not lose it, this knowledge, but he did not realize it yet.

He moved building materials from one place to another, and when they needed a group of men to complete a task, he became essential. But he did not know the English words. Most of the others did, but there was no one from his country here. Sometimes they would slowly explain to him the more difficult tasks, and every day, it seemed, the work became more intricate. The father moved his head so they would think he had understood, but he did not understand one word. He began to sense that words were not necessary; he could learn by observation and then repeat what he saw. In his own country he had not been an expressive man. Even as a child he had only used words when absolutely necessary. People often thought he was mute or he was from another country or his mind was dull. But all of that did not matter; he had learned to cook and he had discovered the love of a woman who did not need him to be someone he was not.

The woman touched the man at the meat of his shoulder and when he felt her, his body relaxed. It was not like coming home when they returned to the Excelsior; the strangeness of the place and the noise of the people there discomfited them. A woman was crying behind the door of the room opposite theirs and they wondered, Has she received some terrible news? Will she be returning to the place she has run away from? The hostel was a sanctuary, but it was also a place of sadness for many, and often it was only the children who gave it life.

"Tomorrow," Emmanuel said to Ernesto, and he touched him lightly on the back and then ran to another floor of the building where he and his mother lived. He did not acknowledge the father and the mother. Alfredo turned so he could say goodbye to his brother's friend, but the boy was already gone. He could not understand how Emmanuel had spent the day with them and could then disappear without a word to him. He, too, wanted a friend, like the children he had played with in his own country.

"Why does he go so fast?" he asked. He felt the smart of Emmanuel's abruptness in his chest.

"He has his own mother," the woman replied. "Maybe he feels bad for leaving her all day."

Alfredo thought about this, about how he would feel if he had left his mother alone in the hostel, and he understood his mother's words. He said, "We will... When... When will we go to the glass hotel?" The words emerged so quickly from him in his agitation they fell over one another.

"We will go one day," the father said as they entered the room. "You will see." It was his secret plan to take his family to the hotel one weekend, when a person could eat a two-course meal at a special rate. He would work on the construction site until he was able to pay for the things they needed, for the money he would send back home. Then they would all spend the day at the glass hotel. Perhaps there would be a swimming pool for his sons. He touched the boy on his head so he would not feel bad about the place they were in, the unfriendly Emmanuel, the people they had left behind.

At night the father dreamed he was in his old kitchen, with the heat and flies and the cries of chickens outside. The mother flew to the beach on their coast and noticed how the moonlight glinted off the waves. Ernesto dreamed of his school friends before they had been forced to scatter, before the fighting had begun. Only Alfredo remained in the new country in his sleep; he was in the glass hotel, in his own room.

The night moved on and then other dreams began, the ones of violence, of rebels and rape and cutlasses arcing through the air. The father began to shudder in his sleep, and then his wife woke. When she realized it was happening again, she reached out and petted him with her club, her smooth paw. She did not know she was doing so; it was instinctive. Ordinarily she concealed the damaged limb. They had severed her hand in the conflict, but she could still feel the life of her fingers as she comforted her man. In the new country, they had offered her a place to go, for the trauma, but she did not want that; she had her boys, her quiet husband. There was a way to function in the world when the world was devastating, everyone careless of each other and of themselves. She knew that now. She had been forced to learn. In a moment her husband was still again and she lay back with her eyes closed, but she did not sleep.

It was a simple thing, a misunderstanding, that caused the confusion the next day. The father traveled to the south to the construction site. By the end of the week he was certain he would have earned enough to send several packages home. But mid-morning the inspectors arrived.

A foreman took him aside. "You have the correct papers?" he asked.

The father looked at him and nodded. He did not understand what was happening. He continued to work as the inspectors spread out. He could not see the other men from the hostel, but he would look for them soon so they could take their lunch break. It was colder today, but he had been working so hard he had been forced to remove his sweater.

They came up the scaffolding, two men with their briefcases and the foreman beside them. From the corner of his eye the father could see the men from the hostel across the road. They were waving to him frantically. The inspectors approached another man and talked quietly with him. They stood where the ladder was situated. The father could not see another way down. He thought, I am in a place I do not understand. The ground is vanishing beneath me. He pictured the boy, his youngest, and he pushed away the fear. He ran to the edge of the platform and grasped the metal pole. He did not look down in case he faltered. He held the pole and allowed gravity to carry him, not knowing how it would end. His hands were cut and then his torso rubbed hard against the brackets. He remembered his sweater lying on the platform. He did not have the strength to manage a smooth descent and his shirt and trousers were torn, but he did not notice these things. His mind was on his folly. If he were caught he would jeopardize everything for his family and he did not know if he could live with himself after that.

He hobbled across the road where the others were waiting for him. He looked behind once to see if he was being followed, but no one was there.

"That was close," one of the men called and clapped him on the shoulder. They all laughed, but he did not laugh with them. He only smiled. His hands and arms were throbbing and the blood had soiled his clothes.

When the mother saw him, she became very quiet. No one spoke. They only fussed around the wounds and the blood and the torn clothing. Their fear was like a fist of bread they could not swallow. The youngest boy began to cry. His brother, Ernesto, was frightened, but excited too. He went and told his friend what had happened. It was like an adventure for him; the blood, the daring escape.

Emmanuel smirked; it only confirmed his thoughts. He said, "He is stupid, your father." He could not help himself. It was the way he was now. Angry. He did not know that he blamed his own father for dying, that it was a wound inside himself that would fail to heal.

Ernesto looked at him, disbelieving, and then he walked away. It was too much, the injured father, the distraught brother, the hurtful friend. Too many things were happening at once and he could make no sense of it. When he returned to the room, his father was resting on his brother's cot. He saw him there, a man who was not slender, a man who hardly spoke. He began to wonder about Emmanuel's words. Was there any truth in them? A seed had been planted now.

Alfredo sat beside his father looking from the carpet to his mother, back to the carpet again. The mother's silence disturbed them all. She tidied the room and soaked the soiled clothes in the bath and seemed not to care about what had happened. Even the father eyed her cautiously, but he did not speak.

"God will help us," the father whispered, so that only the youngest heard.

The boy remained silent. At length he asked, "Where is God, Papa?"

The father sighed and looked at his son. "He is in the room. He is here with us. All around." He lifted his arms and waved his fat fingers to illustrate.

The boy looked around the room, but he did not understand. Ernesto followed his gaze, but he did not know what they were looking at.

"You are a chef, you are not a laborer!" the mother shouted. "You cannot cook with your hands torn like this! Do you understand?" She had gone from silence to blind rage in an instant. She shook her fist, but held the arm where her hand had been severed tight against her stomach. She did not care if other people heard through the thin walls. She was tired of holding everything in. "How can we make a new life if you cannot work because you are injured? Did you think what would happen if they caught you with no papers, what would happen to us, the boys? We cannot go back to that place where they are killing us! Soon they will allow us to stay and you can do whatever job you like. But still you cannot wait! You are ready to risk everything."

The boys looked from their wounded father to their mother as she stood over him. They took in the damp walls, the orange carpet with the kink by the bathroom door, the window that overlooked the street where the girls walked at night and people roared sometimes in their misery.

"I am going to see Emmanuel," Alfredo said after no one had spoken in minutes. He closed the door quietly and ran along the corridor and down the stairs. He did not stop running when he came to the street or to the busy road where the cars and buses clamored. A tall man, wrapped in a soiled duvet, strode along the street peering into rubbish bins. Shrieking. Alfredo continued to run. He mingled with people as they waited for permission to cross the road. A woman moved away from him as if he were a street urchin. When he reached the other side he began to run again. He did not look behind for fear of seeing his father or his mother or anyone from the hostel. He ran and ran until he arrived at the hotel and when he was through its glass doors he stood still and breathed deeply.

He said he had been going to see Emmanuel, but ten minutes later, the friend knocked at the door looking for Ernesto. All the anger in the room vanished. They searched the lounge where the television was, and the breakfast room, and the reception, but they could not find him. No one had seen him disappear. The mother was shaking now and the other son was mute with anxiety.

"We must look outside. Alfredo!" the father called. "He cannot go far from here. Where can he go? Alfredo!" He was bellowing now. He was not aware of the strength of his own voice. Ernesto looked at him, his eyes wide with trepidation.

The man at the reception desk said the staff would scour the hostel to ensure Alfredo was not hiding anywhere. "Where could a little boy go?" he asked.

Emmanuel thought suddenly he knew where he was. He said in English, "Maybe he goes to the hotel," and he pointed.

They did not know the boy was already in the elevator of the glass hotel, rising above the street, looking out at the city they had recently arrived in. There seemed to be nothing between him and the world outside except a thin sheet of glass. When he peered down at the retreating traffic he found he was not afraid. He came out on the top floor and approached the long corridor. He began to try the handles of all the rooms he passed. He was looking for his own room, but he knew he needed a key. He did not know whom to ask. A man opened a door he had tried and squinted at him and closed it quickly. Otherwise it was quiet. He saw no people. He was anxious now and tired and he did not know what to do.

A woman opened a door near the end of the corridor and a cloud of light fell across his path. She did not notice him. She removed some objects from a trolley and then re-entered the room. He came to the door and stood for a moment, waiting for her, but he was very tired now. He sat on the carpet in the corridor, trying to remain alert, but his head hung down.

"Who are you?" the woman said to him.

He jerked his head up. He was not sure whether he had fallen asleep, whether time had passed—had she simply come out as soon as he had sat down? He looked at her, but he could not understand all the words she spoke.

"Are you lost?" she asked. "Are you looking for someone?" She did not seem angry, but he did not know how to make her understand.

He said, "The room," with all the English he could muster, but he knew it was not enough.

The woman gazed at him and spoke some words in her own language and he was amazed he could understand her completely. He had thought his family were the only ones in this new place.

"Come," she said. She pushed open the door of the room she had been cleaning and showed him in: the wide bed so perfectly made, the large face of the television set, the gleaming marble in the bathroom. He walked to the window and knelt on a chair and looked out at the vast city. He could not hear the sounds of traffic far below, he could not see the river of people entering the railway stations, he could not see the lost ones shuffling to and fro on the street. He saw only rooftops and sunlight and all the space in the world between the earth and the sky that seemed like emptiness, that was untouched and beautiful. He turned and climbed on to the bed. He did not worry about the woman or his mother and father or when he should return to the hostel. He was too tired for any of that. The boy slept. Again, he did not have bad dreams. He did not even dream of his own country. He saw the green grass in the park that Sunday afternoon, his mother's five fingers searching for his face, his father and brother, even the angry friend, Emmanuel, sitting on the bed in the hotel room, looking for the face of God.

.

Jungfrau

Mary Watson—winner of the 2006 Caine Prize

It was the Virgin Jessica who taught me about wickedness.

I once asked her why she was called the Virgin Jessica. She looked at me with strange eyes and said that it was because she was a special person, like the Blessed Mary.

"A virgin is someone who can do God's work. And if you're very, very clean and pure you can be one of the 144 virgins who will be carried in God's bosom at the end of the world. And if you're not..."

She leaned towards me, her yellow teeth before my eye. I thought she might suck it out, she was so close. She whispered, "If you're not, then God will toss you to the devil who will roast you with his horn. Like toasted marshmallows. You don't want the devil's evil horn to make a hole in your pretty skin, now do you?"

She kissed my nose—my little rabbit's nose, she called it—and walked away, her long white summer dress falling just above her high, high red heels. Her smell, cigarette smoke and last night's perfume, lingered around my eyeball. I wanted to be like the Virgin Jessica. I wanted a name like hers.

We called her Jez for short.

My mother Annette was the Virgin Jessica's adopted sister. She was older and tireder. The Virgin had no children while my mother had 43. She was a schoolteacher in one of those schools where the children wore threadbare jerseys and had hard green snot crystallized around their noses and above their crusty lips—lips that could say *poes* without tasting any bitterness. Or that secret relish of forbidden language.

Sometimes my mother would have them—her other children, her little smelly children—over at our house. They would drape themselves around our furniture like dirty ornamental cherubs and drink hot pea soup. The steam melted the snot, which then ran down into the soup. It did not matter to them because they ate their boogers anyway.

I hated my mother's other children. I glared at them to let them know, but they stared back without much expression. Their faces had nothing to say—I could read nothing there. Jessica found them amusing.

"Sweet little things," she mumbled, and laughed into her coffee. Her shoulders shook epileptically.

After the Virgin told me how important it was to be clean, I tolerated them in the haze of my superiority. I was clean—I bathed every night—and they were filthy, so obviously God wouldn't want to touch them.

The Virgin spent hours in the bathroom every evening. Naked she walked to her bedroom, so lovely and proud she seemed tall; I followed faithfully, to observe a ritual more awesome than church. With creams and powders she made herself even cleaner for God. How he must love her, I thought. She spread his love upon her as she rubbed her skin until it glowed and her smell spread through the house, covering us all with the strength of her devotion. Then she went out, just after my father came home, and stayed out until late.

The Virgin Jessica had a cloud of charm twenty centimeters around her body. Strangers hated her because they thought that anyone that beautiful could only be mean. But it was not her pretty black eyes or her mouth that made her beautiful. She was beautiful because she was wrapped in a cloud of charm. And when you breathed in the air from the cloud, you breathed in the charm and it went down your veins and into your heart and made you love her. If you came close enough, she would smile her skew smile, pretending to love you with her slitted eyes, and the charm would ooze out like fog from a sewer and grab you and sink into your heart and lungs. Even I who had known her all my life would feel the charm with a funny ache. She had a way of leaning forward when she spoke, claiming the space around her with her smell, her charm. And my father, who didn't speak or laugh, he too would be conquered.

"What's the old man up to tonight?" she would say, leaning towards him with a wink, her eyes laughing; and he would fold his newspaper and look pleased, even grunt contentedly.

I tried saying those same words, leaning forward the way Jez did, and he looked at me coldly. So cold that my wink froze halfway and my laugh caught in my throat. Embarrassed, I transformed the laugh into a cough and rubbed my eyes like a tired child. I think it was then that I realized that his love for me was bound to me as his little girl. And my love for him bound me to my little girl's world.

I took pains to keep my girl's world intact after that. When boys teased me at school, I felt the walls of my father's favor tremble. One of them phoned and sang a dirty song into my hot ear. My head burnt for days after that. I felt the fires of hell from that phone call. I feared that the fires would start inside me, catching my hair and eating the strands like candlewick, melting my skin like wax, dripping and staining mommy's carpets (she would be very cross). The fire would eat the horrid children in the schoolroom, then crawl towards my mother, burn her slowly and then finish with her chalk-stained fingers. Her glasses would shrivel up and her mouth crease with silent screams. Unsatisfied, the fire would move towards my father, crackling his newspaper; the smoke would cloud his glasses. Beneath them, his eyes would have that same cold look—but not cold enough to douse the flames. The fire would then stagger towards the Virgin. Leering, it would grab her ankles and eat her white frock, turning it to soot. She would cry out and her head would toss, her hair unravel and she would scream from the force of the flames. The Virgin Jessica's screams in my head made me put a knife on the windowsill of her bedroom so that she could undo the burglar bars and escape.

The image of flames and screams resounded in my head for several days. They surged whenever the other girls in their shortened school dresses lit cigarettes in the toilets. They could not see how the flames would get bigger. I checked all the stubs carelessly tossed into the sink and bin to make sure that the fire did not escape. The slight thrill I had once received from the boys teasing me in the safety of the schoolyard, away from my father's fearsome eyes, faded. I spent my intervals at the far end of the yard, eating sandwiches and talking to the dogs through the wire fence. I had to coax them across the road with my milk and the ham from my bread. I was found one day, squatting on my haunches and telling Nina and Hildegarde about a garden of moss. I felt a shadow; it made me shiver, and I looked up to see if God was angry. Instead I saw Ms. Collins above me, her eyes made huge by her glasses. I was scared that she'd be cross. I wanted to pee; some dripped down my leg, so I crouched and shut my eyes tightly, praying fervently that I would not pee. She reached out for my hand and asked me to make some charts for her in exchange for some biscuits and cool drink. From then on I spent my breaks helping Ms. Collins in her art room and she would give me yogurt and fruit and sometimes chocolate. I never ate these. Instead I put them on the steps of the white Kirk on the way home. Ms. Collins tried to ask me questions, but I was shy and would only whisper, "I don't know." She would speak relentlessly. She told me about her baby daughter who ate grass.

I preferred just to look at her. I liked looking at her big, ugly eyes and her pretty hair. But I think she got tired of me: maybe my silence wore her down; maybe the sound of her own voice scared her, for it must have been like talking to herself. She probably thought she was going mad, talking and talking to still brown eyes. But the day I went into her art room and found a boy from my class helping her with the charts, I remembered the fires of hell and ran away. Maybe she wanted me to burn; maybe she wasn't a virgin either.

It must have been the sound of midnight that woke me. The house without my mother felt unguarded. It seemed her presence warded off a fury of demons. I sat upright in my clean girl's bed, trying to feel the pulse of the night. I slipped my feet over the side of the bed and listened. The darkness is covered by a haze that makes the still corners move.

I knew that my mother had not returned. The wild child with snot streaming from his nose and eyes, he had her still. I sat at the lounge window, watching the sea, hating the wild child. He had come after supper, his little body panting like a steam engine. He ran up the hill in the rain, he had run all the way from the settlement. He sobbed, buried his head in my mother's trousers.

"Please, please, *asseblief,* please," his broken voice scratched.

Wishing so very hard that he hadn't come, I watched the boy cry until my mother barked, "Evelyn, get out of here."

I prayed that the wild child would leave: go back to your plague, I screamed silently. It was too late. He had brought his plague with him. It wandered about our house and muffled my warnings. So she did not hear me, and let the child take her away.

Her trousers soiled with tears and mucus, she rushed into her bedroom, where I was watching one of those endless sitcoms about silly teenagers. She grabbed her car keys.

"Don't wait up for me."

I would not have waited for her. Even now, in the dark hour, I was not waiting for her.

I must have stayed at the window for at least an hour. I saw the sea roar-smash-roar against the rocks. I saw the stillness of the midnight road, the white line running on towards the mountain. The road was empty; but then I saw two people walking up the hill. They walked slowly and closely in their midnight world. The walk was a stagger.

They fell pleasantly against each other. I saw them walk towards the house and only then did I see who they were.

When Jessica and my father entered the house, quietly and with the guilty grace of burglars, they were glowing from the wind and walking and waves and the wildness of the night's beauty. The haze inherent in the darkness was centered around them. I looked on with envy, for I too wished to walk the empty night with them. Jessica let out a startled sound when she saw me curled up on the windowsill.

"Look at you," she fussed, "hanging around dark windows like a sad little ghost."

Her face was close to mine and her breathing deep.

"Have you been watching for your mother? Has she come home yet?"

I shook my head. I had not been waiting for my mother.

She held my hands in her cold, cold fingers. "Your hands are freezing," she said.

"You need some Milo. How long have you been sitting here? Long?"

"Your father and I went to see if your mother was coming home. I wish she'd phone, but then they probably don't have one. I really don't understand why Annette involves herself in other people's business. But I suppose you should count your blessings. When we were small, Annette and me, all we had to play with was scrap metal."

Jessica chattered on, repeating the stories I had heard so many times.

My mother came home while I was clutching my Milo. I was playing the mournful ghost, the sick patient, and all the while glowing in the attention of both my father and Jessica. Jessica was chattering brightly, so bright that she made the darkness her own while I huddled in its shadows. My father was silent, his eyes as dark as mine. Jessica's words tripped out of her mouth and drew circles around us.

Then Annette stepped into our enchanted circle. She asked for tea. As Jessica made the tea her words stumbled then stopped. My father went to bed, taking my hand as he left the kitchen. I did not want to go to bed. I wanted to be in the kitchen with just my father and Jessica and me.

I stood on a rock in the garden and stared down at the people watching my sea. They were dotted across the small beach, the wind twisting their hair around their necks and forcing them closer into their jackets. They lifted their fingers to point, just like in a seaside painting.

Their mouths were wide with laughter and their eyes bright, yet all the while I knew that they were posing, as if for an invisible artist. Their minds could sometimes glimpse his black beret, his paint-splattered smock in this idyllic scene.

I went down to the sea. There were too many whale-watchers trampling the sand, my desecrated temple, with their flat feet and stubby toes. I glared at the fat children who clung to their parents, hanging on to their arms and legs.

146

"Beast with two backs," I muttered.

They smelt suburban. Their odor of white bread and Marmite drifted unpleasantly into the sea air. They huddled into their windbreakers and yawned at the ocean.

"It's just a dark blob," they whined, their winter-paled faces cracking beneath the noon sun. They shivered from the wind nuzzling their necks.

I sat near the water's edge and buried my pretty toes in the sand. The crowd, the people who came to see the whales, were noisy and their noise ate into my ears as they crunched their chips and the packets crackled in the wind.

"Go home," I hissed to a solitary toddler who wandered near me.

I turned to see a woman scoop him up and pretend to eat his angel curls. My coward's face smiled at her.

I stayed there for a while, watching the people watch the whales. Then I noticed some of my mother's children playing in the water on the other side of the beach. They shrieked and laughed; some played in their dirty clothes, others in varying stages of nakedness.

They sang a ditty with filthy words while roughly shoving and splashing each other with the cold water. They knocked down their friends and made them eat sand. The suburban children's parents shook their heads, pulled their young ones and walked away, still shaking their heads, as though the shaking would dispel the image from their minds. They soon forgot all about those children who haunted the corners of my world, my mother's chosen children.

She came to call me for lunch. She did not see her young ones, who had moved towards the tidal pool, and I did not tell her about them.

I sneaked my mother off the beach, chattering too brightly. We walked towards the hill. Someone came running behind us, but we carried on walking, for my mother didn't seem to hear the footsteps—maybe I was too bright. I walked faster and we crossed Main Road. When we reached the other side, I felt a light strong-hard knock like a spirit just made solid. I turned to see the wild child hugging my mother, her arms wrapped around him. He gave her a flower and ran back. When the wild child crossed the road, he was hit by whale people in a blue car. The driver got out, my mother ran to her child. The driver, annoyed and red, complained that he hadn't seen anyone, there was nobody there.

"Just a shadow flitted across my eyes," his wife wailed. "Just a dark shadow."

The driver said that he would fetch help. He and his wife drove off in their blue car—the dent was slight—and didn't come back. Perhaps to him there really was nobody there: the dent was so very slight, and those children are so thin, after all.

My mother lifted the wild child in her arms. She waited and while she waited, her mouth got tighter and tighter and she wept. When one hundred blue cars had passed by, she slowly got up from the pavement. With the wild child in her arms, she walked up the hill. She did not speak to me, her mouth was tight and her hair unbound from its ponytail.

At our house Jessica and my father hovered awkwardly around her, their legs and arms looking wrong on their bodies, as if they had taken them off and put them back the wrong way. They moved slowly and clumsily, like they had wound down. My mother lay her child on my clean girl's bed and stayed by his side.

"Stephen, get the doctor quickly," she barked at my father.

I ate my Sunday roast. I paid little attention to the doctor's arrival or the child's crying or my mother's pacing. Her tight face had shut me out. I sat in the lounge and watched the sea, picking at the meat. When the violet hour came, the beach was empty and my room smelt of the wild child and the barest hint of my mother's love. But they were both gone.

I stayed in the lounge with my father and the Virgin, who brought us tea. We played cards and laughed the soft, covered laughs of forbidden frivolity. We munched biscuits and watched the Virgin's teasing eyes as she tried to cheat, as she toasted marshmallows over a candle flame, as she spoke, smiled, sighed. The wild child and my mother were forgotten. I did not think of the bruised bundle on my bed.

Then the quiet beneath our laughter became too insistent. It was guilt that sent me in search of her. It was the guilt of the betrayer for the betrayed, because guilt is more binding than passion.

There was not a trace of my mother and the wild child in my bedroom. There was no mark of my mother's care or her chosen child's blood staining the sheets. There were no cup rings on my dressing table, no dent on the pillow. I looked for my mother in my bedroom. I hunted in every corner but could not find the slightest whisper of her smell.

I could find nothing of her in the lounge—that was my father's room. Their bedroom was green and clinical and did not contain either of them. The kitchen was heavy with the Virgin's presence, which smelt of rose water with a burny undertone. I sat down on the floor, perplexed.

Agitated, I realized that I could not remember if her smell had been in the house the day before. Or the previous week. I went to the garage, which she used as a schoolroom. As I opened the door, a fury of smells came screaming towards me. There were the wild children's smells of pain and fear and anger. And she was there, entangled in this foul mix. Nothing of her remained in the house because it was all concentrated here. Delicately it cushioned and enveloped the rawness of the children as it wove itself into them. The force of this beauty, this tenderness made me want to weep with jealousy. Such sadness, such terror. I left the dim garage knowing that my mother had been gone for a long time. I had not noticed because I had been coveting the Virgin. I went back to the house.

Jessica tilted her head slightly and focused her skew eyes on me. I had not seen her standing in the doorway, slim and graceful (she was so beautiful), watching me.

"What are you sniffing around for? Does something smell bad?" She seemed anxious.

"Not in here," I replied. "I was just smelling. Smelling to see where my mother has gone."

"You funny, funny child," she said, wrapping her precious arms around me. I pretended to squirm. "What else can that incredible snout of yours sniff out? Can you smell where your father is?"

I was surprised, because she didn't understand me at all. I looked at her and saw an odd dullness in her pretty face.

"It doesn't happen with my nose," I tried to explain. "It happens inside somewhere, same as when Daddy and I go to the moss garden. I don't see it with my eyes."

She regarded me with a slight frown shadowing her eyes and making her face sulky.

"What moss garden?"

"Secrets."

I smiled sweetly at her and she lost her frown and said, "Don't you trouble your pretty little head about your inner eyes and ears, you are much too young for such worries."

She coaxed me into helping her make sandwiches, which was easy because I loved doing anything with her. But she still did not know what I meant.

I sought out my mother after that. I lavished attention upon her, for I felt that I had betrayed her. I betrayed her with my unholy, selfish love for the Virgin. I placated her with tokens of love, with tea and wild flowers picked along the road to the beach. I feared that the Blessed Mary would not be pleased that in my heart of hearts I had turned my love from my flesh mother to another. My guilt was augmented by my jealousy of her chosen children, and because I denied her my love yet begrudged her theirs. As my guilt grew so her nocturnal visits to the township increased.

"There's so much fear out there, you couldn't imagine it, Evie. You're a lucky, lucky girl. I remember being so poor that my hunger nearly drove me insane. We were like wild flowers growing on the side of the road."

I resented my mother's childhood poverty. I resented her hunger and I resented being made to feel guilty about not being hungry.

"You could so easily have been one of those children, look at Auntie Carmelita, the way her children run around, that's the inmates ruling the asylum. So you just be grateful that you're not like them. You think about that if it makes you sad when I go out at night."

It did not make me sad when she went out at night. I was jealous but not sad, because her absence set my nights free. I would stare at the midnight sea; I would walk the moss garden with my father.

I sought her greedily with endless cups of tea and awkwardly asked her how her day had been—did she not think the weather was fine for this time of year?—smoothed her hair, kissed her cheek with my Judas lips and fussed about her as much as Jessica did.

And she would be propped in her chair, my mother, my failed heroine, and I would talk and talk and she would say, "Not now, Evie, I'm tired, tired," and my guilt would grow and I would leave unhappy yet relieved. Her eyes would hold mine and she would say, "Thanks, Evie," and the guilt grew and grew because there was trust and affection in her eyes, doggy brown eyes that I did not want to love.

Those eyes changed one day and she became cross. Her breath was thin and tinny, like she did not want to take air in, let air out. The tedium of breathing seemed to offend her, so she resisted it. That was when she started smoking cigarettes. She took some of Jessica's cigarettes, shrugged like Jessica and laughed.

"Makes breathing interesting," she tittered. "Besides, we're all going to die anyway," she cackled, looking at the danger signs on the box. She laughed and laughed but it was a cross laugh.

It crept out of the silences, was born between a glance held, then turned away. This guilt would not be contained. It was in the air as plain as the tingling cold of sunny winter days. It kept me awake those cold August nights. So cold that my fingers would ache as I lay awake, feeling the ice in the walls, the breathing of the house, the numbness of my mother's nocturnal absences. I sighed and turned the other cheek, hoping to find sleep with my back to the wall, then my face, then my back again.

There is no rest for the wicked.

"Be a good girl," my father had said as he kissed me that night. "Be a good girl for your old father."

He kissed me again and pulled the covers up to my chin. When he got up from the bed, the mattress rose as the weight lifted. I felt safe then, as the rain and wind struck down on the roof.

It was still raining as I lay staring at the ceiling in the small hours of the morning.

There is no rest for the wicked.

Sighing an old woman's sigh, I kicked my tired sore legs to the right, the side where I always raised myself from the bed. I wandered to the kitchen seeking leftovers from the Virgin's dinner, because I was famished. Trying to be the good child exhausted me and then left me sleepless. I could hear my father snoring. He sounded like a wailing wolf. I was surprised that he slept. When I wandered around the rooms at night, I felt the alertness of a house that did not slumber nor sleep.

I found the Virgin in her kitchen. She was eating. She stuck her fork into the mince and rammed it into her mouth. Again and again she stuffed forkfuls into her mouth, sometimes pausing to mix the mince with spaghetti, her delicate fingers swiftly swirling it around the fork. The apple-pie dish lay empty before her.

When she looked up and saw me, spaghetti was hanging down the side of her mouth, from those sweet red lips. She let go of the fork. She seemed embarrassed, but she had no need to be because I knew that she had been fasting. The Virgin often fasted to deny herself the pleasures of the flesh. I admired her for that because I could not fast no matter how hard I tried. But looking at her with spaghetti on her chin and mince on her white nightgown, I felt ill. Surely she would make herself sick, eating like that. She looked up and saw me, and it frightened me because she looked old. The guilt had etched itself there too. I was frightened because I thought that the Virgin was pure. I chased those naughty thoughts from my mind. I chased them until my beloved Virgin seemed young again. Then unbidden, the words came to my mouth.

"There's no rest for the wicked," I said.

My words hurt her; she placed her head in her hands. The guilt was what made me do it, the guilt, it made words come to my mouth. My secret joy at releasing suppressed words sank into my flesh and I felt my skin tauten. My hands were wet so I wiped my mouth, but it would not be clean. When she left the room, my mind screamed for her mercy, for forgiveness. She did not hear me; she took none of that with her. I sat in her chair and waited and waited.

I longed for my mother then. I longed to press my burning face, my wet nose into her trousers and sob. I wanted her to leave her bed at night and come to me and to choose me as her child and I would choose her as my mother and the guilt would go away and we would be happy. I went to where I knew I would find some of her.

The schoolroom door creaked slightly and my white slippers upon the cold cement floor made a featherlight crunch. I stood in the dark waiting to feel her and the children, waiting for sounds that were long gone. I crossed my arms around myself and waited. And then they came to me—the sighs, the hushed tinkles of laughter, the moans and the whimpers. The room was drenched in sorrow. I listened excitedly as the ghosts of yesterday came to me. The sounds grew less and less faint. They were calling to me. The shadows started taking shape and I saw that everything had fallen into a woven mass, a moving tapestry in the corner of the schoolroom. I saw my mother as a she-wolf, her hair tangled and glowing, licking her young ones, her tongue moving over furry flesh. I wanted to join her pack and have her lick my sins away. I moved towards them, then stopped, for the shadows changed again. My mother now had Jessica's face, an unfamiliar Jessica face with enormous slanted glowing eyes, feral biting teeth that dipped to the whimpering flesh beneath her. My mother was gone.

"Mommy?" I whispered. "Mommy?" It was shrill and anxious. I did not know what magic I had conjured.

"Mommy?"

Everything stopped moving. The tapestry froze and then unraveled.

And then I saw them. I had not imagined the moving tapestry in the corner of the schoolroom, nor had I imagined Jessica licking the furry flesh. As my eyes accustomed themselves to the dim light, I saw that it was my father with Jessica. They were clumsily covering their bodies, hiding themselves, and I thought that was silly—I had seen it all before. But I had not known that he shared the moss garden with her. I left the garage. I heard them calling after me and I walked away.

Jambula Tree

Monica Arac de Nyeko—winner of the 2007 Caine Prize

I heard of your return home from Mama Atim, our next-door neighbor. You remember her, don't you? We used to talk about her on our way to school, hand in hand, jumping, skipping, or playing runandcatchme. That woman's mouth worked at words like ants on a cob of maize. Ai! Everyone knows her quack-quack-quack-mouth. But people are still left wordless by just how much she can shoot at and wreck things with her machine-gun mouth. We nicknamed her Lecturer. The woman speaks with the certainty of a lecturer at her podium claiming an uncontested mastery of her subject. I bet you are wondering how she got to know of your return. I could attempt a few guesses. Either way, it would not matter. I would be breaking a promise. I hate that. We made that promise never to mind her or be moved by her. We said that after that night. The one night no one could make us forget. You left without saying goodbye after that. You had to, I reasoned. Perhaps it was good for both of us. Maybe things could die down that way. Things never did die down. Our names became forever associated with the forbidden. Shame.

Anyango—Sanyu.

My mother has gotten over that night. It took a while, but she did. Maybe it is time for your mother to do the same. She should start to hold her head high and scatter dust at the women who laugh after her when she passes by their houses. Nakawa Housing Estates has never changed. Mr. Wangolo, our SST teacher, once said those houses were just planned slums with people with broken dreams and

155

unplanned families for neighbors. Nakawa is still over one thousand families on an acre of land they call an estate. Most of the women don't work. Like Mama Atim, they sit and talk, talk, talk and wait for their husbands to bring home a kilo of offal. Those are the kind of women we did not want to become. They bleached their skins with Mekako skin lightening soap till they became tender and pale like a sun-scorched baby. They took over their children's *dool* and *kwepena* catfights till the local councillor had to be called for arbitration. Then they did not talk to each other for a year. Nakawa's women laugh at each other for wearing the cheapest sandals on sale by the hawkers. Sanyu, those women know every love charm by heart and every *juju* man's shrine because they need them to conjure up their husbands' love and penises from drinking places with smoking pipes filled with dried hen's throat artery. These women know that an even number is a bad sign as they watch the cowry shells and coffee beans fall onto cowhide when consulting the spirits about their husbands' fidelity. That's what we fought against when we walked to school each day. Me and you hand in hand, towards school, running away from Nakawa Housing Estate's drifting tide, which threatened to engulf us and turn us into noisy, gossiping and frightening housewives.

You said it yourself, we could be anything. Anything coming from your mouth was seasoned and alive. You said it to me, as we sat on a mango tree branch. We were not allowed to climb trees, but we did, and there, inside the green branches, you said—we can be anything. You asked us to pause for a moment to make a wish. I was a nurse in a white dress. I did not frighten children with big injections. You wished for nothing. You just made a wish that you would not become what your father wanted you to be—an engineer, making building plans, for his mansion, for his office, for his railway village. The one he dreamed about when he went to bed at night.

Sanyu, after all these years, I still imagine shame trailing after me tagged onto the hem of my skirt. Other times, I see it, floating into your dreams across the desert and water to remind you of what lines we crossed. The things we should not have done when the brightness of Mama Atim's torch shone upon us—naked. How did she know exactly when to flash the light? Perhaps asking that question is a futile quest for answers. I won't get any! Perhaps it is as simple as accepting that the woman knows everything. I swear if you slept with a crocodile under the ocean, she would know. She is the only one who knows first-hand whose husband is sleeping with whose daughter at the estates inside those one-bedroomed houses. She knows whose son was caught inside the fences at Lugogo Show Grounds; the fancy trade fair center just across Jinja Road, the main road which meanders its way underneath the estates. Mama Atim knows who is soon dying from gonorrhoea, who got it from someone, who got it from so-and-so who in turn got it from the soldiers who used to guard Lugogo Show Grounds, two years ago. You remember those soldiers, don't you? The way they sat in the sun with their green uniforms and guns hanging carelessly at their shoulders. With them the AK47 looked almost harmless—an object that was meant to be held close to the body—black ornament. They whistled after young girls in tight mini-skirts that held onto their bums. At night, they drank Nile Lager, tonto, Mobuku and sung *harambe, Soukous* or *Chaka-Chaka* songs.

Eh moto nawaka mama
Eh moto nawaka
I newaka tororo
Nawaka moto
Nawaka moto
Nawaka moto
Eh fire, burns mama
Eh fire, burns
It is burning in Tororo
It is burning
It is burning
It is burning

Mama Atim never did pass anywhere near where they had camped in their green tents. She twisted her mouth when she talked about them. What were soldiers doing guarding Lugogo? she asked. Was it a frontline? Mama Atim was terrified of soldiers. We never did find out why they instilled such fear in her. Either way it did not matter. Her fear became a secret weapon we used as we imagined ourselves being like goddesses dictating her fate. In our goddess-hands, we turned her into an effigy and had soldiers pelt her with stones. We imagined that pelting stones from a soldier was just enough to scare her into susuing in her XXL mothers' union panties. The ones she got a tailor to hem for her, from left-over materials from her children's nappies. How we wished those materials were green, so that she would see soldiers and stones in between her thighs every time she wore her green soldier color, stone-pelting color, and AK-47 color. We got used to the sight of green soldiers perched in our football fields. This was the new order. Soldiers doing policemen's work! No questions, *Uganda yetu, hakuna matata*. How strange it was, freedom in forbidden colors. Deep green—the color of the morning when the dew dries on leaves to announce the arrival of shame and dirt. And everything suddenly seems so uncovered, so exposed, so naked.

Anyanyo—Sanyu.

Mama Atim tells me you have chosen to come back home, to Nakawa Housing Estates. She says you refuse to live in those areas on the bigger hills and terraced roads in Kololo. You are coming to us and to Nakawa Housing Estates, and to our many houses lined one after another on a small hill overlooking the market and Jinja Road, the football field and Lugogo Show Grounds. Sanyu, you have chosen to come here to children running on the red earth, in the morning shouting and yelling as they play *kwepena* and *dool*—familiar and stocked with memory and history. You return to dirt roads filled with thick brown mud on a rainy day, pools of water in every pothole, and the sweet fresh smell of rain on hard soil. Sanyu, you have come back to find Mama Atim.

Mama Atim still waits for her husband to bring the food she is to cook each night. We used to say, after having nine sons and one daughter she should try to take care of them. Why doesn't she try to find a job in the industrial area like many other women around the housing estates? Throw her hips and two large buttocks around and play at entrepreneurship. Why doesn't she borrow a little *entandikwa* from the micro-finance unions so she can buy at least a bale of second-hand clothes at Owino market where she can retail them at Nakawa market? Second-hand clothes are in vogue, for sure. The Tommy Hilfiger and Versace labels are the in "thing" for the young boys and girls who like to hang around the estates at night. Second-hand clothes never stay on the clothes hangers too long, like water during a drought, they sell quickly.

Mummy used to say those second-hand clothes were stripped off corpses in London. That is why they had slogans written on them such as—"You went to London and all you brought me was this lousy T-shirt!" When Mummy talked of London, we listened with our mouths open. She had traveled there not once, not twice, but three times to visit her sister. Each time she came back with her suitcase filled up with stories. When her sister died, Mummy's trips stopped like that bright sparkle in her eye and the Queen Elizabeth stories, which she lost the urge to retell again and again. By that time we were grown. You were long gone to a different place, a different time and to a new memory. By then, we had grown into two big girls with four large breasts and buttocks like pumpkins and we knew that the stories were not true. Mummy had been to Tanzania—just a boat trip away on Lake Victoria, not London. No Queen Elizabeth.

Mama Atim says you are tired of London. You cannot bear it any more. London is cold. London is a monster which gives no jobs. London is no cozy exile for the banished. London is no refuge for the immoral. Mama Atim says this word immoral to me—slowly and emphatically in *Japadhola*, so it can sink into my head. She wants me to hear the word in every breath, sniff it in every scent so it can haunt me like that day I first touched you. Like the day you first touched me. Mine was a cold, unsure hand placed over your right breast. Yours was a cold, scared hand, which held my waist and pressed it closer to you, under the jambula tree in front of her house. Mama Atim says you are returning on the wings of a metallic bird—Kenya Airways. You will land in the hot Kampala heat which bites at the skin like it has a quarrel with everyone. Your mother does not talk to me or my mother. Mama Atim cooks her kilo of offal which she talks about for one week until the next time she cooks the next kilo again, bending over her charcoal stove, her large and long breasts watching over her saucepan like cow udders in space. When someone passes by, she stops cooking. You can hear her whisper. Perhaps that's the source of her gonorrhoea and Lugogo Show Ground stories. Mama Atim commands the world to her kitchen like her nine sons and one daughter. None of them have amounted to anything. The way their mother talks about me and you, Sanyu, after all these years, you would think her sons are priests. You would think at least one of them got a diploma and a low-paying job at a government ministry. You would think one of them could at least bring home a respectable wife. But *wapi!* Their wives are like used bicycles, ridden and exhausted by the entire estate manhood. They say the monkey which is behind should not laugh at the other monkey's tail. Mama Atim laughs with her teeth out and on display like cowries. She laughs loudest and forgets that she, of all people, has no right to urinate at or lecture the entire estate on the gospel according to St. Morality.

Sometimes I wonder how much you have changed. How have you grown? You were much taller than I. Your eyes looked stern; created an air about you—one that made kids stop for a while, unsure if they should trample all over you or take time to see for sure if your eyes would validate their preconceived fears. After they had finally studied, analyzed, added, multiplied, and subtracted you, they knew you were for real. When the bigger kids tried to bully me, you stood tall and dared them to lay a finger on me. Just a finger, you said, grinding your teeth like they were aluminium. They knew you did not mince words and that your anger was worse than a teacher's bamboo whipping. Your anger and rage coiled itself like a python around anyone who dared, anyone who challenged. And that's how you fought, with your teeth and hands but mostly with your feet. You coiled them around Juma when he knocked my tooth out for refusing to let him have his way on the water tap when he tried to cheat me out of my turn.

I wore my deep dark green uniform. At lunch times, the lines could be long and boys always jumped the queue. Juma got me just as I put my water container to get some drinking water after lunch. He pushed me away. He was strong, Sanyu. One push like that and I fell down. When I got up, I left my tooth on the ground and rose up with only blood on the green; deep green, the color of the morning when the dew dries off leaves.

You were standing at a distance. You were not watching. But it did not take you too long to know what was going on. You pushed your way through the crowd and before the teachers could hear the commotion going on, you had your legs coiled around Juma. I don't know how you do it, Sanyu. He could not move.

Juma, passed out? Hahahahahahaha!

I know a lot of pupils who would be pleased with that. Finally his big boy muscles had been crushed, to sand, to earth, and to paste. The thought of that tasted sweet and salty like grasshoppers seasoned with onion and *kamulari*—red, red-hot pepper.

Mr. Wangolo came with his hand-on-the-knee-limp and a big bamboo cane. It was yellow and must have been freshly broken off from the mother bamboos just outside the school that morning. He pulled and threatened you with indefinite expulsion before you let big sand-earth-paste Juma go. Both you and Juma got off with a two-week suspension. It was explicitly stated in the school rules that no one should fight. You had broken the rules. But that was the lesser of the rules that you broke. That I broke. That we broke.

Much later, at home, your mother was so angry. On our way home, you had said we should not say how the fight started. We should just say he hit you and you hit him back. Your house was two blocks from ours and the school was the nearest primary school to the estate. Most of the kids in the neighborhood studied at Nakawa Katale Primary School all right, but everyone knew we were great friends. When your mother came and knocked upon our door, my mother had just put the onions on the charcoal stove to fry the goat's meat. Mummy bought goat's meat when she had just got her salary. The end of the month was always goat's meat and maybe some rice if she was in a good mood. Mummy's food smelt good. When she cooked, she joked about it. Mummy said if Papa had any sense in his head, he would not have left her with three kids to raise on her own to settle for that slut he called a wife. Mummy said Papa's new wife could not cook and that she was young enough to be his daughter. They had to do a caesarean on her when she gave birth to her first son. What did he expect? That those wasp hips could let a baby's head pass through them?

When she talked of Papa, she had that voice. Not a "hate voice" and not a "like voice," but the kind of voice she would use to open the door for him and tell him welcome back, even after all these years when he never sent us a single cent to buy food, books, soap or Christmas clothes. My Papa is not like your Papa, Sanyu. Your Papa works at the Ministry of Transport. He manages the Uganda railways, which is why he wants you to engineer a railway village for him. You say he has gotten so intoxicated with the railway that every time he talks of it, he rubs his palms together like he is thinking of the best ever memory in his life. Your father has a lot of money. Most of the teachers knew him at school. The kids had heard about him. Perhaps that is why your stern and blank expression was interpreted with slight overtones. They viewed you with a mixture of fear and awe: a rich man's child. Sometimes Mummy spoke about your family with slight ridicule. She said no one with money lived in Nakawa Housing Estates of all places. If your family had so much money, why did you not go to live in Muyenga, Kololo, and Kansanga with your Mercedes-Benz lot? But you had new shoes every term. You had two new green uniforms every term. Sanyu, your name was never called out aloud by teachers, like the rest of us whose parents had not paid school tuition on time and we had to be sent back home with circulars.

Dear Parent,
This is to remind you that unless this term's school fees are paid out in full, your daughter/son.......... will not be allowed to sit for end of term exams....
Blah blah blah...

Mummy always got those letters and bit her lip as if she just heard that her house had burnt down. That's when she started staring at the ceiling with her eyes transfixed on one particular spot on the brown tiles. On such days, she went searching through her old maroon suitcase. It was from another time. It was the kind that was not sold in shops any more. It had lost its glitter and I wished she never brought it out to dry in the sun. It would be less embarrassing if she brought out the other ones she used for her Tanzania trips. At least those ones looked like the ones your mother brought out to dry in the sun when she did her weekly house cleaning. That suitcase had all Mummy's letters—the ones Papa had written her when, as she said, her breasts were firm like green mangoes. Against a kerosene lamp, she read aloud the letters, reliving every moment, every word and every promise.

I will never leave you.
You are mine forever.
Stars are for the sky, you are for me.
Hello my sweet supernatural colors of the rainbow.
You are the only bee on my flower.
If loving you is a crime I am the biggest criminal in the world.

Mummy read them out aloud and laughed as she read the words on each piece of stained paper. She had stored them in their original Air Mail envelopes with the green and blue decorations. Sometimes papa had written to her in aerogram. Those were opened with the keenest skill to keep them neat and almost new. He was a prolific letter-writer, my papa, with a neat handwriting. I know this because often times I opened her case of memories. I never did get as far as opening any letter to read; it would have been trespassing. It did not feel right, even if Mummy had never scolded me for reading her "To Josephine Athieno Best" letters.

I hated to see her like that. She was now a copy-typist at Ramja Securities. Her salary was not much, but she managed to survive on it, somehow, somehow. There were people who spoke of her beauty as if she did not deserve being husbandless. They said with some pity, "Oh, and she has a long ringed neck, her eyes are large and sad. The woman has a voice, soft, kind and patient. How could the man leave her?" Mummy might have been sad sometimes, but she did not deserve any pity. She lived her life like her own fingernails and temperament: so calm, so sober and level-headed, except of course when it came to reading those Papa letters by the lantern lamp.

I told you about all this, Sanyu. How I wished she could be always happy, like your mother who went to the market and came back with two large boys carrying her load because she had shopped too much for your papa, for you, for your happy family. I did not tell you, but sometimes I stalked her as she made her way to buy things from the noisy market. She never saw me. There were simply too many people. From a distance, she pointed at things, fruit ripe like they had been waiting to be bought by her all along. Your mother went from market stall to market stall, flashing her white Colgate smile and her dimpled cheeks. Sometimes I wished I were like you; with a mother who bought happiness from the market. She looked like someone who summoned joy at her feet and it fell in salutation, humbly, like the *kabaka* subjects who lay prostrate before him. When I went to your house to do homework, I watched her cook. Her hand stirred groundnut soup. I must admit, Mummy told me never to eat at other people's homes. It would make us appear poor and me rather greedy. I often left your home when the food was just about ready. Your mother said, in her summon-joy-voice: "Supper is ready. Please eat." But I, feigning time consciousness, always said, "I have to run home, Mummy will be worried." At such times, your father sat in the bedroom. He never came out from that room. Every day, like a ritual, he came home straight from work.

"A perfect husband," Mummy said more times than I can count.

"I hate him," you said more times than I could count. It was not what he didn't do, you said. It was what he did. Those touches, his touches, you said. And you could not tell your mother. She would not believe you. She never did. Like that time she came home after the day you taught Juma a good lesson for messing around with me. She spoke to my mother in her voice which sounded like breaking china.

"She is not telling me everything. How can the boy beat her over nothing? At the school tap? These two must know. That is why I am here. To get to the bottom of this! Right now!"

She said this again and again, and Mummy called me from the kitchen where I had escaped just when I saw her knock on our back door holding your hands in hers and pulling you behind her like a goat!

"Anyango, Anyangooooo," Mummy called out.

I came out, avoiding your eyes. Standing with her hands held in front of me with the same kind of embarrassment and fear that overwhelmed me each time I heard my name called by a teacher for school fees default.

They talked for hours. I was terrified, which was why I almost told the truth. You started very quickly and repeated the story we had agreed on our way home. Your mother asked, "What was Anyango going to say again?" I repeated what you had just said, and your mother said, "I know they are both lying. I will get to the bottom of this at school in two weeks' time when I report back with her." And she did. You got a flogging that left you unable to sit down on your bum for a week.

When you left our house that day, they talked in low voices. They had sent us outside to be bitten by mosquitoes for a bit. When they called us back in, they said nothing. Your mother held your hand again, goat style. If Juma had seen you being pulled like that, he would have had a laugh one hundred times the size of your trodden-upon confidence. You never looked back. You avoided looking at me for a while after that.

Mummy had a list of "don'ts" after that for me too. They were many.

Don't walk back home with Sanyu after school.
Don't pass by their home each morning to pick her up.
Don't sit next to her in class.
Don't borrow her text books. I will buy you your own.
Don't even talk to her.
Don't, don't, don't do any more Sanyu.

It was like that, but not for long. After we started to talk again and look each other in the eyes, our parents seemed not to notice, which is why our secondary-school applications went largely unnoticed. If they complained that we had applied to the same schools and in the same order, we did not hear about them.

1. St. Mary's College Namagunga.
2. Nabisunsa Girls' School.
3. City High School.
4. Modern High School.

You got admitted to your first choice. I got my third choice. It was during the holidays that we got a chance to see each other again. I told you about my school. That I hated the orange skirts, white shirts, white socks and black boy's Bata shoes. They made us look like flowers on display. The boys wore white trousers, white shorts, white socks and black shoes. At break time, we trooped like a bunch of moving orange and white flowers to the school canteens, to the drama room, and to the football field.

You said you loved your school. Sister Cephas, your Irish headmistress, wanted to turn you all into Black English girls. The girls there were the prettiest ever and were allowed to keep their hair long and held back in puffs, not one inch only like at my school.

We were seated under the jambula tree. It had grown so tall. The tree had been there for ages with its unreachable fruit. They said it was there even before the estate houses were constructed. In April, the tree carried small purple jambula fruit which tasted both sweet and tangy and turned our tongues purple. Every April morning when the fruit started to fall, the ground became a blanket of purple.

When you came back during that holiday, your cheeks were bulging like you had hidden oranges inside them. Your eyes had grown small and sat like two short slits on your face. And your breasts, the two things you had watched and persuaded to grow during all your years at Nakawa Katale Primary School, were like two large jambulas on your chest. And that feeling that I had, the one that you had, that we had—never said, never spoken—swelled up inside us like fresh mandazies. I listened to your voice rise and fall. I envied you. I hated you. I could not wait for the next holidays when I could see you again. When I could dare place my itchy hand onto your two jambulas.

That time would be a night, two holidays later. You were not shocked. Not repelled. It did not occur to either of us, to you or me, that these were boundaries we should not cross nor should think of crossing. Your jambulas and mine. Two plus two jambulas equals four jambulas—even numbers should stand for luck. Was this luck pulling us together? You pulled me to yourself and we rolled on the brown earth that stuck to our hair in all its redness and dustiness. There in front of Mama Atim's house. She shone a torch at us. She had been watching steadily, like a dog waiting for a bone it knew it would get; it was just a matter of time.

Sanyu, I went for confession the next day, right after Mass. I made the sign of the cross and smelt the fresh burning incense in St. Jude's church. I had this sense of floating on air, confused, weak, and exhausted. I told the priest, "Forgive me, Father, for I have sinned. It has been two months since my last confession." And there in my head, two plus two jambulas equals four jambulas...

I was not sorry. But I was sorry when your father with all his money from the railways got you a passport and sent you on the wing of a bird; hello London, here comes Sanyu.

Mama Atim says your plane will land tomorrow. Sanyu, I don't know what you expect to find here, but you will find my mummy; you'll find that every word she types on her typewriter draws and digs deeper the wrinkles on her face. You will find the Housing Estates. Nothing has changed. The women sit in front of their houses and wait for their husbands to bring them offal. Mama Atim's sons eat her food and bring girls to sleep in her bed. Your mother walks with a stooped back. She has lost the zeal she had for her happiness-buying shopping trips. Your papa returns home every day as soon as he is done with work. My Mummy says, "That is a good husband."

I come home every weekend to see Mummy. She has stopped looking inside her maroon case. But I do; I added the letter you wrote me from London. The only one I ever did get from you, five years after you left. You wrote:

A.
I miss you.
S.

Sanyu, I am a nurse at Mengo Hospital. I have a small room by the hospital, decorated with two chairs, a table from Katwe, a black and white television and two paintings of two big jambula trees which I got a downtown artist to do for me. These trees have purple leaves. I tell you, they smile.

I do mostly night shifts. I like them, I often see clearer at night. In the night you lift yourself up in my eyes each time, again and again. Sanyu, you rise like the sun and stand tall like the jambula tree in front of Mama Atim's house.

Poison

Henrietta Rose-Innes—winner of the 2008 Caine Prize

L ynn had almost made it to the petrol station when her old Toyota ran dry on the highway. Lucky me, she thought as she pulled onto the roadside, seeing the red and yellow flags ahead, the logo on the tall façade. But it was hopeless, she realized as soon as she saw the pile-up of cars on the forecourt. A man in blue overalls caught her eye and made a throat-slitting gesture with the side of his hand as she came walking up: no petrol here either.

There were twenty-odd stranded people, sitting in their cars or leaning against them. They glanced at her without expression before turning their eyes again towards the distant city. In a minibus taxi off to one side, a few travelers sat stiffly, bags on laps. Everyone was quiet, staring down the highway, back at what they'd all been driving away from.

An oily cloud hung over Cape Town, concealing Devil's Peak. It might have been a summer fire, except it was so black, so large. Even as they watched, it boiled up taller and taller into the sky, a plume twice as high as the mountain, leaning towards them like an evil genie.

As afternoon approached, the traffic thinned. Each time a car drew up, the little ceremony was the same: the crowd's eyes switching to the new arrival, the overalled man slicing his throat, the moment of blankness and then comprehension, eyes turning away. Some of the drivers just stood there, looking accusingly at the petrol pumps;

others got back into their cars and sat for a while with their hands on the steering wheels, waiting for something to come to them. One man started up his car again immediately and headed off, only to coast to a halt a few hundred meters down the drag. He didn't even bother to pull off onto the shoulder. Another car came in, pushed by three sweaty black men. They left the vehicle standing in the road and came closer, exchanging brief words with the petrol attendants. Their forearms were pumped from exertion and they stood for a while with their hands hanging at their sides. There was no traffic at all going into the city.

Over the previous two days, TV news had shown pictures of the N1 and N2 jam-packed for 50 kilometers out of town. It had taken a day for most people to realize the seriousness of the explosion; then everybody who could get out had done so. Now, Lynn supposed, lack of petrol was trapping people in town. She herself had left it terribly late, despite all the warnings. It was typical; she struggled to get things together. The first night she'd got drunk with friends. They'd sat up late, rapt in front of the TV, watching the unfolding news. The second night, she'd done the same, by herself. On the morning of this, the third day, she'd woken up with a burning in the back of her throat so horrible that she understood it was no hangover, and that she had to move. By then, everybody she knew had already left.

People were growing fractious, splitting into tribes. The petrol attendants and the car-pushers stood around the taxi. The attendants' body language was ostentatiously off-duty: ignoring the crowd, attending to their own emergency. One, a woman, bent her head into the cab of the taxi, addressing the driver in a low voice. The driver and the *gaardjie* were the only people who seemed relaxed; both were slouched low on the front seats, the driver with a baseball cap tilted down over his eyes. On the other side of the forecourt was a large Afrikaans family group that seemed to have been traveling in convoy: mother, father, a couple of substantial aunts and uncles, half a dozen blonde kids of different sizes. They had set up camp, cooler bags and folding chairs gathered around them. On their skins, Lynn could see speckles of black grime; everybody coming out of the city had picked up a coating of foul stuff, but on the white people it showed up worse. A group of what looked like students—tattoos, dreadlocks—sat in a silent line along the concrete pad that supported the petrol pumps. One, a dark, barefoot girl with messy black hair down her back, kept springing to her feet and walking out into the road, swiveling this way and that with her hands clamped under her armpits, then striding back. She reminded Lynn a little of herself, ten years before. Skinny, impatient. A fit-looking man in a tracksuit hopped out of a huge shiny bakkie with *Adil's IT Bonanza* on its door and started pacing alertly back and forth. Eventually the man—Adil himself?—went over to the family group, squatted on his haunches and conferred.

Lynn stood alone, leaning against the glass wall of the petrol-station shop. The sun stewed in a sulfurous haze. She checked her cellphone, but the service had been down since the day before. Overloaded. There wasn't really anyone she wanted to call. The man in the blue overalls kept staring at her. He had skin the color and texture of damp clay, a thin, villain's mustache. She looked away.

The black-haired girl jumped up yet again and dashed into the road. A small red car with only one occupant was speeding towards them out of the smoky distance. The others went running out to join their friend, stringing themselves out across the highway to block the car's path. By the time Lynn thought about joining them, it was already too late—the young people had piled in and the car was driving on, wallowing, every window crammed with hands and faces. The girl gave the crowd a thumbs-up as they passed.

A group was clustering around one of the cars. Peering over a woman's shoulder, Lynn could see one of the burly uncles hunkered down in his shorts, expertly wielding a length of hose coming out of the fuel tank. His cheeks hollowed, then he whipped the hose away from his mouth with a practiced jerk, stopped the spurt of petrol with his thumb, and plunged the other end of the hose into a jerry-can. He looked up with tense, pale eyes.

"Any more?" he asked in an over-loud voice.

Lynn shook her head. The group moved on to the next car.

She went to sit inside, in the fried-egg smell of the cafeteria. The seats were red plastic, the table-tops marbled yellow, just as she remembered them from childhood road trips. Tomato sauce and mustard in squeezy plastic bottles crusted around the nozzle. She was alone in the gloom of the place. There were racks of chips over the counter, shelves of sweets, display fridges. She pulled down two packets of chips, helped herself to a Coke and made her way to a window booth. She wished strongly for a beer. The sun came through the tinted glass in an end-of-the-world shade of pewter, but that was nothing new; that had always been the color of the light in places like this.

Through the glass wall, she watched absently as the petrol scavengers filled up the tank of *Adil's IT Bonanza*. They'd taken the canopy off the gleaming bakkie to let more people climb on. The uncles and aunts sat around the edge, turning their broad backs on those left behind, with small children and bags piled in the middle and a couple of older children standing up, clinging to the cab. What she'd thought was a group had been split: part of the white family was left behind on the tar, revealing itself as a young couple with a single toddler, and one of the sweaty car-pushers was on board. The blue-overalled guy was up front, next to Adil. How wrong she'd been, then, in her reading of alliances. Perhaps she might have scored a berth, if she'd pushed. She sipped her Coke thoughtfully as the bakkie pulled away.

Warm Coke: it seemed the electricity had gone too, now.

Lynn started distractedly picking at the strip of aluminium that bound the edge of the table. It could be used for something. In an emergency. She opened a packet of cheese and onion chips, surprised by her hunger. Lynn realized she was feeling happy, in a secret, volatile way. It was like ditching school: sitting here where nobody knew who she was, where no one could find her, on a day cut out of the normal passage of days. Nothing was required of her except to wait. All she wanted to do was sit for another hour, and then another hour after that, at which point she might lie down on the sticky vinyl seat in the tainted sunlight and sleep. She hadn't eaten a packet of chips for years. They were excellent. Crunching them up, she felt the salt and fat repairing her headache. Lynn pushed off her heeled shoes, which were hurting, and untucked her fitted shirt. She hadn't dressed practically for mass evacuation.

The female petrol attendant pushed open the glass door with a clang, then smacked through the wooden counter-flap to go behind the till. She was a plump, pretty young woman with complexly braided hair. Her skin, Lynn noticed, was clear brown, free from the soot that flecked the motorists. She took a small key on a chain from her bosom and opened the till, whacking the side of her fist against the drawer to jump it out. Flicking a glance across at Lynn, she pulled a handful of 50-rand notes from the till, then hundreds.

"Taxi's going," she said.

"Really? With what petrol?"

"He's got petrol. He was just waiting to fill the seats. We arranged a price—for you, too, if you want."

"You're kidding. He was just waiting for people to *pay*? He could have taken us any time?"

The woman shrugged, as if to say, *taxi-drivers*. She stroked a thumb across the edge of the wad of notes. "Are you coming?"

Lynn shrugged back at her.

"You don't want to come in a taxi?"

"No, it's not that—it's just, where would we go? I'm sure someone will come soon. The police will come. Rescue services."

The woman gave a snort and exited the shop, bumping the door open with her hip. The door sucked slowly shut, and then it was quiet again.

Lynn watched through the tinted window as the money was handed over, which seemed to activate the inert *gaardjie*. He straightened up and started striding back and forth, clapping his hands, shouting and hustling like it was Main Road rush hour. The people inside the taxi edged up in the seats and everyone else started pushing in. The driver spotted Lynn through the window and raised his eyebrows, pointing with both forefingers first at her and then at the kombi and then back at her again: *coming?* When she just smiled, he snapped his fingers and turned his attention elsewhere. People were being made to leave their bags and bundles on the tar.

Lynn realized she was gripping the edge of the table tightly. Her stomach hurt. Getting up this morning, packing her few things, driving all this way... it seemed impossible for her to start it all again. Decision, action, motion. She wanted to curl up on the seat, put her head down. But the taxi was filling up.

Her body delivered her from decision. All at once her digestion seemed to have sped up dramatically. Guts whining, she trotted to the bathroom.

Earlier, there'd been a queue for the toilets, but now the stalls were empty. In the basin mirror, Lynn's face was startlingly grimed. Her choppy dark hair was greasy, her eyes as pink as if she'd been weeping. Contamination. Sitting on the black plastic toilet seat, she felt the poisons gush out of her. She wiped her face with paper and looked closely at the black specks smeared on to the tissue. Her skin was oozing it. She held the wadded paper to her nose. A faint coppery smell. What was this shit? The explosion had been at a chemical plant, but which chemical? She couldn't remember what they'd said on the news.

She noticed the silence. It was the slightly reverberating stillness of a place from which people have recently departed.

There was nobody left on the forecourt. The battered white taxi was pulling out, everyone crammed inside. The sliding door was open, three men hanging out the side with their fingers hooked into the roof rim. Lynn ran after it onto the highway, but the only person who saw her was the blond toddler crushed against the back windscreen, one hand spread against the glass. He held her gaze as the taxi picked up speed.

The cloud was creeping higher behind her back, casting a dull murk, not solid enough to be shadow. She could see veils of dirty rain bleeding from its near edge. Earlier, in the city, she had heard sirens, helicopters in the sky; but there were none out here. It was silent.

Standing alone on the highway was unnerving. This was for cars. The road surface was not meant to be touched with hands or feet, to be examined too closely or in stillness. The four lanes were so wide. Even the white lines and the gaps between them were much longer than they appeared from the car: the length of her whole body, were she to lie down in the road. She had to stop herself looking over her shoulder, flinching from invisible cars coming up from behind.

She thought of the people she'd seen so many times on the side of the highway, walking, walking along roadsides not designed for human passage, covering incomprehensible distances, toiling from one obscure spot to another. Their bent heads dusty, cowed by the iron ring of the horizon. In all her years of driving at speed along highways, Cape Town, Jo'burg, Durban, she'd never once stopped at a random spot, walked into the veld. Why would she? The highways were tracks through an indecipherable terrain of dun and gray, a blur in which one only fleetingly glimpsed the sleepy eyes of people standing on its edge. To leave the car would be to disintegrate, to merge with that shifting world. How far could she walk, anyway, before weakness made her stumble? Before the air thickened into some alien gel, impossible to wade through, to breathe?

It was mid-afternoon but it felt much later. Towards the city, the sky was thick with bloody light. It was possible to stare straight at the sun—a pink bleached disk, like the moon of a different planet. The cloud was growing. As she watched, a deep rose-colored occlusion extended towards her, pulling a wash of darkness across the sky. A strange horizontal rain came with it, and reflexively she ducked and put her hands to her hair. But the droplets were too big and distinct, and she realized that they were in fact birds, thousands of birds, sprinting away from the mountain. They flew above her and around her ears: swift starlings, laboring geese. Some small rapid birds were tossed up against the sky, smuts from a burning book.

As they passed overhead, for the first time Lynn was filled with fear.

Approximately 50 packets of potato chips, assorted flavors. Eighty or so chocolate bars, different kinds. Liquorice, wine-gums, Smarties. Maybe 30 bottles of Coke and Fanta in the fridges, different sizes. Water, fizzy and plain: fifteen big bottles, ten small. No alcohol of any kind. How much fluid did you need to drink per day? The women's magazines said two liters. To flush out the toxins. Would drinking Coke be enough? Surely. So: two weeks, maybe three. The survival arithmetic was easy. Two weeks was more than enough time; rescue would come long before then. She felt confident, prepared.

Boldly, she pushed through the wooden flap and went behind the counter. The till stood open. Beyond were two swing doors with head-high windows, and through them a sterile steel-fitted kitchen, gloomy without overhead lighting. Two hamburger patties, part-cooked, lay abandoned on the flat steel plate of the griller, and a basket of fries sat in a vat of opaque oil. To the right was a back door with a broad metal pushbar. She shoved it.

The door swung open on to a sudden patch of domesticity: three or four black bins, a metal skip, sunlight, some scruffy bluegums and an old two-wire fence with wooden posts holding back the veld. A shed with a tilted, corrugated-iron roof leaned up against the back wall. The change in scale and atmosphere was startling. Lynn had not imagined that these big franchised petrol stations hid modest homesteads. She'd had the vague sense that they were modular, shipped out in sections, everything in company colors. Extraneous elements—employees—were presumably spirited away somewhere convenient and invisible at the end of their shifts. But this was clearly somebody's backyard. It smelt of smoke and sweat and dishwater, overlaying the burnt grease of the kitchen. Through the doorway of the shed, she could see the end of an iron bed and mattress. On the ground was a red plastic tub of the kind used to wash dishes or babies. Two plastic garden chairs, one missing a leg. A rusted car on bricks.

Lynn laughed out loud. Her car! Her own car, twenty years on: the same model blue Toyota, but reduced to a shell. The remaining patches of crackled paint had faded to the color of a long-ago summer sky. The roof had rusted clean through in places, and the bottom edges of the doors were rotten with corrosion. Old carpeting was piled on the back seat and all the doors were open. Seeing the smooth finish gone scabrous and raw gave Lynn a twinge at the back of her teeth.

She walked past the car. There was a stringy cow on the other side of the fence, its pelt like mud daubed over the muscles. A goat came avidly up to the wire, watching her with its slotted eyes, and she put her arm through and scratched between its horns. The cow also mooched over in an interested way. Smelling its grassy breath, Lynn felt a tremor of adventure. She could be here for *days*. She felt no fear at the prospect: nobody else was here, nobody for miles around (although briefly she saw again: the hand sliding across the throat…).

Out back here, the sky looked completely clear, as if the petrol station marked the limit of the zone of contamination. She shot her fingers at the goat and snapped them like the taxi-man, and spun round in a circle, humming.

She breathed in sharply, stepping back hard against the wire. "Jesus Christ."

Someone was in the car. The pile of rugs had reconstituted itself into an old lady, sitting on the backseat as if waiting to be chauffeured away.

Lynn coughed out a laugh, slapping her chest. "Oh god, sorry," she said. "You surprised me."

The old lady worked her gums, staring straight ahead. She wore a faded green button-up dress, a hand-knitted cardigan, elasticized knee stockings and slippers. Gray hair caught in a meager bun.

Lynn came closer. "Um," she began. *"Hello?"* Afrikaans? Lynn's Afrikaans was embarrassingly weak. "Hallo?" she said again, giving the word a different inflection. Ridiculous.

No response. Poor thing, she thought, someone just left her here. Would the old lady even know about the explosion? "Sorry... *tannie?*" she tried again. She'd never seriously called anyone *"tannie"* before. But it seemed to have some effect: the old lady looked at her with mild curiosity. Small, filmed, black eyes, almost no whites visible. A creased face shrunken onto fine bones. An ancient mouse.

"Hi. I'm Lynn. Sorry to disturb you. Ah, I don't know if anyone's told you—about the accident? In Cape Town."

The woman's mouth moved in a fumbling way. Lynn bent closer to hear.

"My grandson," the old lady enunciated, slowly but clearly. Then she smiled faintly and looked away, having concluded a piece of necessary small talk.

"He told you about it?"

No answer.

So. Now there was another person to consider, an old frail person, someone in need of her help. Lynn felt her heaviness return. *"Tannie,"* she said—having begun with it she might as well continue—"There's been an accident, an explosion. There's chemicals in the air. Poison, *gif.* It might be coming this way. I think we should go out front. There might be people coming past who can help us. Cars. Ambulances."

The old lady seemed not averse to the idea, and allowed Lynn to take her arm and raise her from her seat. Although very light, she leaned hard; Lynn felt she was lugging the woman's entire weight with one arm, like a suitcase. Rather than negotiate the complex series of doors back through the station, they took the longer route, clockwise around the building on a narrow track that squeezed between the back corner of the garage and the wire fence. Past the ladies, the gents, the café. As they walked, it started to rain, sudden and heavy. The rain shut down the horizon; its sound on the forecourt canopy was loud static. Lynn wondered how tainted the falling water was. She sat the old lady down on a sheltered bench outside the shop, and fetched some bottles of water and packets of chips from inside. Then she urgently had to use the bathroom again.

The toilet was no longer flushing. Her empty guts felt liquid, but strained to force anything out. The headache was back. When she got back outside, the rain had stopped again, as abruptly as it started, leaving a rusty tang in the air. The old lady had vanished.

Then Lynn spotted movement out on the road: her car door was open. Coming closer, she saw that the woman was calmly eating tomato chips in the back seat. Having transferred herself from the wreck in the backyard to the superior vehicle out front, she was now waiting for the journey to commence. A neat old lady, Lynn noted: there were no crumbs down her front. She seemed restored by the chips. Her eyes gleamed as she whipped a small plastic tortoiseshell comb out of a pocket and started snatching back wisps of hair, repinning the bun into place with black U-bend pins that Lynn hadn't seen since her own grandmother died. In contrast, she felt increasingly disheveled, and embarrassed about her dump of a car: the empty Heineken bottles on the floor, the tissues in the cubbyhole. She should have kept things cleaner, looked after things better.

"My grandson," the woman said to Lynn, with a nod of reassurance.

"Of course," said Lynn.

Evening was coming. The clouds had retreated somewhat and were boiling grumpily over the mountain. The brief rain had activated an awful odor: like burnt plastic but with a metallic bite, and a whiff of sourness like rotten meat in it too. Lynn sat in the front seat, put the

178

keys into the ignition and gripped the steering wheel. She had no plan. The sky ahead was darkening to a luminous blue. The silent little woman was an expectant presence in her rear-view mirror. Feeling oppressed, Lynn got out of the car again and stood with her hands on her hips, staring east, west, willing sirens, flashing lights. She ducked back into the car. "I'll be back in a sec. Okay? You're all right there?"

The old woman looked at her with polite incomprehension.

She just needed to walk around a bit. She headed off towards the sun, which was melting messily into smears of red and purple. The mountain was no longer visible. The road was discolored, splattered with lumps of some tarry black precipitate. She counted five small bodies of birds, feathers damp and stuck together. Blades of grass at the side of the road were streaked with black, and the ground seemed to be smoking, a layer of foul steam around her ankles. It got worse the further she walked, and so she turned around.

There was someone standing next to her car. At once she recognized the mustache, the blue overalls.

Her first impulse was to hide. She stood completely still, watching. He hadn't seen her.

The clay-faced man was holding something... a box. No, a can. He had a white jerry-can in his hands and he was filling her car with petrol. Suddenly her stomach roiled and she crouched down at the side of the road, vomiting a small quantity of cheese-and-onion mulch into the stinking grass. When she raised her chin, the man was standing looking back at the petrol station.

Deciding, she made herself stand, raising her hand to wave—but in that moment he opened the door and got in; the motor turned immediately and the car was rolling forward. She could see the back of the old woman's head, briefly silver as the car turned out into the lane, before the reflection of the sunset blanked out the rear windscreen. The Toyota headed out into the clear evening.

Lynn sat in the back of the rusted car and watched the sky turn navy and the stars come out. She loved the way the spaces between the stars had no texture, softer than water; they were pure depth. She sat in the hollow the old lady had worn in the seat, ankles crossed in the space where the handbrake used to be. She sipped Coke; it helped with the nausea.

She'd been here three days and her head felt clear. While there'd been a few bursts of strange rain, the chemical storm had not progressed further down the highway. It seemed the pollution had created its own weather system over the mountain, a knot of ugly cloud. She felt washed up on the edge of it, resting her oil-clogged wings on a quiet shore.

Sooner or later, rescue would come. The ambulances with flashing lights, the men in luminous vests with equipment and supplies. Or maybe just a stream of people driving back home. But if rescue took too long, then there was always the black bicycle that she'd found leaned up against the petrol pump. The woman's grandson must have ridden here, with the petrol can, from some place not too far down the road. It was an old postman's bike, heavy but hardy, and she felt sure that if he had cycled the distance, so could she. Maybe tomorrow, or the day after. And when this was all over, she was definitely going to go on a proper detox. Give up all junk food, alcohol. Some time soon.

Lynn snapped open a packet of salt-'n'-vinegar chips. Behind her, the last of the sunset lingered, poison violet and puce, but she didn't turn to look. She wanted to face clear skies, sweet-smelling veld. If she closed her eyes, she might hear a frog, just one, starting its evening song beyond the fence.

Waiting

EC Osondu—winner of the 2009 Caine Prize

My name is Orlando Zaki. *Orlando* is taken from Orlando, Florida, which is what is written on the t-shirt given to me by the Red Cross. *Zaki* is the name of the town where I was found and from which I was brought to this refugee camp. My friends in the camp are known by the inscriptions written on their t-shirts. Acapulco wears a t-shirt with the inscription, *Acapulco*. Sexy's t-shirt has the inscription *Tell Me I'm Sexy*. Paris's t-shirt says *See Paris And Die*. When she is coming toward me, I close my eyes because I don't want to die.

Even when one gets a new t-shirt, your old name stays with you. Paris just got a new t-shirt that says *Ask Me About Jesus*, but we still call her Paris and we are not asking her about anybody. There was a girl in the camp once whose t-shirt said *Got Milk?* She threw the t-shirt away because some of the boys in the camp were always pressing her breasts forcefully to see if they had milk. You cannot know what will be written on your t-shirt. We struggle and fight for them and count ourselves lucky that we get anything at all. Take Lousy, for instance; his t-shirt says *My Dad Went To Yellowstone And Got Me This Lousy T-shirt*. He cannot fight, so he's not been able to get another one and has been wearing the same t-shirt since he came to the camp. Though what is written on it is now faded, the name has stuck. Some people are lucky: London had a t-shirt that said *London* and is now in London. He's been adopted by a family over there. Maybe I will find a family in Orlando, Florida, that will adopt me.

Sister Nora is the one who told me to start writing this book, she says *the best way to forget is to remember and the best way to remember is to forget.* That is the way Sister Nora talks, in a roundabout way. I think because she is a Reverend Sister she likes to speak in parables like Jesus. She is the one who has been giving me books to read. She says I have a gift for telling stories. This is why she thinks I will become a writer one day.

The first book she gave me to read was *Waiting For Godot*. She says the people in the book are waiting for God to come and help them. Here in the camp, we wait and wait and then wait some more. It is the only thing we do. We wait for the food trucks to come and then we form a straight line and then we wait a few minutes for the line to scatter, then we wait for the fight to begin, and then we fight and struggle and bite and kick and curse and tear and grab and run. And then we begin to watch the road and wait to see if the water trucks are coming, we watch for the dust trail, and then we go and fetch our containers and start waiting and then the trucks come and the first few containers are filled and the fight and struggle and tearing and scratching begin because someone has whispered to someone that the water tanker only has little water in it. That is, if we are lucky and the water tanker comes; oftentimes, we just bring out our containers and start waiting and praying for rain to fall.

Today we are waiting for the photographer to come and take our pictures. It is these pictures that the Red Cross people send to their people abroad who show them to different people in foreign countries and, after looking at them, the foreign families will choose those they like to come and live with them. This is the third week we have been waiting for the photographer, but he has to pass through the war zone so he may not even make it today. After taking the photographs, we have to wait for him to print it and bring it back. We then give it to the Red Cross people and start waiting for a response from abroad.

I want to go and join my friend under the only tree still standing in the camp. Acapulco is raising a handful of red dust into the air to test for breeze; the air is stagnant and the red earth falls back in a straight line.

"Orlando, do you think the photographer will come today?" he asks.

"Maybe he will come."

"Do you think an American family will adopt me?"

"Maybe, if you are lucky."

"Will they find a cure for my bedwetting?"

"There is a tablet for every sickness in America."

"I am not sick, I only wet myself in my sleep because I always dream that I am urinating outside and then I wake up and my knickers are wet because it was only a dream, but the piss is real."

"The same dream every night?"

"Yes."

"Do you think that if I go to America, my parents will hear about me and write to me and I will write to them and tell my new family to let them come over and join me?"

"When the war ends, your parents will find you."

"When will the war end?"

"I don't know, but it will end soon."

"If the war will end soon, why are the Red Cross people sending us to America?"

"Because they don't want us to join the Youth Brigade and shoot and kill and rape and loot and burn and steal and destroy and fight to the finish and die and not go to school."

This was why Acapulco was always sitting alone under the tree: because he always asked a lot of questions. Sister Nora says it is good to ask questions, that if you ask questions you will never get lost. Acapulco begins to throw the sand once more, testing for breeze. Pus is coming out of his ears and this gives him the smell of an egg that is a little rotten. This was another reason people kept away from him. A fly is buzzing around his ear; he ignores it for some time and at the exact moment the fly is about to perch, he waves it away furiously.

"I wish I had a dog," he said.

"What do you want to do with the dog?"

"I will pose with the dog in my photograph that they are sending to America because white people love dogs."

"But they also like people."

"Yes, but they like people who like dogs."

"London did not take a picture with a dog."

"Yes, London is now in London."

"Maybe you will soon be in Acapulco," I said, laughing.

"Where is Acapulco?"

"They have a big ocean there, it is blue and beautiful."

"I don't like the ocean, I don't know how to swim, I want to go to America."

"Everyone in America knows how to swim; all the houses have swimming pools."

"I will like to swim in a swimming pool, not the ocean. I hear swimming pool water is sweet and clean and blue and is good for the skin."

We are silent. We can hear the sound of the aluminium sheets with which the houses are built. They make an angry noise like pin-sized bullets when going off. The houses built with tarpaulin and plastic sheets are fluttering in the breeze like a thousand plastic kites going off. Acapulco raises a handful of dust in the air. The breeze carries it away. Some of it blows into our faces and Acapulco smiles.

"God is not asleep," he says. I say nothing.

"There used to be dogs here in the camp." He had been in the camp before me. He is one of the oldest people in the camp.

There were lots of black dogs. They were our friends, they were our protectors. Even though food was scarce, the dogs never went hungry. The women would call them whenever a child squatted down to shit and the dogs would come running. They would wait for the child to finish and lick the child's buttocks clean before they ate the shit. People threw them scraps of food. The dogs were useful in other ways too. In those days, the enemy still used to raid the camp frequently. We would bury ourselves in a hole and the dogs would gather leaves and other stuff and spread it atop the hole where we hid. The enemy would pass by the hole and not know we were hiding there.

But there was a time the Red Cross people could not bring food to the camp for two weeks because the enemy would not let their plane land. We were so hungry we killed a few of the dogs and used them to make pepper-soup. A few days later, the Red Cross people were let through and food came. The dogs were a bit wary, but they seemed to understand it was not our fault.

And then, for the second time, there was no food for a very long time. We were only able to catch some of the dogs this time. Some of them ran away as we approached, but we still caught some and cooked and ate them. After that, we did not see the dogs again; the ones that ran away kept off. One day, a little child was squatting and having a shit. When the mother looked up, half a dozen of the dogs that had disappeared emerged from nowhere and attacked the little child. While the mother screamed, they tore the child to pieces and fled with parts of the child's body dangling between their jaws. Some of the men began to lay ambush for the dogs and killed a few of them. They say the dogs had become as tough as lions. We don't see the dogs any more. People say it is the war.

I decided I was going to ask Sister Nora. As if reading my mind, Acapulco told me not to mention it to anyone. He said people in the camp did not like talking about the dogs.

"I am not sure the photographer will still come today," I said.

"Sometimes I think there is a bullet lodged in my brain," Acapulco said.

"If you had a bullet in your brain, you would be dead."

"It went in through my bad ear. I hear explosions in my head, bullets popping, voices screaming, *banza, banza bastard, come out we will drink your blood today*, and then I smell carbide, gun-smoke, burning thatch. I don't like smelling smoke from fires when the women are cooking with firewood; it makes the bullets in my brain begin to go off."

"You will be fine when you get to America. They don't cook with firewood; they use electricity."

"You know everything, Zaki. How do you know all these things though you have never been to these places?"

"I read a lot of books, books contain a lot of information, sometimes they tell stories too," I say.

"I don't like books without pictures; I like books with big, beautiful, colorful pictures."

"Not all books have pictures. Only books for children have pictures."

"I am tired of taking pictures and sending them abroad to families that don't want me, almost all the people I came to the camp with have found families and are now living abroad. One of my friends sent me a letter from a place called Dakota. Why have no family adopted me? Do you think they don't like my face?"

"It is luck; you have not found your luck yet."

"Sometimes I want to join the Youth Brigade, but I am afraid; they say they give them we-we to smoke and they drink blood and swear an oath to have no mercy on any soul, including their parents."

"Sister Nora will be angry with you if she hears you talking like that. You know she is doing her best for us, and the Red Cross people too, they are trying to get a family for you."

"That place called Dakota must be full of rocks."

"Why do you say that?"

"Just from the way it sounds, like many giant pieces of rock falling on each other at once."

"I'd like to go to that place with angels."

"You mean Los Angeles."

"They killed most of my people who could not pronounce the name of the rebel leader properly, they said we could not say *Tsofo*, we kept saying *Tofo* and they kept shooting us. My friend here in the camp taught me to say Tsofo, he said I should say it like there is sand in my mouth. Like there is gravel on my tongue. Now I can say it either way."

"That's good. When you get to America, you will learn to speak like them. You will try to swallow your tongue with every word, you will say *larer, berrer, merre, ferre, herrer.*"

"We should go. It is getting to lunch time."

"I don't have the power to fight. Whenever it is time for food, I get scared. If only my mother was here, then I would not be *Displaced*. She would be cooking for me; I wouldn't have to fight to eat all the time."

We both looked up at the smoke curling upwards from shacks where some of the women were cooking *dawa*. You could tell the people that had mothers because smoke always rose from their shacks in the afternoon. I wondered if Acapulco and I were yet to find people to adopt us because we were displaced and did not have families. Most of the people that have gone abroad are people with families. I did not mention this to Acapulco; I did not want him to start thinking of his parents who could not say *Tsofo*. I had once heard someone in the camp say that if God wanted us to say *Tsofo* he would have given us tongues that could say *Tsofo*.

"Come with me, I will help you fight for food," I say to Acapulco.

"You don't need to fight, Orlando. All the other kids respect you, they say you are not afraid of anybody or anything and they say Sister Nora likes you and they say you have a book where you record all the bad, bad, things that people do and you give it to Sister Nora to read and when you are both reading the book both of you will be shaking your heads and laughing like *amariya* and *ango*, like husband and wife."

We stood up and started walking towards the corrugated-sheet shack where we got our lunch. I could smell the *dawa*, it was always the same *dawa*, and the same green-bottle flies and the same bent and half-crumpled aluminium plates and yet we still fought over it.

Kimono saw me first and began to call out to me, he was soon joined by Aruba and Jerusalem and Lousy and I'm Loving It and Majorca and the rest. Chief Cook was standing in front of the plates of *dawa* and green soup. She had that look on her face, the face of a man about to witness two beautiful women disgrace themselves by fighting and stripping themselves naked over him. She wagged her finger at us and said: No fighting today, boys. That was the signal we needed to go at it; we dived. *Dawa* and soup were spilling on the floor. Some tried to grab some into their mouth as they fought to grab a plate in case they did not get anything to eat at the end of the fight. I grabbed a lump of *dawa* and tossed it to Acapulco and made for a plate of soup but as my fingers grabbed it, Lousy kicked it away and the soup poured on the floor. He laughed his crazy hyena laugh and hissed, saying: the leper may not know how to milk a cow, but he sure knows how to spill the milk in the pail. Chief Cook kept screaming, hey no fighting, one by one, form a line, the *dawa* is enough to go round. I managed to grab a half-spilled plate of soup and began to weave my way out as I signaled to Acapulco to head out. We squatted behind the food shack and began dipping our fingers into the food, driving away large flies with our free hand. We had two hard lumps of *dawa* and very little soup. I ate a few handfuls and wiped my hands on my shorts, leaving the rest for Acapulco. He was having a hard time driving away the flies from his bad ear and from the plate of food, and he thanked me with his eyes.

I remembered a book Sister Nora once gave me to read about a poor boy living in England in the olden days who asked for more from his chief cook. From the picture of the boy in the book, he did not look so poor to me. The boys in the book all wore coats and caps and they were even served. We had to fight, and if you asked the chief cook for more, she would point at the lumps of *dawa* and the spilled soup on the floor and say we loved to waste food. I once spoke to Sister Nora about the food and fights, but she said she did not want to get involved. It was the first time I had seen her refuse to find a solution to any problem. She explained that she did not work for the Red Cross and was their guest like me.

I was wondering how to get away from Acapulco. I needed some time alone but I did not want to hurt his feelings. I told him to take the plates back to the food shack. We did not need to wash them because we had already licked them clean with our tongues.

As Acapulco walked away to the food shack with the plates, I slipped away quietly.

Stickfighting Days

Olufemi Terry—winner of the 2010 Caine Prize

Thwack, Thwack, the two of them go at it like madmen, but the boys around them barely stir with excitement. They both use one stick and we find this swordy kind of stickfighting a bit crappy. Much better two on one or two on two—lots more skill involved and more likelihood of blood.

I turn to Lapy. "Let's go off and practice somewhere. This is weak." Lapy likes any stickfight, but almost always does what I say. His eyes linger ruefully on Paps and the other boy—don't know his name but I see him a lot—and then he follows me.

I run almost full tilt into Markham and he gives me a grin, like we're best pals and he's been looking for me. Markham is my rival. We've beaten each other roughly the same number of times. Well, six to five in his favor, but one of my victories was a beauty, a flowing sequence of sticks that even I couldn't follow before I smashed his nose in nicely. Almost broke it. The satisfaction of Markham's watery-eyed submission that day makes me smile easily back at him.

"Wanna mix it up?" Markham's eyes aren't smiling any more; he won the last one and thinks he's on a roll. I know better.

"We could," I come back smoothly, "but it wouldn't mean much." I hold up Mormegil. I've told no one I've named my sticks though I'm not ashamed. I love Mormegil, but I don't think the others would understand. "I've only got one stick with me." I cock my head to one side enquiringly at him. To be honest, I've been leaving Orcrist, my other, so I don't have to get into any serious battles. Everyone knows

I'm a two-stick man. But I'm not ready to go up against Markham again just yet. Or any of the other top stickfighters. I've been trying some new moves. I feel close to a breakthrough in terms of technique. But it's not quite there and until it is, I only carry Mormegil. Mormegil is as long as our regulations allow, a lovely willow poke, dark willow—that's why I chose the name. It means black sword in Tolkien's language. A sword with a mind of sorts. Turin wielded it, and it would cut anything, anyone, eagerly. In the end it took his own life to avenge those he killed. My Mormegil has little knobs at the joint and one tip is nicely pointed—we're not allowed to sharpen sticks—but this is natural. Mormegil is a killing machine, even though I've never done for anyone yet. But I will. I like Markham, but I'd like to kill him. I dream of doing it in front of a huge pack of boys. Clinically.

Markham's henchman, Tich, is a one-stick man but he now holds up two. "You can use this one." He throws it to me and I catch it easily, angry at being forced to fight. I force a deep gulp of air into my lungs. Fighting angry is bad! Only Simon ever did it effectively and where's he now? I give Lapy a confident look, taking the measure of the unfamiliar stick as I do. It's rubbery, too bendy but unlikely to break. It's also too light. Much too light.

Markham's not much one for warm-ups, he bounces from one toe to another like a boxer, rolls his head, then gestures to me that he's ready. I already see a ring of boys forming around us, keen for a real spar and not that sword stuff.

He comes at me, neither quick nor slow, his arms wide. One of his sticks, an ash thing, is almost as good as Mormegil. He let me hold it once, before we were rivals. Stiff as hell and with a good weight, maybe an inch shorter than my beauty. I fend him off easily. Markham is good, but he's cautious. He knows I'll not risk much with an unknown stick. I could keep him off with Mormegil, but I feel I've got to try one of my new moves. No one'll attach too much to this particular fight so I can afford to be bold. But I'm cunning too. That's what got me to where I am. That and good reflexes.

I hold Mormegil in my left hand and the unfamiliar stick in my right, gripped in the middle—an outdated form I know, but very good for riposting against an over-eager opponent. Here he comes, Markham, his sticks a blur more from technique than power. In goes

Mormegil to break that rhythm and then I bring my whippy stick in to catch the one in Markham's left. It is too bendy to give me much opening, but I am quick, and I know not to go for a body blow; the opportunity is small and he'd be able to retaliate. I bang Mormegil against the outside of his wrist, the bony bit, all the while twirling my right hand to keep him caught up. I try for his knuckles but he is no fool, Markham. He pulls back a step, wiping his forehead with the back of his hand. I watch him change his grip to match mine. There's no sweat on me yet! He's not angry enough to make a serious error, but I feel in my gut, now's the time to let him—all the boys—see what I've been working on. I drop my right grip so that I'm holding both sticks sword like. I bang them together once, and advance on him. This is me at my most fearsome: my speed frightens opponents and no one knows exactly what I've got planned so it's now or never. Our sticks clatter against each other left to left, right to right and cross-wise. I use the bendy stick to hold his every thrust and I am glad that the whippiness absorbs much of the power. Markham settles into a pattern and at the last second, I drop one of my parries so that his stick whistles on, at the same time lowering Mormegil so that my face is unprotected. Markham falls for it and doesn't try to halt his stroke, lunging at my face with gangs of force. Trust him to try and maim me—and this contest means nothing. Both his sticks are held high... so I fall to one knee with both of mine ready, my mind blotting out the murmured wave of anticipation from the crowd. I've thought long about this, long enough that there's no need to think now. It's not enough to go for the balls, the most vulnerable spot. No, a quick stickfighter can inflict double damage. I stab with Mormegil at his crotch, relishing its rigidness and the pain it will cause, yet pulling the stroke a little, for I am a boy also, I know what it means to strike full strength there. Better to kill someone with a temple blow than that. At the same time, I bang the bendy stick on the ball of his knee as hard as I can and roll.

I come to my feet expecting to see Markham in the toils of agony. He feigns total indifference at first, then allows us to see he's in some pain, but only from his knee. He hobbles backward a step, kicking it out to ease it. I wait, tasting the moment but puzzled as to why he isn't clutching his balls howling.

A deep voice rolls out, that of the judge: "Halt, boys!" Markham turns to him, a mixture of reluctance and relief on his face. I'm glad, and now every boy there turns toward the judge. He's not a stickfighter. Not even a boy, the judge. His real name is Salad but we use both. I don't know whether he gave us the art of stickfighting, but he knows the rules and enforces them when he's around. Sometimes he's unseen for days, but his word is binding always, and not because we're afraid. The judge has a fearsome appearance, he's all muscle, like carved wood, his arms bulge and this seems the reason for his shabby shirts—it isn't—and the strain of his thighs against his corduroys makes his hands seem normal, fragile even. But the judge, Salad, is sick. At times, he can't stop coughing and, somehow, it is known among us that the muscles have surrendered their strength though they are preserved in form. The judge's voice is what commands our respect, mostly. He is very fair too.

"What's in your pants, Markham?" the judge is quietly stern. He stands with his hands behind his back. Some of the boys are already taller than him. Markham knows he'll be forced to prove that he didn't cheat, so with little ado, he pulls out through the top of his pants a thick sponge, much squashed, and hands it over to Salad. I grin, but joy is short lived. The judge pronounces: "Markham is disqualified. Match annulled." Damn! I was certain he'd award me a victory, but now it's worked against me that the match wasn't a proper one. And everyone who matters has seen my new move, too, so the element of surprise, my tactical advantage, is lost. I don't waste time trying to appeal to the judge; he's very strict, and this is why we respect him. I walk away too quickly for anybody to speak to me, Lapy at my shoulder.

In the evening I practice my forms with Lapy, who'd be a good stickfighter if he could be bothered. He never says much, but I like him for this. He's no pushover, Lapy. If he tells me something, I listen; he knows what he's about. He's got the manner of a champion stickfighter: you can never tell what's on his mind and he never seems afraid. When he feels like being scarce, even I won't see him.

Finally, I light a cigarette butt I found and ask him the question that's burned on my lips for hours. "What d'you think of the judge's decision earlier?"

He stops to glance at me in the middle of a stick maneuver. "Pretty bog-standard. He cheated, but the judge didn't want to give you a total victory. Psychologically, that would have demoralized Markham too much." I watch him ponder whether to say more before he begins to weave his sticks once more. Sometimes, I think of giving up this stickfighting lark altogether. I'm 13 and getting too big to spend hours practicing my sticks. The smart boys spend their days poking and scouring the dump. There's a lot of valuable stuff here—it's not just home.

The judge surprises me early the next morning; he's been watching me from behind a car wreck. Usually I'm about early, practicing my sticks, snooping on what others are doing. When I notice him, I wonder how he escaped my eye for so long; it's hard to conceal such a bulky body.

He says, his voice hoarse: "Well met, Raul." The judge—Salad, I want to call him as the older boys do—talks like this sometimes. He moves out from behind the wreck heavily, though I know just how agile he is.

"Salad," I say, continuing my single stick forms. I'm not exactly angry, but it won't hurt if he thinks I am. He likes me. I feel him waiting; his silence tells me something of his mood.

"My decision yesterday was based on what I felt was fair." I wait, hoping he'll blurt something. "I know you and Markham are rivals. I know how evenly matched you two are. I know you feel betrayed, you think I've given him the edge because he's seen your new moves." I'm so stunned by Salad's words that my stick hangs momentarily in the air. It's best to neither confirm nor deny, so I continue practicing, keeping my face flat. My thoughts race. I now feel sheepish, angry, afraid, and resentful of the judge all at once so I push these feelings away. My concentration is so strong that when I stop to breathe a few minutes later, Salad is no longer there. At first I'm glad, and not just because my chest is heaving. But then it hits me that he wanted to tell me something and then didn't. I am hurt rather than curious. Even if it is just more stories—it is Salad after all who tells us about Mormegil, Turin, and Beren—he should have said his piece.

I practice with Lapy much of that day, in a remote bit of the dump. He's a good partner, cagey. I use my new moves a couple of times but with no success. By the evening our feet blister from acid waste, and I feel like crap. My sadness has nothing to do with fighting sticks.

I feel no better the next day and decide perhaps what I need is not more practice but to trade blows with someone. I go in search of Markham, but before I find him, I come upon a group formed up in a circle around two boys, 15-year-olds. I know one of them, Malick—he's a brute—but I've never seen the other. They're going at it. Malick uses a lone stick, swings it like a club although it's regulation thickness. His fights are popular because he's sly, savage. We've seen the judge pull him off people a time or two. Malick is actually not so brutish, in my opinion. I think he plays it up because he's not liked and wants to disgust us even more. The other boy uses two sticks and is very good. He blends power and finesse very well; he's strong on both hands. I wonder if he's from the dump. Malick will lose and so I stay to watch, even though I'm eager to fight this morning. His opponent seems popular, the crowd murmur his name, Peja, in a way that I detest, despite his skill. When he disarms Malick a little later, it's done without viciousness so that Malick stands empty-handed but unhurt. His eyes roll wildly in his head as he considers his options. I feel sure Malick is on the point of throwing himself at Peja to grapple him to the ground, but he doesn't. The fight is over.

Before anyone can move off, Salad pushes another boy forward by the shoulders, into the circle, and points to me. The judge only occasionally proposes fights in this way—it's not the role of a judge, really, is it? But when he does, there's excitement. This boy is a little shorter than me, sandy-haired, compact. His face is bland and I know with a jolt in my belly that he'll be good, probably better than Markham. Salad has put me on the spot, but happily I'm spoiling for a fight. I step forward with a readiness that's very like a thrill for blood. I don't know him, I may never see him again, but I want badly to hurt him in unusual ways with my sticks. Break his wrist or knock out his front teeth. Around us, as we prepare, lots of younger boys, tens and elevens. A trio of Malick's friends hang about too.

We both take time to limber up. For me it's a chance to study my opponent. With a signal, the judge gets us going. Sandy hair comes right in, quick as mercury, and hits my knuckles, surprisingly hard. He does not dance back and we spar up close so my longer reach is a disadvantage. He manages to catch my other knuckles. He's done something to his sticks, this one; they are somehow very hard. Being hit twice so quickly calms me. I'm sweating already and my mind is blank save for a desire to humble this boy. His quickness is at least equal to mine, I think, without dismay. I don't know that he'll tire before me either; my stomach is a pit and my vision blurs round the edges. I should've eaten something, but that's not a thought for the present. The next time he launches an attack I go back at him equally hard. His right hand is a little weaker, his ripostes less certain on that side, so I force him to retreat with Orcrist, trying to double his wrist back on itself. He sidles away, but I follow, banging his elbow. He tries to reply and succeeds in getting his right hand free. The crowd has been quiet, and as we take a moment to breathe, it feels like we all take in air together. This time when he closes with me, Mormegil keeps him away, but I cannot do this for long and I only want him to think I'm tired. He is cautious too—his elbow is likely giving him pain and he teases me with his left hand, batting at Mormegil. I launch myself at him once more, feeling like I did against Markham, that it is now or never. I'm not sure what I'll do, but I feel confident enough to respond to anything. He's quick as lightning and rash—going for the eyes when he could have thumped my knuckles again. But he's in close once more and we trade blow and parry until my arms feel they might fall from my shoulders and my breathing fills my ears. I force him to aim a blow at my ribs, leaving my left side open, knowing he'll take the opening. It stings—I feel the skin redden almost instantly—and I drop to one knee, reeling a little bit. He pauses—he lacks the killer instinct—one stick above his shoulder; the other is pointed at me to ward off any blow that may come. But my stroke is aimed once again at the knee, too low for his block, and I lunge rather than swing, to jab him full on the ball of his kneecap, twisting Orcrist—not Mormegil—to cause more pain. He stumbles back, almost dropping a stick as he hops to clasp his injured knee. Mormegil comes up as I shoot up off my own knee like it's a launch pad though it hurts like hell to do that. I pull my stroke at the last second, grudgingly.

There's something in his eyes—he's not afraid—but I see recognition beyond fear—and acceptance of what I'm about to do, of what I am.

Killer. I pull the blow, or push it rather so I miss his temple—the thought flashes through me, through my entire body like a lash, that I don't know this boy and can't kill him. Mormegil lacerates his ear instead. And having changed the stroke, I drop my stick. My knuckles sear again as if in sympathy with him. And I breathe once more, like a bellows, exhausted and desperate suddenly to sit. Sandy hair still clutches his knee, ignoring his torn ear. He's on the ground now in agony and my sorrow is complete. Salad eyes me gravely, but I can't abide his eyes on mine; there's only shame in this win. It takes all my willpower to not leave Orcrist and Mormegil as I walk off. Part of me notices—and is bitter—that no one chooses to follow me, to ask what's wrong.

I feel shunned, but the dump is actually a big place and boys here have enough of a struggle to survive not to worry over someone feeling down. I cannot find Lapy and even the lazy search of a day does not turn him up. Hunger attacks my insides suddenly and I hunt for food for hours. I even leave the dump to see what can be scavenged outside. I take Mormegil, tucked under my clothes—for protection. The fearful looks, the clutched purses of the outside are somehow welcome, an escape from loneliness. At least I'm noticed. People on the outside are scared of me but not because I fight sticks. I'm an urchin, a snot-faced, scuffed boy in rags that they want to pity but can't. I stuff my head with stale old chicken and bacon cadged from a greasy restaurant and go back to the dump, hating and enjoying the nervous looks.

When I can't take any more loneliness, I decide to go and find him, the one I nearly killed. That's how I think of him, and I can't shut him out of my thoughts. I'm resolved to go and see how he is. To explain myself. Perhaps to even say sorry, even though I don't know what for. The thing is, I don't know where he stays, perhaps he's not even a dump kid. I ask boys I know and even boys I don't, describing him, hoping they saw the fight. I get a jumble of answers; short sandy-haired boys are a dime a dozen anywhere, I suppose. I give up, then bump into him as I go in search of Lapy once more, just to keep active. He's practicing with some mates. They stop as I draw near. He gives me an almost friendly nod, though I notice his eyes are guarded, like when a madman's in the room. Talking is an effort, my tongue feels thick and ashy, and I have to ask him for a word twice before he understands. We go some way away and he makes a show of dropping his sticks, to impress his friends, I suspect. I conceal my smile.

I say it all at once, afraid to stop even for breath: "Look, I don't even know your name, and I'm not sure this will come out the right way, but I just wanted to say sorry. It was a good fight, you're a good fighter. I know what I did wasn't technically illegal, but I feel an apology is needed." I wrestle down the urge to go on. Laconic Lapy. I must be like him. Like the Spartans too. Sandy hair thrusts his hand at me like we've just played tennis or some other cruddy gentlemanly sport. There are no bruises on him; the ear looks whole. For an instant I think I imagined the whole thing.

"Tuor," he introduces himself. I smile again but not with relief, with real amusement. He's no Tuor. Salad's stories! "It was even steven," he continues. "A good fight like you said, and I would've done the same in your place." And abruptly as that there's nothing left to say for either of us. I try to give him a smile that's not so grateful, friendlier, before I swivel and make off. The clacking of sticks starts up again immediately and I feel less guilty.

Days pass before I pick up my sticks again. When I do, I have a strange sense that it's not me that swings Mormegil or stabs with Orcrist, but some unseen beast that slips into me. The feeling leaves me quite numb. I try to explain it to Lapy, but he looks at me as if I've lost my marbles. He's not afraid to practice with me though, our friendship is the same. I neither avoid Markham nor seek him out, but he's in my thoughts. Concede to Markham, give up this whole racket, my ambitions as a stickfighter, pass Mormegil on to some eight-year-old coming up, and do something less deadly, less emotionally sapping. That's what part of me feels. I, too, could lose an eye, or be killed.

It rains for what feels like a week and the dump is in wretched mood. There's nothing to do all day but take shelter. I experience strange exhilarations, tire myself with mad quests that keep me out in the rain. Lapy doesn't try to settle me down; he's known me too long. The morning of the third day, I wake shivering, still muddy and wet from the evening before, and with both sticks clenched in my left fist like a lifeline. Lapy gives me water, tries to swaddle me but I'm already too hot. I'm also too weak to push off the stinking kerosene-smelling blanket which suffocates me. I wake from dreams in which the sandy-haired Tuor sets me alight with a burning stick. Other boys I have fought look on, bored rather than excited.

When I wake properly, the sun peers thinly through high clouds. I smell smoke somewhere not far off, but the sight and warmth of the sun is rousing enough. Lapy has left me, likely in disgust at my screams and moans. I'm surprised at how steady I feel on my feet. Awake, I remember that Salad was also in my fever dreams and I'm suddenly dying to know what he wanted to tell me when he came to watch me practice. But first I wander aimlessly, hoping for water and perhaps a bite. I know where I can sometimes get food from someone. Not a stickfighter, but he's so good at scavenging he doesn't care if we steal from him. Sometimes.

I'm ravenous and tear at some bread so fresh it must be from yesterday, and not crust either. I've seen virtually no one but a radio is playing nearby, a warbly song I recognize but can't put a name to. I sit next to the scavenger's sleeping den long after I've wolfed his food, somehow more wobbly from having eaten. I stand, and there he is. Tauzin—I think, watching me smugly. He's a lanky, knobbly thing, all bony knees and thrust-out elbows, not at all tough so I don't expect him to try anything.

He speaks before I can thank him. "That bread was poisoned. I left it as bait for whoever's been stealing my stuff. Rat poison," he adds unnecessarily. "Bet you didn't know I was a master poisoner. Had no idea it was you, but I don't care really. You might not even die." He's talking too much, yabbering on as though we're in a classroom somewhere, or mates, and what he says really matters. I stick my hand down my craw, squeezing my fingers into a point and forcing them as hard as I can past my gullet. He stops, stunned, and I aim the flood of mush that comes spurting out at him even though he's not stupid, he stopped and stood about ten feet away. A second smaller gush of puke rises, and now I'm sure it's all out. I smile.

"Too late," he tells me, but he's no longer so cool, and not just because I took him by surprise emptying my stomach. No, he's shitless now 'cause I'm advancing on him, both sticks suddenly, magically, in my left hand, a trick I've practiced loads to get really good at. He backs up a couple of steps, shuffling as though he'll wet himself if he lifts his feet.

"The poison's already working on your system."

"I've plenty of time to kill you though." I don't mean the words; I just want to scare him. I've no idea if he's actually poisoned me, but as I utter the threat, I know with certainty I'll carry it through. No one's around and this sniveling rat of a poisoner doesn't deserve such a quick end as he'll get. If I am poisoned, I'll be too weak later, too doubled-over in pain to kill him.

It's done almost quicker than thought. He turns to run but his long legs are more hindrance than use and I trip him easily, kicking one foot against the other. He falls like a rag doll, making no effort to keep on his feet, and it's contempt at this weakness that sets my arm in motion. Standing bent over him, I swing the two sticks in my left hand easily, a bit like a golfer, I think, and hard enough that wind whistles through the tiny space between Orcrist and Mormegil. The strike is precise enough to kill; I feel the rubbery give of his temple beneath the tip of my sticks. But once more shame comes on me, so suddenly I taste it mingling with the acid of vomit. I walk away without checking that he's dead. I feel weak again, the return of a fever.

A strange wind comes up that doesn't stir the bushes but pulls at my shorts, keens to me like a dead baby. I stand, clutching my head, afraid I'll fall if I try to walk. The dump suddenly doesn't seem empty after all. Boys are skulking all about, may even have seen me kill Tauzin, and they're just waiting for the right moment to ambush me. I would take one or two of them with me, and the certainty steadies me slightly. After some minutes, I begin walking again, with purpose. To find someone who never moves from his spot.

Aias is awake but looks like he's about to die; his eyes are gummy and he holds as ever the tell-tale plastic bottle in his dainty fingers. Aias looks like shit, but his smile is that of a boy who loves the world. He used to be one of the very best stickfighters. One of only two legends we have in the dump. There are almost as many stories about him as about Turin. A champion with two sticks or with a single one. You were lucky if Aias fought you with a single stick; very good if he used two. It was before my time, though Aias cannot be older than 17. His smile is jolly, but only if you don't look too closely. He has all his teeth, but they are very nearly black, the gums too.

"Aias," I whisper. It seems rude to speak normally around him, to disturb the sleepy peace of glue life. "Aias. Got any glue?" It takes him an eon to look at me, to turn one muddy and one clear eye towards me. He's got the trembles. I wish I had food to offer him. The hand he extends shakes uncontrollably. He's never selfish with his glue. Involuntarily, I wipe the bottle mouth with my shirt, suck on it hard. There's not much left, barely any in fact. I suck a minute, taking small breaths through my nose and watching Aias turn his head as though it's buried in a slurry of mud. I feel a mixture of pity and stomping contempt before the warmth invades my mouth and throat. It would be easy to kill him, end his half-life, easier even than with Tauzin. I wouldn't even have to use my sticks, he's like a twig. One wrench would snap his neck. Up close, his happy smile seems more a grin of pain. Glue's supposed to be a happy drug. It warms you, it's true, it's a help on cold nights. But it makes me think of blood. I get a bit twitchy on glue, my mind's full of gore. The longer you do it, the more it kills the brain, rots it, or those bits of the brain that make you fight. I suck so hard I get a headache with my warm feeling. I hand the bottle back to him, trying not to gag at his stink. His feet are dotted with yellow shit specks. I walk away with a muzzy head, concentrating on putting one foot in front of the other and clutching at the warmth spreading all the way to my fingertips. It feels like a layer on my skin and yet it's gotten beneath the surface at the same time, sending rays into my bones.

I almost bump heads with Markham. He steps back a pace as if to get a good look, says "you have your sticks, good. Salad thinks we should do a rematch." I think my answering nod is calm, but he has a bad habit of catching me off guard. He spins and walks ahead. I follow, his two friends moving in to flank me so it feels like I have an honor guard. I clutch my sticks in anticipation. Markham's own sticks hang from the loops of his shorts; he looks ridiculous.

If anything, I start to feel warmer as I walk. When we find Salad my headache is gone. I'm swollen with energy, and even more eager than usual. More boys draw up. Salad has a few words with us, in a stern tone. He's tireder than ever, and coughs hoarsely. His voice is normal and his muscles have the same rubbery, hard look they always do. For the first time I notice he and I are almost the same height. His words bleed out of his mouth, I think because of the glue, and I hear nothing of what he says. I need to release the force building inside me. I can't let it escape before I finish Markham, and I know I will. Snarls echo in my head. Markham will never again challenge me.

I don't limber up; Markham eyes me, perhaps taking note of my confidence. I stand still to avoid wasting the killing essence in me; I don't want it to escape.

So that when Salad gives the signal I go for Markham harder, I think, than I've ever gone for anyone. He's ready though, and our sticks swirl faster and more intricately than I've seen in some time. A trick of the glue makes them catch alight. My limbs are weightless and Mormegil, like its namesake, is keen to drink. No wrist blows, no knuckle raps. I go for his throat and he aims for my head. He'll tire before my supercharged arms so I swing and swing, using a good deal of my strength in each stroke. He sweats, I am dry and I watch his eyes dart about trying to follow my sticks.

He doesn't give ground, I admire that. I'm pressed up almost against him and not once does he hunt for space. But I have cunning too, and when the glue in my veins gives me the signal, I switch tactics. I swing with Orcrist a second too slowly, and he rises to the bait. His parry becomes harder, faster, he drives at my neck. I slip the blow, stepping back and aside, tilting my head ever so slightly so that it misses me. He tries to recover—he's almost as quick as I am—but there's time for me to smash the top of his earlobe, to parry his own return stroke and aim Mormegil's tip at his throat. Let the beast slake its thirst. He dives backward to escape, almost as though he's been hit. He thinks I'll give him time to regain his footing, but I don't. Instead I'm on him, and on his back he tries to sweep my leg with his foot just as I stab again, for his groin. Mormegil catches the inside of his thigh—the twisty fucker—and before I can strike again, with perfect accuracy this time, Salad's arm is in front of me, a barrier of muscle the size of my head. "Fight over," he announces, his voice coming from a long way off. "Raul wins." My skin tingles with the remains of the glue's warmth. My arms, my body still hum with unused force. I close my eyes a second for calm but I cannot turn away. What happens must. I start to swing before my eyes open, I feel bold, so ready. The judge blocks with his forearm, as if he expects this. It must sting like hell even wrapped in muscle like that. His eyes are on mine without expression, but the watching boys release a gasp of shock. I smile. They do not know it, but I'm freeing them from the tyranny of authority. My next blow follows so hard on the heels of the first that Salad cannot possibly counter, and he doesn't. To his credit, he only falls to one knee; I expected a hit on the temple would end him. Stunned, he's at the right height now for me to use maximum power and I hit him again cleanly across the nose. He keels forward not even putting out his hands to catch himself. I give him a chance to roll onto his back, but before I can pick my next spot, another blow lands. Markham's. He hits the judge's knee, a downward chop like an axe stroke, and then pokes at his crotch with the other stick. A spasm crosses Salad's face, the first one. He pulls himself into a ball, his knees up as I stab for his eyes. Markham is circling, looking for an opening, and it's like we're the only two alive in that place, the other boys are all frozen, so still as to be almost empty shells. Markham thrusts into his other eye and Salad's face splashes blood. He still makes no sound.

I'd dreamed of a killing blow, the single cut that cleanly ends life, but I've done that already, with Tauzin earlier. It was sweet. But now's not the time for precision. I swing and thrust, mindlessly raining blows, and Markham is with me, shares my aim for we club at the judge's head with no thought for accuracy. Even when he no longer moves, Markham and I swing for some minutes. Then I stop.

Hitting Budapest

NoViolet Bulawayo—winner of the 2011 Caine Prize

We are on our way to Budapest: Bastard and Chipo and Godknows and Sbho and Stina and me. We are going even though we are not allowed to cross Mzilikazi Road, even though Bastard is supposed to be watching his little sister Fraction, even though Mother would kill me dead if she found out; we are going. There are guavas to steal in Budapest, and right now I'd die for guavas, or anything for that matter. My stomach feels like somebody just took a shovel and dug everything out.

Getting out of Paradise is not so hard since the mothers are busy with hair and talk. They just glance at us when we file past and then look away. We don't have to worry about the men under the jacaranda either since their eyes never lift from the draughts. Only the little kids see us and want to follow, but Bastard just wallops the naked one at the front with a fist on his big head and they all turn back.

We are running when we hit the bush; Bastard at the front because he won country-game today and he thinks he rules, and then me and Godknows, Stina, and finally Chipo, who used to outrun everybody in Paradise but not any more because her grandfather made her pregnant. After crossing Mzilikazi, we slither through another bush, gallop along Hope Street past the big stadium with the glimmering benches we'll never sit on. Finally we hit Budapest. We have to stop once for Chipo to rest.

"When are you going to have the baby, anyway?" Bastard says.

Bastard doesn't like it when we have to stop for her. He even tried to get us not to play with her altogether.

"I'll have it one day."

"What's one day? Tomorrow? Thursday? Next week?"

"Can't you see her stomach is still small? The baby has to grow."

"A baby grows outside. That's the reason they are born. So they grow."

"Well, it's not time yet. That's why it's still a stomach."

"Is it a boy or girl?"

"It's a boy. The first baby is supposed to be a boy."

"But you're a girl and you're a first-born."

"I said supposed."

"You. Shut your mouth, it's not even your stomach."

"I think it's a girl. I don't feel it kicking."

"Boys kick and punch and butt their heads."

"Do you want a boy?"

"No. Yes. Maybe. I don't know."

"Where exactly does a baby come out of?"

"From the same way it gets into the stomach."

"How exactly does it get into the stomach?"

"First, God has to put it in there."

"No, not God. A man has to put it in there, my cousin Musa told me. Didn't your grandfather put it in there, Chipo?"

She nods.

"Then if a man put it in there, why doesn't he take it out?"

"Because it's women who give birth, big-head. That's why they have breasts to suckle the baby."

"But Chipo's breasts are small. Like stones."

"They will grow when the baby comes. Isn't it, Chipo?"

"I don't want my breasts to grow. I don't want a baby. I don't want anything, just guavas," Chipo says, and takes off. We run after her, and when we get right in the middle of Budapest, we stop. Budapest is like a different country. A country where people who are not like us live.

But not an ordinary country—it looks like everybody woke up one day and closed their gates, doors and windows, picked up their passports, and left for better countries. Even the air is empty; no burning things, no smell of cooking food or something rotting; just plain air with nothing in its hands.

Budapest is big, big houses with the graveled yards and tall fences and durawalls and flowers and green trees, heavy with fruit that's waiting for us since nobody around here seems to know what fruit is for. It's the fruit that gives us courage, otherwise we wouldn't dare be here. I keep expecting the streets to spit and tell us to go back to the shanty.

We used to steal from Chipo's uncle's tree, but that was not *stealing* stealing. Now we have finished all the guavas in his tree so we have moved to strangers' houses. We have stolen from so many, I cannot even count. It's Godknows who decided that we pick a street and stay on it until we have gone through all the houses. Then we go to the next street. This is so we do not confuse where we have been with where we are going. It's like a pattern, and Godknows says this way we can be better thieves.

Today we start a new street and so we carefully scout around. We pass SADC Street, where we already harvested every guava tree two weeks ago. We see white curtains part and a face peer from a window of the cream home with the statue of a urinating boy with wings. We stand and stare, looking to see what the face will do, when the window opens and a small voice shouts for us to stop. We remain standing, not because the voice told us to stop, but because none of us has started to run, and because the voice does not sound dangerous. Music pours out of the window onto the street; it's not *kwaito*, it's not dance hall, it's not anything we know.

A tall, thin woman opens the door and comes out of the house. She is eating something, and she waves as she walks toward us. Already we can tell from the woman's thinness that we are not even going to run. We wait for her, so we can see what she is smiling for, or at; nobody really ever smiles at us in Paradise. Except Mother of Bones, who smiles at anything. The woman stops at the gate; it's locked, and she didn't bring the keys to open it.

"Jeez, I can't stand the heat, and the hard earth, how do you guys ever do it?" the woman asks in her not-dangerous voice. She takes a bite of the thing in her hand, and smiles. A nice, pink camera dangles from her neck. We all look at the woman's feet peeking out from underneath her long skirt. They are clean and pretty feet, like a baby's. She is wiggling her toes. I don't remember my own feet ever looking like that, maybe when I was born.

Then I look up at the woman's red, chewing mouth. I can tell from the vein at the side of her neck, and the way she smacks her big lips, that what she is eating tastes good. I look closely at her long hand, at the thing she is eating. It is fat, and the outer part is crusty. The top looks creamy and soft, and there are coin-like things on it, a deep pink, the color of burn wounds. I also see sprinkles of red and green and yellow, and finally the brown bumps, like pimples.

"What's that?" Chipo asks, pointing at the thing with one hand and rubbing her stomach with the other. Now that she is pregnant, Chipo likes to play with her stomach every time she talks. The stomach is the size of a soccer ball, not too big. We all look at the woman's mouth and wait to hear what she will say.

"Oh, this? It's a camera," the woman says, which we know. She wipes her hand on her skirt and pats the camera. She then aims what is left of the thing at the bin by the door, misses, and laughs, but I don't see anything funny. The woman looks at us, like maybe she wants us to laugh since she is laughing, but we are busy looking at the thing, flying in the air like a dead bird before hitting the ground. We have never seen anyone throw food away. I look sideways at Chipo.

"How old are you?" the woman says to Chipo, looking at her stomach like she has never seen anybody pregnant.

But Chipo is not even listening, she is busy looking at the thing lying there on the ground.

"She is ten," Godknows replies for Chipo. "We are nine, me and her, like twinses," Godknows says, meaning him and me. "And Bastard is eleven and Sbho is eight, and Stina we don't know."

"Wow," the woman says, playing with her camera.

"And how old are you?" Godknows asks her. "And where are you from?" I'm thinking about how Godknows talks too much.

"Me? Well, I'm 33, and I'm from London. This is my first time visiting my dad's country."

"I ate some sweets from London once. Uncle Polite sent them when he first got there, but that was a long time ago. Now he doesn't even write," Godknows says. The woman's twisted mouth finishes chewing. I swallow with her.

"You look fifteen, like a child," Godknows says. I am expecting the woman to slap Godknows's big mouth for saying that, but then she only laughs like she has been told something to be proud of.

"Thank you," she says. I look at her like what is there to thank? and then at the others, and I know they think the woman is strange too. She runs a hand in her hair, which looks matted and dirty; if I lived in Budapest I would wash my whole body every day and comb my hair nicely to show I was a real person living in a real place.

"Do you guys mind if I take a picture?"

We do not answer because we are not used to adults asking us anything; we just look at the woman take a few steps back, at her fierce hair, at her skirt that sweeps the ground when she walks, at her pretty peeking feet, at her big jewelry, at her large eyes, at her smooth brown skin that doesn't even have a scar to show she is a living person, at the earring on her nose, at her T-shirt that says "Save Darfur."

"Come on, say cheese, say cheese, cheese, cheeeeeeeese," the woman enthuses, and everyone says "cheese." Myself, I don't really say, because I am busy trying to remember what cheese means exactly, and I cannot remember. Yesterday Mother of Bones told us the story of Dudu the bird, who learned and sang a new song whose words she did not really know the meaning of, and was caught, killed, and cooked for dinner because in the song she was actually begging people to kill and cook her.

The woman points at me, nods, and tells me to say "cheeeeeese" and I say it because she is smiling like she knows me really well. I say it slowly at first, and then I say, "cheese" and "cheese," and I'm saying "cheese cheeeeese" and everyone is saying "cheese cheese cheese" and we are all singing the word and the camera is clicking and clicking and clicking. Then Stina, who never really speaks, just starts and walks away.

The woman stops taking pictures and says, "Are you okay?" but Stina does not stop. Then Chipo walks away after Stina, rubbing her stomach, then the rest of us all walk away after them.

We leave the woman standing there, taking pictures. Bastard

stops at the corner of SADC and starts shouting insults at her, and I remember the thing, and that she threw it away without even asking us if we wanted it, and I begin shouting too, and everyone else joins in. We shout and we shout and we shout; we want to eat the thing she was eating, we want to make noise in Budapest, we want our hunger to go away. The woman just looks at us, puzzled, and hurries back into the house and we shout after her still. We get hoarse shouting. Our throats itch. When the woman closes her door and disappears, we stop and slowly walk away to find guavas.

Bastard says when we grow up we will stop stealing guavas and move to bigger things inside the houses. When that time comes, I'll not even be here; I'll be living in America with Aunt Fostalina, doing better things. But for now, the guavas. We decide on IMF Street, on a white house so big it looms like a mountain. In front is a large swimming pool, empty chairs all around it.

The good thing with this pretty house is that the mountain is set far back in the yard, and our guavas are right within reach, as if they heard we were coming and ran out to meet us. It doesn't take long to climb over the durawall, onto the tree, and fill our plastic bags with bull guavas. These ones are big, like a man's fist, and do not ripen to yellow like the regular guavas; they stay green on the outside, pink and fluffy on the inside. They taste so good I cannot even explain it.

* * *

Going back to Paradise, we do not run. We walk nicely like Budapest is now our country, eating guavas along the way and spitting the peels all over to make the place dirty. We stop at the corner of AU Street for Chipo to vomit. Today her vomit looks like urine, but thicker. We leave it there, uncovered.

"One day I will live here, in a house just like that," Sbho says, biting a thick guava. She looks to the left and points to a big blue house with the long row of steps, flowers all around it. Her voice sounds like she knows what she is talking about.

"How are you going to do that?" I ask.

Sbho spits peels on the street and says, with her big eyes, "I just know it."

"She is going to do it in her dreams," Bastard says to the sun, and throws a guava at the durawall of Sbho's house. The guava explodes and stains the wall pink. I bite into a sweet guava. I don't like grinding the bull guava seeds especially because they are tough and it takes a long time to do, so I just grind them gently, sometimes swallow them whole even though I know what will happen.

"Why did you do that?" Sbho looks at the now-dirty durawall of her house, and then at Bastard. Bastard giggles, throws another guava. It misses the wall but hits the gate. The gate does not make noise like a real gate is supposed to.

"Because I can. Because I can do what I want. Besides, what does it matter?"

"Because you just heard me say I like the house, so you are not supposed to do anything to it. Why don't you pick another house that I don't care about?"

"Well, that doesn't make it your house, does it?" Bastard wears a black tracksuit bottom that he never takes off, and a faded orange T-shirt that says "Cornell." He takes off the Cornell T-shirt, ties it over his head, and I don't know if it makes him look ugly or pretty, if he really looks like a man or woman. He turns and starts walking backwards so he can walk facing Sbho. He always likes that whomever he is quarreling with look right at him. He has beaten us all, except Stina.

"And besides, Budapest is not a toilet where anyone can just walk in. You can never live here."

"I'm going to marry a man from Budapest. He'll take me away from Paradise, away from the shacks and Heavenway and Fambeki and everything else," Sbho says.

"Ha ha. You think a man will marry you with your missing teeth? I wouldn't even marry you myself," says Godknows, shouting over his shoulder.

He and Chipo and Stina walk ahead of us. I look at Godknows' shorts, torn at the back, at his pitch-black buttocks peeping like strange eyes through the dirty white fabric.

"I'm not talking to you, big-head!" Sbho shouts at Godknows. "Besides, my teeth will grow back. Mother says I will even be more beautiful, too!"

Godknows flings his hand and makes a "whatever" sign because he has nothing to say to that. Everybody knows that Sbho is pretty, prettier than all of us here, prettier than all the children in Paradise. Sometimes we refuse to play with her if she won't stop talking like we don't already know it.

"Well, I don't care, I'm going out of the country myself. I will make a lot of money and come back and buy a house in this very Budapest or Los Angeles, even Paris," Bastard says.

"When we were going to school, my teacher, Mr. Gono, said you need an education to make money, that's what he said, my own teacher." Chipo rubs her stomach, and says Mr. Gono's name so proudly like he is her own father, like he is something special, like maybe it's him inside her stomach.

"And how will you do that when we are not going to school?" Chipo adds.

"I don't need school to make money. What Bible did you read that from, huh?" Bastard screams at Chipo, bringing his face close to hers like he will bite her nose off. Chipo caresses her stomach and eats the rest of her guava quietly. She walks faster, away from us.

"I'm going to America to live with my Aunt Fostalina; it won't be long, you'll see," I say, raising my voice so they can all hear. I start on a brand new guava; it is so sweet I finish it in just three bites. I don't even bother chewing the seeds.

"America is too far," Bastard says, bored. "I don't want to go anywhere where I have to go by air. What if you get stuck there and you can't come back? Me, I'm going to South Africa or Botswana. That way, when things get bad, I can just get on the road without talking to anybody; you have to be able to easily return from wherever you go."

I look at Bastard and think what to say to him. A guava seed is stuck between my gum and my last side teeth and I try to reach for it with my tongue. I finally use my finger. It tastes like earwax.

"America is far," Chipo says, agreeing with Bastard. She stops briefly, her hand under her stomach, so we can catch up with her. "What if something happens to your plane when you are in it? What about the terrorists?"

I think fat-face, soccer-ball-stomach Chipo is only saying it to please ugly-face Bastard since he just screamed at her. I give her a talking eye, but my mouth just keeps chewing.

"I don't care, I'm going," I say, and walk fast to catch up with Godknows and Stina because I know where the talk will end if Chipo and Bastard gang up on me.

"Well, go, go to that America and work in nursing homes and clean poop. You think we have never heard the stories!" Bastard screams to my back, but I just keep walking.

I think about turning right around and beating Bastard up for saying that about my America. I would slap him, butt him on his big forehead, and then slam my fist into his mouth and make him spit his teeth. I would pound his stomach until he vomited all the guavas he has eaten, pin him to the ground. I would jab my knee into his back, fold his hands behind him and then pull his head back till he begged for his life. But I shut up and walk away. I know he is just jealous. Because he has nobody in America. Because Aunt Fostalina is not his aunt. Because he is Bastard and I am Darling.

* * *

By the time we get back to Paradise the guavas are finished and our stomachs are so full we are almost crawling. We will just drink water for the night, listen to Mother of Bones tell us a story, and go to sleep. We stop to defecate in the bush. It is best to do so before it gets too dark, otherwise no one will accompany you; you have to pass the cemetery to get to the bush and you might meet a ghost.

We all find places, and me, I squat behind a rock. This is the worst part about guavas; all those seeds get you constipated when you eat too much. When it comes to defecating, we get in so much pain, like trying to give birth to a country. Minutes and minutes and minutes pass and nobody shouts, "I'm done, hurry up."

We are all squatting like that, in our different places, and I'm beating my thighs with fists to make a cramp go away when somebody screams. Not the kind of scream that comes from when you push too hard and a guava seed cuts your anus; it says "come and see," so I stop pushing, pull up my underwear and abandon my rock. And there, squatting and screaming, is Godknows. He is also pointing ahead in the thick trees, and we see it, a tall thing dangling in a tree.

"What's that?" somebody, I don't know who, whispers. Nobody answers because now we can all see what it is. A woman dangles from a green rope. The sun squeezes through the leaves, and gives everything a strange color that makes the woman's light skin glow like there are red-hot coals inside her.

The woman's thin arms hang limp at the sides, and her hands and feet point to the ground, like somebody drew her there, a straight line hanging in the air. Her eyes are the scariest part, they look too white, and her mouth is open wide. The woman is wearing a yellow dress, and the grass licks the tip of her shoes.

"Let's run," Stina says. They are the first words Stina has spoken since country-game. When Stina speaks, you know it's something important, and I get ready to run.

"Coward, can't you see she's hanged herself and now she's dead?" Bastard picks a stone and throws; it hits the woman on the thigh. I expect something will happen, but then nothing does, the woman just does not move.

"See, I told you she is dead." Bastard says, in that voice he uses when he is reminding us who is the boss.

"God will punish you for that," Godknows says.

Bastard throws another stone. It hits the woman on the leg with a *khu* sound. The woman still does not move.

I am terrified; it is like she is looking at me from the corner of her white, popped eye. Looking and waiting for me to do something, I don't know what.

"God does not live here, idiot," Bastard says. He throws another stone that only grazes the woman's yellow dress, and I am glad he missed.

"I will go and tell my mother," Sbho says, sounding like she wants to cry. Stina starts to leave, and Sbho and Godknows and I follow him. Bastard stays behind for a little while, but when I look over my shoulder, I see him right there behind us. I know he can't stay in the bush by himself, with a dead woman, even though he wants to make like he is the president of Paradise. We start walking together again, but then Bastard jumps in front of us.

"Wait, who wants bread?" he says, tightening the Cornell T-shirt on his head. I look at the wound on Bastard's chest, just below his left breast. It's almost pink, like the inside of a guava.

"Where is it?" I say.

"Listen, did you notice how that woman's shoes look almost new? If we can get them then we can sell them and buy a loaf, or maybe even one-and-a-half. What do you say?"

We all turn around and follow Bastard back into the bush, and we are rushing, then we are running, then we are running and laughing and laughing and laughing.

Bombay's Republic

Rotimi Babatunde—winner of the 2012 Caine Prize

The old jailhouse on the hilltop had remained uninhabited for many decades, through the construction of the town's first grammar school and the beginning of house-to-house harassment from the affliction called sanitary inspectors, through the laying of the railway tracks by navvies who likewise succeeded in laying pregnancies in the bellies of several lovestruck girls, but fortunes changed for the building with the return of Color Sergeant Bombay, the veteran who went off with the recruitment officers to Hitler's War as a man and came back a spotted leopard.

Before Bombay's departure, when everything in the world was locked in its individual box, he could not have believed such metamorphosis was possible. A man was still a man and a leopard a leopard while the old jailhouse was a forsaken place not fit for human habitation. A white man was the District Officer who went by in an impressive white jacket and a black man was the Native Police constable who saluted as the white man passed. This was how the world was and there was no reason to think it could be otherwise. But the war came and the bombs started falling, shattering things out of their imprisonment in boxes and jumbling them without logic into a protean mishmash. Without warning, everything became possible.

* * *

Months preceding the arrival of the military bands, news had been filtering in that the foreign powers were clawing at each other's throats. In the papers, there were cartoons showing how bad things would be if Hitler won. Posters appeared all over town encouraging the young men to enlist and then the recruitment officers showed up accompanied by drum majors who conducted smartly uniformed bands through the streets. Unmoved by the marching songs and colorful banners flying above the parades, not a single volunteer stepped out. Shrugging, people just said, the gecko and the lizard may decide to get married, fine for them, but it would be silly for the butterfly to dance its garments to shreds at their wedding celebration. The next day, traditional drums accompanied the bands to rouse enthusiasm, but this also failed to inspire, and speculations became rife that conscription would be used as in some other places. But that was not to be because reports came that Hitler himself was waiting with his ruthless army at the border and that, with him, things were going to be much worse than the imagination could conceive. Those he didn't pressgang into slavery would be roasted alive for consumption by his beloved dogs, this was the word on the street, and panic began spreading with virulent haste.

* * *

When the bugle sounded and Bombay woke with a jerk in the darkness, he didn't know where he was or what on earth he was doing there. The space in which he found himself was too large to be his bedroom. Its array of double bunks stretching away into the dimness was spooky in the waning moonlight and the shrouded figures rousing on the bunks seemed like creatures materializing out of a bad dream. The bugle sounded once more and it all came flooding back to Bombay, the long truck ride from his hometown with the other recruits and the thickness of the dust on their bodies and, on arrival at the camp, the granite face of the warrant officer who supervised the distribution of kits to the lost-looking recruits. Bombay's joints still ached from the rattling of the wooden floorboard where he had sat, cramped with his colleagues in the truck's rear like livestock huddling together for warmth. He didn't wait for the third and final bugle before jumping down from his bed.

That was the beginning of his first day at training camp.

He went mechanically through the warm-up exercises and completed the arduous challenge of the roadwork. After a quick breakfast, he stood ramrod stiff as the drill sergeant moved between the files barking instructions. Later that day, with his muscles sore and his head throbbing from the day's long exertions, it suddenly struck him that he liked it. Everything in military life was clear and ordered. That was what he wanted and he found nothing more satisfactory.

At dinner time, listening to the recruits drawn from distant places on the continent speaking a plethora of languages he did not know existed, Bombay marveled at his superior officers' ability to whip that Babel with just a few commands into a single martial unit. As he continued eating, the polyglot buzz of impenetrable speech swirled on around the dining hall without unleashing bedlam, contrary to what Bombay would have predicted. There are many things I know nothing of in this world, Bombay exhaled as he shoveled another spoonful of barracks mess into his mouth. Things he never knew were possible.

* * *

Bombay had to like Ceylon, if only because it provided an escape from the nausea. In the weeks at sea, he had vomited so much he would have loved any land, but the coconut-dotted beaches of Ceylon and the bullock carts plodding down the lanes and the monkeys that sneaked into their base to dash off with whatever was not secured made Bombay's fondness for the island easier.

The recruits had completed their basic training before setting sail. On disembarking, they began preparations for jungle combat. Their base was in a village just outside Colombo. The training at the village was good. As the recruits jogged past, the women picking leaves in the tea estates would stop to look. Every evening a cart brought down containers of coconut wine for the soldiers to drink and, sometimes, Bombay dared the local gin that tasted fierier than gasoline.

Bombay did not mind that the baths were segregated, one for the African soldiers and another for the Europeans. The village headman often came around when the men were bathing. As the days went by, the crowd that came with him grew larger. The visitors always headed straight to scrutinize the Africans as they washed but never bothered to check out the lathering Europeans. It was then Bombay became puzzled about what was going on. He made enquiries and was assured that the villagers meant no harm. Reports had come that the pants of the African soldiers were sewn three-quarter length to conceal their tails and the headman was bringing his villagers to confirm if this was the case. Bombay was not angry. He simply found it interesting people could assume he had a tail. The chance of anyone having such a belief was something he had not considered possible.

* * *

Bombay's discoveries of the possible would come faster than the leeches in Burma's crepuscular jungles. At first, Bombay's tasks were limited to mule driving and porting baggage. If there are people trying to kill me, it would be stupid of me not to be in a position to kill them also, he repeatedly grumbled to his superiors. To shut him up, he was posted to a combat unit.

The campaign to recapture Buthidaung was in progress. Bombay's unit was deployed to a swampy pass of the Kaladan Valley where they got isolated from the main army for weeks. Their situation got dire and it seemed they would have to feed on wild bananas lined with pawpaw-like seeds but tasting like detergent. Then Bombay's squad ran into enemy ambush. They had no option but to dive for cover as hostile gunfire reduced the vegetation above their heads to shreds. Their ammunitions had already gone too low to mount a credible resistance but Bombay thought it wiser to go down fighting and his squad agreed. They charged shrieking at the machine-gun position with pangas raised, their common howling and bawling coming as if from a primeval horde of lunatics hell-bent on murder. The firing stopped. Perhaps a freakish mistake damaged the enemy's equipment mid-operation, anyone would have assumed. When the manic charge Bombay led reached its destination, the enemy was gone. The squad met three machine guns and several abandoned magazines, the operators of the weapons long melted into the greenery like frost crystals blown into the jungle's humid oven. To Bombay's astonishment, all the firearms were in excellent working condition. The captured guns ensured the squad's return to base. On arrival Bombay was made a lance corporal, the first of the promotions that would elevate him to the rank of sergeant and carrier of the regimental flag, and given the Distinguished Conduct Medal for bravery, one of the three medals he would be awarded on the front.

Shortly before the decoration ceremony, Bombay protested to his Lieutenant that he had taken his action not because of bravery but out of fear, and deserved no honor for valor. The officer smiled. That was the first time Bombay had seen him grinning. Oh poor you, so you don't even know why the Japs fled, the Lieutenant said. The stories that preceded you to this war said that the Africans are coming and that they eat people. We fueled those rumors by dropping leaflets on the enemy, warning them that you will not only kill them but you also will happily cook them for supper. The Japanese, as you very well know, are trained to fight without fear of death. They don't mind being killed but, like anyone else, they are not in any way eager to be eaten. Their training didn't prepare them for that. That was why they scrammed when they saw you screaming towards them like bloodthirsty savages. But anyway, that you know nothing about the situation only makes your action more courageous. Report in an hour to receive your decoration. Okay?

Bombay saluted. The normally stern-faced Lieutenant, recalling the incident, was tickled out of his reserve. He started chuckling as he walked away, finding the comedy of the engagement with the Japanese so hilarious that tears streamed down his cheeks as he burst into outright laughter. He contemplated the emotions experienced by the Japanese soldiers as Bombay's squad bore down on them and the terror that must have gripped the enemy on concluding it was a clan of cannibals from Henry Rider Haggard's gory tales making a sortie for lunch. His laughter was still sounding a minute later when he made his entrance into the canteen, desiring to calm the mirthful paroxysms rocking him with a drink.

In the Lieutenant's wake, Bombay stood perplexed for a long spell, trying to come to grips with the revelation he had just received. Perhaps human flesh may be prime-grade meat, but he had never imagined eating anyone for a meal or even as a quick snack. Thinking more about it, Bombay's stomach got queasy and he had to steady his rising urge to puke. That people would imagine he was a cannibal was something he had not thought was possible.

* * *

Bombay would never hear the Lieutenant laugh again. Some weeks after Bombay's decoration, the Lieutenant's unit was separated from the division by blazing howitzers during a large push to drive the Japanese out of the winding road leading to Kalewa. Before nightfall, everyone in the group was accounted for except the Lieutenant.

Bombay admired the officer despite his mirthless countenance. The tactics he deployed when he led a tricky assault on a troublesome hilltop battery had struck Bombay as brilliant and, in those anxious moments only a cigarette could relieve, the man did not need to be asked before offering his last half-stick to whoever needed it the most. Oftentimes he had sat late with Bombay, sharing stories about his childhood on a farm bordered by a tiny lake near the Cumbrian Mountains and lamenting how much he missed the mooing of the cows when they were being led back from grazing in the unpredictable fog. This was why Bombay was happy to be included in the party tasked with finding the missing officer.

It was a dangerous mission. The more tenacious pockets of enemy combatants were still booby-trapping the jungle. The captain who led the search had recently arrived from Europe at the front. The men complained about his dismissive bossiness and the way he bragged about himself as if he was the special one sent to conclude the war singlehandedly. Someone once wondered why a man who could not even relate well with his own people was given charge over soldiers from a continent whose cultures he knew nothing about. Bombay, though, never griped about things like that. The front had been a good teacher to him. He was confident that the captain, by the time he ceased being a sophomore under the jungle's tutelage, would learn that life and war were more complex than the textbooks he had read in the military academy.

The lessons provided by the search expedition would be brutal on the new officer. It was the height of the monsoon and, for weeks, the rains had been coming down with pestilential resolve. The search was just beginning when the downpour became even more oppressive. The dampness was no longer news. Squelching around in soggy boots and dripping fatigues was a constant drudge they endured with amphibious fortitude, and the men found the captain's continuous bitching about the weather irritating. He stopped talking when they came upon a mound of charred enemy corpses in a ditch which served as a gun pit. Their burns were clearly not from grenades or kindred explosives. The corpses had been incinerated by their vanquishers with flame throwers to prevent disease. Executing such cremations had long become routine for Bombay. The mission moved on.

Dim shards of light constituted all the brightness able to breach the vegetation canopy. In the half-dark, having to beat new paths through the undergrowth was a thankless chore. Far more vicious than the stinging nettles and topping the jungle's sundry tortures was the omnipresent menace of the tiger leeches. The bloodsuckers were like fair punishment on both sides for their collaborative orgy of mass slaughter.

Since the encounter with the immolated bodies, the captain had been in increasing distress. His condition worsened after the party chanced on one of their soldiers who had fallen into an enemy poison pit. No one could say if he had bled to death from gashes inflicted by the sharp bamboo spikes or if he had succumbed to blood poisoning from the rotten meat with which the spikes were laced. From his advanced state of decomposition, it was evident he had been there for a while. The group advanced after retrieving the soldier's name tag and noting the location. By then, the captain had become a liability to the expedition. His constant lagging behind was hampering the group's progress and his unbroken whimpering and jabbering was only tolerated because the muffling drone of the rain made it a manageable risk. The next-ranking officer had taken de facto command and, with night rapidly approaching, he was thinking of calling off the search mission when the flashlights of Bombay and his colleagues picked up a figure. The man was stripped stark naked and tied to a tree, as if on death row awaiting his executioners. It was the missing Lieutenant. He was dead but there was no sign that he had been shot. His body had been severally pierced. The spectacle of his entrails spilling out of his excavated stomach and drooling down to his toes could not have been ghastlier. Bombay winced. The pain eternally howling from the Lieutenant's frozen face left no doubt that he had been used as bayonet practice by his enemy captors while still alive.

Confronted by that horror, the captain's visage turned ashen. It seemed his dilating eyes would soon pop out of their sockets. His breathing deteriorated into a sharp gasping for air, as if from lungs compromised by pneumonic failure. Then the captain began weeping, slobbering for his dead mother to emerge from her grave and save her innocent son from the Japanese and the gluttonous leeches, to take him away from the monstrous labyrinth of the jungle because he had no idea what he was doing there and how to get himself out of it. The oblivious blankness of his eyes confirmed that something had snapped. The captain's own volition could not sustain him on his feet. Two soldiers on either side had to support him back to base.

Over the next few days, the captain's condition deteriorated. He stayed in bed all day, shivering and whimpering. Everything terrified him, including daylight, and he kept his face shrouded with a blanket. The stench reeking from him became overpowering because the bed which he never left also served him as toilet, and at night he was always sedated because of fears his impromptu yelling could provide bearings to troops attacking in the darkness.

The captain's dead mother did not come over to spirit him away from the jungle, possibly from a dread counterpart to her son's for the enemy's eviscerating bayonets. Instead, it was a single-engine Moth that could only evacuate one patient at a time which finally flew him to a psychiatric hospital. Bombay was deeply shocked by the captain's fate. He remembered the white-jacketed District Officer back home with his manicured nails and the imperious airs of one in absolute control of the cosmos, the white man oozing superiority over the khaki-clad Native Police constables as if merely exercising his natural birthright. That the captain, a countryman of the colonial administrator, had disintegrated to a condition that pitiful meant the impeccable District Officer could likewise descend to the same animal depths. Bombay had seen a lot in the war. Diarrheic

Europeans pestered by irreverent flies while the men shat like domestic livestock in the open. Blue eyes rolling in mortal fear as another enemy shell whistled past. But never before had he imagined one of his imperial masters degenerating into a state so wretched. He found it good to know that was also possible.

* * *

Bombay's universe of the feasible continued expanding with inflationary acceleration. Buthidaung was successfully occupied and his division advanced down the Mayu Valley, maneuvering into position as part of the pincer movement to prevent the Japanese escaping through the Kaladan corridor. In the Mayu basin, Bombay's platoon had to traverse an extensive stretch of elephant grass. The plants were especially tall and their leaves slashed like a field of razors, lacerating the face and making progress on foot through their scarifying gauntlet interminable. In the middle of that grassy stretch, the platoon came upon corpses from a friendly battalion. The European cadavers were left whole but the African ones had been chopped up.

The Japs are convinced black soldiers resurrect, said an officer, so they dice the corpses to forestall having to kill them twice.

Bombay was incredulous. You mean... they believe it is possible we rise up to continue fighting them after we are killed? he asked.

Yes, the officer replied, chuckling.

Every one of us?

Yes.

Just like Lazarus?

Why?

And like Jesus Christ, your saviour?

A scowl had replaced the smile on the officer's lips. Yes, he said.

In the silence afterwards, the only sound came from the rustling of the elephant grass. I could not have reckoned anyone would think black people can rise from the dead, Bombay thought. He would never forget that. The platoon moved on.

* * *

At Bombay's new base, a bombardier was grounded after roughing up a fellow airman competing with him for the attentions of a pretty military nurse. The affections of the nurse belonged to his rival but the bombardier still carried her picture, like an ancestral amulet, in his wallet. He had to be restrained within a makeshift stockade when his unrequited passion spiked up his aggressiveness.

A few days into his confinement, the bombardier broke out in the small hours and overpowered the soldier guarding the corral. Bombay was standing as sentry outside the barracks that night. The manic bombardier had killed one man and injured another three with the Bren gun he seized from his guard before Bombay shot him. Once. The bombardier died on the spot.

Afterwards, smoking as daylight began reddening the east, Bombay remembered his countryman Okonkwo, whose story would become famous some years after the war when it was told in a book titled *Things Fall Apart*. Decades before, Okonkwo had killed an arrogant constable of the new colonizers. To deprive the white men of the pleasure of doing the same to him, Okonkwo hanged himself. Yes, those Bombay had been killing in the war were of a lighter hue than he was, but they were not white men and, even then, their killing had been sanctioned by his imperial overlords. Now, Bombay had killed a white man, not the black servant of the white man or the alien antagonists of Europe. Bombay vowed to take the brave route of Okonkwo rather than having anyone lead him to the gallows.

The next day, Bombay received a letter from his commanding officer. To Bombay's shock, it commended Bombay for his quick thinking, which had prevented a bigger carnage from decimating the barracks.

* * *

So Bombay was surprised to know it was possible to be praised for killing a white man, as he would also be astounded in the Kabaw Valley on observing that the Japanese snipers were still resolute in their refusal to target his side's stretcher bearers. This was the same enemy who not only slaughtered their opponent's wounded in captured hospitals but also shot their own injured men if they lacked the resources to evacuate them during hasty withdrawals, yet here they were still refusing to shoot at their opponent's stretcher carriers. Bombay shook his head in confusion, lost in bewilderment, as he would the evening his platoon leader told him that a strategic bridge over a tributary of the River Irrawaddy no longer needed to be taken.

What about the enemy soldiers on the other side? Bombay asked.

We no longer have any enemy on the other side, the platoon leader said.

They were still shooting only a short while ago.

Yes, but we no longer have any enemy on the other side.

Bombay could not get it, but he shrugged off his befuddlement. If they are gone, that means we will soon be going to Malaya, he said. People are saying we will soon be invading Malaya since there is not much fight going on here any more.

We won't be going anywhere.

Bombay noticed that the platoon leader looked unusually exhausted. What is happening? Bombay asked, his apprehension mounting.

Nothing. The war is already over, you know. Nothing will be happening except our respective journeys home, the platoon leader replied.

The big bomb had sprouted its mushrooms over a week before. The documents of surrender were already signed, but news of the ceasefire was slow in getting to the troops who, in their ignorance, were still fighting on days after the war had been declared ended.

We have won the godforsaken war, said the platoon leader, without any euphoria. The only place we are going now is home.

Considering both men's downcast looks, they might as well have lost. Along with the crudity, the war had brought along its own kindergarten certainty, kill or be killed, and the confirmation of its end brought no joy, only difficulty in comprehending the sudden evaporation of the matter which had dominated their recent years. On arrival at the front, Bombay like every other soldier was buoyed by the deluded faith that, unlike those dying around him, he would survive the enemy's bullets. With time such thoughts went extinct and the only things he bothered about were pragmatic routines, like drying out his wet boots and getting his gun loaded and enduring the fangs of the ever-thirsty tiger leeches. In that robotic existence,

Bombay had no luxury to indulge in speculations about victory or defeat. Now, the war was over. To his surprise, he was still alive and he had to begin thinking of the return journey home which only minutes earlier was so remote it wasn't a practical possibility.

We should begin packing our bags, Bombay said.

Yes.

The platoon leader began walking away and then he turned back to Bombay.

On your way home don't worry about what you will tell your loved ones or your friends about the part we played in this war, the platoon leader said. No-one will know where you were and, if you try informing them, they will not know where this is. We call this the Forgotten Front and we call ourselves the Forgotten Army. That is the lie we flatter ourselves with. I tell you, this is not the Forgotten Front and we are not the Forgotten Army. Nobody has ever heard of us so they can't even begin forgetting about us. That is the plain truth. To the world, we might never have existed.

The platoon leader, a no-nonsense combatant from the Welsh highlands, was almost in tears as he pondered the destiny of their common struggle on that neglected front, an effort that, true to his prophecy, would remain anonymous, like the travails of faceless and nameless characters forever entombed in a book of fiction that will never be written. The platoon leader plodded away with heavy steps, his spirit sapped to the lees by his valedictory agonies.

Bombay watched him go. He sighed. Bombay didn't care much about memory or forgetting. For him, things would never be locked in boxes again and that consciousness, the irreversible awareness handed out not by charity to Bombay but appropriated by him from the jungle without gratitude and by right, was enough recompense from the war. With the campaign over, the only thing that mattered to Bombay was the brand-new universe of possibilities he would be taking home with him from the front.

* * *

Politics was pungent in the air when Bombay returned to his homeland. The nationalist leaders had gotten more clamorous in their criticism of the colonialists and there were editorials in the dissident newspapers denouncing the big bomb's deployment as racist because it wouldn't have been dropped on Europeans. The atmosphere was spiced up by the evening assemblies under the acacia tree near the market. Having discovered the necessities of parliamentary representation and the right to self-rule during their travels, the brightest of the veterans freshly returned from Burma zealously quoted Gandhi and Du Bois at incendiary gatherings which constables from the Native Police Authority oftentimes had to break up.

Much was expected of the veteran who had distinguished himself above the lot by receiving not only the Distinguished Conduct Medal and the George Cross but also the rarely awarded Victoria Cross for conspicuous bravery. People were disappointed, though, because Color Sergeant Bombay showed not the slightest interest in populist agitation. The taciturn man seemed content strutting around in his blue PT gear and staring with unseeing blankness through the eyes of anyone who looked in his direction. Whenever grown-ups asked him if the Japanese were really as brutal as the other veterans reported, Bombay would reply with one of his newfound cryptic sentences. We did them no harm and they did us no harm, he would say, we only tried to kill each other as often as we could. And when people pressed him further to say something concrete about the war and his Japanese enemies he would truncate the discussion by saying, the white man dropped the big bomb on them but they are talking with each other now. They were good friends before and they are back as good friends again.

It became obvious Bombay was more comfortable chatting with the younger ones. He spoke to them of the tiger leeches and the horror that surges through the body at the instant you feel their fangs sinking into you, the discharged Sergeant schooling the wide-eyed children about how the leeches must not be plucked out because they leave their fangs behind and, instead, should be scorched off with a match or lighter since burn marks are kinder on the skin than the sepsis festered by their abandoned fangs. He exposed his torso and the children saw the dark stains singed by the flames all over his skin, like rosettes on a leopard's coat. This is the story of how I became a spotted leopard, he said, and his juvenile audience gleefully sprang back in mock fright when he snarled at them like the feline beast.

He got the name which replaced his original one from the tales he told about Bombay. The city was called Bombay because its streets were littered with bombs through which pedestrians must carefully tiptoe, the veteran said, except if one fancied levitating sky high as blown-up mincemeat.

The youngsters had overhead their teachers speaking in school about the Black Hole of Calcutta. They asked Bombay if he came across the hole during his sojourn abroad and the man replied, Of course. Bombay described the sinister darkness of the abyss into which, after dropping a coin, you could wait for all eternity without the shadow of an echo returning from the fathomless deep. That is why it is called the Black Hole of Calcutta, the veteran said. When sheep fell into the hole, an occurrence whose regularity wasn't surprising since they were the most foolish creatures alive, continued Bombay, the sheep tumbled for days on end down the Black Hole of Calcutta which ran straight through the center of the earth but he assured his enraptured listeners that, luckily for the foolish sheep, their owners always found the dazed animals grazing happily on the other side of the globe close to where they popped out of the pitch-black shaft.

The children were pleased to hear him narrate his barehanded battles with the crocodiles lurking beneath the muddy waters of the Irrawaddy, the veteran whispering to them that the females had gold nuggets for eyes and the males stared coldly at the world with fist-sized diamonds which, if plucked from their sockets, would be sold for an amount large enough to make the wealthiest man around seem the most miserable pauper.

The story the kids requested he repeat over and over was the one about the clan of weeping jinni who followed him for seven days and seven nights through the jungle pleading to buy his rare African soul with the most fabulous riches this world has to offer. A bit envious of the attention Bombay was giving the youngsters, some grown-ups made mockery that, considering the strange light burning in Bombay's eyes, it was not impossible that the veteran, as substitute to his three-medaled soul, had bartered off a slice of his sanity to the desperate creatures.

Wit morphed into reality when confirmation came that Bombay had taken possession of the long-empty jailhouse, disregarding the accounts of ghosts and dreadful presences which had long kept everyone away from the building. On the day of housewarming, Color Sergeant Bombay lowered the imperial flag in his new residence and proceeded to declare his person and his house thenceforth independent from the British Empire. That action got many people wondering if the ravenous leeches Bombay moaned so much about had not sucked his head hollow during the jungle war, siphoning out his brains and leaving behind only the most idiotic dregs for him to bring home to Africa.

* * *

The morning the tax collectors visited the old jailhouse, Bombay was drinking from a large gourd of palm wine and puffing a cigarette on the landing attached to the upper floor. In front of the building, a flag with a spotted leopard leaping in its center fluttered its sedition in place of the colonial banner whose deposition by Bombay had been the high point of his eccentric housewarming ceremony. The newest free nation of the world, this was how the veteran referred to his newly inaugurated People's Republic of Bombay.

Near the mast, rough-hewn busts commemorated the founding fathers of the infant republic. The figures increased in scale from the first to the last, concretizing Bombay's perception of their order of importance. Major General "Fluffy" Ffolkes, Commander of Bombay's Division in Burma. Lieutenant General Slim, Commander of all the Divisions of the Forgotten Army. Lord Louis Mountbatten, Supreme Commander over the Allied Armies in the eastern theater. And, finally, triumphant at the apogee of that evolution as if he was the Seal of the Generals, stood the bust of Color Sergeant Bombay, pioneer President and Commander in Chief of the newborn Republic of Bombay.

The visiting tax collectors interrupted their progress towards the veteran's residence to read the names etched below the figures, bemused by the cheekiness of the iconography informing Bombay's diminutive Mount Rushmore Memorial. They were still laughing at the veteran's impudence when they reached the staircase winding up to the upper floor of the old jailhouse. Bombay had been watching them all along, panting with rage as the visiting bureaucrats jabbed their fingers in ridicule at his ancestral totems. The collectors were surprised when they looked up to see Bombay standing right above them. They greeted him. He didn't reply. After some seconds, he spoke. Did you collect the necessary visas?

The taxmen were stumped.

Are you deaf? I said did any of you collect a visa before crossing the border?

We are tax collectors. Bring out your tax receipt.

Bombay got angry. This is an independent republic, he thundered. And get this into your rotten heads, this nation is not part of your bloody Commonwealth and it will never join. You and your children will always need visas to enter here. Next time you trespass into this territory, you will be shot dead. Like the enemy spies you all are. Every one of you. Is that clear?

The threat of gunfire brought about nervous movements from the taxmen. Their leader, who was accustomed to being dreaded rather than confronted, tried to assert his authority as delicately as he could. We simply came here to do our job, he said. We are not here to make trouble but if you give us trouble then we will be forced to give you trouble in return.

Is it that clown, Charles, who sent you here?

Charles? We were not sent by any Charles. We are tax collectors. The District Officer would be annoyed if we report you to him. Of course, you would not want that to happen, would you?

Ah, the District Officer. The goat is called Charles. Isn't that his name?

You are calling DO, the white man... like any name.... that he is a goat. The DO is the DO. You are looking for big trouble, said the scandalized team leader.

Charles is the name his father gave him, so let him use it. From today on you must call him by his first name, Charles, not DO. Is that clear?

Bombay had threatened to shoot. In the silence, the uneasy tax collectors kept an alert eye on the wine-guzzling veteran looming over them like murder. They fidgeted with anxiety about where the situation was heading.

Call him what you like and we will call him what we like, one of them mustered the courage to say. But please tell us, have you paid your hut tax? We are here to collect your hut tax. If you don't co-operate, we will call the Native Police and they will take you straight to prison.

Bombay laughed. Tell Charles that this is a big building built of stone. It is not a hut and it is much larger than that useless house he lives in, wasting his evenings planting flowers that can't grow in this weather and rearing cats like a white witch. How dare you come here asking for something as ridiculous as my hut tax? It is a shame that, in your slumber, you all choose to point your empty heads in a single direction. If your employer Charles is a blind fool, are you all also dumb that you can't tell him this is not a hut but a free and independent republic which he has no right to invade?

But that wasn't really the point, the collectors were explaining when Bombay stormed in, banging the door on their explanations that the tax was necessary for the smooth running of the colony.

The taxmen were discussing their next course of action when Bombay came out dressed in full ceremonial uniform, the Victoria Cross glistening in concert with the other medals dangling around his neck. He bellowed at the officials and demanded to know where they were when, after crossing the River Chindwin, ten men from his division died drinking from a lake the enemy had poisoned. He asked them what they were doing when his superior officers told him not to take his pants off as he washed in a stream so as not to frighten people with the exposure of his monkey tail. Still screaming with fury at the taxmen, Bombay asked if Charles, the stupid fellow who calls himself the District Officer, knew anything about Kabaw where, in the Valley of Death, tiger leeches descended on his platoon like an ambush of assassins and if any of them, arrogant white master or cringing black servants, will ever in their petty lives visit Rangoon where a full General decorated him with one of the many medals around his neck while, resplendent, a military band trumpeted its exultation. Then Bombay stopped talking. He fiddled with his trousers and began roaring a Gurkha song whose lyrics were in a language none of the collectors could understand.

Later, in the report they gave the District Office on their return to Colony House, the tax collectors would admit that they thought Bombay had exhausted his mulishness and was making to bring out his hut tax from his trouser pockets so they were caught unawares when the veteran's penis popped out instead and urine began jetting down at them like a waterfall from above. Being bathed in excrement is a taboo in our culture, they would note, so we had to scamper back from the disgusting horror sprinkling towards our heads.

They ran even faster when the first gunshot sounded. The taxmen, who on the evidence of that day might have made a good career for themselves as Olympic sprinters, were already at the compound's gate when the second shot came. A good distance from the building, the only one among the collectors who had the courage to glance back saw the golden liquid still shooting out of Bombay's fly, the endless torrent fed by the gallons of palm wine the man had been imbibing since daybreak.

The District Officer pondered over the incident for several days. Bombay was adamant in his refusal to pay his tax and he had scared away representatives of the Crown so he deserved to be arrested. An utterly contemptible cad, this was how the District Officer described Bombay. The colonial administrator, though, was not so naive as to conclude that the resolution could be so simple. He regretted Bombay's possession of firearms, which complicated the issue. Yes, there were enough arms-bearing Native Police constables to execute a successful storming of the old jailhouse, but the veteran was a screwball with sufficient knowledge of warfare to mount a stiff and suicidal resistance from his hilltop position, an engagement that could also be fatal to a good number of the constables. An Empire-tired MP could take interest in the affair and, notwithstanding the fact that Bombay was no more than another native conscript, the rebellious veteran could become a poster boy for the Empire's detractors, held up by the home country's troublemakers because of his status as a multiply decorated war hero. The District Officer did not fancy having to defend the slaughter of such a person at the Foreign Office or in Parliament. Involvement in a messy situation like that could very well be it for his career.

To worsen the scenario, the native firebrands campaigning for independence could latch on to the matter as a fulcrum on which to hinge their campaign. It was that final realization that clinched the District Officer's decision for him. Better let sleeping dogs lie, he reasoned. Bombay was like a disease which had quarantined itself. There was nothing smarter than letting him be, if only to guarantee his disconnection from wider political activity, the District Officer resolved, grudgingly allowing Bombay an independence whose legitimacy the veteran could not recognize because he had long before then unilaterally imposed the same upon himself.

* * *

The District Officer's reasoning proved sound. Bombay stayed away from the nationalist agitators, devoting his efforts instead to drafting a 792-page constitution for his hilltop republic and sending communiqués to the world press about the first general elections in the domain which, inevitably, returned the enclave's sole citizen as President.

Many years after Bombay's renegade republic was inaugurated, the colonial flag descended for the last time in the veteran's abandoned nation. Bombay wrote to his counterpart in his nation of birth, congratulating him on the belated independence and promising that Bombay's older republic would be glad to volunteer wisdom to the rookie state whenever necessary. The letter was never acknowledged, but that rebuff only fired President Bombay's resolve.

He wrote endless letters to the heads of state of the newly independent nations of Africa and granted interviews to any pressman who wanted one. Soon, people began paying attention. Impressed by his credentials as a war hero and intrigued by his rhetoric, national leaders from all over Africa invited him to grace ceremonies in their countries. Bombay called these trips state visits. He always reminded his hosts that giving your guest something good to take away, if possible cash, was a venerable African tradition so he never returned empty-handed from his trips. Whenever there was a coup or a regime change, Bombay's Republic was one of the first to grant recognition to the new government. In appreciation, more gifts came Bombay's way and the GDP of his republic kept up a healthy annual growth.

The longer he stayed in power, the more Color Sergeant Bombay found it necessary to give himself ever more colorful titles. Lord of All Flora and Fauna. Scourge of the British Empire. Celestial Guardian of the Sun, Moon and Stars. Sole Discoverer of the Grand Unified Theorem. Patriarch of the United States of Africa. Chief Commander of the Order of the Sahara Desert and the Atlantic Ocean. Father of the Internet. When Bombay ventured out of his hilltop republic, it was in a convoy of siren-blaring vehicles as interminable as those of the rulers he hobnobbed with during his continent-wide trips, and he always flew into a rage if anyone failed to address him as His Excellency, President of the People's Republic of Bombay, followed by a listing of his titles which were so numerous that not even Bombay could remember them all.

Bombay would rewrite his republic's constitution eleven times and serve as the enclave's President for 47 arbitrary tenures after elections won with landslide support from his republic's sole citizen, himself, until death finally unseated him from office.

The obituary, titled "Bombay's Republic," penned by a columnist working for a newspaper published in Bombay's birth country, would have pleased the veteran. Color Sergeant Bombay, war hero and perpetual president, was loved without exception by all the citizens of his People's Republic of Bombay, so ended the tribute. No-one argued with the claim since it was only natural for a person to love himself without reservations.

Before Hitler's War spawned possibilities in his universe like body bags on the Burma front, Color Sergeant Bombay would not have believed an obituary so affecting could come from a newspaper based in a country he considered foreign.

.

Miracle

Tope Folarin—winner of the 2013 Caine Prize

Our heads move simultaneously, and we smile at the tall, svelte man who strides purposefully down the aisle to the pulpit. Once there, he raises both of his hands then lowers them slightly. He raises his chin and says *let us pray*.

"Dear Father, we come to you today, on the occasion of this revival, and we ask that you bless us abundantly, we who have made it to America, because we know we are here for a reason. We ask for your blessings because we are not here alone. Each of us represents dozens, sometimes hundreds of people back home. So many lives depend on us, Lord, and the burden on our shoulders is great. Jesus, bless this service, and bless us. We ask that we will not be the same people at the end of the service as we were at the beginning. All this we ask of you, our dear saviour, Amen."

The pastor sits, and someone bolts from the front row to the piano and begins to play.

The music we hear is familiar and at the same time new; the bandleader punches up a preprogramed beat on the cheap electronic piano and plays a few Nigerian gospel songs to get us in the mood for revival. We sing along, though we have to wait a few moments at the beginning of each song to figure out what he's playing. We sing joyful songs to the Lord, then songs of redemption, and then we sing songs of hope, hope that tomorrow will be better than today, hope that, one day soon, our lives will begin to resemble the dreams that brought us to America.

The tinny Nigerian gospel music ends when the pastor stands, and he prays over us again. He prays so long and so hard that we feel the weight of his words pressing down on us. His prayer is so insistent, so sincere, that his words emerge from the dark chrysalis of his mouth as bright, fluttering prophecies. In our hearts we stop asking *if* and begin wondering *when* our deeply held wishes will come true. After his sweating and shaking and cajoling he shouts another *Amen*, a word that now seems defiant, not pleading. We echo his defiance as loudly as we can, and when we open our eyes we see him pointing to the back of the church.

Our eyes follow the line of his finger, and we see the short old man hunched over in the back, two men on either side of him. Many of us have seen him before, in this very space; we've seen the old man perform miracles that were previously only possible in the pages of our Bibles. We've seen him command the infirm to be well, the crippled to walk, the poor to become wealthy. Even those of us who are new, who know nothing of him, can sense the power emanating from him.

We have come from all over North Texas to see him. Some of us have come from Oklahoma, some of us from Arkansas, a few of us from Louisiana and a couple from New Mexico. We own his books, his tapes, his holy water, his anointing oil. We know that he is an instrument of God's will, and we have come because we need miracles.

We need jobs. We need good grades. We need green cards. We need American passports. We need our parents to understand that we are Americans. We need our children to understand they are Nigerians. We need new kidneys, new lungs, new limbs, new hearts. We need to forget the harsh rigidity of our lives, to remember why we believe, to be beloved, and to hope.

We need miracles.

We murmur as the two men help him to the front, and in this charged atmosphere everything about him makes sense, even the irony of his blindness, his inability to see the wonders that God performs through his hand. His blindness is a confirmation of his power. It's the burden he bears on our behalf; his residence in a space of perpetual darkness has only sharpened his spiritual vision over the years. He can see more than we will ever see.

When the old man reaches the pulpit, his attendants turn him around so he's facing us. He's nearly bald—a few white hairs cling precariously to the sides of his shining head—and he's wearing a large pair of black sunglasses. A bulky white robe falls from his neck to the floor. Beneath, he's wearing a flowing white *agbada*.

He remains quiet for a few moments—we can feel the anticipation building, breath by breath, in the air. He smiles. Then he begins to hum. A haunting, discordant melody. The bandleader tries to find the tune among the keys of his piano, but the old man slaps the air and the bandleader allows the searching music to die.

He continues to hum and we listen to his music. Suddenly he turns to our left and points to a space somewhere on the ceiling:

"I DEMAND YOU TO LEAVE THIS PLACE!" he screams, and we know there is something malevolent in our midst. We search the area his sightless eyes are probing, somewhere in the open space above our heads. We can't see anything, but we raise our voices in response to the prophet's call. Soon our voices are a cacophonous stew of Yoruba and English, shouting and singing, spitting and humming, and the prophet from Nigeria speaks once more:

"We must continue to pray, ladies and gentlemen! There are forces here that do not wish for this to be a successful service. If we are successful in our prayers that means they have failed! They do not wish to fail! So we cannot expect that our prayers will simply come true; we must fight!"

We make our stew thicker; we throw in more screams and prayers until we can no longer distinguish one voice from another. Finally, after several long minutes, the prophet raises his hands:

"We are finished. It is done."

And we begin to celebrate, but our celebration lacks conviction—we haven't yet received what we came here for.

The prophet sways to the beat of our tepid praise. The man on his left stands and dabs his forehead. The prophet clears his throat and reaches forward with his right hand until he finds the microphone. He grabs it, leans into it.

"I have been in the US for two months now..." he begins, rhythmically moving his head left and right, "I have been to New York, to Delaware, to Philadelphia, to Washington, to Florida, to

Atlanta, to Minnesota, to Kansas, to Oklahoma, and now, finally, I have arrived here."

We cheer loudly.

"I will visit Houston and San Antonio before I leave here, and then I will go to Nevada, and then California. I will travel all over this country for the next month, visiting Nigerians across this great land, but I feel in my spirit that the most powerful blessings will happen *here*."

We holler and whoop and hug each other, for his words are confirmation of the feelings we've been carrying within ourselves since the beginning of the service.

"The reason I am saying that the most powerful blessings will happen here is because God has told me that you have been the most faithful of his flock in the US. You haven't forgotten your people back home. You haven't forgotten your parents and siblings who sent you here, who pray for you every day. You have remained disciplined and industrious in this place, the land of temptation. And for all your hard work, for your faithfulness, God is going to reward you today."

Some of us raise our hands and praise the Father. A few of us bow our heads, a few of us begin to weep with happiness.

"But in order for your blessings to be complete, you will have to pray today like you have never prayed before. You will have to believe today like you have never believed before. The only barrier to your blessing is the threshold of your belief. Today the only thing I will be talking about is belief. If I have learned anything during my visits to this country, it is that belief is only possible for those who have dollars. I am here to tell you that belief comes *before* dollars. If you have belief, then the dollars will follow."

Silence again. We search our hearts for the seedlings of doubt that reside there. Many of us have to cut through thickets of doubt before we can find our own hearts again. We use the silence to uproot our doubt and we pray that our hearts will remain pure for the remainder of the service.

"Let me tell you, great miracles will be performed here today. People will be talking about this day for years and years to come. And the only thing that will prevent you from receiving your share is your unbelief…"

At this moment he begins to cough violently, and the man on his right rushes forward with a handkerchief. He places the handkerchief in the prophet's hand, and the prophet coughs into it for a few seconds, and then he wipes his mouth. We wait anxiously for him to recover.

He laughs. "I am an old man now. You will have to excuse me. Just pray for me!"

"We will pray for you, Prophet!" we yell in response.

"Yes, just pray for me, and I will continue to pray for you."

"Thank you, Prophet! Amen! Amen!"

"And because you have been faithful, God will continue to bless you, he will anoint you, he will appoint you!"

"Amen!"

"Now God is telling me that there is someone here who is struggling with something big, a handicap that has lasted for many, many years."

We fall quiet because we know he is talking about us.

"He's telling me that you have been suffering in silence with this problem, and that you have come to accept the problem as part of yourself."

We nod in agreement. How many indignities have we accepted as a natural part of our lives?

"The purpose of my presence in your midst is to let you know that you should no longer accept the bad things that have become normal in your lives. America is trying to teach you to accept your failures, your setbacks. Now is the time to reject them! To claim the success that is rightfully yours!"

His sunglasses fall from his face, and we see the brilliant white orbs quivering frantically in their sockets, two full moons that have forgotten their roles in the drama of the universe. His attendants lunge to the floor to recover them, and together they place the glasses back on his ancient face. The prophet continues as if nothing happened.

"I do not perform these miracles because I wish to be celebrated. I perform these miracles because God works through me, and he has given me the grace to show all of you what is possible in your *physical* and *spiritual* lives. And now God is telling me: you, come up here."

We remain standing because we don't know to whom he is referring.

"YOU! You! You! YOU! Come up here!"

We begin to walk forward, shyly, slowly. I turn around suddenly, and I realize I'm no longer a part of the whole. I notice, then, that the lights are too bright, and the muggy air in the room settles, fog-like, on my face. Now I am in the aisle, and I see the blind old man pointing at me.

"You, young man. Come here. Come up here for your miracle!"

I just stand there, and I feel something red and frightening bubbling within me. I stand there as the prophet points at me, and I feel hands pushing me, forcing me to the front. I don't have enough time to wrap up my unbelief and tuck it away.

Then I'm standing on the stage, next to the prophet.

The prophet moves closer to me and places a hand on top of my head. He presses down until I'm kneeling before him. He rocks my head back and forth.

"Young man, you have great things ahead of you, but I can sense that something is ailing you. There is some disease, some disorder that has colonized your body, and it is threatening to colonize your soul. Tell me, are you having problems breathing?"

I find myself surprised at his indirect reference to my asthma. But now the doubts are bombarding me from every direction. Maybe he can hear my wheezing? It's always harder for me to breathe when I'm nervous, and I'm certainly nervous now.

"Yes sir," I reply.

"Ah, you do not need to confirm. I now have a fix on your soul, and the Holy Spirit is telling me about the healings you need." He brushes his fingers down my face, and my glasses fall to the ground. Everything becomes dim.

"How long have you been wearing glasses, my son?"

"Since I was five, sir."

"And tell me, how bad is your vision?"

Really bad. I have the thickest lenses in school, the kind that make my eyes seem like two giant fish floating in blurry, separate ponds.

"It's bad, sir."

The prophet removes his hand from my head and I can feel him thrashing about, as if he's swimming in air, until an attendant thrusts a microphone into his groping hand.

"As you guys can see, I know a little about eye problems," he booms, and although it sounds like he's attempting a joke, no one laughs, and his words crash against the back wall and wash over us a second time, and then a third.

"And no one this young should be wearing glasses that are so thick!" The congregation cheers in approval. I hear a whispered *yes, prophet.*

"I can already tell that you have become too comfortable with your handicap," he roars, "and that is one of the main problems in this country. Handicaps have become *normal* here." I see the many heads nodding in response. "People accept that they are damaged in some fashion, and instead of asking God to intervene, they accept the fact that they are broken!"

More head nodding, more *Amens.*

"Let me tell you something," he continues. He's sweating profusely; some of it dribbles onto my head. My scalp is burning. "God gives us these ailments so that we are humbled, so that we are forced to build a relationship with him. That is why all of us, in some way or another, are damaged. And the reason they have come to accept handicaps in this country is because these Americans do not want to build a relationship with God. They want to remain forever disconnected from His grace, and you can already see what is happening to this country."

The *Amens* explode from many mouths; some louder, some softer, some gruff, some pleading.

"So the first step to getting closer to God, to demonstrating that you are a serious Christian, is declaring to God all of your problems and ailments, and asking him to heal you."

A few *Amens* from the back overwhelm everything. I squint to see if I can connect the praise to the faces, but I can only see the featureless faces swathed in fog.

"So now I'm going to ask God to heal this young man who has become accustomed to his deformity. But before I touch you, before I ask the Holy Spirit to do its work, I must ask you, before everyone here—are you ready for your miracle?"

I stare at the congregation. I see some nodding. I've never thought of a life without glasses, but now my head is filled with visions of perfect clarity. I can see myself playing basketball without the nerdy, annoying straps that I always attach to my glasses so they won't fall off my face. I imagine evenings without headaches, headaches that come after hours spent peering through lenses that give me sight while rejecting my eyes.

"Are you ready?" he asks again, and I can feel the openness in the air that exists when people are waiting for a response. I know I'm waiting for my response as well.

"I'm ready."

"Amen!"

"AMEN! AMEN!" Their *Amens* batter me; I bow beneath the harsh blows of their spiritual desperation.

"My son, you are ready to receive your gift from God."

His two attendants scramble from his side, drag me to my feet, and bring me down to the floor. One positions himself next to me, the other behind me. When I look over my shoulder I see the attendant standing there with his arms extended before him.

"I feel something very powerful coursing through my spirit," the prophet yells. "This is going to be a big miracle. Bring me to the boy!"

The attendant beside me strides up to the stage and helps the prophet down the steps. He positions the prophet before me, and I notice that the prophet seems even shorter than before. He is only a few inches taller than me. His hot breath causes my eyes to water; I resist the urge to reach up and rub them.

The prophet suddenly pulls off his sunglasses. He stares at me with his sightless eyes. I become uncomfortable, so I lean slightly to the right and his face follows. I lean slightly to the left and his face does the same. A sly smile begins to unfurl itself across his face. My heart begins to beat itself to death.

"Do not be frightened. I can see you through my spiritual eyes," he says. "And after this miracle, if you are a diligent Christian, you will be able to do the same."

Before I can respond, his right hand shoots forward, and he presses my temples. I stumble backwards but maintain my balance. I turn to gaze at all the people in front of me, and though I can't see individual faces I see befuddlement in its many, various forms. I see random expressions contort themselves into a uniform expression of confusion. I actually manage to separate my brother from the masses because his presence is the only one in the room that seems to match my own. We're both confused, but our confusion isn't laced with fear.

The prophet presses my temples again, and again, and each time I regain my balance. His attendants are ignoring me now. They're both looking down at the prophet, inquiring with their eyes about something. I'm not sure what. Then I hear the shuffling feet, and I know that the people are becoming restless.

"The spirit of bad sight is very strong in him, and it won't let go," the prophet yells.

Life returns to the church like air filling up a balloon. I see the prophet's attendants nod, and the new *Amens* that tunnel into my ears all have an edge of determination.

"This healing will require special Holy Ghost healing power. Come, take my robe!" The attendant closest to me pulls the robe from his back, and the prophet stands before me even smaller and less imposing than before. "While I am working on this spirit everyone in this room must pray. You must pray that I will receive the power I need to overcome this spirit within him!"

I see many heads moving up and down in prayer, and I hear loud pleading, and snapping, and impassioned howling.

"That is very good!"

The prophet steps forward and blows in my eyes, and then he rubs my temples. I remain standing. He blows and rubs again. The same. He does it again, and again, and each time the praying grows louder and more insistent. The prophet moves even closer to me, and this time when he presses my temples he does not let go. He shoves my head back until I fall, and the attendant behind me eases me to the floor. I finally understand. I remain on the floor while his attendants cover me with a white sheet. Above, I hear the prophet clapping his hands, and I know that he's praying. The fluorescent lights on the ceiling are shining so brightly that the light seems to be huddling in the sheet with me. I hug the embodied light close.

After a few minutes the prophet stops clapping.

"It is finished! Pick the young man up."

His attendants grab my arms and haul me up. I hear a cheer building up in the crowd, gaining form and weight, but the prophet cuts everything off with a loud grunt.

"Not yet. It is too soon. And young man, keep your eyes closed." I realize that my eyes are still closed, and I wonder how he knows.

I begin to believe in miracles. I realize that many miracles have already happened; the old prophet can see me even though he's blind, and my eyes feel different somehow, huddled beneath their thin lids. I think about the miracle of my family, the fact that we've remained together despite the terror of my mother's abrupt departure, and I even think about the miracle of my presence in America. My father reminds my brother and me almost every day how lucky we are to be living in poverty in America, he claims that all of our cousins in Nigeria would die for the chance, but his words were meaningless before. Compared to what I have already experienced in life, compared to the tribulations that my family has already weathered, the matter of my eyesight seems almost insignificant. *Of course I can be healed! This is nothing. God has already done more for me than I can imagine. This healing isn't even for me. It is to show others, who believe less, whose belief requires new fuel, that God is still working in our lives.*

Then the Prophet yells in my ear: "OPEN YOUR EYES."

My lids slap open, and I see the same fog as before. The disembodied heads are swelling with unreleased joy. I know what I have to do.

"I can see!" I cry, and the loud cheers and sobbing are like new clothing.

"We must test his eyes, just to make sure! We are not done yet!" yells the prophet, and nervousness slowly creeps up my spine like a centipede. "We have to confirm so the doubters in here and the doubters in the world can know that God's work is real!"

One of his attendants walks a few feet in front of me and holds up a few fingers. I squint and lean forward. I pray I get it right.

"Three!" I yell, and the crowd cheers more loudly than before.

"Four!" I scream, and the cheers themselves gain sentience. They last long after mouths have closed.

"One!" I cry, and the mouths open again, to give birth to new species of joy.

* * *

This is what I learned during my first visit to a Nigerian church: that a community is made up of truths and lies. Both must be cultivated in order for the community to survive.

The prophet performed many more miracles that day. My father beamed all the way home, and I felt that I had been healed, in a way, even if my eyes were the same as before.

That evening, after tucking my brother and me in, my father dropped my glasses into a brown paper bag, and he placed the bag on the nightstand by my bed.

"You should keep this as evidence, so that you always remember the power of God," he whispered in my ear.

The next morning, when I woke up, I opened my eyes, and I couldn't see a thing. I reached into the bag and put on my glasses without thinking. My sight miraculously returned.

My Father's Head

Okwiri Oduor—winner of the 2014 Caine Prize

I had meant to summon my father only long enough to see what his head looked like, but now he was here and I did not know how to send him back.

It all started the Thursday that Father Ignatius came from Immaculate Conception in Kitgum. The old women wore their Sunday frocks, and the old men plucked garlands of bougainvillea from the fence and stuck them in their breast pockets. One old man would not leave the dormitory because he could not find his shikwarusi, and when I coaxed and badgered, he patted his hair and said: "My God, do you want the priest from Uganda to think that I look like this every day?"

I arranged chairs beneath the avocado tree in the front yard, and the old people sat down and practiced their smiles. A few people who did not live at the home came too, like the woman who hawked candy in the Stagecoach bus to Mathari North, and the man whose one-roomed house was a kindergarten in the daytime and a brothel in the evening, and the woman whose illicit brew had blinded five people in January.

Father Ignatius came riding on the back of a bodaboda, and after everyone had dropped a coin in his hat, he gave the bodaboda man 50 shillings and the bodaboda man said, "Praise God," and then rode back the way he had come.

Father Ignatius took off his coat and sat down in the chair that was marked, "Father Ignatius Okello, New Chaplain," and the old

247

people gave him the smiles they had been practicing, smiles that melted like ghee, that oozed through the corners of their lips and dribbled onto their laps long after the thing that was being smiled about went rancid in the air.

Father Ignatius said, "The Lord be with you," and the people said, "And also with you," and then they prayed and they sang and they had a feast; dipping bread slices in tea and, when the drops fell on the cuffs of their woollen sweaters, sucking at them with their steamy, cinnamon tongues.

Father Ignatius' maiden sermon was about love: love your neighbor as you love yourself, that kind of self-deprecating thing. The old people had little use for love, and although they gave Father Ignatius an ingratiating smile, what they really wanted to know was what type of place Kitgum was, and if it was true that the Bagisu people were savage cannibals.

What I wanted to know was what type of person Father Ignatius thought he was, instructing others to distribute their love like this or like that, as though one could measure love on weights, pack it inside glass jars and place it on shelves for the neighbors to pick as they pleased. As though one could look at it and say, "Now see: I have ten loves in total. Let me save three for my country and give all the rest to my neighbors."

It must have been the way that Father Ignatius filled his mug—until the tea ran over the clay rim and down the stool leg and soaked into his canvas shoe—that got me thinking about my own father. One moment I was listening to tales of Acholi valor, and the next, I was stringing together images of my father, making his limbs move and his lips spew words, so that in the end, he was a marionette and my memories of him were only scenes in a theatrical display.

Even as I showed Father Ignatius to his chambers, cleared the table, put the chairs back inside, took my purse, and dragged myself to Odeon to get a matatu to Uthiru, I thought about the millet-colored freckle in my father's eye, and the 50-cent coins he always forgot in his coat pockets, and the way, each Saturday morning, men knocked on our front door and said things like, "Johnson, you have to come now; the water pipe has burst and we are filling our glasses with shit," and, "Johnson, there is no time to put on clothes even; just come the way you are. The maid gave birth in the night and flushed the baby down the toilet."

Every day after work, I bought an ear of street-roasted maize and chewed it one kernel at a time, and, when I reached the house, I wiggled out of the muslin dress and wore dungarees and drank a cup of masala chai. Then I carried my father's toolbox to the bathroom. I chiseled out old broken tiles from the wall, and they fell onto my boots, and the dust rose from them and exploded in the flaring tongues of fire lapping through chinks in the stained glass.

This time, as I did all those things, I thought of the day I sat at my father's feet and he scooped a handful of groundnuts and rubbed them between his palms, chewed them, and then fed the mush to me. I was of a curious age then: old enough to chew with my own teeth, yet young enough to desire that hot, masticated love, love that did not need to be indoctrinated or measured in cough-syrup caps.

The Thursday Father Ignatius came from Kitgum, I spent the entire night on my stomach on the sitting-room floor, drawing my father. In my mind I could see his face, see the lines around his mouth, the tiny blobs of light in his irises, the crease at the part where his ear joined his temple. I could even see the thick line of sweat and oil on his shirt collar, the little brown veins that broke off from the main stream of dirt and ran down on their own.

I could see all these things, yet no matter what I did, his head refused to appear within the borders of the paper. I started off with his feet and worked my way up and in the end my father's head popped out of the edges of the paper and onto scuffed linoleum and plastic magnolias and the wet soles of bathroom slippers.

I showed Bwibo some of the drawings. Bwibo was the cook at the old people's home, with whom I had formed an easy camaraderie.

"My God!" Bwibo muttered, flipping through them. "Simbi, this is abnormal."

The word "abnormal" came out crumbly, and it broke over the sharp edge of the table and became clods of loam on the plastic floor covering. Bwibo rested her head on her palm, and the bell sleeves of her cream-colored caftan swelled as though there were pumpkins stacked inside them.

I told her what I had started to believe, that perhaps my father had had a face but no head at all. And even if my father had had a head, I would not have seen it: people's heads were not a thing that one often saw. One looked at a person, and what one saw was their face: a regular face-shaped face, that shrouded a regular head-shaped head. If the face was remarkable, one looked twice. But what was there to draw one's eyes to the banalities of another's head? Most times when one looked at a person, one did not even see their head there at all.

Bwibo stood over the waist-high jiko, poured cassava flour into a pot of bubbling water and stirred it with a cooking oar. "Child," she said, "how do you know that the man in those drawings is your father? He has no head at all, no face."

"I recognize his clothes. The red corduroys that he always paired with yellow shirts."

Bwibo shook her head. "It is only with a light basket that someone can escape the rain."

It was that time of day when the old people fondled their wooden beads and snorted off to sleep in between incantations. I allowed them a brief, bashful siesta, long enough for them to believe that they had recited the entire rosary. Then I tugged at the ropes and the lunch bells chimed. The old people sat eight to a table, and with their mouths filled with ugali, sour lentils, and okra soup, said things like, "Do not buy chapati from Kadima's Kiosk—Kadima's wife sits on the dough and charms it with her buttocks," or, "Did I tell you about Wambua, the one whose cow chewed a child because the child would not stop wailing?"

In the afternoon, I emptied the bedpans and soaked the old people's feet in warm water and baking soda, and when they trooped off to mass I took my purse and went home.

The Christmas before the cane tractor killed my father, he drank his tea from plates and fried his eggs on the lids of coffee jars, and he retrieved his Yamaha drum-set from a shadowy, lizardy place in the back of the house and sat on the veranda and smoked and beat the drums until his knuckles bled.

One day he took his stool and hand-held radio and went to the veranda, and I sat at his feet, undid his laces, and peeled off his gummy socks. He wiggled his toes about. They smelt slightly fetid, like sour cream.

My father smoked and listened to narrations of famine undulating deeper into the Horn of Africa, and, when the clock chimed eight o'clock, he turned the knob and listened to the death news. It was not long before his ears caught the name of someone he knew. He choked on the smoke trapped in his throat.

My father said: "Did you hear that? Sospeter has gone! Sospeter, the son of Milkah, who taught Agriculture in Mirere Secondary. My God, I am telling you, everyone is going. Even me, you shall hear me on the death news very soon."

I brought him his evening cup of tea. He smashed his cigarette against the veranda, then he slowly brought the cup to his lips. The cup was filled just the way he liked it, filled until the slightest trembling would have his fingers and thighs scalded.

My father took a sip of his tea and said: "Sospeter was like a brother to me. Why did I have to learn of his death like this, over the radio?"

Later, my father lay on the fold-away sofa, and I sat on the stool watching him, afraid that, if I looked away, he would go too. It was the first time I imagined his death, the first time I mourned.

And yet it was not my father I was mourning. I was mourning the image of myself inside the impossible aura of my father's death. I was imagining what it all would be like: the death news would say that my father had drowned in a cesspit, and people would stare at me as though I were a monitor lizard trapped inside a manhole in the street. I imagined that I would be wearing my green dress when I got the news—the one with red gardenias embroidered in its bodice—and people would come and pat my shoulder and give me warm Coca Cola in plastic cups and say: "I put my sorrow in a basket and brought it here as soon as I heard. How else would your father's spirit know that I am innocent of his death?"

Bwibo had an explanation as to why I could not remember the shape of my father's head.

She said: "Although everyone has a head behind their face, some show theirs easily; they turn their back on you and their head is all you can see. Your father was a good man and good men never show you their heads; they show you their faces."

Perhaps she was right. Even the day my father's people telephoned to say that a cane tractor had flattened him on the road to Shibale, no-one said a thing about having seen his head. They described the rest of his body with a measured delicacy: how his legs were strewn across the road, sticky and shiny with fresh tar, and how one foot remained inside his tire sandal, pounding the pedal of his bicycle, and how cane juice filled his mouth and soaked the collar of his polyester shirt, and how his face had a patient serenity, even as his eyes burst and rolled in the rain puddles.

And instead of weeping right away when they said all those things to me, I had wondered if my father really had come from a long line of obawami, and if his people would bury him seated in his grave, with a string of royal cowries round his neck.

"In any case," Bwibo went on, "what more is there to think about your father, eh? That milk spilled a long time ago, and it has curdled on the ground."

I spent the day in the dormitories, stripping beds, sunning mattresses, scrubbing PVC mattress pads. One of the old men kept me company. He told me how he came to spend his sunset years at the home—in August 1998 he was at the station waiting to board the evening train back home to Mombasa. When the bomb went off at the American Embassy, the police trawled the city and arrested every man of Arab extraction. Because he was 72 and already rapidly unraveling into senility, they dumped him at the old people's home, and he had been there ever since.

"Did your people not come to claim you?" I asked, bewildered.

The old man snorted. "My people?"

"Everyone has people that belong to them."

The old man laughed. "Only the food you have already eaten belongs to you."

Later, the old people sat in drooping clumps in the yard. Bwibo and I watched from the back steps of the kitchen. In the grass, ants devoured a squirming caterpillar. The dog's nose, a translucent pink doodled with green veins, twitched. Birds raced each other over the frangipani. One tripped over the power line and smashed its head on the moss-covered electricity pole.

Wasps flew low over the grass. A lizard crawled over the lichen that choked a pile of timber. The dog licked the inside of its arm. A troupe of royal butterfly dancers flitted over the row of lilies, their colorful, gauze dancing skirts trembling to the rumble of an inaudible drumbeat. The dog lay on its side in the grass, smothering the squirming caterpillar and the chewing ants. The dog's nipples were little pellets of goat shit stuck with spit onto its furry underside.

Bwibo said, "I can help you remember the shape of your father's head."

I said, "Now what type of mud is this you have started speaking?"

Bwibo licked her index finger and held it solemnly in the air. "I swear, Bible red! I can help you and I can help you."

Let me tell you: one day you will renounce your exile, and you will go back home, and your mother will take out the finest china, and your father will slaughter a sprightly cockerel for you, and the neighbors will bring some potluck, and your sister will wear her navy-blue PE wrapper, and your brother will eat with a spoon instead of squelching rice and soup through the spaces between his fingers.

And you, you will have to tell them stories about places not-here, about people that soaked their table napkins in Jik bleach and talked about London as though London were a place one could reach by hopping onto an Akamba bus and driving by Nakuru and Kisumu and Kakamega and finding themselves there.

You will tell your people about men that did not slit melons up into slices but split them into halves and ate each of the halves out with a spoon, about women that held each other's hands around street lamps in town and skipped about, showing snippets of gray Mother's Union bloomers as they sang:

Kijembe ni kikali, param-param
Kilikata mwalimu, param-param

You think that your people belong to you, that they will always have a place for you in their minds and their hearts. You think that your people will always look forward to your return.

Maybe the day you go back home to your people you will have to sit in a wicker chair on the veranda and smoke alone because, although they may have wanted to have you back, no-one really meant for you to stay.

My father was slung over the wicker chair on the veranda, just like in the old days, smoking and watching the hand-held radio. The death news rose from the radio, and it became a mist, hovering low, clinging to the cold glass of the sitting-room window.

My father's shirt flapped in the wind, and tendrils of smoke snapped before his face. He whistled to himself. At first the tune was a faceless, pitiful thing, like an old bottle that someone found on the path and kicked all the way home. Then the tune caught fragments of other tunes inside it, and it lost its free-spirited falling and rising.

My father had a head. I could see it now that I had the mind to look for it. His head was shaped like a butternut squash. Perhaps that was the reason I had forgotten all about it: it was a horrible, disconcerting thing to look at.

My father had been a plumber. His fingernails were still rimmed with dregs from the drainage pipes he tinkered about in, and his boots still squished with *ugali* from nondescript kitchen sinks. Watching him, I remembered the day he found a gold chain tangled in the fibres of someone's excrement, and he wiped the excrement off against his corduroys and sold the chain at Nagin Pattni, and that evening, hoisted high upon his shoulders, he brought home the red Greatwall television. He set it in the corner of the sitting room and said, "Just look how it shines, as though it is not filled with shit inside."

And every day I plucked a bunch of carnations and snipped their stems diagonally and stood them in a glass bowl and placed the glass bowl on top of the television so that my father would not think of shit while he watched the evening news.

I said to Bwibo, "We have to send him back."

Bwibo said, "The liver you have asked for is the one you eat."

"But I did not really want him back, I just wanted to see his head."

Bwibo said, "In the end, he came back to you and that should account for something, should it not?"

Perhaps my father's return accounted for nothing but the fact that the house already smelt like him—of burnt lentils and melting fingernails and the bark of bitter quinine and the sourness of wet rags dabbing at broken cigarette tips.

I threw things at my father: garlic, incense, salt, pork, and when none of that repelled him, I asked Father Ignatius to bless the house. He brought a vial of holy water, and he sprinkled it in every room, sprinkled it over my father. Father Ignatius said that I would need further protection, but that I would have to write him a check first.

One day I was buying roast maize in the street corner when the vendor said to me, "Is it true what the vegetable-sellers are saying, that you finally found a man to love you but will not let him through your door?"

That evening, I invited my father inside. We sat side by side on the fold-away sofa, and watched as a fly crawled up the dusty screen between the grill and the window glass. It buzzed a little as it climbed. The ceiling fan creaked, and it threw shadows across the corridor floor. The shadows leapt high and mounted doors and peered through the air vents in the walls.

The wind upset a cup. For a few seconds, the cup lay lopsided on the windowsill. Then it rolled on its side and scurried across the floor. I pulled at the latch, fastened the window shut. The wind grazed the glass with its wet lips. It left a trail of dust and saliva, and the saliva dribbled down slowly to the edge of the glass. The wind had a slobbery mouth. Soon its saliva had covered the entire window, covered it until the rosemary brushwood outside the window became blurry. The jacaranda outside stooped low, scratched the roof. In the next room, doors and windows banged.

I looked at my father. He was something at once strange and familiar, at once enthralling and frightening—he was the brittle, chipped handle of a ceramic tea mug, and he was the cold yellow stare of an owl.

My father touched my hand ever so lightly, so gently, as though afraid that I would flinch and pull my hand away. I did not dare lift my eyes, but he touched my chin and tipped it upwards so that I had no choice but to look at him.

I remembered a time when I was a little child, when I stared into my father's eyes in much the same way. In them I saw shapes: a drunken, talentless conglomerate of circles and triangles and squares. I had wondered how those shapes had got inside my father's eyes. I had imagined that he sat down at the table, cut out glossy figures from coloring books, slathered them with glue, and stuck them inside his eyes so that they made rummy, haphazard collages in his irises.

My father said, "Would you happen to have some tea, Simbi?"

I brought some, and he asked if his old friend Pius Obote still came by the house on Saturdays, still brought groundnut soup and pumpkin leaves and a heap of letters that he had picked up from the post office.

I said, "Pius Obote has been dead for four years."

My father pushed his cup away. He said, "If you do not want me here drinking your tea, just say so, instead of killing-killing people with your mouth."

My father was silent for a while, grieving this man Pius Obote whose name had always made me think of knees banging against each other. Pius Obote used to blink a lot. Once, he fished inside his pocket for a biro and instead withdrew a chicken bone, still red and moist.

My father said to me, "I have seen you. You have offered me tea. I will go now."

"Where will you go?"

"I will find a job in a town far from here. Maybe Eldoret. I used to have people there."

I said, "Maybe you could stay here for a couple of days, Baba."

The Sack

Namwali Serpell—winner of the 2015 Caine Prize

There's a sack.

    A sack?

    A sack.

Hmm. A sack. Big?

Yes. Gray. Like old *kwacha*. Marks on the outside. No. Shadows. That's how I know it is moving.

Something is moving inside it?

The whole sack is moving. Down a dirt road with a ditch on the side, with grass and yellow flowers. There are trees above.

Is it dark?

Yes, but light is coming. It is morning. There are some small birds talking, moving. The sack is dragging on the ground. There is a man pulling it behind him.

Who is this man?

I can't see his face. He is tallish. His shirt has stains on the back. No socks. Businessman shoes. His hands are wet.

Does he see you?

I don't know. I'm tired now. Close the curtains.

Yes, *bwana*.

J. left the bedroom and went to the kitchen. The wooden door was open but the metal security gate was closed. The sky looked bruised. The insects would be coming soon. They had already begun their electric clicking in the garden. He thought of the man in the

257

bedroom, hating him in that tender way he had cultivated over the years. J. washed the plates from lunch. He swept. A chicken outside made a popping sound. J. sucked his teeth and went to see what was wrong.

The *isabi* boy was standing outside the security gate. The boy held the bucket handle with both hands, the insides of his elbows splayed taut. His legs were streaked white and gray.

How do you expect me to know you are here if you are quiet? J. asked as he opened the gate. The boy shrugged, a smile dancing upwards and then receding into the settled indifference of his face. J. told the boy to take off his *patapatas* and reached for the bucket. Groaning with its weight, J. heaved the unwieldy thing into the sink. He could just make out the shape of the bream, flush against the inside of the bucket, its fin protruding. J. felt the water shift as the fish turned uneasily.

A big one today, eh? J. turned and smiled.

The boy still stood by the door, his hands clasped in front of him. His legs were reflected in the parquet floor, making him seem taller.

Do you want something to eat?

The boy assented with a diagonal nod.

You should eat the fish you catch. It is the only way to survive, J. said.

I told him about the first dream but I did not tell him about the second. In the second dream, I am inside the sack. The cloth of it is pressing right down on my eyes. I turn one way, then the other. All I can see is gray cloth. There is no pain but I can feel the ground against my bones. I am curled up. I hear the sound of the sack, sweeping like a slow broom. I have been paying him long enough—paying down his debt—that he should treat me like a real *bwana*. He does his duties, yes. But he lacks deference. His politics would not admit this, but I have known this man since we were children. I know what the color of my skin means to someone of our generation. His eyes have changed. I think he is going to kill me. I think that is what these dreams are telling me. Naila. I cannot remember your hands.

They lifted the bream out of the bucket together, the boy's hands holding the tail, J.'s hands gripping the head. The fish swung in and out of the curve of its own body, its gills pumping with mechanical panic. They flipped it on to the wooden board. Its side was a jerking plane of silver, drops of water magnifying its precise scaling. The chicken outside made a serrated sound.

Iwe, hold it down!

The boy placed his hands on either end of the body. J. slid a knife beneath the locking, unlocking gills. Blood eased over their hands. The fish bucked once, twice. Stopped.

I needed your help, J. smiled.

He deboned and gutted the fish. The boy wiped the chopping board, hypnotized by his own hand tracking thin loops of purple and yellow entrails across it. J. fried the fish in cooking oil with salt and onions and tomatoes. He served a piece of it to the boy, setting the plate on the floor. He set a portion of the fish aside for himself and took a plate with the rest of it to the man in the bedroom.

The room was dark but for an orange patch on the wall from the street lamp.

Who is here?

The *isabi* boy. J. put the plate on the side table and turned on the lamp.

The man began to cough, the phlegm in his chest rattling as he heaved and hacked. J. helped him sit up and rubbed his back until the fit ceased. When it was done, the man was tired.

Why is the fish boy still here? Did you not pay him?

I gave him supper.

As if I have food to spare, the man grunted. He took the plate on to his lap and began eating.

In the first dream, the sack is full and it is being dragged. In the second dream, I am inside it. What will the third dream reveal? You laugh. You say that dreams move forwards, not back. That I am imagining things. But that is why you chose me, Naila. Or at least that is what I fancied then. Now I am not so sure. Some days, I think you loved me for my hands. Other days, I think you threw stones to decide.

The plate on the kitchen floor was empty. The boy was gone. A tongue cleaned that plate, J. thought as he went to the doorway. The security gate was scaly with insects now, some so heavy their bodies chimed against the hollow metal bars. J. opened it and descended the short set of steps outside. He squatted to open the thatched door of the coop. He could hear the creaking, purring sound of the birds. Light from the house slivered the dark. J. inched along, his hipbone clicking as he went from one chicken to the next. They pivoted their heads and puffed their feathers. The last chicken sat upright on its nest, but it wasn't moving. J. heard a shudder and scanned the wall. The boy. Crouching in the corner, light-mottled.

J. turned back to the chicken and inched closer, reaching for it. The feathers were strung with light brittle spines. The bird fell limp in his hand. Then he saw them, hordes of them, spilling down the chicken's body, rolling around its neck, massing from its beak. J. started back. The chicken caved in as a flood of ants washed over it. J. stood, hitting his head on the thatched roof. The chickens were yelping and flapping, feathers rising from the ground. The ants snipped at his skin. As he hunched his way out of the coop, a chicken beat its way past his ribs and loped across the yard, head at full piston. Methodically, J. brushed his body off. Then he reached back and pulled the shaking child from the shadows.

My chest is full of cracked glass. That is how it feels when I cough. But the glass never shatters—there is not even that relief of complete pain. I am sick, Naila. Working for me has only made him stronger. Why does he bother? I thought at first that it was the money. But now I think he has been waiting. I wonder at the dwindling of our cares. We began with the widest compass, a society of the people, we said. But somehow we narrowed until it was just us three. Jacob, Joseph, Naila. You replaced yourself with the baby you birthed. So there were still three. But then your family took our son away. And now there are only two. Every day this sickness bites into my body and soon there will be only one. In the dream that just woke me, I am on the ground. It is night. The man kneels at my side. The face is melted, but his hairline has washed back with a froth of white hair and he has those same strong arms. His hands are wet. He is tugging the mouth of the sack up over my thighs. This must be when he puts my body into it. We are in the garden. I woke to the smell of smoke.

J. burned the coop. The four chickens left—one had disappeared in the night, snatched by a lucky dog—huddled in a makeshift corral. The fire smelled good; the dead chicken was practically fresh-cooked. From the kitchen doorway, J. watched the last of the smoke coiling up to join the clouds above. The sun took its time. His saliva was bitter and when he spat in the sink, he saw that it was gray. The boy was sleeping on a blanket on the kitchen floor. J. leaned against the counter, watching the boy's chest catch and release. His skinny legs were clean now, greased with Vaseline. J. had hosed the ants off him and anointed the rash of bites. J. made a cup of tea—Five Roses, milk, no sugar—and balanced it on a tray.

The bedroom was ripe with the metallic smell of dried blood. A copper dawn lit the window: *Kwacha! Ngwee...*

The man looked up when J. entered the room. What was that fire?

I burned the chicken coop.

Why?

J. put the tray on the side table and began to leave the room.

Do not walk away from me. The man spat.

J. wiped the spit from the floor with his sleeve. White ants, he said.

Bloody superstitions. The man sucked his teeth. Is that bloody fish boy still here? I don't like people coming here. They find out who I am and ask for money.

He doesn't know who you are. He's too young. This boy has no family, J. said. We could use the help.

The man lifted his cup, his hand trembling. He sipped the hot tea and winced with pleasure.

The boy goes. I can't afford such things.

The light had gone from copper to white gold, the day spending itself freely. J. squatted on the stoop outside, shelling groundnuts to cook a dish of pumpkin leaves. Students in pale-blue uniforms flirted in the dirt road. J. watched them with fond pity as he pressed the knuckle of his thumb to the belly of a shell. He hadn't tasted *chibwabwa ne'ntwilo* in twenty years. Naila's favorite. When he returned to the kitchen, he could hear voices in the living room. J. looked through the gap between the door and the frame. The man was leaning against the far wall, his pajamas low on his hips. J.'s eyes narrowed: the man hadn't left his bed in weeks. He was shouting at the boy, who stood with his back to J.

Isa kuno, the man said sternly. Come here! Are you deaf?

The boy moved hesitantly over to him and the man's hand fell trembling on to the bony shoulder. He used the boy as a crutch, levering himself to the sofa. His breathing rasped, shaving bits of silence off the air. In the dull light of the living room, the boy's skin was the color of a tarnished coin.

There, the man pointed at a picture frame face down on the floor near the sofa. What is that?

J. opened the door. Leave him, he said.

The boy rushed to J.'s side.

He broke it, the man snarled, picking up the framed photograph.

He doesn't know, J. said, looking down at the boy leaning against his leg.

I don't want him here, the man panted.

I owe it to him, J. said.

The man gaped, a laugh catching in his throat. The only debt you owe is to me, old man.

J. pushed the boy ahead of him into the kitchen.

I did not think I would walk again. These dreams give me strength. Not enough. I only got halfway to the kitchen, to the knives in the drawer. They wait like a flat bouquet: their thick wooden stems, their large silver petals. I will gather them up in my tired hands and I will hold them out to you. Naila. Look at you. There is a crack over your face because that bastard boy dropped the picture. But you are lovely in your green *salwar kameez*. Why do you look down? I never noticed before. Your eyelids are like smooth stones in this picture. I am a fool beside you. We reek of arrogance, all of us, J. with his Nehru shirt. How far he has fallen, sweeping and cooking for me like I'm a *musungu*. This picture must have been taken before the

Kalingalinga rally, the one that led to the riot. Do you remember? We were so hopeful. So very young.

J. stood above the sleeping man. He watched him for a moment then slapped his hand against the wall to wake him. A gecko in the corner shimmied upwards, its eyes a black colon punched in its face. The man's head fell forwards and he began coughing himself awake. When the phlegm had settled, he blinked.

Supper, J. said, placing a hand under the man's armpit to help him up. The man swept his weight against J. like a curtain falling from its rails. J. guided him back towards the bedroom, but the man raised his hand.

No. I'll eat in there, he nodded his head at the kitchen door. J. shrugged and they proceeded slowly in the other direction. J. kicked the door to the kitchen open and, as the *isabi* boy watched warily, he lowered the man into a chair by a small table.

Fish again? the man smiled at the boy.

J. placed a plate of food before the man and a bowl for the boy on the floor. The man stared at his plate. The fish was in pieces, its skin a crimped silver, its eye a button. When J. went to sit on the stoop, the man complained: Join me, he said.

My dream in the living room was short. A man is holding an ankle in each hand on either side of his hips. He drags the body towards the empty sack. It leaves a dark irregular trail on the ground. J. was standing over me when I woke up. You would say that these visions are an old man's nonsense. That no man dreams backwards. Can you see us sitting across from each other now? He eats in silence. The boy on the floor hums a rally song. J. must have taught him that. They are trying to confuse me. I know this boy is not my son, but I have to concentrate to keep it in mind. I insisted on this last supper. I am resigned to it. You laugh: you know I am resigned to nothing. You escaped my wilfulness only by dying. I will see this out. We will wrestle like Jacob and the angel.

I do not want the eye, the man said. J. reached for the plate.

Am I a child that you must cut my food?

J. stood and wiped his hand on his trousers. He walked around the boy on the floor who was already burrowing into his *nsima*, humming a song in loops, and opened a drawer and took out a short knife with a wooden handle.

Yes, that one, the sharp one, the man said.

J. sat back down, watching the man insert the point of the knife into the cavity in the fish's head and cut the eye out carefully, tipping it on to the edge of the plate. He put the knife on the table and began to eat in that slow noisy way of his.

So, the man said, picking at his teeth with his fingernail. J. was at the sink, rinsing pots. What will we do about that broken picture?

I can get it fixed. We are still comrades, that glass cutter and me, J. said.

Comrades? He sucked his teeth.

J. leaned against the counter, his arms, damp from dishwater, folded across his chest. What word would you prefer? Friend?

What do you know about that word? The man sucked his teeth again. The boy looked up at them, his cheeks dotted with white bits of *nsima*.

Yes, *bwana*. I know nothing of friendship, J. said.

The man looked at him. Rage beat across the air between them. Eating across from each other at a table again had kindled something.

I did not take her from you. J. released the words one at a time.

I've been having dreams, the man whispered.

No. I will not listen to your dreams. I have had dreams, *friend*. J. spat. He paced the room with the easy vigor of an animal, flaunting his vitality. His words cut through the smell of fish and illness, through the boy's whimpering hum.

I dream of her cunt, J. said. The English word was steely in his mouth. I pull a baby from her cunt. The baby's stomach is round and full and I can see through the skin, I see another baby inside it, five fingers pressed strong against the inside. I look at her face, sweating from labor, and I say, How is this possible? She laughs. Then I know that this is what happens when you use a woman with a used cunt.

The man looked away first. J. strode to the sink and spat in it. The boy was gone, his bowl upside down like an eye on the floor.

J. stooped to pick it up and looked back at his boss. The man's eyes were closed, his hands under the table.

We should not talk about that woman.
    She is gone.
    She has been gone a long time.
    And the boy?
    The boy is gone too.
    The man turned on to his side, gingerly hitching up his knees. J. looked down at him. J. had long ago decided to hate that woman: a feeling which had clarity and could accommodate the appetite he had once felt for her body. But he knew that the man still loved her, that he scratched invisible messages to her in the sheets. J. was sorry for his old friend. But to say sorry would be preface to leaving and he would not leave until it was done. The sick man hiccupped in his sleep like a drunk or a child. J. switched off the lamp and left the room.

When the door clicked shut, the man's eyes opened. He reached under his pillow and the blade snipped him. The tiny pain in his thumb pulsed inside the throng of pain in his body, a whining in the midst of a howling. The man sucked the blood from his thumb and carefully nestled his hand back under the pillow to grasp the knife handle. He could not slow the reversed momentum of these dreams, but he would not succumb like a dog. He kept his eyes open as long as he could.

    A man shuffles through the dark, carrying a body over his shoulder. The legs dangle down the man's front and bounce as he moves unsteadily down a corridor. He faces forwards but steps backwards. He turns and fumbles with a door knob. The bedroom door opens with a sucking sound. He bends slowly and lays the body on the bed. It tumbles down piecemeal, buttocks, then torso, then arms. The man stands and looks at it for a long time. All of a sudden, he pitches over the body. He seems grappled to it. A moan lifts and trips and falls into a scream cut short.

    Which comes first? The knife handle abrading his palm? Or the wide agony in his chest? The man's eyes open, he gasps. J.'s face floats above as if he had exhaled him: flat as day, dark as night. His fist is pressed hard to his own chest, his palm around the knife's handle. J.'s fingers are wrapped around his, their hands a bolus of flesh and bone, wood and blade. Together, they wrench the knife free of its home. Blood washes over him, its temperature perfect.

The boy stood in the doorway of the kitchen, looking out. It was night. His *bwana* was at the bottom of the garden, busy with a black lump and a gray sack. The boy's mind was empty but for a handful of notions—love, hunger, fear—darting like birds within, crashing into curved walls in a soundless, pitiless fury.

Memories We Lost

Lidudumalingani—winner of the 2016 Caine Prize

There was never a forewarning that this thing was coming. It came out of nowhere, as ghosts do, and it would disappear as it had come. Every time it left, I stretched my arms out in all directions, mumbled two short prayers, one to God and another to the ancestors, and then waited on my terrified sister to embrace me. The embraces, I remember, were always tight and long, as if she hoped the moment would last forever.

Every time this thing took her, she returned altered, unrecognizable, as if two people were trapped inside her, both fighting to get out, but not before tearing each other into pieces. The first thing that this thing took from her, from us, was speech, and then it took our memories. She began speaking in a language that was unfamiliar, her words trembling as if trying to relay unthinkable revelations from the gods. The memories faded one after the other until our past was a blur.

Some of the memories that have remained with me are of her screaming and running away from home. I remember when she ran out to the fields in the middle of the night, screaming, first waking my mother and me and then abducting the entire village from their sleep. Men and boys emerged from their houses carrying their knobkerries as if out to hunt an animal. Women and children stayed behind, frightened children clutching their mothers' nightgowns. The men and boys, disorientated and peeved, shuffled in the dark and split into small groups as instructed by a man who at the absence of a clear plan crowned himself a leader. Those with torches flicked them on and pushed back the darkness. Some took candles; they squeezed their bodies close and wrapped blankets around themselves in an attempt to block the wind, but all their matches extinguished before they could light a single candle.

Those without torches or candles walked on even though the next step in such darkness was possibly a plunge down a cliff. This was unlikely, it should be said, as most of them were born in the village, grew up there, got married there, had used that very same field as their toilet for all their lives, and had in overlapping periods only left the village when they went to work for the white man in large cities. They had a blueprint of the village in their minds; its walking paths, its indentations, its rivers, its mountains, its holes where ghosts lived were imprinted in their blood.

Hours later, the first small group of men and boys, and then another and another, emerged from the darkness. They did not find her. They had looked everywhere, at least they had claimed. They were worried about not finding my sister or annoyed at being woken in the middle of the night—I could not tell. Morphed into defeated men, their faces drooped to the floor, and their bodies slouched as if they had carried a heavy load. Each group was not aware of the other groups' whereabouts. They did not even know if the other groups still existed or if the night had swallowed them. They had last seen them when they wished them luck when they split up. They had heard them yell my sister's name, in the dark, before going silent.

She did not scream.

She did not cry.

She did not scream.

She did not cry.

She did not respond to the calls.

Each group chanted with great terror. With each group that emerged, I hoped that it would chant something else, but nothing changed; the chant was, as if it had been rehearsed for a long time, repeated the same each time, tearing my heart apart.

She did not scream.

She did not cry.

She did not scream.

She did not cry.

She did not respond to our screams.

The chant went on until all groups had returned.

Mother, a woman of tall build and wide hips, only returned home when the sun was way up in the sky the next day, carrying my sister on her back.

She would scream in intervals as if to taunt me, my mother said.

I remember another time my sister banged her head against the wall until she bled. She and I were racing around the rondavel to see who would return first to our starting point. I think we were 12 and 15 then. She had begun to grow breasts, and she was telling me how sensitive they were. She had brushed her fingers over them and a sensation she had never felt before had pulsed through her body. She did not know what was going on or what had caused her body to tingle apart from that touch. I remember trying to interject that she was becoming a woman, she was becoming sexual—not that I knew anything myself.

She dismissed me teasingly, in the gentle manner that she dismissed things, leaving one not convinced whether she was in agreement or not. You know nothing about breasts, she told me after examining my chest. I told her that I was a late bloomer. The lie came out of me as naturally as truth comes to others. I had made my mother, and anyone else who knew, promise that she must never know the truth about how my chest had no breasts. She teased me for a long time that day and days after. It was nothing malicious, it was in the manner that a sibling tells another sibling that they have a big head but get upset when someone else says the words.

Then it arrived. I did not see it approaching. I had always hoped that I would so that I could stop it. At the time, I was convinced that if one observed more carefully one could see it coming, with horns, spikes, and an oversized head—that's how I imagined it looked. I don't know if she ever saw it coming, but I hope not. The horror of seeing a monster coming for you and not being able to run even though one is not in a dream would have been unbearable for her.

I was telling her how once I fooled the boys in my class that I had grown breasts. It was a Friday. I stuffed pantyhose into my shirt, to look like breasts, and wore my mother's bra. The stupid boys never stopped to wonder at the improbability of the situation. How is it possible that my breasts had grown in one day?

So the boys stared at me the whole day, convinced that I had suddenly bloomed in the night, I said to her.

I stared out into the landscape that began in my mother's garden and stretched far beyond sight. The sun was setting behind the forest and dust was floating everywhere. Where the dust was dense, one could see it sway this way and that way as if in the middle of a dance. A sophisticated dance, the kind that, I imagined, happened in other worlds, very far from the village. The village was settling into repose. The cold summer air had begun to torment the villagers' bare legs and arms. Everything was in silhouette, including the horses that trotted across the veld, the cattle that lowered their heads to graze, and the water that flowed down the cliff. The mountains, ancient but nevertheless still standing, were casting giant shadows over the landscape. The shadows stretched so far from the mountain that they began to exist as if they were solid entities on their own.

In the middle of a story I was telling her, she gently rocked back and forth then began hitting the back of her head against the wall. For a short time I thought she was providing rhythm for my anecdote. It was only when she began to scream, in an attempt to churn this thing out of her, that I became alarmed. By then she had smashed her head and left blood on the wall. She had transformed into someone else. She was not here. I tried to grab her or whatever was there. I tried to make her stop. I held her hands, bound them behind her back, laid my body against hers, but she pushed me away easily with a strength that came to her only when this thing tore her apart. Had it not been a mud wall, an old one at that, she would have cracked her skull open. Instead, she cracked the wall with her head.

The bloodstain remained visible on the wall long after my mother scraped it off; long after she had applied three layers of mud and new water paint. The stains stayed long after the sangoma came and cleansed the spot where my sister had bludgeoned her head. I began to smell the bloodstains in my dreams, in my clothes, in everything. The smell of blood lingered after many sunsets had come; even after the rain had come.

The other time that I remember this thing entering my sister was when she threw hot porridge on me. This thing arrived in her and abducted her while she hovered over a hot porridge pot. In the middle of a joke she never finished, she flung the pot across the room. It only just missed my face but my chest was not that fortunate. I don't remember opening the bottom half of the door of the rondavel but I found myself standing outside, naked, having pulled my dress off. The pain was unbearable. Hours later, when she gained consciousness, she was shocked and devastated about what had happened to me. I told her I had poured hot water on myself by mistake. She would never forgive herself.

Though it had been tough in other months, it was in November that things got worse. This thing, this thing that took over her followed her to school and she had to drop out. It arrived while she was in class. She was so strong, so out of control, that she flung a desk across the room and smashed a window. When I arrived in her class, everyone was standing around watching. She had broken a chair against the wall, too, and she was screaming words I did not understand. I stood at a short distance from her. All she had to do was look into my eyes. Please look into my eyes, I begged. Her eyes had turned red and her entire body was shaking. When she did look at me, after scanning the bewildered faces of the crowd, she stopped screaming. She knew me. I stared right into her eyes and I could see this thing leave; I could see my sister returning.

After that incident I went truant from school. Every morning I threw up. I convinced my mother that I was sick. She asked a boy who went to the same school to tell my class teacher that I had come down with an illness.

I want to be in the same class with you, I said to my sister, so I am going to wait until you are fine so we can go to school together.

They will never allow that. Mother, the teachers, the principal.

Yes they will. It is not like I want to study a grade higher. I want to study with you in the same class.

She and I spent that week doing sketches. With a pencil she could sketch me onto the paper such that it appeared as if I was alive on the page, another me, more happy, less torn, existing elsewhere.

She begged and begged me to go to school and promised me that she would be fine and that every day when I came back she would have new sketches for me.

We spent our days talking, one ear listening out for my mother's footsteps. We would know she was coming by the sound of the door closing when she walked out of the main house, then her shadow would come first through the door of our house.

My mother took my sister to more sangomas and more churches and gave her more bottles of medication. She became unresponsive. She only nodded and shook her head at irrelevant moments—there was nothing else. It turned out later, when I went back to school, that my week of absence had gone unreported. This bothered neither my class teacher nor me. Over the years my sister had missed so much school that I had caught up with her and was, in fact, two grades above her.

A few weeks after I had returned to school, the teacher told us about schizophrenia and I knew then that this is what my sister had and that all the medication she had been taking would never help her. Instead, it was destroying her. The teacher told us that there is no cure for this thing, but I knew that my sister deserved to feel something, anything.

The first thing my sister and I got rid of was her arsenal of medication. This is going to be our secret, I said. On our long walks, away from our mother, we dug holes and buried the roots she had to chew. The way to get rid of the medication drink, I demonstrated to her, was to pour it into the mug and take an empty sip, then when no-one was looking throw it out the back window that had grass growing below it. The window also opened to a large landscape where the cattle grazed. When mother asks if I have given you your medication you must nod, I told her.

I came back from school the following Monday afternoon and she took me to our house and poured her medication, took an empty sip, and threw it out the window with a smile. It was our game.

She began to recognize herself. She and I began to communicate again. We invented our own language because she had stopped talking. We simply gestured to each other and then over time we inserted a few words here and there.

We began to love each other again. I remember the day we connected again. We were in the same room we had always sat in, staring, as we always did, into the landscape, over the mountains, at the horizon, into the sun, until our eyes could not take us any further. It was a day of looking out, smiling, laughing, crying, holding hands.

We sat there and watched the day go by. We didn't even attempt to say a word. I realized then that she and I needed no words.

In the afternoon that day it began to rain. I dragged her out of the house. We jumped in the rain, begging it to pour on us so we could be tall, big, strong, bold. In that moment, my sister returned; she smiled, laughed. That day we began to form new childhood memories, filling the void left by the one that had been wiped out.

We lay on the wet ground, stretched out our arms and legs, rain falling on our faces, and felt free. But my mother had seen us laugh and jump and thought that this thing was going to come again.

The following day the entire village gathered outside our house for yet another ritual meant to cure my sister. She had been through all these rituals and church sermons and nothing had changed. Each time sangomas and pastors promised that she would be healed within days. There was once, at least according to the elders, a glimpse of these sangomas healing. The tobacco, meat, and matches that had been put in the rondavel for the ancestors to take at night, in one of the many rituals, were not there by morning, leading them to believe that the ancestors had healed her. It was not long after that this thing came again, proving that the tobacco, meat, and matches had simply been stolen by thieves.

The day of the ritual, I remember how the clouds moved across the sky in a hurry, and how thick fog hung on to the grass, the mountains, the riverbanks, and forests as if to announce death. It hung so low that people appeared to be floating with their legs cut off below their knees. The women's chatter and songs reached us long before the crowd was visible. It appeared as if the fog had swallowed them and that the women would never come into sight; all the same, they did. They ululated and chanted songs as they approached our home.

Men came in silence, arms folded behind their backs, carrying sticks.

A few minutes after the women arrived, smoke escaped the fireplace into the sky, dancing with the moving clouds as if the sky was their dance floor. The children ran around and kicked soccer balls that had been made by stuffing papers into plastic bags. Everyone moved in a chaotic choreography. That way went an obese woman balancing a bucket of water on her head; this way went a child with a tablecloth; that way went a dog with a bone; this way went chickens; that way stood women gossiping about my sister. From our house, I could see the chaos amplifying as more people arrived.

I looked at my sister and found her face, as it had become in earlier months, emotionless. In the past few days she had given me hope that she had returned. Now tears rolled down our cheeks. I knew then that she still felt something, that the last few days of holding hands, laughing, and jumping in the rain were not a dream.

The fog began to clear and everything came into focus. The mountains, landscape, river, and the other villages were there, unmoved.

An old man who had been smoking his pipe behind the kraal emptied it and stuffed it in his pockets. The ritual began. Knives were drawn and the goat was first stabbed in the stomach to summon our ancestors from their enclaves, and then it was meat.

After some time, an old aunt came for us, calling for us to come out of the house. We hugged tightly, my sister and I, wiped each other's tears. It was only after we had heard her footsteps approaching our house that we walked out, holding hands, fingers tightly entwined. The only way to have torn me away from her would have been to cut us apart.

The villagers shouted insults at the "thing," as it remained unknown to them. For what felt like an entire lifetime, while my sister and I sat at a corner in the kraal, our heads bowed, the elders kept referring to this thing as the devil's work and demons. None of them knew my sister; none of them cared. The sun was up now, thick shadows gathering around the house. Even though there was no wind, the windmill by the fields made a creaking sound.

My mother was torn and defeated and questioned why God gave this thing to my sister—and my father. Secrets stay buried for so long but one day they rise to open like seeds breaking free from the earth. Nobody had ever mentioned that my father had this thing. That he had left one day on his horse, to see distant relatives, and had never come back. To only be seen in the way the deceased are seen after their death, in dreams and hallucinations.

He had been seen in some village at least twice, my mother told me. The person who had seen him yelled and waved, but he never bothered to look. They were not sure if it was my father but they were convinced that it had to be. He was never buried, though it is now twenty years later. There was nothing to bury. I have no memory of my father. There was always hope that he would return from somewhere; nobody knew where, nobody cared, as long as he returned.

The night of the ritual, my sister and I slept lying the same way, instead of in different directions. I woke up and she was holding me, squeezing me, and she had sunk her teeth in the pillow so she would not cry. She jerked for a few minutes and then fell asleep in my arms.

In the morning, I went to milk the goat. I saw two human shadows hovering above the kraal. At first, though it was unusual, I thought nothing of it even as they mumbled something to each other. In the shadows that leaped inside the kraal, with the smell of manure, I saw that it was my mother and an uncle who had come to stay with us for the ritual. It was as if their heads were bound together into one, creating a giant head, a ghost even. I had meant to get up but when I heard them mention my sister, I put the jug of milk down and crouched, leaning on the goat so it did not move. My mother and Smellyfoot, the man who had moved in with my mother, were making plans to take my sister away.

The medication and the rituals did not work, my mother said. The way she saw it, my sister needed to go see Nkunzi. This thing is going to come back, she said.

Nkunzi was a sangoma from a remote village in which houses were lined miles apart from one another; he was famous for "baking" people like my sister, claiming to cure them. It is said that whenever there was a car approaching his village, people would shout for Nkunzi to come out. Your demons are here, they would say.

Smellyfoot, a name that my sister had given him, agreed with my mother. We were not his kids; why would he care? And that was it, they decided: the next day my sister would be taken to Nkunzi to be baked. This is what they did with people who heard voices or demons, as they called them; they baked them until the demons left them. What was even more terrible than the baking was that people had come to be convinced of it.

I had heard of how Nkunzi baked people. He would make a fire from cow dung and wood, and once the fire burned red he would tie the demon-possessed person onto a section of zinc roofing then place it on the fire. He claimed to be baking the demons and that the person would recover from the burns a week later. I had not heard of anyone who had died but I had not heard of anyone who had lived either.

I could not allow this to happen to my sister.

After sunset I got my things and we left together. The twilight was approaching. I couldn't think where to go. We wandered first onto the main road; then I spotted many eyes staring at us so I changed direction and sank into the valley. My sister held tightly on to my hand. I did not tell her anything she did not need to know. We were going to see an aunt who had suddenly fallen ill. We have to see her before the sun rises tomorrow, I told her.

There was no aunt who was ill.

We walked in the valley, on the banks of the river, then up a wet mound and over a fence that had once stood but was now lying broken on the ground. We came to a bridge with a tar road and because we were both scared of water we crossed the bridge and walked on the road alongside the river.

We hardly noticed that it had become night; suddenly a giant moon had sneaked above us and stars had weaved patterns only gods understood. Mountains and landscape were now mere shapes, giant and indistinct, leaving us, tiny as we were then, the only things present in the world.

We walked by the river and then abandoned it, walked up a mountain and down the other side into a village. I was not sure whether it was Philani or another village. I had only ever been there once before and that visit was not even physical. My mother had mentioned it in one of her stories before she moved us into the new house—before a week later replacing our father, and us, with the Smellyfoot.

Once we descended the mountain and found ourselves in a strange village we would knock on the first house that had its light on and sleep there. That had been the initial plan, but it was flawed. Everyone in the villages knew everyone. I was convinced that whomever we asked for a place to sleep, even if we were to lie and give them false names, tell them that we were heading to the next village but something had delayed us, they would have recognized us, either because we have my grandfather's ears or my mother's nose or that they had seen us when we were toddlers, even stroked our buttocks. It had always been said that my sister had my grandfather's forehead. The plan was too risky.

We are close, I told my sister. Close to where, I had no idea. All the same, we were going forward, and it felt like we had reached where we were going, which was nowhere in particular. All that mattered was that we were now far from home.

We had no idea where we were going to sleep, what we were going to eat or how we were going to live, but returning home was not an option. Maybe when my mother dies, I said, maybe then we can return.

We crossed Philani village—I was still not sure which village it was—with dogs barking at us, or at something else, perhaps a pole that had always stood there. In no time at all we reached another village. My sister stopped asking me why we were leaving home. She squeezed my hand every now and then and I hers.

Many times, I contemplated telling my sister why we were running away from home, but I could not. I did not know where to begin. There was and still is no perfect place to begin; the real story would destroy her.

My mother preferred her numb. I preferred a sister. A laughing sister, a talking sister, and a sister who looked into my eyes and cried and laughed. Imagine the reflections that suddenly appear when one stares into water and beats it. That is what happens to my sister. I want to tell her she has a mental disorder that makes it impossible for her to tell fiction from reality.

We could not see any lights. People had long gone to sleep. We had no idea where we were but we knew that we had reached another village. The moon had disappeared and the stars were now only dots in the sky. Morning was close, I thought, and I told my sister who nodded and smiled.

We had no idea what time it was but it had been a long time since we left home, and our feet hurt. We decided to sleep under a tree, to wake once the sun was up and walk again, to somewhere.

The Story of the Girl Whose Birds Flew Away

Bushra al-Fadil—winner of the 2017 Caine Prize
Translated by Max Shmookler

There I was, cutting through a strange market crowd—not just people shopping for their salad greens, but beggars and butchers and thieves, prancers and Prophet-praisers and soft-sided soldiers, the newly arrived and the just retired, the flabby and the flimsy, sellers roaming and street kids groaning, god-damners, bus-waiters and white-robed traders, elegant and fumbling. And there in the midst, our elected representatives, chasing women with their eyes and hands and whole bodies, with those who couldn't give chase keeping pace with an indiscreet and sensual attention, or lost in a daydream.

I cut, sharp-toothed, carving a path through the crowd when a passer-by clutched his shoulder in pain, followed by a "Forgive me!" Then a scratch on a lady's toe was followed with a quick "Oh no!" Then a slap to another's cheek, after which was heard "Forgiveness is all I seek!" So lost in dreams I could not wait for their reply to my apology.

The day was fresher than a normal summer day, and I could feel delight turbaned around my head, like a Bedouin on his second visit to the city. The working women were not happy like me, nor were the housewives. I was the son of the Central Station, spider-pocketed, craning my neck to see a car accident or the commotion of a thief being caught. I was awake, descending into the street, convulsing from hunger and the hopeless search for work in the "cow's muzzle," as we say. I suppressed my unrest. The oppressed son of the oppressed but despite all of that—happy. Could the wretched wrest my happiness from me? Hardly. Without meaning to, I wandered through these thoughts. The people around me were a pile of human watermelons, every pile awaiting its bus. I approached one of the piles and pulled out my queuing tools—an elbow and the palm of my hand—and then together they helped my legs to hold up my daily depleted and yearly defeated body. I pulled out my eyes and began to look... and look... in all directions and to store away what I saw.

I saw a blind man looking out before him as if he were reading from that divine book which preceded all books, that book of all fates. He kept to himself as he passed before me, but still I felt the coins in my pocket disappear. Then I saw a woman who was so plump that when she called out to her son—"Oh Hisham"—you could feel the greasy resonance of the "H" in your ears. I saw a frowning man, a boy weaving an empty tin can along the ground with his feet. I saw voices and heard boundless scents and then, suddenly, in the midst of all of that, I saw her. The dervish in my heart jumped. I saw her: soaring without swaying, her skin the color of wheat—not as we know it but rather as if the wheat were imitating her tone. She had the swagger of a soldier, the true heart of the people. And if you saw her, you'd never be satiated.

I said to myself, "This is the girl whose birds flew away."

Her round face looked like this:

Her nose was like a fresh vegetable and by God, what eyes! A pharaonic neck with two taut slender cords, only visible when she turned her head. And when she turned her head, I thought all the women selling their mashed beans and salted sunflower seeds would flee, the whole street would pick up and leave only ruts where they had been, the fetid stench of blood would abandon the places where meat was sold. My thoughts fled to a future I longed for. And if you poured water over the crown of her head, it would flow down past her forehead. She walked in waves, as if her body were an auger spiralling through a cord of wood.

She approached me. I looked myself over and straightened myself out. As she drew closer, I saw she was holding tight to a little girl who resembled her in every way but with a child's chubbiness. Their hands were woven together as if they had been fashioned precisely in that manner, as if they were keeping each other from straying. They both knitted their eyebrows nonchalantly, such that their eyes flashed, seeming to cleanse their faces from the famished stares of those around them.

"This is the girl whose birds flew away," I said.

I turned to her sister and said, "And this must be the talisman she's brought to steer her away from evil. How quickly her calm flew from her palm."

I stared at them until I realized how loathsome I was in comparison. It was this that startled me, not them. I looked carefully at the talisman. Her mouth was elegant and precise as if she never ate the stewed okra that was slowly poisoning me. I glanced around and then I looked back at them, looked and looked—oh how I looked!—until a bus idled up and abruptly saved the day. Although it was not their custom, the people made way for the two unfamiliar girls, and they just hopped aboard. Through the dust kicked up by the competition around the door I found myself on the bus as well.

We lumbered forward. The man next to me was smoking and the man next to him smelled as if he were stuffed with onions. If the day were not so fresh, and were it not for the girl and her talisman and their aforementioned beauty, I would have got off that wretched bus without a word of apology. After five minutes, the onionized man lowed to the driver: "This's my stop, buddy."

He got off and slammed the door in a way that suggested the two of them had a long and violent history. The driver rubbed his right cheek as if the door had been slammed on him. He grumbled to himself, "People without a shred of mercy."

The onion man reeled back around and threw a red eye at the driver. "What?" he exploded. "What'd you say?"

"Get going, by God!" I yelled. "He wasn't talking about you."

As the bus pulled away, the onionized man's insults and curses blended with the whine of the motor. As if the driver wanted to torment us, he continued the argument as a monologue, beginning, "People are animals..." He blamed the matter on human nature, such as it was, and railed and cursed until we hit a pothole in the main road. The bus hopped up like a frog, croaking until he floored the gas and it bolted forward, roaring "Zamjara zamjara" like some wild animal.

The cruel movements of the bus began to hurt my back. But when I looked over at the girls, I figured they must have taken the shape of their seats, as they did not seem to be in pain nor was their flesh being shaken from the bone. Finally we arrived. They got off and I followed, unable to hear their footsteps over the sound of my own hooves, audible to all. I nearly reached for my ears. Had they grown longer? I trailed behind them. This was not the Sudanese way and, before I saw them, I would always walk alongside my fellow pedestrians. Yet they seemed to be walking to the rhythm of my thoughts, so I said to myself, let them walk ahead. The rhythm should lead the tune anyway. They walked in front, a music of excessive beauty, and I walked behind, confused and off-beat.

Then suddenly they spun round, beautiful, their faces colored with an ornate rage.

The older said, "What's with you? Why're you following us?"

"No, no, my cousin," I said, trying to loosen the strings of their fury. "I already have someone just as beautiful as you. And anyway I am not the kind to chase after beauty in the streets with a rifle."

"We've heard that a thousand times!" she said.

"You don't believe me. I was trying to say that I already have a girl. I love her and she loves me and my camel loves her she-camel.[1]

---

1 A well-known couplet from a poem by the pre-Islamic poet al-Munakhkhal al-Yashkuri (580-603).

A thousand times I've come to her angry and left with a smile, as if she lived in some sort of joy factory. This morning, I left so full of her that people catcalled me in the street."

Instead of laughter, a pure melody slipped out of the throat of the girl whose birds flew away. Then we fell silent.

My mind turned to the memory of my beloved. What a devilish afreet she was![2] So sure of herself, that girl, so confident. Once, when the summer was at its most intense, she said to me as we were returning from a concert: "My grandmother was so beautiful that Suror himself used to sing to her."[3]

"Suror and the other singers were slowly crushed by the Haqiba poets,"[4] I told her, "until they began to moan and cry and oscillate as if enchanted by the melodic rounds and dirty words."

"What do you mean?" she asked.

"Their poets are like butchers selling women by the pound. When a man goes down to the butcher's shop, he hears a voice singing and hollering 'Breast! Breast! Cheek! Cheek!' So he rifles through the selection of female parts, turning over those bits that please him while the voice draws his attention to the beauty of those pieces he may have missed. He leaves after buying a breast with onion or a flank garnished with arugula, and those who have guests would buy a whole rump."

My love said, "Knock off that dirty talk and pull back your tongue. Have you forgotten that Khalil Farah was one of the singers?"[5]

She left me speechless. That must have been my daydreams returning because when I looked around I could not find a trace of the girl whose birds flew away nor her sister.

I turned my senses into a tracking device. My ears became two microphones, my eyes two cameras, my nose a chemlab and my tongue a newscast. The device worked perfectly, unlike the products

---

2 Afreet: a mischievous, otherworldly creature of Sudanese mythology.

3 Al-Haj Mohammed Ahmed Suror (1901-1946), one of the founders of modern Sudanese song.

4 The Haqiba school of song and poetry appeared in Sudan in the 1920s, advocating modernization and promoting the erotic in poetry.

5 Khalil Afandi Farah (1894-1932)—an anti-colonial Sudanese poet and activist.

made in our factories these days. From there I monitored the situation like a mouse following the movements of its age-old enemy in order to protect itself. But then the girl's radar picked me up. I quickened my step, afraid she would insult me, but she ran behind me, saying, "You've been tormenting me. What do you want?"

"Nothing," I said, "except to see you. To sing of you and dream of you! There's no need for pain between us. There's no doubt that it's a one-sided attraction, for I'm enamored of one like you but I feel in front of her a certain... inferiority." The girl laughed and scrutinized me, as if seeking to identify what it was that was strange about me, and so I persisted:

"Made of red blood, are you? And was your heart a single rose struck by tragedy after tragedy until it folded back upon itself?"

She laughed again and my heart felt the soothing snow of contentment and joy.

"A poet?" she asked.

"So they say," I said, adding: "Who told you?"

"We've heard," she said.

"And who's with you such that you address yourself in the plural? Why, your face is light and your voice light and you a mirror suspended in my tears illuminated, and so I cry."

"Beautiful," she said dryly. "I had misunderstood you but now the truth comes out. You know the young men these days, so inane and brazen."

"But dig deep and you'll find precious metals not found on the surface," I said. "My friends are more numerous than the ants and most of them understand and are understood."

The girl whose birds flew away skipped ahead out of joy. Her form wavered until she disappeared, the sweet ring of her bells still in my ear. The image of her eyes remained in my mind, growing bright then dim then bright again, her face still nourishing my memory with joy. Her birds flew away. Away. Away.

And just like that we became friends. For an entire month our meetings continued in the streets: skipping, laughing, discussing— without reaching her true depths—and fearing she had only touched my surface. And so, one Wednesday, I asked her:

"Who is that little girl on your right?"

"My sister," she said. "I need her when we're walking in the markets. She protects me from the evil of the cars."

"A talisman?" I asked.

"What?" she said.

"Like a charm or a spell. She protects you from envious eyes, no?" Then I said to myself: But if death has already sunk its claws in, no talisman will help. I stared in the faces of the two beautiful girls for a long moment. The younger one shrunk away, her strength drained like an ox at the water wheel. No doubt her endless chores had made her grow old before her years. I got on board the bus with them again. The passengers' eyes, like glass saws, flew over the thighs and eyes and faces of the young girls. I turned. All around me, the passengers' mouths gaped like empty salt dishes. Their eyes had taken flight, leaving two holes in every face. My glasses may have held back my eyes, but they could not hold back my innate curiosity and the deep pleasure I took in statistics: On their bodies I counted a total of 99 round eyes. Strange, I thought, to add up to an odd number, until I looked around and saw a man with only one eye.

I returned home angry and rummaged through my papers until I found what I had been looking for. I resolved to return immediately. It was already midday. The sun was wide awake and I was furious. I found the bus door flung open like a gaping maw and entered. It was like Noah's Ark inside. Every face imaginable. All kinds of peoples. Once seated, it was easy to slip into distracted daydreaming. I sat down and released my strong-hooved stallions from their stables to gallivant through the fields of my imagination and fantasy.

It was as if I had lost my voice. As if it had evaporated. My worries barked and yapped at me, but neither my own two eyes nor anyone else's woke me. I was the son of the heaping portion, the steaming dinner plate, but they filled me with despair instead of millet and milk. In return, I filled others with joy, for my fate was miserable while theirs was better (and good for them!). It was as if I had been created to ensure their survival and they survived to torment me.

And yes, I am the comatose son of sleep, the son of long anticipation and unfulfilled promises. A beloved I have in memory and longing only. Someone like me only hopes for someone like her. And someone like her would never be satisfied with someone like me. So who am I like? *You cow*, I said to myself, *you beast. Man stuffed with disease, with bacteria, with transformations and shake-ups, with ascents and long, tumbling falls. Women searching for happiness clamor around him only to find suffering under the whip. Those searching for a friend he treats as an enemy; and around him gather those women whose birds have flown away—and yet, there is nothing around which he clamors. And despite all of this, he claims that he is one who understands, who is aware, who has chosen to pick a fight and rebel.*

I returned to my state of despair to find myself still on the damned bus, the people around me butting heads and locking horns, the men refusing to relinquish their seats to the women, the women not sparing the men a single curse from the dictionary. I needed to get off before Bagheeti Station and, when I did, I saw before me a train of humanity propeled by curiosity towards the hospital. My own curiosity was no less than theirs but perhaps I was more arrogant. I rode the wave of the crowd after I had exhausted every expression and exclamation of surprise.

"What's going on?" I yelled, but my question was lost in the din of similar questions. Several interpretations came to me, each independent of the next, pulling together certain details and disregarding others. The responses of onlookers did nothing but catapult me forward, toward the source of my curiosity. I was swept away by the crush of the people around the vortex, closer and closer until I screamed—

"Blood!"

It was as if a razor had cut the light from my eyes. As if I had died. A bloodbath. A bath whose dye was blood and impact. The talisman stained with blood and terror. And the blood of two girls just like them—the dye of henna. Blood on their hands like murderers, and on their legs like the murdered, and elsewhere, everywhere, such that you could not tell from where it was seeping. I said out loud: "Must've been a traffic accident, no doubt."

"No way," yelled an agitated man with a rounded face.

"What, then?" I asked myself.

I turned with the rest of the gaping onlookers to a calm-voiced boy. "They were on the beach," he said. "Twisted just like that and unconscious. A heavy-set man found them and went to the police station."

"It was a traffic accident!" I screamed.

My neighbor, who happened to be among the crowd, turned to me. "Have you gone mad?" he demanded. "A traffic accident on the beach? What the hell does that mean? A boat collided with them? Or perhaps a fish jumped from the water and smacked into them?"

A traffic accident, no doubt, I said to myself. Then I turned towards the wide avenue, calling out in a laughing scream, a sobbing, playful sermon: "No, no, no. No! Her birds flew away! Her birds flew away! Her birds flew... flew... flew..."

Some of the passers-by glanced at me, shaking their heads, and then, certain I was mad, they turned away.

"Flew... flew... flew."

A man stopped his car. His jugular bulged with laughter as he asked me, "What flew off?"

"Her birds..." I replied.

The driver laughed until the tarmac shook and the car stalled and emitted a cloud of fumes. He restarted the engine and disappeared.

Flew... flew... flew... Could it be? It must be that some force took them to that place. Some sort of deception, some trickery. Did I not see the terror and fear on their faces? The terror of the talisman and the shock of the girl whose birds flew away? No... she landed... landed... landed.

Around me a crowd had gathered. They were all staring at me as if I were responsible for the accident. I nearly screamed at them: "They flew away! She flew away!" But the tarmac spread before me and so I began to walk. And walk and walk. That terrible day! I did not reach the well-spring of my dreams, nor my house. The river was closer and the eyes of the lovers there more reassuring. So I decided to go there, perhaps to cleanse myself or lay my head in the darkness of their pupils and sleep in their solid whiteness. *He filled my void and arose from sleep to fight what had been ordained for me.*[6] As long

---

6 A partial line from the praise poem of al-Mutanabbi (died 965), dedicated to his patron Sayf al-Dawla.

as the innocent birds were struck with stones and selfish desires, they would continue to land in such ugly places against their will, in patches full of violence and hate.

Translated from the Arabic by Max Shmookler, with support from Najlaa Osman Eltom.

Fanta Blackcurrant

Makena Onjerika—winner of the 2018 Caine Prize

She was our sister and our friend, but from the time we were totos, Meri was not like us. If the Good Samaritans who came to give us foods and clothes on Sundays asked us what we wanted from God, some of us said going to school; some of us said enough money for living in a room in Mathare slums; and some of us, the ones who wanted to be seen we were born-again, said going to heaven. But Meri, she only wanted a big Fanta Blackcurrant for her to drink every day and it never finish.

God was always liking Meri. In the streets when we opened our hands and prayed people for money, they felt more mercy for Meri. They looked how she was beautiful with a brown mzungu face and a space in front of her teeth. They asked Meri, where is your father and where is your mother? They gave her ten bob and sometimes even twenty bob. For us who were color black, just five bob.

All of us felt jealousy for Meri, like a hot potato refusing to be swallowed. We thieved things from her nylon paper. Only small things: her bread, her razor blade, her tin for cooking. But some of us felt more jealousy for Meri and we wished bad things to fall on her head.

And then one day Meri was put in the TV. It happened like this: a boy called Wanugu was killed by a police. This Wanugu he was not our brother or our friend, but some boys came to the mjengo where we were staying carrying sticks and stones. They said all chokoraas, boys and girls, must go to the streets to make noise about

Wanugu. Fearing them, we went and shouted "Killers, killers, even chokoraas are people" until TV people came to look our faces with their cameras.

All of us wanted to be put in the TV. Quickly, quickly we beat dust out of our clothes; we stopped smiling loudly to hide our black teeths; we pulled mucus back inside our noses. All of us told the story of Wanugu, how he was killed with a gun called AK47 when he was just sitting there at Jevanjee gardens, breathing glue and hearing the lunchtime preacher say how heaven is beautiful. He was not even thinking which car he could steal the eyes or mirrors or tires. All of us told the story, but at night when we went to the mhindi shops to look ourselves in the TVs being sold in the windows, we saw only Meri. She was singing Ingrish:

"Meri hada ritro ramp, ritro ramp, ritro ramp."

Some of us looked Meri with big eyes because we had not heard that before she came to the streets she had been taken to school, from standard one to three.

We said, "Meri, speak Ingrish, even us we hear."

We beat her some slaps and we laughed, but inside all of us started fearing that someone was coming to save Meri from the streets. All of us remembered how last year people came to save a dog because it found a toto thrown away in the garbage. We felt jealousy for Meri. She was never thinking anything in her head. Even if she was our sister and our friend, she was useless, all the time breathing glue and thinking where she could find a Fanta Blackcurrant. If anyone came to save Meri, all of us were going to say we were Meri. Some of us started washing in Nairobi river every day to stop smelling chokoraa; some of us went to the mhindi shops every day to listen how people speak Ingrish on the TVs; some of us started telling long stories about how long time ago even us we had lived in a big house.

But no one came to save Meri. Days followed days and years followed years. We finished being totos and blood started coming out between our legs. And Meri, from staying in the sun every day, she changed from color brown to color black just like us. Jiggers entered her toes. Her teeth came out leaving ten spaces in her mouth. Breathing glue, she forgot her father's name and her mother's name. Every day her head went bad: she removed her clothes and washed herself with soil until we chased her. We caught her. We sat on her. We pinched her. We beat her slaps. We pulled her hair. We didn't stop until tears came out of her eyes.

All of us were now big mamas. When we prayed people for money in the streets, they looked how we had big matiti hanging on our chests like ripe mangoes. We felt shame because they were seeing we were useless. In the end, all of us stopped praying people in the streets. Even Meri, she followed us at night when we went to see the Watchman at the bank.

He said, "Me, I am only helping you because I feel for you mercy."

He said, "You only pay me ten bob and remain with ten bob."

He said, "I will find you good customers."

He said he was our friend, but when we asked him how to remove the toto inside Meri's stomach, he chased us away, calling us devils.

He said, "Who told you me I know how to kill totos?"

All of us felt mercy for Meri. Maybe one time after a customer finished, she had forgotten to wash herself down there with salt water. Some of us said we knew a way to remove the toto using wires; some of us knew a way using leaves from a tree in Jevanjee gardens; some of us started crying, fearing even us we had a toto inside.

But Meri, she was just breathing glue and singing a song to herself. In the mjengo where we were staying, with two walls and one side of the roof removed, she sat the whole day under the stairs going nowhere, telling us which man had put the toto inside her stomach. First it was a man walking with a stick who gave her a new 100 bob, and then she said it was a mzungu talking Ingrish through his nose, and then she scratched the jiggers in her toes and the lice in her hair and said no, it was the man who took her in a new car to a big house and washed her body and applied her nice smelling oil, asking her, does she see how she can be beautiful. We asked ourselves if she was thinking to find that man. If she was thinking he was going to marry her and take her to live in that big house, eating breads and drinking milks.

All of us pulled air through our teeth to make long sounds at her because she was thinking like an empty egg. But some of us, looking how Meri was happy, we gave her presents—soap remaining enough for washing three times; a comb broken some teeth; a mango still color green. We wanted that when the toto came out she could not refuse for us to carry it and touch it on the stomach to make it laugh. Some of us started telling her which name was the best for the toto. We wished it to be a girl, even if boys are better, because boys can search inside garbage for tins, papers and bottles and take them to a place in Westlands to be paid some money. But girls are beautiful and you can plait their hairs and wear them clothes of many colors. All of us thought like this, but all of us could see the troubles coming to fall on Meri's head.

We prayed the Watchman for her again, but he said, "No, no, no. Customers don't want someone with a toto inside her stomach."

We had helped her the most. We could not share our moneys with Meri. She started standing outside a supermarket and following the people coming out with nylon papers full of things for their totos: milks, breads and sugars. She opened her hand for them, saying, "Saidia maskini." Some of the people threw saliva on the ground, thinking Meri was wanting to touch them.

But God was always liking Meri. Looking how she was wearing a mother-dress with holes and no shoes, Good Samaritans felt mercy for her. Before lunchtime, she was given 40 or 50 bob. But outside that supermarket, there were also beggars sitting on the ground showing people their broken legs and their blind eyes. They felt jealousy for Meri. When people were not looking, they stood up and chased Meri away, beating her.

From there Meri went to open her hand for people sitting in traffic jam at the roundabout near Globe Cinema. She showed them crying eyes, saying, "Mama, saidia maskini." But they did not feel mercy. They closed their windows and looked her from the other side, thinking she wanted to run away with their Nokias like a chokoraa boy. And sometimes cars came very fast almost knocking her and then heads came out of the windows and shouted, "Kasia, get out of the road or I will step you." Breathing glue, Meri did not feel bad in her heart.

But that area was for beggar mamas and their totos. These beggar mamas, every day their work was looking the people passing and telling their totos which people to follow and pray for money. When these mamas saw Meri being given a 10 bob, they caught her and beat her some slaps, saying even them they needed to put food in their mouths.

We said, "Meri, stop fearing those women."

We said, "Meri, Nairobi is not theirs."

We said, "Meri, in the streets it is a must to survive."

But all of us knew Meri was not Doggie who if you tried to take her things she could eat your fingers. Meri could not kick a chokoraa boy like Kungfu between his legs when he came to look for her at night. All of us felt mercy for Meri, but we had helped her the most.

She stayed sleeping on her sacks for two days and then her food finished. She put all her things inside a nylon paper and tied them with a shuka on her back, like a toto. She didn't say where she was going.

One day, two days, three days we did not think about Meri. Sleeping on our sacks; washing our faces at night and applying powders; waiting in the streets for customers to stop their cars and say kss-kss-kss for us to come quickly; counting our moneys and looking at the presents we had been given—plastic bangles, a box remaining two biscuits, a watch with the glass broken—all that time, we were thinking our own things. Some of us were thinking if we had jiggers in our toes. Some of us were thinking how we would be if our mothers and fathers had not died in Molo clashes. All of us breathed glue and counted on our fingers the days remaining until we finished being chokoraas.

Four days, five days, six days, and then we started fearing for Meri. We asked ourselves what if chokoraa boys had found her staying alone? What if City Council had caught her and thrown her inside a truck to be taken to the police station? Some of us, who had never been inside a police station, closed their eyes and ears when we told them our stories of being put in a cell with cockroaches and rats and big people criminals and one bucket for doing toilet in front of everyone.

They asked us, "How did you come out of the police station?"

We told them the story. We said, "Those police they do not even give you ten bob, not like customers."

And then Meri came back. She was wearing a dress we had never seen and on top, a bigger sweater that was hiding her stomach. She had washed with soap and clean water. We could see her nylon paper was not full the same way it was when she went away. We saw she was not just carrying the normal things for surviving in the streets: plastic Kasuku for keeping food given by Good Samaritans, bottles for fetching water, papers and sticks for starting fire, cloths for catching blood, salt, and tins for cooking. She was not just carrying things collected in the streets like shoes and slippers not matching each other, one earring, a cup broken the handle, a paper written interesting things. Long time ago, she had lost the things she brought when she came to the streets: her mother's rothario; the knife that killed her father; a song her brother sang for her.

We only wanted to see inside her nylon paper. We did not do something bad, just seeing. Even her she had seen inside our nylon papers many times before, but now she was sitting alone under the stairs going nowhere, singing to her stomach: "Lala, mtoto, lala." Some of us said her head had gone bad. Some of us said she was selfish. The way she was holding her nylon paper, we asked ourselves, was she thinking we wanted to thief her things? Even us we had our things, our moneys, our food. When she went to toilet, we went quickly quickly and looked inside her nylon paper and said, "Waa, waa."

Meri was carrying three breads, four milks and two sugars. She was carrying sweets tied in a handkerchief and cabbages and rice. We could smell the chicken and chips she had not shared with us. In the bottom, she had two soaps, a plastic flower for putting in her hair and three Fanta Blackcurrants, remaining only the bottles.

We did not do something bad, but she shouted at us, "Thieves, thieves."

She removed the breads from our mouths and put everything back in her nylon paper. Remembering the way we helped her, we wanted to beat her slaps, to pull her hair and to bite her. We wanted to pinch her and put soil in her mouth. But because of the toto in her stomach, some of us felt bad in our hearts. We went to say sorry to Meri and sit with her under the stairs going nowhere.

We said, "Meri, we are not going to tell anyone."

We said, "Meri, do you remember who shared with you her toothbrush?"

But Meri refused to tell us her secret. At night when we went to see the Watchman, Meri was left sleeping in our mjengo, not even fearing chokoraa boys could find her alone. In the morning, when we came back, she was not there and when she came back, she was carrying more things. All of us knew Meri was thieving somewhere.

Days followed days and then a week, and then Meri was caught.

It was January and the sun was smiling loudly in the middle of the sky. The wind was chasing nylon papers and going under office women's skirts. Makangas were shouting for people to enter their matatus and be taken to Kahawa, Kangemi, and other places. People were refusing to enter the matatus because the fare was 40 bob instead of 20 bob. Some of us were sleeping and feeling we were dying; some of us were starting fires to cook our food; some of us were jumping a rope and remembering the days we were totos. Some of us, breathing glue, were seeing dreams of eating chips and chicken.

We heard Meri running and then she passed under the mabati fence surrounding our mjengo. All of us saw she was not carrying her nylon paper and then four men entered behind her. There was a tall man, a short man, a man wearing a red shirt, and the leader carrying a big stick. They did not say to us anything. They went where Meri was hiding under the stairs going nowhere and covered her mouth for her not to scream. Some of us breathed glue and looked far away; some of us closed our ears and covered ourselves under our sacks.

Now we knew where Meri was thieving. From office women wearing nice clothes that shaped them a figure eight. She was following them behind slowly slowly, looking everywhere in the streets if there were any police or City Council. Office women do not walk fast, wearing those sharp shoes and looking themselves in all the windows of shops. At the place for crossing the road they stop because they do not want to be splashed dirty water by cars and matatus. This is the time Meri went quickly quickly and opened her hand and said, "Saidia maskini."

If the office woman gave her some money, Meri did not do anything, but if the woman said something bad to her, calling her a malaya or asking her what she was thinking when she opened her legs, Meri removed a nylon paper she was hiding under her sweater. Every day Meri was carrying under her sweater what she toileted in the morning. In a small voice she told the office woman to give her money or be applied toilet and go back to the office smelling badly. And because office women fear toilet, they gave her 100 bob or even 200 bob.

And then, Meri was very clever: she did not run away. Before the office woman shouted she was a thief, Meri started talking to herself and falling down and applying toilet on her face until people started thinking she was a mad woman.

God was liking Meri, but she did not know that area was the area of big criminal thieves. They felt jealous how Meri was thieving cleverly. Four big criminal thieves came to our mjengo to beat her with the big stick; they kicked her with their big shoes, pom, pom, pom like a sack of beans being removed the dry skins. They cut her new dress and her sweater. Blood came out from her head, her neck, her hands and between her legs. They did not feel mercy for Meri.

All of us wanted to help Meri. All of us were hearing the screams inside her covered mouth. All of us wanted to run and call the people in the streets, the police and the City Council. But all of us were thinking, if the big criminal thieves did not feel mercy for Meri, with her big swollen stomach, how much would they feel mercy for us?

Days followed days, and Meri was sleeping on her sacks, not moving or talking to us. We brought for her water. We put food in our mouths to chew and put it in her mouth soft soft. Even if her head was an empty egg, she was our sister and our friend. We removed her dress and her sweater and washed them in Nairobi river. We poured soil where blood had come out of her body. We put her dead toto in a nylon paper and threw it in a garbage far away. Tears came out of our eyes for Meri. Some of us said in a small voice Meri was dying. They said we go find another mjengo where to live, far away from Meri. We beat them slaps. We pulled their hair. We put soil in their mouths. Meri was our sister and our friend.

We said, "Meri, it is better like this, you will see."

We said, "Meri, now the Watchman can find customers for you again."

We said, "Meri, this is the life of chokoraa."

But Meri was not hearing. Days followed days and every day, she was talking to herself. And then one day, she put all her things in a nylon paper and tied it on her back with a shuka, like a toto. She passed us and the mabati fence surrounding our mjengo. She closed her eyes a little because the sun was jumping everywhere—on the windows of cars, on the heads of passing people, on the roads shining black. She passed matatus blowing their horns and splashing mud-water on people. She passed hawkers running away from City Council. She passed watchmen outside banks and offices. She passed chokoraa boys climbing on garbage to find tins, papers and bottles for selling in Westlands. She passed streetlights looking down with yellow and black eyes. She passed a man being thieved his shoes, his pockets, his clothes. Everywhere, we followed her asking her many times:

"Meri, where are you going?"

"Meri, where are you going?"

Days followed days and then years followed years. Some of us were caught by police and City Council. We were taken to the police station and from there to the Jaji who looked us through the mirrors in front of his eyes to see if we were good or bad. He beat his table with a wood hammer and sent some of us to Langata to stay with big women criminals and some of us to a school to cut grasses. Some of us were killed by police with a gun called AK47. Some of us were killed by people we do not know. Some of us we decided to become the wives of chokoraa boys. Some of us, after many years, we had enough money for living in a house in Mathare slums and we started finding customers for ourselves. And some of us, because of breathing too much glue, our heads went bad and we started removing our clothes and chasing people in Nairobi.

But Meri, she crossed Nairobi river and then we do not know where she went.

Skinned

Lesley Nneka Arimah—winner of the 2019 Caine Prize

The unclothed woman had a neatly trimmed bush, waxed to resemble a setting sun. The clothed women sneered as she laid out makeup and lotion samples, touting their benefits. "Soft, smooth skin, as you can see," she said, winking—trying, and failing, to make a joke of her nakedness. Chidinma smiled in encouragement, nodding and examining everything Ejem pulled out of the box. Having invited Ejem to present her wares, she would be getting a free product out of this even if none of her guests made a purchase.

Ejem finished her sales pitch with a line about how a woman's skin is her most important feature and she has to take care of it like a treasured accessory. The covered women tittered and smoothed their tastefully patterned wife-cloth over their limbs. They wore them simply, draped and belted into long, graceful dresses, allowing the fabric to speak for itself. They eyed Ejem's nakedness with gleeful pity.

"I just couldn't be uncovered at your age. That's a thing for the younger set, don't you think?"

"I have a friend who's looking for a wife; maybe I can introduce you. He's not picky."

Ejem rolled her eyes, less out of annoyance than to keep tears at bay. Was this going to happen every time? She looked to Chidinma for help.

"Well, I for one am here for lotions, not to discuss covered versus uncovered, so I'd like this one." Chidinma held up the most expensive cream. Ejem made a show of ringing it up and the other women were embarrassed into making purchases of their own. They stopped speaking to Ejem directly and began to treat her as if she were a woman of the osu caste. They addressed product questions to the air or to Chidinma, and listened but did not acknowledge Ejem when she replied. Ejem might have protested, as would have Chidinma, but they needed the sales party to end before Chidinma's husband returned. It was the only stipulation Chidinma had made when she'd agreed to host. It was, in fact, the only stipulation of their friendship. Don't advertise your availability to my husband. Chidinma always tried to make a joking compliment of it—"You haven't had any kids yet, so your body is still amazing"—but there was always something strained there, growing more strained over the years as Ejem remained unclaimed.

The woman who had first addressed Chidinma instead of Ejem, whom Ejem had begun to think of as the ringleader, noticed them glancing at the clock, gave a sly smile, and requested that each and every product be explained to her. Ejem tried, she really did, whipping through the product texts with speed, but the clock sped just as quickly and eventually Chidinma stopped helping her, subdued by inevitable embarrassment. Before long, Chidinma's husband returned from work.

Chance was all right, as husbands went. He oversaw the management of a few branches of a popular bank, a job that allowed them to live comfortably in their large house with an osu woman to spare Chidinma serious housework. He could even be considered somewhat progressive; after all, he had permitted his wife's continued association with her unclothed friend, and he wasn't the sort to harass an osu woman in his employ. True, he insisted on a formal greeting, but after Chidinma had bowed to him she raised herself to her tiptoes for a kiss and Chance indulged her, fisting his hands in the wife-cloth at the small of her back.

But he was still a man, and when he turned to greet the women his eyes caught on Ejem and stayed there, taking in the brown discs of her areolae, the cropped design of hair between her legs, whatever parts of her went unhidden in her seated position. No one said anything, the utter impropriety of an unclaimed woman being in the house of a married man almost too delicious a social faux pas to interrupt. But, as Chidinma grew visibly distressed, the ringleader called the room to order and the women rose to leave, bowing their heads to Chance, giving Chidinma's hands encouraging little squeezes. No doubt the tale would make the rounds—"the way he stared at her"—and Chidinma wouldn't be able to escape it for a while. The women walked by Ejem without a word, the message clear: Ejem was beneath them.

Chidinma tried to distract her husband by asking about his day. Chance continued to stare at Ejem while he answered. Ejem wanted to move faster, to get out as quick as she could, but she was conscious of every sway of her breasts, every brush of her thighs as she hurried. Chance spoke to Ejem only as she was leaving, a goodbye she returned with a small curtsy. Chidinma walked her to the door.

"Ejem, we should take a break from each other, I think," she said with a pained air of finality, signaling that this break wasn't likely to be a temporary one.

"Why?"

"You know why."

"You're going to have to say it, Chidinma."

"Fine. This whole thing, this friendship, was fine when we were both uncovered girls doing whatever, but covered women can't have uncovered friends. I thought it was nonsense at first, but it's true. I'm sorry."

"You've been covered for thirteen years and this has never been a problem."

"And I thought by this time you'd be covered too. You came so close with that one fellow, but you've never really tried. It's unseemly."

"He's only seen me this once since you made it clear–'

"Once was enough. Get covered. Get claimed. Take yourself off the market. Until then, I'm sorry, but no."

Chidinma went back inside the house before Ejem could respond. And what could she say anyway? I'm not sure I ever want to be claimed? Chidinma would think her mad.

Ejem positioned her box to better cover her breasts and walked to the bus stop. Chidinma hadn't offered her a ride home, even though she knew how much Ejem hated public transportation—the staring as she lay the absorbent little towel square on her seat, the paranoia of imagining every other second what to do if her menstrual cup leaked.

At the stop, a group of young men waited. They stopped talking when they saw Ejem, then resumed, their conversation now centered on her.

"How old you think she is?"

"Dude, old."

"I don't know, man. Let's see her breasts. She should put that box down."

They waited and Ejem ignored them, keeping as much of herself as possible shielded with the box and the cosmetic company's branded tote.

"That's why she's unclaimed. Rudeness. Who's gonna want to claim that?"

They continued in that vein until the bus arrived. Even though the men were to board first, they motioned her ahead, a politeness that masked their desire for a better view. She scanned the passengers for other uncovered women—solidarity and all that—and was relieved to spot one. The relief quickly evaporated. The woman was beautiful, which would have stung on its own, but she was young, too, smooth-skinned and firm. Ejem stopped existing for the group of young men. They swarmed the woman, commenting loudly on the indentation of her waist, the solid curve of her arm. The young woman took it all in stride, scrolling a finger down the pages of her book.

Ejem felt at once grateful and slighted, remembering how it had been in her youth, before her waist had thickened and her ass drooped. She'd never been the sort to wear nakedness boldly, but she'd at least felt that she was pleasant to look at.

The bus took on more passengers and was three-quarters full when an osu woman boarded. Ejem caught herself doing a double take before averting her gaze. It wasn't against the law; it just wasn't done, since the osu had their own transport, and the other passengers looked away as well. Embarrassed. Annoyed. Even the bus driver kept his eyes forward as the woman counted out her fare. And when she finally appeared in the center aisle, no one made the polite shift all passengers on public transportation know, that nonverbal invitation to take a neighboring seat. So even though there were several spots available, the osu woman remained standing. Better that than climb her naked body over another to sit down. It was the type of subtle social correction, Ejem thought, that would cause a person to behave better in the future.

But as the ride progressed, the osu woman squeezing to let by passengers who didn't even acknowledge her, Ejem softened. She was so close to becoming an unseen woman herself, unanchored from the life and the people she knew, rendered invisible. It was only by the grace of birth that she wasn't osu, her mother had said to her the very last time they spoke. "At least you have a choice, Ejem. So choose wisely." She hadn't, had walked away from a man and his proposal and the protection it offered. Her parents had cut her off then, furious and confounded that she'd bucked tradition. She couldn't explain, not even to herself, why she'd looked at the cloth he proffered and seen a weight that would smother her.

At her stop, Ejem disembarked, box held to her chest. With the exception of a few cursory glances, no one paid attention to her. It was one of the reasons she liked the city, everybody's inclination to mind their own business. She picked up the pace when she spotted the burgundy awning of her apartment building. In the elevator, an older male tenant examined her out of the corner of his eye. Ejem backed up until he would have had to turn around to continue looking. One could never tell if a man was linked or not, and she hated being inspected by men who'd already claimed wives.

In her apartment she took a long, deep breath, the type she didn't dare take in public lest she draw unwanted attention. Only then did she allow herself to contemplate the loss of Chidinma's friendship, and weep.

When they were girls, still under their fathers' covering, she and Chidinma had become fast friends. They were both new to their school and their covers were so similar in pattern they were almost interchangeable. Ejem remembered their girlhood fondly, the protection of their fathers' cloth, the seemingly absolute security of it. She had cried when, at fifteen, her mother had come into her bedroom and, stroking her hair, told Ejem that it was time to remove her cloth. The only people who could get away with keeping their daughters covered for long were the wealthy, who often managed it until the girls could secure wife-cloth. But Ejem's father had grown up a poor man in a village where girls were disrobed as early as possible, some even at age ten, and it was beyond time as far as he was concerned. He knew what happened to the families of girls who stayed covered beyond their station, with the exception of girls bearing such deformities that they were permitted "community cloth" made from donated scraps. But if a girl like Ejem continued to be clothed, the town council would levy a tax that would double again and again until her father could not pay it. Then his girl would be disrobed in public, and her family shamed. No, he couldn't bear the humiliation. Things would happen on his terms.

The day Ejem was disrobed was also the day her father stopped interacting with her, avoiding the impropriety of a grown man talking to a naked girl. Ejem hadn't wanted to go to school or market or anywhere out of the house where people could see her. Chidinma, still under her father-cloth, told her (horrified, well-off) parents that she, too, felt ready to disrobe so that she and Ejem could face the world together, two naked foundlings.

Chidinma's parents had tried to spin it as piousness, a daughter disrobed earlier than she had to be because she was so dedicated to tradition. But it'd had the stink of fanaticism and they'd lost many friends, something for which, Chidinma confided, her parents had never forgiven her.

A part of Ejem had always believed they'd be claimed at the same time, but then Chidinma had secured a wife-cloth at twenty, with Ejem as her chief maid. And then Chidinma gave birth to a boy, then two girls, who would remain covered their entire lives if Chidinma had anything to say about it. And through it all, Ejem remained uncovered, unclaimed, drifting until the likelihood passed her by.

She downed a mug of wine in one huge gulp, then another, before sifting through yesterday's mail. She opened the envelope she'd been avoiding: the notice of her upcoming lease renewal, complete with a bump in monthly rent. With the money she'd earned today, she had enough to cover the next two months. But the raised rent put everything in jeopardy, and Chidinma's abandonment meant Ejem could no longer sell to her wealthy set. If she couldn't secure income some other way, a move to a smaller town would soon be a necessity.

When she'd first leased the apartment, Ejem had been working at the corporate headquarters of an architecture firm. Though her nakedness drew some attention, there were other unclaimed women, and Ejem, being very good at what she did, advanced. Just shy of a decade later, she was over 30, the only woman in upper management, and still uncovered.

Three months ago, Ejem had been delivering a presentation to a prospective client. As usual, she was the only woman in the room. The client paid no attention to her PowerPoint, focusing instead on what he considered to be the impropriety of an unclaimed woman distracting from business matters. Ejem was used to this and tried to steer the conversation back to the budget. When the man ignored her, none of her co-workers bothered to censure him, choosing instead to snicker into their paperwork. She walked out of the room.

Ejem had never gone to Human Resources before; she'd always sucked it up. The HR manager, a covered woman who was well into her fifties, listened to her with a bored expression, then, with a pointed look at Ejem's exposed breasts, said: "You can't seriously expect a group of men to pay attention to pie charts or whatever when there is an available woman in the room. Maybe if you were covered this wouldn't happen. Until you are, we can no longer put you in front of clients."

Ejem walked out of the building and never returned. She locked herself away at home until Chidinma came knocking with a bottle of vodka, her youngest girl on her hip, and a flyer for home-based work selling makeup.

Now that lifeline was gone, and it would be only a matter of time until Ejem exhausted her savings. She switched on the TV, and flipped channels until she reached an uncovered young woman relating the news. The woman reported on a building fire in Onitsha and Ejem prepared dinner with the broadcast playing in the background, chopping vegetables for stir-fry until she registered the phrase "unclaimed women" repeated several times. She turned up the volume.

The newscaster had been joined by an older man with a paternal air, who gave more details.

"The building was rumored to be a haven of sorts for unclaimed women, who lived there, evading their responsibilities as cloth makers. Authorities halted firefighters from putting out the blaze, hoping to encourage these lost women to return to proper life. At least three bodies were discovered in the ashes. Their identities have yet to be confirmed."

That was the other reason Ejem wanted to remain in the metro area. Small towns were less tolerant of unclaimed women, some going so far as to outlaw their presence unless they were menials of the osu caste. They had a certain freedom, Ejem thought—these osu women who performed domestic tasks, the osu men who labored in the mines or constructed the buildings she'd once designed—though her envy was checked by the knowledge that it was a freedom born of irrelevance. The only place for unclaimed women, however, as far as most were concerned, was the giant factories, where they would weave cloth for women more fortunate than they.

The town's mayor appeared at a press conference.

"This is a decent town with decent people. If folks want to walk around uncovered and unclaimed, they need to go somewhere else. I'm sorry about the property loss and the folks who couldn't get out, but this is a family town. We have one of the world's finest factories bordering us. They could have gone there." The screen flipped back to the newsman, who nodded sagely, his expression somehow affirming the enforcement of moral values even as it deplored the loss of life.

Ejem battled a bubble of panic. How long before her finances forced her out into the hinterlands, where she would have to join the cloth makers? She needed a job and she needed it fast.

What sorts of jobs could one do naked? Ejem was too old for anything entry-level, where she'd be surrounded day after day by twentysomethings who would be claimed quickly. Instead, she looked for jobs where her nudity would be less of an issue. She lasted at a nursing home for five weeks, until a visiting relative objected to her presence. At the coffee shop she made it two and a half hours until she had to hide in the back to avoid a former co-worker. She quit the next day. Everywhere she went heightened how sheltered she'd been at her corporate job. The farther from the center of town she searched, the more people stared at her openly, asking outright why she wasn't covered when they saw that she didn't bear the mark of an osu woman. Every once in a while Ejem encountered osu women forced outside by errands, branded by shaved heads with scarification scored above one ear. Other pedestrians avoided them as though they were poles or mailboxes or other such sidewalk paraphernalia. But Ejem saw them.

As her search became more desperate, every slight took a knife's edge, so that Ejem found herself bothered even by the young girls still covered in their father-cloth who snickered at her, unaware or not caring that they, too, would soon be stripped of protection. The worst were the pitying Oh, honey looks, the whispered assurances from older covered women that someone would eventually claim her.

After a while she found work giving massages at a spa. She enjoyed being where everyone was disrobed; the artificial equality was a balm. Her second week on the job, a woman walked in covered with one of the finest wife-cloths Ejem had ever seen. She ordered the deluxe package, consisting of every single service the spa offered.

"And may I have your husband's account number?"

"My account number," the woman emphasized, sliding her card across the counter.

The desk girl glared at the card, glared at the woman, then left to get the manager. Everyone in the waiting room stared.

The manager, a woman close to Ejem's age, sailed in, her haughty manner turning deferential and apologetic as soon as she caught sight of the client. "I'm so sorry. The girl is new, still in father-cloth. Please excuse her." The finely clothed one remained silent. "We will, of course, offer you a significant discount on your services today. Maria is ready to start on your massage right away."

"No," the woman said firmly. "I want her to do it." Ejem, who'd been pretending to straighten products on the shelves, turned to see the woman pointing at her.

Soon she was in one of the treatment rooms, helping the woman to disrobe, feeling the texture of the cloth, wanting to rub it against her cheek. She left to hang it and encountered the manager, who dragged her down the hall and spoke in a harsh whisper.

"Do you know who that is? That is Odinaka, *the* Odinaka. If she leaves here less than pleased, you will be fired. I hope I'm clear."

Ejem nodded, returning to the massage room in a nervous daze. Odinaka was one of a handful of independently wealthy women who flouted convention without consequences. She was unclaimed, but covered herself anyway, and not in modest cloth, either, but in fine, bold fabric that invited attention and scrutiny. She owned almost half the cloth factories across the globe. This unthinkable rebellion drew criticism, but her wealth ensured that it remained just that: words but no action.

Odinaka sat on the massage table, swinging her legs. At Ejem's direction, she lay on her stomach while Ejem warmed oil between her hands. She coated Odinaka's ankles before sliding up to her calves, warming the tissue with her palms. She asked a few casual questions, trying to gauge whether she was a talker or preferred her massages silent. She needn't have worried. Not only did Odinaka give verbose replies, she had questions for Ejem herself. Before long, she had pried from Ejem the story of how she'd come to be here, easing muscle tensions instead of pursuing a promising career as an architect.

"It doesn't seem fair, does it, that you have to remain uncovered?"

Ejem continued with the massage, unsure how to reply to such seditious sentiments.

"You know, you and I are very similar," Odinaka continued.

Ejem studied the woman's firm body, toned and slim from years of exercise. She considered the other ways in which they were different, not least that Odinaka had never had to worry about a bill in her life. She laughed.

"You are very kind, but we're nothing alike, though we may be of the same age," she responded, as lightly as she could, tilting the ending into a question. Odinaka ignored it, turning over to face her.

"I mean it; we are both ambitious women trying to make our way unclaimed in male-dominated fields."

Except, Ejem didn't say, you are completely free in a way I am not, as covered as you wish to be.

"Covering myself would be illegal—" she started.

"Illegal-smeagle. When you have as much money as I do, you exist above every law. Now, wouldn't you like to be covered too?"

308

Odinaka was her saviour. She whisked Ejem away from her old apartment, helping her pay the fee to break her lease, and moved her into a building she owned in one of the city's nicest neighborhoods.

Ejem's quarters, a two-bedroom apartment complete with a generously sized kitchen, had the freshness of a deep clean, like it had been long vacant, or had gone through a recent purge, stripped of the scent and personality of its previous occupant. The unit had a direct intercom to the osu women who took care of the place. Ejem was to make cleaning requests as needed, or requests for groceries that later appeared in her fridge. When Ejem mentioned the distance from the apartment to her job, Odinaka revealed that she didn't have to work if she didn't want to, and it was an easy choice not to return to the spa. The free time enabled her to better get to know the other women in the building.

There was Delilah, who seemed like a miniature Odinaka in dress and mannerisms, but in possession of only half as much confidence. Doreen, a woman close to forty, became Ejem's favorite. She owned a bookstore—one that did well as far as bookstores went—and she had the air of someone who knew exactly who she was and liked it. She eschewed the option to self-clothe.

"Let them stare," Doreen would declare after a few glasses of wine. "This body is a work of art." She would lift her breasts with her hands, sending Ejem and the other women into tipsy giggles.

The remaining women—Morayo, Mukaso and Maryam—were polite but distant, performing enough social niceties to sidestep any allegations of rudeness, but only just. Ejem and Doreen called them the three Ms or, after a few drinks, "Mmm, no," for their recalcitrance. They sometimes joined in Odinaka's near-nightly cocktail hour, but within a few weeks the cadre solidified into Odinaka, Delilah, Doreen and Ejem.

With this group of women, there were no snide remarks about Ejem's nakedness, no disingenuous offers to introduce her to a man—any man—who could maybe look past her flaws. Odinaka talked about her vast business, Doreen about her small one, and they teased each other with terrible advice neither would ever take. Ejem talked some about the career she'd left behind, but didn't have much to add. And for the first time, her shyness was just shyness, not evidence of why she remained unclaimed, nor an invitation to be battered with advice on how she could improve herself.

Besides, Odinaka talked enough for everyone, interrupting often and dominating every topic. Ejem didn't mind, because of all of them, Odinaka had had the most interesting life, one of unrelenting luxury since birth. She'd inherited the weaving company from her father when he retired, almost a decade ago, which had caused an uproar. But if one of the wealthiest dynasties wanted a woman at the helm, it was a luxury they could purchase. And if that woman indulged in covering herself and collecting and caring for other unclaimed women, who had the power to stop her?

"I imagine creating a world," Odinaka often said, "where disrobing is something a woman does only by choice."

On Ejem's first night in the building, Odinaka had brought a length of cloth to her, a gift, she said, that Ejem could wear whenever she wanted. Ejem had stared at the fabric for hours. Even in the confines of the building, in her own unit, she didn't have the courage to put it on. At Odinaka's cocktail hour, Doreen would sit next to her and declare, "It's us against these bashful fuckers, Ejem," setting off an evening of gentle ribbing at everyone's expense.

"You really go to your store like that?" Ejem asked Doreen one afternoon. "Why don't you cover yourself? No one will say anything if they know you're one of Odinaka's women, right?" She was trying to convince herself that she, too, could don the cloth and go out in public without fear.

Doreen stopped perusing invoices to give Ejem all her attention. "Look, we have to live with this. I was disrobed at age ten. Do you know what it feels like to be exposed so young? I hid for almost a decade before I found myself, my pride. No one will ever again make me feel uncomfortable in my own skin. I plan to remain unclaimed and uncovered for as long as I live, and no one can say a damn thing about it. Odinaka rebels in her own way, and I in mine. I don't yearn for the safety of cloth. If the law requires me to be naked, I will be naked. And I will be goddamned if they make me feel uncomfortable for their law."

The weeks of welcome, of feeling free to be her own person, took hold and, one night, when Ejem joined the other women in Odinaka's apartment, she did so covered, the cloth draped over her in a girl's ties, the only way she knew how. Doreen was the first one to congratulate her, and when she hugged Ejem, she whispered, "Rebel in your own way," but her smile was a little sad.

Odinaka crowed in delight: "Another one! We should have a party."

She mobilized quickly, dispensing orders to her osu women via intercom. Ejem had yet to see any of the osu at work, but whenever she returned to her quarters from Odinaka's or Doreen's, her bed was made, the bathroom mirror cleared of flecks, the scabs of toothpaste scrubbed from the sink, and the rooms themselves held an indefinable feeling of having only just been vacated.

In less than the hour it took Ejem and the other residents to get themselves ready for the party, Odinaka's quarters had become packed. Men and women, all clothed except Doreen, mingled and chatted. Doreen held court on the settee, sipping wine and bestowing coy smiles.

Ejem tried to join in, but even with the self-cloth, she couldn't help feeling like the uncovered woman she'd been her entire adult life. Odinaka tried to draw Ejem into her circle of conversation, but after Ejem managed only a few stilted rejoinders, she edged away, sparing herself further embarrassment. Ejem ended up in a corner watching the festivities.

She was not aware that she herself was being watched until a man she'd seen bowing theatrically to Odinaka leaned against the wall next to her.

"So, you're the newest one, huh?"

"I suppose I am."

"You seem reasonable enough. Why are you unclaimed?"

Ejem tensed, wary.

"What's that supposed to mean, 'reasonable'?"

He ignored the question.

"Do you know I have been trying to claim that woman ever since she was a girl?" He nodded toward Odinaka. "Our union would have been legendary. The greatest cloth weaver with the greatest cotton grower. What do you think?"

Ejem shrugged. It was really none of her business.

"Instead she's busy collecting debris."

Stunned by his rudeness, Ejem turned away, but he only laughed and called to someone across the room. Suddenly every laugh seemed directed at her, every smile a smirk at her expense. She felt herself regressing into the girl who'd needed Chidinma's tight grip in hers before she could walk with her head high. She ducked out, intending to return to her quarters.

She ran into Delilah, who held a carved box under her arm, a prized family heirloom Ejem recognized from their many gatherings. It was one of the few objects Odinaka envied, as she could not secure one herself, unable to determine the origin of the antique. She was forever demanding that Delilah bring it out to be admired, though Delilah refused to let Odinaka have it examined or appraised, perfectly content to let her treasure remain a mystery.

Ejem didn't particularly like Delilah. She might have been a mini Odinaka but, unlike Odinaka, Delilah was pretentious and wore her fine breeding on her sleeve. Ejem's distress was visible enough that Delilah paused, glancing between her and the door that muted the soirée.

"Is everything okay?" she asked.

Ejem nodded, but a tight nod that said it was not. She watched Delilah's concern war with the promise of fun on the other side of the door. Delilah's movements, a particular twist in her shoulders, the way she clenched her fist, an angled tilt of her head, suddenly brought to Ejem's mind the osu woman on the bus. Something must have crossed her face because Delilah lifted a furtive, self-conscious hand to pat her hair into place—right where an identifying scar would have been if a government midwife had scored it into her head when she was six months old, and then refreshed it on return visits every two years until she turned eighteen. That practice was the extent of Ejem's osu knowledge. Her people lived side by side with the osu and they knew nothing of each other.

Looking at Delilah's box, it occurred to Ejem that an osu girl— if she were clever enough, audacious enough, in possession of impossibly thick hair—could take her most prized possession—say, a fine carved box that had been in the family for many generations— and sneak away in the middle of the night. She could travel farther than she had ever been in her life, to a city where no one knew her. And, because she was clever, she could slip seamlessly into the world of the people she knew so well because she'd had to serve them all her life.

Before the thought could take hold, the uncertainty in Delilah's face was replaced by an artificial sweetness, and she patted Ejem's shoulder, saying, "Rest well, then," before escaping into the party.

Ejem was awoken at dawn by the last of the revelers leaving. She stayed in her apartment till eight, then took advantage of Odinaka's open-door policy to enter her benefactor's apartment. If she hadn't been there herself, she would never have believed it had been filled with partiers the night before. In three hours, someone, or several someones, had transformed the wreckage of 50 guests—Ejem remembered at least two spilled wineglasses and a short man who'd insisted on making a speech from an end table—back into the clean, modern lines preferred by one of the wealthiest women in the world. A woman who apparently collected debris, like her. She wasn't exactly sure what she wanted to say to Odinaka—she couldn't childishly complain that one of the guests had insulted her—but she felt injured and sought some small soothing.

She found Odinaka lounging in her bed, covers pulled to her waist.

"Did you enjoy yourself, Ejem? I saw you talking to Aju. He just left, you know." She wiggled her brows.

Well. Ejem couldn't exactly condemn him now. "We had an interesting conversation," she said instead.

"'Interesting,' she says. I know he can be difficult. Never mind what he said."

Odinaka pressed the intercom and requested a breakfast tray, then began to recap the night, laughing at this and that event she didn't realize Ejem hadn't been there to see.

After ten minutes, she pressed the intercom again. "Where is my tray?" she demanded, a near shout.

Catching Ejem's expression, she rolled her eyes.

"Don't you start as well."

Ejem opened her mouth to defend the osu women, but shut it just as quickly, embarrassed not only by the unattractive revolutionary bent of what she'd almost said, but also because it felt so much like a defense of herself.

"You are just like Doreen," Odinaka continued. "Look, I employ an army of those women. They have a job and they need to do it. You remember how that goes, right?" Odinaka turned on the television. A commercial advertised a family getaway that included passes to a textile museum where the children could learn how cloth was made. Ejem recalled a documentary she'd seen in school that showed the dismal dorms to which unclaimed women were relegated, the rationed food, the abuse from guards, the "protection" that was anything but. It had been meant to instil fear of ending up in such a place, and it had worked.

When the program returned, Odinaka turned up the volume until it was clear to Ejem she had been dismissed.

Ejem decided that her first foray in her new cloth would be to visit Doreen in her shop. Doreen would know just what to say to ease the restless hurt brewing inside her. She may even know enough of Delilah's history to put Ejem's runaway suspicions to rest. Doreen had invited her to visit the bookstore many times—"You can't stay in here forever. Come. See what I've done. See what an unclaimed woman can build on her own."

Wearing self-cloth in the safety of Odinaka's building was one thing. Ejem dawdled in front of the mirror, studying the softness of her stomach, the firm legs she'd always been proud of, the droop of her breasts. She picked up the cloth and held it in front of her. Much better. She secured it in a simple style, mimicking as best as she could the draping and belting of the sophisticated women she'd encountered.

For the first time in her adult life, no one stared at her. When she gathered the courage to make eye contact with a man on the sidewalk and he inclined his head respectfully, she almost tripped in shock. It was no fluke. Everyone—men and women—treated her differently, most ignoring her as yet another body on the street. But when they did acknowledge her, their reactions were friendly. Ejem felt the protective hunch of her shoulders smooth itself out, as though permission had been granted to relax. She walked with a bounce in her step, every part of her that bounced along with it shielded by the cloth. Bound up in fabric, she was the freest she'd ever felt.

Ejem was so happy that, when she saw a familiar face, she smiled and waved before she remembered that the bearer of the face had disowned their friendship some months ago. Chidinma gave a hesitant wave in return before she approached Ejem, smiling.

"You're covered! You're claimed! Turn around; let me see. Your wife-cloth is so fine. I'm upset you didn't invite me to the claiming ceremony."

The words were friendly but the tone was strained, their last exchange still echoing in the air.

"There wasn't a ceremony. There was nothing to invite you to."

Chidinma's smile faded. "You don't have to lie. I know I was awful to you; I'm sorry."

"No, really, there wasn't." Ejem leaned closer, yearning to confide, to restore their former intimacy. "It's self-cloth. I covered myself."

It took Chidinma a moment to absorb this. Then she bristled, pulling back any lingering affection. Her smile went waxy and polite.

"You must be very happy with your husband."

"Chidinma, I don't have a husband. I'm covering myself."

Chidinma's look turned so vicious that Ejem stepped back, bumping into a man who excused himself.

"Are you, now? A self-cloth, is it? Someone from a good family like yours? I don't believe it." Unlike Ejem, Chidinma didn't lower her voice, earning startled glances from passers-by. Ejem shushed her.

"Oh, are you ashamed now? Did something you're not entirely proud of?"

When Ejem turned to leave, Chidinma snatched her by the cloth. Now she whispered, "You think you're covered, but you're still naked. No amount of expensive 'self-cloth'—how ridiculous!—will change that."

It was a spiteful and malicious thing to say, meant to hurt, and it did. Ejem tried to pull her cloth from her old friend's fist, but Chidinma didn't let go. She continued, her voice cracking with tears.

"You don't get to be covered without giving something up; you don't get to do that. It's not fair. After everything I did for you, it's not fair."

Chidinma cried openly now and Ejem used the opportunity of her weakened grip to twist away, near tears herself.

It had been easy, Ejem thought, in the opulence of Odinaka's house, to forget that they were breaking laws. Easy, too, to clink glasses night after night. What had some woman given up so that Ejem could have this cloth? Was she a weaver by choice or indentured, deemed past her prime and burdened to earn the care of the state? The fabric felt itchy now, as though woven from rough wire.

Ejem hurried back the way she had come, to the safety of Odinaka's building. On the verge of panic, she fumbled with the keys to her apartment and let herself in. Once inside, she leaned against the door and slid to the floor, head to knees, catching her breath. She felt... something, that made her look around, and that's when she saw the osu woman standing in the corner. Her skin was light, almost blending into the dusky beige of the wall, her scar a gristly, keloided mass on the side of her head. She appeared to be Ejem's age or older. She held a bottle of cleaning solution and a rag. She was naked.

It was clear by the hunch of her shoulders and the wary look in her eye that it was not a nakedness she enjoyed. How long had it been since Ejem had carried that very look on her own face? How long since she'd felt shame so deep she'd nearly drowned in it?

The day she'd lost her father-cloth, she'd pleaded with her father, fought him as he'd attempted to rip the fabric away. Her mother had cried to her to bear it with some dignity, but Ejem had gone mindless. When her father had finally taken all of the cloth, uncurling her fingers to snatch even the frayed strip she'd held on to, Ejem had curled into herself, making a cover of her appendages. Each day since had been a management of this panic, swallowing it deep in her belly where it wouldn't erupt.

The osu woman nodded to Ejem, then slipped through a panel in the wall and disappeared. The panel slid back into place soundlessly, and when Ejem went to the wall she could feel no seam. She clawed at it, bending and breaking her nails, trying to force a way in. Finding no entry from her side, she pounded and called out, seeking a welcome.

About the authors

Leila Aboulela was born in Cairo, grew up in Khartoum and moved in her mid-twenties to Aberdeen. She is the author of five novels: *The Translator* (1999), *Minaret* (2005), *Lyrics Alley* (2011), *The Kindness of Enemies* (2015), and *Bird Summons* (2019). Her latest story collection, *Elsewhere, Home* (2018), won the Saltire Fiction Book of the Year Award. Her work has been translated into fifteen languages and she has been longlisted three times for the Orange Prize for Fiction. Her plays, including *The Insider* and *The Mystic Life*, have been broadcast on BBC Radio.

Segun Afolabi was born in Kaduna, Nigeria, grew up in Canada, the Congo, Indonesia, Germany and Hong Kong, and now lives in London. His first short-story collection, *A Life Elsewhere,* was published in 2006 and was shortlisted for the Commonwealth Writers' Prize. His first novel *Goodbye Lucille* (2007) won the Authors' Club Best First Novel award in the UK.

Monica Arac de Nyeko is a Ugandan who studied at Makerere University and the University of Groningen but now lives in Nairobi. She is a leading member of the Ugandan women writers' association FEMRITE. Her essay "In the Stars" won first prize in the Women's World, Women in War Zones essay-writing competition. Her short fiction, poetry and essays have appeared in many publications, including the anthologies *Memories of the Sun* and *Tears of Hope, The Nation, IS* magazine, and *Poetry International*.

Lesley Nneka Arimah was born in the UK but grew up in Nigeria and wherever else her father was stationed for work. Her debut short-story collection *What It Means When a Man Falls from the Sky* won the 2017 Kirkus Prize and the 2017 New York Public Library Young Lions Fiction Award, among other honors. Arimah is a 2019 United States Artists Fellow in Writing. She currently lives in Las Vegas and is working on a novel about you.

Rotimi Babatunde is a playwright and writer who currently lives in Ibadan, Nigeria. He won the Meridian Tragic Love Story Competition (organized by the BBC World Service) and the AWF Cyprian Ekwensi Prize for Short Stories. His plays have been broadcast on the BBC World Service and performed at venues including Riksteatern, the Royal Court Theatre, and Halcyon Theatre.

NoViolet Bulawayo was born and raised in Zimbabwe. She earned her MFA at Cornell University where she was a recipient of the Truman Capote Fellowship. She was a Stegner Fellow at Stanford University, where she now teaches as a Jones Lecturer in Fiction. Her first novel *We Need New Names* (2013) won the LA Times Book Prize Art Seidenbaum Award for First Fiction, the Pen/Hemingway Award, and the Etisalat Prize for Literature; it was also shortlisted for the Man Booker Prize.

Brian Chikwava was born in Victoria Falls, Zimbabwe, and went to school in Bulawayo before studying civil engineering at Bristol University in Britain. After his short story "Seventh Street Alchemy" won the 2004 Caine Prize, he settled in London, where he has since worked as a writer and musician. His album *Jacaranda Skits* (2004) combined his words with township music, jazz and blues. His first novel *Harare North* was published in 2015.

Bushra al-Fadil is a Sudanese poet and writer. He holds a PhD in Russian language and literature, and lectured in this at Khartoum University until he was expelled from the country after participating in protests against the military coup by Omar al-Bashir. He currently lives in Saudi Arabia. He has published four collections of short stories in Arabic and won the Altayeb Salih Short Story Award in 2012.

Tope Folarin was born in Utah and raised in Texas as part of a Nigerian immigrant family. He was educated at Morehouse College, and the University of Oxford, where he earned two Master's degrees as a Rhodes Scholar. He is the recipient of writing fellowships from the Institute for Policy Studies and Callaloo. He currently lives and works in Washington DC. His first novel, *A Particular Kind of Black Man*, was published in August 2019.

Helon Habila was born in Nigeria, where he studied English at the University of Jos and later worked as literary editor of the *Vanguard* newspaper. In 2005, Habila became the first Chinua Achebe Fellow at Bard College, New York, and subsequently became professor of Creative Writing at George Mason University in Fairfax, Virginia. His first volume of short stories, *Prison Stories*, was published in 2000. He is the author of four novels—*Waiting for an Angel* (2002); *Measuring Time* (2007) *Oil on Water* (2010), and *Travelers* (2019)—and the non-fiction book *The Chibok Girls* (2017).

Lidudumalingani is a writer, filmmaker and photographer. He was born in the Eastern Cape province of South Africa, in a village called Zikhovane. Lidudumalingani has published short stories, non-fiction and criticism in various publications. His films have been screened at various film festivals.

Okwiri Oduor was born in Nairobi, Kenya. Her novella *The Dream Chasers* was highly commended in the Commonwealth Book Prize 2012. Her work has appeared in *The New Inquiry, Kwani?, Saraba, FEMRITE,* and *African Writing Online.* She directed the inaugural Writivism Festival in Kampala, Uganda. She is currently working on her first full-length novel.

Makena Onjerika began writing at the age of 15, went on to study fiction at Amherst College, and graduated from the MFA Creative Writing program at New York University. Her short stories have been published in *Urban Confustions, Wasafiri,* and *New Daughters of Africa.* She lives in Nairobi, Kenya, and is currently working on a short-story collection and a fantasy novel.

EC Osondu was born in Nigeria, where he worked as an advertising copywriter for many years before moving to New York to attend Syracuse University, where he gained an MFA for Creative Writing and is now a Fellow. He has won the Nirelle Galson Prize for Fiction. His debut collection of short stories *Voice of America* was published in 2010. He is on the Board of Trustees of the pan-African literary initiative Writivism.

Yvonne Adhiambo Owuor was born in Nairobi and studied English at Kenyatta University before gaining postgraduate qualifications in film and creative writing in Britain and Australia. She has worked as a screenwriter and from 2003 to 2005 was the Executive Director of the Zanzibar International Film Festival. Her story "The Knife Grinder's Tale" became a short film, released in 2007. She is the author of two novels: *Dust* (2014) and *The Dragonfly Sea* (2019). She won Kenya's top literary prize, the Jomo Kenyatta Prize for Literature, in 2015.

Henrietta Rose-Innes was born in Cape Town, South Africa. She has a PhD in Creative and Critical Writing from the University of East Anglia and has held various artist's residencies around the world, including in the US, Italy, Germany, and Switzerland. She is the author of four novels—*Shark's Egg* (2000), *The Rock Alphabet* (2004), *Nineveh* (2016), and *Green Lion* (2017)—and one short-story collection, *Animalia Paradoxa* (2019). She has also compiled an anthology of South African writing, *Nice Times! A Book of South African Pleasures and Delights* (2006).

Namwali Serpell was born in Lusaka, Zambia. She is currently associate professor of English at UC Berkeley in the US. Her first book of literary criticism, *Seven Modes of Uncertainty,* was published in 2014. Her short fiction has been widely published and anthologized. Her first novel, *The Old Drift*, was published in 2019.

Olufemi Terry was born in Sierra Leone of African and Antillean parentage. He grew up in Nigeria, the UK and Côte d'Ivoire before attending university in New York. He received an MA in Creative Writing at the University of Cape Town in 2008. His work has appeared in *The Guardian, Chimurenga,* and the *LA Review of Books* and has been performed on stage in Germany, Switzerland and Austria. He is working on his first novel, a preliminary excerpt from which appeared in the anthology *One World Two* (2016). He was one of the judges of the 2019 Caine Prize.

Binyavanga Wainaina founded the influential Kenyan literary magazine *Kwani?* with the money he received for winning the 2002 Caine Prize with his story "Discovering Home." He had a huge impact on literature from and about Africa, not least with his influential satirical essay "How to Write About Africa," published in *Granta* in 2005. He wrote widely for international publications, including *The East African, National Geographic,* the *Sunday Times* (South Africa), the *New York Times, The Guardian,* and *Chimurenga*. His only book was the memoir *One Day I Will Write About This Place* (2011). He died of a stroke at the age of 48 in 2019.

Mary Watson grew up in Cape Town where she worked as an art museum custodian, library assistant, actor in children's musicals and university lecturer. Her doctorate was in film studies. At sixteen, she had a vivid dream about a girl and her father that grew into a collection of connected short stories, *Moss* (2004)—this included her Caine Prize-winning story "Jungfrau." She now lives in Galway, Ireland. She is the author of three novels: *The Cutting Room* (2013); *The Wren Hunt* (2018), and *The Wickerlight* (2019).